I0451710

The Light Don't Shine No More

Rod Williams

Rod Williams

ISBN: 978-1-62420-526-2

Credits
Cover Artist: Terry McCutchen
Editor: Sherry Derr-Wille

Published in the United States of America

Dedication

Always for Darcie Jane

Chapter One

From her four-poster bed with its great green-and-violet canopy, through the thick milky panes of the iron-grilled windows, Rachel Demeter strained to make out the Flatirons jutting skyward from the foothills. The stone faces consisted of shale and sandstone, with small distinct veins of chlorite threaded throughout. The chlorite deposits had given this town its name of Greenstone. Rachel's bedroom oversaw a small glen sparkling with new snowfall. The foothills rose into the dark beginnings of a forest studded with Ponderosa pines and blue spruce.

Outside, the temperature read five degrees above zero. It was early December, just after Thanksgiving and just before Christmas, and the windowpanes were etched with icy lacework. The late afternoon sun struck the snow and amplified its searing whiteness.

Rachel's body was failing fast. One consequence was her dimming vision, but now her other senses seemed sharper than ever. For instance, the variety of scents in her room commingled to form an oddly fragrant atmosphere of herbal blackberry green tea, orange marmalade and apricot preserves, narcissus and grape hyacinth from a small glass bowl on her nightstand, the acrid bouquet of lemon ammonia from the adjoining bathroom.

Unfortunately, though, there was also the rising smell of her own body funk permeating the room, the reek of her progressing disease.

Her health had declined dramatically over the past several weeks. Her nerve endings had grown hypersensitive. She now felt every small current of air, be it the slightest draft from an open door or a warm gust from the central heating system as a flensing blade dragged along the skin of her arms and legs. She experienced heat and cold in extremes, raising gooseflesh along her arms, inflaming dry red patches on her shins and scalp.

In addition, her ears picked up every sound in and around the big two-story home. Not just the midnight moans of copper pipes behind fifty-year-old walls or the intermittent creaking of the tongue-in-groove floors. Not only the ticking of each of the house's fourteen clocks, or the sporadic clicking of the oven, the clatter of the icemaker, or the sighs made by the home's settling bricks and river rock. Lying with one ear pressed to the pillow, her hair an unwashed nest of gray wires, Rachel could even hear the schussing of soft-soled shoes across the den's plush carpets downstairs. Someone coughed and released a series of groans and mild oaths. Grace was about, busy with her daily dusting, polishing, mopping, and cooking. The homecare worker was prone to humming old show tunes as she worked. Rachel now recognized an off-key version of "The Surrey with the Fringe on Top." It brought a weak smile to her face.

Using her spindly arms, Rachel leveraged herself into a sitting position, leaning back against two plump pillows. The effort exhausted her. Forty, fifty years ago, those same arms had been tanned and well-toned. It was so terribly difficult to think of herself as an old woman, to gaze into a mirror and see the crone staring back. She'd never had to fight for breath before, monitor her diet, or squinch her eyes to make out simple shapes in afternoon light.

The worst of it was the blurriness, the fuzzy silhouettes of once-familiar objects. The prospect of going blind terrified her. All her life, she'd taken pride in her keen eyesight, thought of it as an integral part of her identity. She could still make out colors somewhat and distinguish her own fingers waggling in front of her face. But for how much longer?

Across the room, hanging on walls and perched upon bureaus, were numerous photographs of the young Rachel Demeter. In one, she was in tennis whites, cradling a racquet. In another, she swung a golf club. Here she was hiking a mountain trail, there taking careful aim on an archery range. With her red-brown hair perpetually windblown, she sat astride an appaloosa, walked along the auburn sands of an anonymous beach, and posed aristocratically in the pilot's seat of her husband Henry's little Cessna. There were a dozen pictures showing her accepting commendations for her hours of community service as a museum docent, homeless shelter volunteer, ESL tutor, soccer coach, fundraiser for the local theater, and more. Rachel couldn't see any of those photos now, but she didn't need to. That young doppelganger, trim in khakis, impossibly strong and healthy, wearing a bright immortal smile, was forever imprinted in her head, infinitely more real to her than the forlorn old woman who mocked her from the mirror.

The scary part was it had all passed in a flash. Yes, all of it, her safe and happy childhood, schoolgirl days, college semesters and sweethearts, marriage, worldly accomplishments, children, the loss of her spouse, the last several twilight years. Everything might have happened yesterday, sometimes the past was that vivid. Then there were days when her mind seemed to trombone back and forth across the years, creating rifts and distortions in her fragile sense of time. She thought it strange, being able to recall facts and faces with such clarity, only to question the reliability of those memories, as if she were channeling another woman's life.

Rachel had never been one to sugarcoat reality. Now, approaching the end of her days, what achievements could she claim as a summation of her life? Well, there were sixty-seven years of regrets, sadness, and physical pain, to be sure. Those she recognized as commonplace earthly dues which nobody, rich or poor, ever escaped. She also had to acknowledge helping to build, and now leaving behind, a strong financial legacy. There were three tall, handsome, well-intentioned, and woefully misguided sons. She had the respect and genuine affection of the movers-and-shakers of Greenstone. Perhaps most significantly, she'd developed a carefully cultivated regard for the symmetries of the natural universe, and for what other people called the *soul*.

Downstairs, Grace was humming, "Get Me to the Church on Time". Rachel smiled again, then winced as a thunderbolt raced up her spine. The pain got worse every day, just as the doctors predicted. She shut her eyes and for a perverse moment imagined the cancer shredding her insides like cheesecloth, eating her liver and intestines, howling through her bones, evil and unstoppable.

As she'd done so many times before, she willed the howl into a whimper by turning her thoughts to her late husband. She'd never believed in heaven, but she had to admit the idea of joining Henry in some fuzzy, secular afterlife felt comforting. She'd missed him these past five years, visited him often up at the shelter through snow, wind, rain, and sunshine. By no means did Rachel consider herself religious or even *spiritual,* a word she detested. All her life she'd trusted in human love and earthly grace, sensing a kind of justice at work in the world's distributions of blessings and burdens. She was not an atheist, nor a nihilist. She believed, she told herself doggedly, in *something.* If she didn't quite buy into the notion of eternal paradise, well, she was dying. Wasn't she entitled to the least little smidgen of hope?

The thing was she visualized a different sort of ending. A heart attack in the middle of a hard-fought tennis match, perhaps, or a sudden aneurysm while moderating a 'Contemporary Poetry' discussion at the independent bookstore. Maybe drowning while whitewater rafting, perishing in a fiery small plane crash. Now those were glorious ways to go. Not like this. Not bedridden, slowly wasting away. The cancer offended Rachel's heightened sense of style. She'd wanted a riveting obituary. 'Died after a long illness' really stuck in her craw. No, she wasn't supposed to go this way.

A distinct sweet-and-sour tang rose into her mouth and nose. A sudden nip of garlic materialized at the back of her throat, and the illusion of cilantro sizzled on her tongue-tip. Yet another of her mysterious responses to the cancer was this jumbled rioting of her taste buds. During the past week, she'd consumed nothing more than saltines, mashed bananas, plain yogurts and taste-free puddings, weak tea, and a terrible greenish chicken broth. Yet at odd and unpredictable moments, her mouth would swim with a bouquet of random flavors. She re-lived her very first tastes of butterscotch, turnips, dark-roasted coffee, peaches, lobster, mushrooms, blueberry pancakes, scallions, merlot. Each taste carried with it a corresponding episode from her newsreeling life. For instance, hot cocoa and gingersnaps transported her to the snowy Christmas when she was six, evoking memories of green garlands, red ribbons, sledding with her brothers, a powerful sense of being cared for, the scents of fresh-cut evergreen. The flashbacks made her shiver sixty-plus years later, her papery skin shrinking from that long-ago holiday cold. She closed her eyes, drifted into a gauzy half-sleep.

She suffered through a vague foreboding dream that caused her body to glaze itself with cold sweat. When her eyes fluttered open, she again discovered she could make out only shadows and the blurred outlines of objects. The permanence of her near blindness struck her, and she felt a self-pitying greediness for the gift of vision, if just for a few more hours. What was the point of life without the ability to see? Instantly, she was ashamed of her weakness and selfishness. Naturally people were born blind, or lost their sight to disease or accident. Many still went on to live fulfilling lives. For Rachel, colors, faces, and landscapes all lost their sacredness when they could not be clearly apprehended, when everything washed out to a pixilated field of grays. Sometimes her church-going friends tried to console her with soup and salvation. She would ask them, not disguising her bitterness, how she was supposed to navigate the hereafter without eyesight. Was she expected to grope her way to the pearly gates on hands and knees? Perhaps with a seeing-eye dog?

What Rachel desperately desired was to see her sons' faces one last time. Bless their hearts, they were all open books, their personalities set without a trace of nuance. Benjamin and his radiant nature, Thomas the charming cynic, Robert, so much like his father, the hard-working, no-nonsense businessman. She adored them with every cell in her body even while acknowledging they were strange and even somewhat shallow men. Oh, they'd tried hard to be normal and to fit in. They couldn't help being born strange, they couldn't be anything else. Was her love for them simply an accident of biology, then? Rachel refused to believe that. For one thing, there were little pieces of Henry and herself scattered throughout the boys' features and gestures. Her intuition also said you could love someone without judgment, love the essence of the person without dwelling on his behaviors. Early in life she understood human beings were, in general, neurotic and insecure. She learned to adjust her expectations and outlooks accordingly.

A few individuals were different, of course. Those folks somehow maintained an emotional integrity through good times and bad, either out of bravery or sheer ignorance of any consequences. Rachel's daughter-in-law, Violet, was one such person. No matter what, Violet remained Violet. She was even-keeled, forgiving, and full of faith, if not innocence. Henry Demeter (never Hank, sometimes H.D.) had been steadfast, well-liked, intelligent, generous, and ambitious. Rachel loved him for over forty years for those qualities and despite his follies. Still, Henry lacked the appealing animal characteristics of constancy and vulnerability.

Somewhere downstairs in the dusk-dimmed house, Grace sang "Some Enchanted Evening" in an unsteady alto.

Rachel's wish was to be cremated. She'd decided on that long ago, had written her desire into her will even prior to Henry's unexpected stroke. She wanted to be cremated and she wanted her ashes and bits of bone strewn with his in the quiet of the forest surrounding the shelter. The shelter was the holiest place she knew. Located just a few winding miles up into the foothills, it had been, over the years, a preferred site for high school bacchanals, weddings, birthday celebrations, amateur rock climbers, quinceaneras, illicit trysts, and suicide pacts. Up there, sunlight assumed an otherworldly glow and even the dust could seem numinous. She welcomed the idea of her poor remains mixed in with the mountain's dirt and rocks. It was Rachel's way of returning to the earth, as close to paradise as an incurable agnostic could get.

It wasn't supposed to end this way. The bitter words came through despite her resolve not to become childish. They were supposed to live well into their eighties, relatively healthy, free of his insurance-and-investment firm and all its pressures. Maybe they'd travel. Maybe they'd take a year off and do nothing, maybe become reacquainted with one another. She'd been looking so forward to his retirement and the better days to come. Instead, Henry died, and everything fell apart after his sudden death. Ben's terrible accident, Robert and Vi's odd arrangement, the cancer, Thomas' self-exile, all of it. In five short years, Rachel's charmed life and expectations were blown apart. *It wasn't supposed to end this way.*

At her bedside were half-a-dozen prescription bottles containing the medicines that helped her stay functional. Tranquilizers, pain pills, blood pressure medication, muscle relaxants, anti-depressants. Anymore, she couldn't read the prescription labels, but she could tell the pills apart by their placement on her nightstand, by their sizes and shapes, and by the colors she could still discern. Blues, yellows, pinks, whites. Pretty, like tiny, impressionistic meadows of wildflowers. She'd been so grateful for them at first. In the past few months, however, she'd grown increasingly aware of her failing body and she no longer was thankful for what little life was left. Her mind remained quick, but so what? She'd never again water-ski, walk the hilly streets of her secluded neighborhood, make love, play the guitar, drive a car. The myth of becoming independent again, which had sustained her through some difficult periods, now vanished with an awful finality.

For a moment, Rachel swore she could hear the end steaming toward her with a sound like a monstrous dark engine. No, it was only Grace's strained whistling version of "My Favorite Things".

Pharmaceuticals had been wonderful and could be wonderful still. You had to do things right, though. One by one, slow and steady. You wanted peace, not permanent brain damage and a ventilator. You did not want the indignity of the pumped stomach and you definitely wanted to avoid a humiliating survival. Slowly and deliberately, Rachel poured a glass of ice-water from the crystal pitcher. She twisted open each of her prescription bottles. One by one, she thought, starting with the blue. Little by little and easy does it. One of Henry's oft-repeated maxims was there was worth, even virtue, in performing tasks incrementally, with patience, attention to detail, and an acceptance of deferred results. Slowly and surely, then. Blue. Yellow. Pink. White. And blue again.

Chapter Two

Robert Demeter straightened his plain dark blue tie and carefully regarded his reflection in the bathroom mirror. The fluorescent lighting turned his skin ghostly and cast his eyes, nose, and lips in a white cheesy smudge. Robert was of medium height and build. He wore his black hair in a businessman's cut and his sideburns fell exactly to mid-ear. His eyes were pale gray.

"Rob? Are you ready? It's almost six."

"Be right there. Two seconds."

They were visiting Mother tonight. She'd been feeling worse lately, so it was the proper thing to do. There was time yet to slap on a mild aftershave, brush the lint from his black trousers, give his shoes one last quick inspection.

His late father never missed the opportunity to remind his sons that 'appearances count'. "Perception is reality", boomed the old man, time after time. "You are the man you present yourself to be. At work, in the community, even with your own family. Always remember that."

Robert had. He'd memorized and internalized and lived out his father's axioms for success in a lifelong struggle to transcend what he thought of as his own ordinary nature. For the third or fourth time, he gave his image a critical review. He regarded the bland, fortyish face in the glass, good-looking in a conventional, uninteresting way. Because he always took pains to be fair-minded, it was easy for him to understand why people underestimated him. Twenty years of military service did little to etch any distinction onto his face; it had remained essentially unchanged since his earliest baby pictures.

He'd enlisted in the Army straight out of high school because he couldn't stand the thought of going to college and because he thought signing up might please his father. He often thought he'd be there still, a nondescript Staff Sergeant possessed of a lackluster dossier, had Henry Demeter survived the major stroke he'd suffered five winters back.

Robert had been comfortable swimming about in the lagoons of the military culture. He'd liked it for many of the same reasons he'd enjoyed playing team sports, for the structure as well as the comforts of comradery, self-discipline, and conformity. The military was one career path where facelessness could be an asset. Just as he'd never been first-string on any varsity sport, he'd never really excelled in his role as a noncom. He might bristle at the bromide 'Good enough for government work', but in truth the Army taught him mediocrity was not necessarily a bad quality. Mediocre meant average, and Robert was nothing if not proud of being an average guy.

He was the first to admit he was no genius, but neither was he a slacker. He readily acknowledged there were folks much better off than him, but also pointed out many more were in far worse shape. His self-image was of a man who got the most out of his limited talents, stamina, and tolerances. He considered himself trustworthy. He bought into the idea that it was Joe Lunchbox who built this country, and who now carried it on his big shoulders. "Sergeants, they're the backbones of the armed forces," he told anyone halfway willing to listen.

One of his warmest memories was of drinking a few beers down at the NCO club with his fellow noncoms after a tedious workday in the motor pool, laughing about clueless officers and swapping war stories.

His favorite joke, which he repeated to every new acquaintance, military or civilian, opened a small peephole into Robert's character. "A sergeant has to take a whiz, so he goes to the latrine. He's at the urinal doing his thing, and when he's just about done, in walks a second lieutenant. The sergeant finishes peeing, zips up, salutes the lieutenant, and starts to walk out of the bathroom. The looie clears his throat and says, 'You know, Sarge, in Officer Candidate School I learned to wash my hands after using the restroom.' This stops the sergeant in his tracks. He pauses, turns around, and replies, 'That's interesting, sir. At the NCO Academy, they taught us not to piss on our hands.'"

Average guy humor, sir, yes sir.

All right, so he was no financial wizard or ground-breaking scientist, no superhuman athlete, no corporate shark. But really, who was? Nobody he knew, anyway. Now, with his military pension and as the head of the company his father built, he was a model citizen who voted faithfully in all elections, belonged to prominent service clubs in town, attended church on Sundays. Under most circumstances, Robert was kind and generous with his family, his few friends, his customers.

Maybe those qualities were what prompted the recent talk of Rob Demeter running for the state legislature. Violet certainly thought it was a splendid idea. She was his biggest booster.

"Rob? Do you have the car keys?"

"Yes."

People chided him for being so vanilla, but one thing they couldn't say was that he was unreliable. You could always count on Robert Demeter. He couldn't understand people who were habitually late for appointments, who made promises they wouldn't keep, who seemed to go out of their way to act flaky. He distrusted men who laughed too easily and women who allowed their emotions to govern their lives. He disliked namedroppers, social butterflies, flirts, rogues, and especially culture-vultures. He thought them all unbearably pretentious. Robert himself drank socially, traveled to Vegas twice a year for the blackjack tables, diligently monitored his diet. Now and then he indulged in salty snacks, and once in a blue moon smoked a joint if the atmosphere was just right.

"All sins in moderation," as his father often lectured. However, he disdained those who went too far in their excesses and entertainments.

When he first received word Henry Demeter had died at his desk at the Foothills Investment Services, Robert found himself unable to interpret his own feelings. He'd always been good at taking orders and following instructions. He'd simply never been in tune with his emotions. He found he couldn't cry. From his barracks at Ft. Dix, he spoke calmly to his mother on the phone. Yes, he would arrange for emergency leave and fly home for the funeral. Yes, it was a shame when it took a tragedy to bring the family together again. Robert sensed he ought to feel something besides vague annoyance at having his routine disrupted.

Where was the fog of sadness, the sudden emptiness he'd heard other men describe when they'd lost a loved one? It helped when his mother's voice was so characteristically dry. She might have been informing him she'd lost her garden to an early cold snap.

Henry's death had come as a total surprise. He'd always been the picture of health. "Never sick a day in my life," as men of his generation liked to boast. "Never sick enough to miss an honest day's work." How fitting then that he'd keeled over at his investment company, his true home. Now there were the endless details of the funeral to plan. Robert envisioned how it would all play out. His mother would be too overwhelmed to deal with the logistics of the services. Benjamin, the youngest, would be her comforter and the comforter of everyone who made the pilgrimage to Henry's open casket. People seemed to naturally gravitate to Ben in times of trouble. The only questions were if he could be contacted and if then he would show up. Thomas, his father's favorite, main recipient of the businessman's meager love and counsel, would, in the long days ahead, vie to be the center of attention. He'd mug, he'd wax poetic. He'd somehow transform Henry's wake into his own performance piece, spinning the right words to evoke tears and laughter from the mourners. Because, no matter what the event, it was always about Thomas.

Robert? Robert would be left to do what was needed, what Ben couldn't do and what Thomas labeled 'the drudge work'. Nothing new there. Robert was expected to be the brother in the background, upholding decorum and seizing responsibility. He would speak with the funeral director. He'd order the flowers. He'd coordinate the catering and call the newspaper about the obituary notice. He'd communicate with the pastor. As usual, he'd be the steady, uncomplaining gofer behind the main scenes. The invisible man. Part of him embraced the role, but another part resented its obscurity. Deep down, he felt he'd never received proper credit for his efforts and sacrifices.

He'd never once considered what his father might've been thinking at the time of his death, if there'd even been time for him to entertain any last thoughts, regrets, revelations. H.D. had never been an introspective man. Robert imagined he wouldn't have changed even with his life ebbing away.

About Heaven and Hell, and where Henry Demeter was fated to spend his eternity, Robert didn't have a clue. In fact, he didn't know what he believed. He didn't spend a lot of time reflecting upon religion, the nature of sin or the afterlife. The Demeters had never been much of a spiritual family, though they'd always been regular churchgoers. Henry's lofty community profile demanded appearances be kept up, and it fell to Robert to carry on the tradition. Thomas grew up to become an atheist who loved gospel music. For a while, Ben seemed attracted to the power and passion of Christianity. Then came his accident, and who knew what he thought about God now. Their mother spoke of her belief in ghosts and astral projections, though not necessarily in a Supreme Being. Robert thought her visits to the shelter, when she'd been well enough to go, a little creepy.

"I'm having a conversation with your father," she'd tell Robert matter-of-factly. "Sure, we still talk. Don't look at me like that."

He'd shake his head and leave her be. His own church attendance was little more than loyalty to his father and a social habit. He'd gone for so many Sundays it never occurred to him not to go.

Now Violet, his bride, his spark and spirit, she was something of a freethinker. She had an open-hearted approach to the world, but she was also pragmatic, which helped keep her grounded. She didn't care for the rituals of church, but generally it wasn't held against her because she was so frank in saying so. Despite her reluctance, she loyally accompanied Robert to services every Sunday, which earned her extra points and forgiveness from their good neighbors.

People whispered they made the strangest couple, a real oil-and-water combination. The line of gossip went something like, "She's pretty enough, and so bright and talented. A little wild, but good-hearted. Why would she marry someone like Robert? Oh, he can be pleasant and solid, though a bit of a stick-in-the-mud. Violet, why, she's extraordinary, isn't she? Well, they do say opposites attract, don't they? But she might have done so much better, don't you think?"

Robert wasn't deaf. He'd heard the talk and had to admit, from time to time, he'd asked himself the same questions. Vi's charms were obvious. Her smile, her gray-green eyes, her fearlessness, were admirable. Then what had she seen in *him*? He wasn't rich or particularly handsome. He wasn't clever like Thomas or sweet-tempered like Ben. Security? Surely not just that. Yes, they'd taken an odd journey together over the years. Their courtship had been long, cautious, slow-burning, full of subtle colors and shadings. They'd never talked much. In truth, they were almost inarticulate in each other's company. Somehow, though, they meshed intuitively, telepathically. Quiet dinners, popular movies, long hikes in the foothills, soft jazz concerts, all without too many words passing between them. Vi's spontaneous nature seemed to offset Robert's slow-and-steady temperament, his hesitancies. His need for consistency and an uncluttered existence seemed to counterbalance her exuberance, her penchant for risk-taking.

At least that's the way Robert viewed matters. He'd never been the sentimental type, but in the first months of their romance he'd been light-headed, impossibly goofy. He thought he understood what it meant to discover your *soulmate*. In his tenderness, he'd felt protective, and longed to pull her close and murmur endearments into her hair, "My darling girl, my shooting star, my sweet little rabbit."

Vi would have none of it. Even when they were first dating, even at her most vulnerable, she'd rejected his infatuated cooing. Growing up she'd had a rough time. She was just coming off an affair that ended badly. It made Robert squirm to think about her history with other men, but most of the time he managed to block it out. Violet matured into a clear-eyed woman with little patience for the cloying language and promises of cheap romance. Giving her flowers was acceptable, and small gifts of jewelry and art and music were always welcome. But spare her the *dear* and *sweetheart* and *honey*, and especially the *little rabbit.* Unless you were spoiling for a fight.

The phone rang. Robert decided to let the answering machine pick up. He and Vi were seeing Mother tonight and he didn't want a delay. It was their scheduled time to visit Mother, who'd been feeling worse than usual lately. She had every right to expect punctuality from her son and daughter-in-law. He'd been grateful, if a little surprised, when Violet and his mother got along so well, although even Rachel seemed mystified by their marriage. At any rate, tonight's plans were set. No unanticipated phone call was going to alter his timetable. *Just leave a message*, he thought as the phone rang again.

Yes, he mused with some satisfaction when the ringing finally stopped. They anchored each other, he and Vi. Outsiders might view him as staid and boring. They might see Vi's passions as mere flightiness. Robert knew better, and now with confidence imagined he had a near-perfect marriage. "No one stands up alone in this hard world," was another of Henry's lessons. Vi played a crucial part in helping Robert mature into the man he'd become. He was proud of being a good son, a devoted husband, a steady employee, an old-fashioned guy who cared about Greenstone and who tried to stay positively involved in community affairs.

Soon, perhaps, he might add 'State Assemblyman' to his resume. Stranger things happened.

"Rob," called Vi, and something in the way she said his name crackled with trouble. He hadn't heard the answering machine click on because Vi had picked up. She appeared in the doorway, phone in hand.

He couldn't read her expression.

She said, "It's the agency. You'd better take it." She added, unnecessarily, "It's about your mother."

Calmly, Robert smoothed his plain blue tie. Fastidiously, he picked at some lint on his shirtsleeve. He ran a hand through his black hair. Then he turned from the mirror to take the phone from his wife to hear the news about his mother.

Chapter Three

Every table was supposed to have an identical set-up. Menus wiped clean and set upright in wooden holders, crystal salt and pepper shakers, silverware tightly rolled in red cloth napkins, a single iris placed upright in a slender cut-glass vase, a candle burning in a small square ceramic dish. Sixteen tables times four place settings equaled sixty-four total units. Sixty-four knives, spoons, salad forks, dinner forks, water glasses, coffee cups, wineglasses, linen placemats. About forty-five minutes of work for Ben.

He was ready. Traditionally, he woke at seven, methodically performed his morning grooming tasks, listened to Fats Domino and Chuck Berry and Jerry Lee Lewis and Buddy Holly to get his blood pumping, fueled himself with a bowl of Raisin Bran, two slices of lightly-buttered cinnamon raisin toast, and a banana, said his prayers, said goodbye to Mr. Whiskers, made double-sure all the doors and windows of his ground-level apartment were locked, then hopped on his custom-made three-wheeler and pedaled the mile-and-a-half through town to his job at Maggiore's.

He never drank coffee or tea, but in his backpack he carried a two-liter bottle of Dr. Pepper to help sugar-jolt him through the day.

Ben had worked at Maggiore's for nearly two years. It was part of his social rehabilitation plan. About a year after the accident, Robert helped him get the job as a step toward Ben regaining some of his independence Ben liked the mathematical structure of his work routine. What was menial work to his co-workers was a comfort for Ben, who performed best when his day was laid out before him like a trustworthy map.

While his fellow employees slipped out the back-screen door to take breaks and pass around a joint, Ben completed his forty-eighth unit. Twelve times four. The task seventy-five percent complete. He didn't quite whistle while he worked, but he did hum under his breath. He also synchronized his movements to the rolls and bumps of various Fifties rock songs. "Blueberry Hill," "Sweet Little Sixteen," "Great Balls of Fire." Anything by Elvis, naturally. Give Ben some vintage music and meaningful work and he was in his own peaceful zone of joy.

"You like those moldy goldy oldies, don't you, Mr. Benjamin?" This was Cynthia, one of the regular waitresses.

"I like that Fat Man. I like The Killer."

Cynthia was by far his favorite co-worker. She was unfailingly nice to him and he considered her very pretty in her black capris and red Maggiore's t-shirt.

"You're a sweet guy, Ben. I'll just bet you have tons of friends." Cynthia flashed him a sunburst smile which spread a tree of warmth throughout his entire body. He felt his cheeks growing hot and knew he was blushing. He ducked his head and went back to work, concentrating mightily on unit number forty-nine. Grinning, Cynthia returned to her own duties. Ben waited till she was out of earshot before exhaling in relief. To soothe himself, he hummed "Roll Over Beethoven."

Cynthia was fine, fine, fine, but she was wrong about Ben having a lot of friends. In fact, if asked, he would declare he had just one true friend, that being his cat, Mr. Whiskers.

Mr. Whiskers was a Heinz 57 feline, a crazy quilt stray who arrived unannounced and out of nowhere on Ben's windowsill at four a.m. one baleful morning last winter. It howled like a cartoon cat, meowing its head off like an ambulance siren. It wouldn't shut up until Ben paid it some serious attention. He finally eased open the window and let it in. The animal bounded to the floor, its fur wet and disheveled. It scoped out the small apartment while Ben went to the kitchen and set out a bowl of milk, opened a can of tuna. On a whim, he placed a few Cheez-Its next to the bowl. The stray devoured everything. It licked its whiskers contentedly at about the same time Ben discovered a pungent puddle of cat pee next to his bedroom closet.

He mopped up the mess and sprayed the floor with Lysol, which he'd heard could kill even the AIDS virus. He tried to lure the beast out his front door by pulling an old shoelace slowly across the carpet and around the door jamb. The cat watched with casual interest but wouldn't take the bait. Instead, it stood its ground and fixed Ben with a flat, superior stare. Ben heaved a sigh and pulled the door shut. From his mother, he'd inherited a love of creatures, and it was this love, plus sheer exhaustion, which caused him to wave the white flag.

"You can stay tonight, Mr. Whiskers," he told the bedraggled cat. "But first thing in the morning, I'm calling the pound."

Mr. Whiskers blinked up at him, yawned, licked a paw, then curled up on the living room floor where it fell dead asleep.

Cat lovers the world over will not be surprised to learn that, when Ben awoke to late morning sunshine, Mr. Whiskers' warm furry body was coiled next to his on the bed. In less than six hours, the stray established squatter's rights. Ben grunted, gave it more milk, some tuna and a Wheat Thin smeared with peanut butter. He added to his weekly grocery list the items *wet/dry cat food* and *kitty litter*.

Mr. Whiskers became the cat's official name. Over time, though, depending upon circumstances, it might be called Mr. Hungry, Mr. Smelly, Mr. Sleepy-head, Mr. Pain-in-the-Butt, Mr. Troublemaker, Mr. Mysterious, and other colorful appellations. Only the title of 'Mr.' remained constant.

It was something of a shock, then, when the vet, providing shots, vitamins, and a routine check-up pronounced Mr. Whiskers a 'she'.

The 'Mr.' tag stuck, though, and slowly Mr. Whiskers' true temperament revealed itself. The first clue should have been her right ear, which was horribly mutilated. It looked as if someone had taken a hole-puncher and methodically employed it around the perimeter of the ear. So, she'd been victimized by a cruel owner sometime in her shadowy, feline past. As things turned out, she was also an instigator, and a tough customer who gave as good as she got. She routinely terrorized the neighborhood at night, picking fights, seducing toms, scratching up the neighbors' screens, bringing birds and snakes into the apartment, howling like a fool at traffic.

Most of Ben's doctors viewed his companionship with Mr. Whiskers as a healthy component of his recovery. The accident had left Ben with what was mystically labeled 'cognitive deficits'. His main symptom seemed to be long-term memory loss. Ben remembered very little about his life prior to the fall. "Very common for a head injury," the therapist told Robert and Violet. In a way, Ben had been fortunate. Everyone said he was blessed to be alive, lucky not to have wound up semi-paralyzed or worse.

His impulse control was mostly good. He didn't suffer from seizures or sleep deprivation. He retained his faith in God. He simply processed information more slowly and incompletely than before. Sometimes his equilibrium went haywire.

After the hospital, there was no question he would stay with Robert and Violet for a while. As he rehabbed, Ben appreciated living in the same house as Vi. She had a clean soap smell about her. She didn't seem to mind his shaved head, or his slurred speech. She catered freely to Ben's sweet tooth. Together they laughed at a lot of the same TV shows. They argued over music, Coltrane and Roy Orbison and Mozart. They discussed God and the mysterious ripples of His universe. At times, Robert could be impatient, but not Vi. Ben thought she was beautiful, and she always saved him a reassuring smile.

Ben couldn't say Robert was unkind. They were brothers after all. One wouldn't be cruel to the other, that wasn't the way brothers behaved. Rob was, however, the cold moon to Violet's shining sun. Ben would not have conceptualized it in this manner, but Robert took the same 'ledger system' approach to his relationships he applied to his work. He calculated what he owed and what was owed him, then attempted to make it all balance. Sometimes, Ben wondered how his brother and Vi ever stayed in tune, but much of the time they seemed to manage.

Ben finished his fifty-fourth unit and took a moment to stretch. Even now, in his diminished capacity, his own relationship with God remained personal. "Faith is no joke," he liked to say. He rarely forgot to thank the Lord for his job, his apartment, his brother and his sister-in-law. He deeply valued their abiding love, his whole blessed existence. Day in, day out, he humbly acknowledged and accepted things might have turned out much, much worse for him. God bless, indeed.

Yet, he remembered enough of Before The Accident to miss the prophecies and revelations which had once lit up the inside of his head with divine fireworks. Those pyrotechnics now remained subdued, flaring only when stress or fatigue worked like a welding torch upon his mind. Those were the only moments when Ben felt anything close to regret or self-pity. He recognized those moments as a test. He had to force himself to remember his accident was all part of a Grand Plan he could never understand but must accept.

Maggiore's was less than an hour away from opening up to the early lunch crowd. The restaurant's employees buzzed about, getting ready for the rush. Ben smiled to himself, hearing the comforting clamor of pots and pans, the salad bar being prepped, his co-workers hurling jokes and uncensored insults among themselves before the arrival of customers. He thought, *All in all, I'm a lucky, lucky man.*

Ben remembered two episodes of violence marring his near-textbook recovery. Those incidents gave his doctors pause when it came time for endorsing his request to live independently.

The first time occurred shortly after his accident. Ben had been released from the hospital and was moved to a convalescent home for a few weeks. There, his behaviors and compliance with medications could be monitored while he received physical therapy. One evening he was sitting by himself in the placid, earth-toned dayroom, gazing indifferently at the crackling TV. In walked an orderly named Kevin. This orderly was a short, sour, dim-witted man with a sad little life and a broad mean streak. Visiting hours were over, no other patients or staff were around, he'd had a shitty day, and he was in the mood to push somebody's buttons. Deliberately, he bumped up against Ben's chair and feigned exasperation, barking, "Move, retard!". To Kevin's immense surprise, Ben responded with a roar and sprang at the stunned worker. He pummeled the man's face bloody and was inflicting major damage on the back and shoulders when staff burst in to break up the one-sided fight. It took four orderlies to restrain Ben who, with his wild swings, scored multiple hits inducing three deep body bruises, two black eyes, and a broken nose.

A tsk-tsk progress note was duly added to Ben's file. His

medications were adjusted, and he underwent twelve weeks of mandatory anger management counseling. Once it was evident the orderly would recover from his injuries, Kevin was gently encouraged to accept a small settlement and to pursue other employment options.

Many months followed without incident. Ben's behavior was impeccable, if somewhat docile. There was no indication of ongoing distress, not a flicker of an outburst. His recovery seemed to be robustly back on track. As part of the plan to mainstream him into society, his caseworker obtained for Ben a part-time janitorial position with a commercial cleaning company. His job coach was Amy, a mild-mannered and waifish dark-haired girl. Amy had a boyfriend by the name of Trevor, and Trevor was a borderline sociopath. He owned all the trademarks of the street-savvy badass ex-con, the gleaming shaved head, jailhouse tattoos on his neck and arms, a silver spike sparkling through his pierced tongue.

Trevor was not allowed to visit Amy at work, but Trevor had no active listening skills. He believed rules were for other people. Being unemployed and not the stay-at-home type, he popped up unannounced at jobsites on a regular basis. At those times, he mainly harangued Amy about her many deficiencies as a girlfriend, such as the way she mishandled money, her lack of house-cleaning skills, her hairstyle, her weight, her inadequacies in the bedroom, her creativity in frying pork chops to inedible cinders, her lousy taste in music, and her general incompetence in pretty much every other area of life. His normal pitch of voice was just below a bellow. He punctuated his tirades by jabbing his hand through the air, pinky and index finger extended. He said "bitch" a lot. He grinned like a baboon when she cowered and whimpered for him to stop.

"Maybe," Ben said hesitantly one afternoon when Trevor was belittling Amy's total lack of fashion sense. It took about three seconds for Trevor to register Ben's presence. When he did, he wheeled slowly, his fanatic's eyes wide with disbelief.

"What? Did you say something?" he hissed.

Ben cleared his throat. "Maybe you should go home, Trevor. Can't you see Amy's really upset? I don't think you're supposed to be here, anyway. Maybe you guys can talk later, when you're a little calmer."

Trevor's eyes blazed like ice-blue death rays. "Back off, queer bait. When I want your fucking input, I'll fucking ask for it."

Badass Trevor never knew what hit him. Ben laid into him like a flesh-and-bone hurricane. He hooked his fist hard into the bald skull, then with the flat of his hand chopped at the blue barbed wire inked around Trevor's neck. While the thug tried to catch his breath, Ben spun him and delivered two hard blows to the kidneys. Trevor sank to his knees, groaning. Ben then let loose with a soccer-style kick below the chin. The tough guy fell to the ground face-first, his legs quivering, unaware that the rest of his body was already unconscious.

Significantly, the therapist's notes later mentioned what he termed Ben's 'inappropriate smiling effect' as Trevor was being scraped off the floor and Amy had been sufficiently tranquilized.

The doctor was also struck by the fact that Trevor lifted weights and was ridiculously muscular, while Ben's physique was more in line with a long-distance runner. It led him to ask Robert and Vi if Ben had ever been prone to violent outbursts before his accident. A troubled look crossed Robert's face. Then he shook his head and soundlessly mouthed "no".

"He was an athlete," Vi was quoted in the report, evidently trying to be helpful. In high school and college, Ben wrestled, rock-climbed, played wide receiver and defensive end on his football teams, even boxed a little. His physical gifts had been inherited from his mother and his competitive nature from Henry. Both Robert and Thomas had been good sandlot ballplayers, playing pick-up basketball, slow-pitch softball, touch football. Neither of them had anything near Ben's natural skills. He brought the same friendly ferocity to the games as his father had exhibited in the business world.

"What are you saying, Vi?" Robert scowled.

"Don't forget, both times he acted out he was provoked. I'm not excusing the violence, of course that's over-the-top, but..." She compressed her lips and struggled to explain herself. "I'm just saying his aggressiveness seems to be brought out by stressful situations and hostile personalities. Those guys he pounded, they were no angels. It's not like he's randomly attacking people on the street. He gets frustrated, so he lashes out."

"So what's your solution? Keep him away from assholes, and maybe he won't go off on them?" Robert was angry. This second lapse of control had shaken the little confidence he'd had in Ben. "Wouldn't that be convenient? For all of us, not just Ben. You know what else would be great? If the assholes would all agree to wear some sort of ID, say, the same colored armband, so you wouldn't have to guess who was who."

"What color would you be wearing, then?" she shot back at him.

"Vi, if Ben is ever going to function on his own again…"

"I know, Rob. I know, I know, I know."

Somehow, they got through it. After many months more of 'appropriate social behavior', Ben regained enough of Robert's trust for Rob to put in a good word at Maggiore's. The restaurant's owner was a Rotary buddy and held some annuities with Rob's firm. Besides, employee turnover was rampant, and he could always use another body at minimum wage.

So began Ben's tenure at Maggiore's. It didn't take long for him to feel at home with the structure of the workday. The crew of high-spirited teenagers, single mothers, amiable miscreants, and grizzled, marginally effective supervisors readily accepted Ben into their dysfunctional fold. They were happy to show him the ropes. Within a few weeks, Ben felt like he'd been there forever. "In a good way," he made sure to add. The first paycheck didn't hurt, either.

He soon learned the rhythm of the restaurant's rush hours and lulls. His co-workers took elaborate pains to teach him their pet names for regular customers. Johnny Fettucine and Marybeth Marinara were an elderly couple that shuffled in for late lunches every Tuesday and Thursday when the staff was busy breaking down the buffet and transitioning to the dinner menu. There was a group of young guys who came in at happy hour most weekdays, the Bruschetta Bunch, looking to forget about their brutal day at the office. They spent a little on appetizers, like mushrooms, calamari, and spinach artichoke dip, and a lot on alcohol. The smoking-hot Tortellini Twins had dinner together on alternate Friday nights and were the targets of much speculation among the male staff as to the true color of their angel hair, the impressive size of their 'gorgeous gorgonzolas, and the presumed skill with which they could hand-bread a cannoli. Their nickname originated when one busboy commented he'd like to 'stuff their tortellini' with six varieties of man-cheese. Other regulars included a short man with a pencil moustache dubbed 'Shrimp Scampi', a lonely, dark-haired woman who sat at the bar and drank red wine till closing time, christened Penne Horndog Picatta, and a favorite, Tito Tiramisu Scaloppini Primavera, Jr. Tito was an overweight, washed-up mobster-looking type.

One of the cooks was an aspiring novelist, and he would narrate a tale noir the moment he laid eyes on Tito. "He lumbered into Maggiore's and collapsed into a chair that groaned beneath his girth. Without so much as glancing at a menu, he ordered ricotta ravioli. As fate would have it, an old enemy came swaggering in as Tito was slurping his matzo ball soup. Tito wasted no time and, without even putting down his spoon, pulled out a pistol and drilled the would-be assailant with three well-placed bullets. The blood ran thick as alfredo sauce, the color of sun-dried tomatoes."

Ben passed muster on this rite of passage one afternoon when he correctly identified Lasagna Larry and his hoity-toity mistress, Rosemary Mozzarella. He was embraced by the Maggiore family. Cynthia took him under her wing, and her kindness went a long way toward helping Ben feel like part of the gang. Whenever he wondered, in those first days at the restaurant, if he would ever feel comfortable in his busboy duties, he needed only an encouraging smile from the pretty waitress to boost his confidence.

Now, he saw Cynthia near the back of Maggiore's, in the small alcove where the pay phones and restrooms were located. She was on the phone and a troubled look clouded her features. She nodded two or three times. From the restaurant's rumor mill, Ben knew there were two ongoing sources of misery for Cynthia. The first was a co-worker, a barely competent cook called Phillip, who was something of a bully and who saw himself as being at the top of Maggiore's pitiful pecking order. Phillip was a swarthy, wisecracking little man of a thousand taunts who was democratic in his coarse treatment of the staff. The grapevine reported he had 'the hots' for Cynthia and, despite consistent rejections, repeatedly pressured her to go out with him.

The other unhappiness in the waitress' life was her father, a widower, with whom she lived. Here, the gossip turned dark and suggestive. Ben hoped what he'd heard about the old man was not even close to being true.

Phillip was in the kitchen whipping up his specialties of charred meats, overdone pastas, and nuked vegetables, so Ben deduced it must be the father on the phone causing Cynthia's distress. Much to his surprise, she turned his way and crooked her finger at him.

"It's for you," she told him, handing him the phone, her sad eyes regarding him in what seemed to Ben a new way. "It's Robert."

Ben listened in silence to his brother on the phone. He remained expressionless as the news was delivered in Rob's clipped, businesslike tones. When Ben hung up, Cynthia squeezed his arm and whispered how very sorry she was.

"Go home, Ben. I'll let everyone know. Are you okay to ride your trike?"

He nodded. Outwardly, he seemed a little stunned, but otherwise fine. Inside, though, something wet and cold coiled in his intestines, something like a whirling black typhoon. He turned away from the waitress and ran to the stockroom where his three-wheeler was parked. His skin broke out in a sheen of cold sweat. Old thoughts and images, many of them half-formed, raged through his head. He found himself alternately flexing and balling his fingers in a helpless anger he couldn't understand. Some memory-shard of yoga classes kicked in then. He recalled his breathing exercises and centered himself as best he could.

Eventually, he rode the three-wheeler home against a rainy headwind. He couldn't stand or comprehend his own feelings, and the stinging rain was almost a welcome distraction. Once home, he made a pot of green tea, one of his mother's favorite beverages. He put on a tape, a homemade compilation of oldies. His hair and clothing were soaked through, his forearms prickled with gooseflesh, but Carl Perkins, Jackie Wilson, and The Drifters slowly sang the warmth back in his blood. Ben collapsed into an old recliner. Mr. Whiskers sauntered by and gave his hand a comforting lick.

The green tea helped. The black typhoon quelled somewhat. And here, where nobody could witness his shame or his guilt or his barely suppressed rage, here in his living room with the curtains drawn and the lights turned off, Ben cried himself to sleep.

Chapter Four

He sensed a certain anticipatory sizzle in the air tonight. Tom took it as an omen this might be a different sort of show for him. Tonight, he planned to tone down the social commentary, the political satire, set aside the celebrity impressions and, for the most part, spare the audience the acid rain of his wit. He didn't know why, but this evening he felt compelled to improvise some new, untested material. If he hadn't learned much else over the past dozen years, at least he'd learned to trust his intuition.

The stage was dark and the theater three-quarters full. A deep, disembodied voice thanked everyone for turning off their pagers and beepers. It then intoned, "Ladies and gentlemen, please welcome tonight's special guest, Mr. Thomas Freeman Demeter."

Polite applause was followed by a thin spotlight. Tom's tall silhouette glided to center stage. He stepped behind the podium to the microphone. A pitcher of iced tea with no lemon and a tall glass was placed on a small table alongside. Lemon, thought Tom, made the tea taste like detergent. He tapped the microphone twice, raised his eyes to scan the audience seated out in the dark. They'd be expecting his usual - The World According to Demeter. Every artist had his greatest hits, right? Demeter's Bill of Rights, which began, "The first, most critical amendment says that all Americans have the right to make their own stupid decisions, and to bear the unhappy consequences.". Behind-the-scenes tales from his cult documentary, *This Hard Life*. Demeter's Ten Commandments. The ever-popular "Wouldn't It Be Great If...?" and "You Can't Make This Shit Up" skits. Grimly comic cautionary tales and contemporary fables from Gotham and Podunkville and The Burbs.

Not tonight, though. Tonight, the audience was in for a little surprise.

"She was not quite human, not quite machine," Tom began, his rich baritone filling the silence. "She was old when memory was young. Her mother was the Earth, her father was the inferno that raged in the heart of the Earth. You could say she was born bubbling up out of the tar pits, conjured by magma, midwifed by plutonic rock. She surfaced to life from the rancid waters and twisted tree roots and old bones of the underworld. She took her first breath in a scrap-metal junkyard, beneath a pewter-gray sky.

"She was blessed with spellbinding beauty. She possessed long platinum hair, coppery eyes, bronzed breasts, a rounded stainless-steel ass. Her loose joints were packed with nickel bearings and her muscles threaded with titanium. She had a young, miraculous body, hammered and buffed to near perfection. It was a body made for speed and motion, for flying, for horseback riding, for lovemaking.

"Her mind, too, was a wonder of engineering. Imagine a brain lit with hundreds of burning strands of tungsten, embedded with tens of thousands of precision-made silicon chips, each sparking with its own colors and magnitudes. Together, they created a high-speed grid of emotions and intelligence. Her nature was hard-wired for equal parts iron will, mercurial temperament, and diamond wit.

"Her name was Rachel, a Biblical name meaning 'the lamb'. A contradiction, perhaps, because she was anything but lamblike. She was a woman of metal and a woman of *mettle*, and also a woman known to occasionally *meddle*. Yet this tough-as-nails creature who was not quite human, not quite machine, *could*, at times, show tenderness. She'd been known to weep at symphonies and sigh over delicate watercolors. Occasionally, she showed a side softened by lifelong charitable work."

Tom paused, partly for effect and partly to pour himself a glass of iced tea. The stage lights were hot. Storytelling was thirsty work.

"The great mystery is how this Rachel, this near-goddess who rose above her beginnings in the dirt and loam and base metals and rocks, who became a gold standard unto herself, how could she ever have stumbled? Why had she willingly stooped to dim her inner lights and weigh down her life by marrying beneath herself? For what earthly reason would she wed a rude, common, unformed lump of lead? What possessed her to give up her bright destiny? Was it rebellion against expectations? An unalloyed rejection of the natural gifts she'd never asked for? A desire to live in a quieter, more commonplace manner?

"Who knows? We won't explore those questions tonight. They'll likely never be answered and, in the end, they probably don't matter. For, dear audience, as you surely know, we're only remembered and measured by our actions, not our intents.

"So, at last, it only matters that Rachel did marry this lowly clod, this unimpressive lump of lead. Through the years, she did what she could to mold him into some sort of presentable sculpture, to shine him up a bit. For better or for worse, they forged a life together. It came to pass that Rachel bore three children, all males. The baby was a golden boy, the middle child a silver-tongued wastrel, and the oldest a cheap-as-tin, gray-as-aluminum dullard.

"Let's begin with the middle boy. He grew up with a brash and brassy charm. He made friends easily, displayed cleverness in his conversations and transactions. This was the silver-tongued son, the one for whom words came as naturally as breathing. His mismatched parents had high hopes for him, but from the beginning he was doomed to disappoint them. See, Silver always seemed to be craning his neck forward, wondering what was coming next. He had the ability to persuade himself that the future was the only happy place possible and perhaps one day he'd dwell there in total contentment. His past? All letdowns, poor decisions, short-sightedness, and a colossal junkpile of regrets. Because it was so painful for him to glance in the rearview mirror, he did so rarely. The present was somewhat better, but also unsatisfactory, mostly a struggle, a dreary and unrewarding slog of maintenance. He viewed today only as a launching pad for his glittering tomorrows. Thus, he never learned to appreciate life as it was happening. He could not live 'in the moment', as it were.

"Gold, on the other hand, had *only* the past to embrace, even if his memories were tragically flawed. This youngest son might have become the smartest of all the boys except for his soft head, which had been dinged and dented through the passing of the years and which ensured he'd never reach his rich potential. He was trustworthy, open-hearted, and hard-working, but his present was fenced in by a carefully planned regimen of chores and rituals. He spent so much effort getting through his days, there was little or no energy left for him to appreciate the routine joys of his existence. The future? He couldn't even conceptualize it. He thought of it as a fuzzier version of today. He was neither optimistic nor cynical about the many tomorrows to come. Tomorrows would come, of course, and they would go. He couldn't connect that natural cycle with the setting and accomplishing of goals. He couldn't fathom meeting new friends, discovering new songs and good wines, experiencing romantic love. His yesterdays, however, remained vivid, disjointed precious yellow flashes inside his damaged head. That was where he came to feel most at home, living within those brilliant, sporadic, fool's gold memories.

"Finally, behold the eldest son, who was pragmatic, plodding, ordinary to a fault, humorless. There was no shine to him at all. He was common as clay. In a word, he was a drone. This tin man, unlike his brothers, was caught in the riptide of the now, incapable of swimming either forward or backward in time. Each morning he woke to a brand-new day without history, without vision. For him, the past was not prologue, but merely the past. Yesterday's news. He understood time flowed in one direction only, and he accepted that idea without ever quite believing in his former selves, the ones who populated his memories. He'd moved on and left them far behind. In this manner, he was able to conveniently re-invent himself and his viewpoints on a day-to-day basis. As for the future, well, the future was too abstract for him to grasp. He'd worry about tomorrow once it became today. Today was within his comfort zone. Today could be seen and heard, touched, tasted, and smelled. Today could be dealt with and savored, or repaired if necessary. There was no sense in stressing over events which had already occurred or might happen someday. The present was tangible and orderly. All else was out of Tin's control."

The audience had fallen dead quiet. Tom paused and allowed himself a small smile. They didn't quite know what to make of him tonight. He wasn't being funny as advertised. They were fidgeting in their seats. *Good, good*, he thought. *I want them off-balance. I want them irked and flummoxed. By the end of the night, when the lights come up, I want to see jaws dropped and eyebrows arched. Tonight, I don't want to be the same old predictable raconteur.*

In a moment of honesty, and with a bit of a shock, he realized *he* wasn't quite sure what to make of himself this evening. He didn't believe in muses, but it did feel as if a force was moving through him, subtly guiding his performance. *Oh?* He heard himself sneer. *A force, is it? Yep, a force, for lack of a better explanation.* It wasn't as overt as a puppet master manipulating his limbs and scripting his every word. It felt more like a dozen voices whispering simultaneously inside his head, all insistently vying for his attention.

His pause had stretched into an uncomfortable thirty seconds. He heard two hundred people breathing in the dark, pictured them staring at him, waiting for him to make some sense of his tale, or at least break the silence. Audiences hated silence. It made them squirm.

Tom gave a little laugh. "Well, I'm afraid that's it for the fable of Rachel and her metallic brood," he told them. "It's either a work-in-progress or a shaggy-dog story, I'm not sure which." He heard some muttering, so he cheerfully added, "Happens to painters all the time. They run out of colors, or else there might be too many colors to choose from. Anyway, how are you supposed to know when a painting is done?" That produced some loud grumbles. *Uh-oh*, he thought, *they're not buying it.* He had good stage presence, though, and went for the save before the catcalls started up.

"Hey, any of you see a little documentary from a few years back called *This Hard Life*?" This seemed to turn the tide a bit. There was light applause and a few appreciative whistles. Tom smiled grimly, nodded, and launched into his well-rehearsed narrative, summoning his movie announcer voice.

Just like that, the audience was hooked. Tom guided the crowd through the film's premise, basically, "Life is hard for most of us, but that doesn't stop human beings from making things harder, does it?" He described the semi-classic scenes, recited the tried-and-true one-liners. Some were familiar with the project, and others seemed eager for an introduction.

30

Tom smiled, relishing the punchline. "And then," he said to the two hundred transfixed people leaning forward, waiting for the payoff. "And then…well, you'll just have to wait for the sequel."

That got a laugh, and Tom knew the rest of the show would go on without a hitch. He cried, "Say, wouldn't it be great if there was one day a year when you could run down slow-moving pedestrians? It could be like a new holiday."

From that point on, the audience was, as the show biz saying goes, putty in his hands.

Backstage, it was the usual post show clusterfuck. The stagehands careened about, cleaning up. The pencil-necked P.R. geek fawned over the performance. The theater manager, Ralph, was the bottom-line type, a real nickel-and-dimer, stern-looking, his feet solidly on the ground and his head jammed way far up his ass. Ralph kept consulting his Timex, anxious to be rid of the weirdo storyteller and to close up shop for the night. When he gazed at his performer, it was as if Tom was gum stuck to the soles of Ralph's cheap brown penny-loafers.

Ralph, in turn, reminded Tom of his brother, Robert.

"Thought you were toast after that Rachel bit," Ralph said, all hostile. "You call that entertainment?"

"Improv," Tom informed him with a tired smile.

He lit a cigarette, which he'd been craving for the past twenty minutes.

"Hmmpf. You're *paid* to entertain, not experiment."

Tom shrugged. "Cash is king," he acknowledged, vowing never to play this shithole again. *Christ, it isn't as if anybody demanded a refund. The Ralphs of the world can all go fuck themselves.*

Now, the box office supervisor, Helen Something-or-Other, she was another story altogether. With her waifish, sleepy-eyed face, Tom scored her as foxy. Not drop-dead gorgeous but delicately pretty. Small in the breasts and around her waist. He felt a familiar pang shoot through his body. She was a brunette, which was also a plus. He'd always professed a weakness for the dark-haired fillies.

It was just a thirty-minute drive home, and he'd bet Donna would have it clocked down to the minute. Otherwise he'd be mighty tempted to cash in on the come-hither signals Helen was beaming his way. *Oh well,* he told himself resignedly. *Down boy. File her face and name away for future reference. Who knows, might pass this way again sometime.* He said his goodbyes, there were handshakes and hugs all around, he took bittersweet pleasure in Helen Something's fleeting look of disappointment. Warm, caramel-brown eyes, too. *Damn, damn, and triple-damn.*

Outside, it was misting. The sky was a tangle of black and gray ribbons throughout which blinked a jaundiced moon. The marquee which read THOMAS FREEMAN DEMETER, FABULIST EXTRAORDINAIRE was now dark. When illuminated, the theater seemed old town chic. Unlit, it looked like any other shabby building in a borderline-leaning-to-scuzzy business district. Really, it wasn't a theater so much as a warehouse for misfit entertainers. Tomorrow, it might host a dreadful local production of *Annie Get Your Gun*, or a dreary autobiographical monologue by some has-been off-Broadway character actor, or a fourth-rate jazz quintet, or some other does-it-really-matter type of show.

Tom climbed into his car, glad to be escaping another sad little venue in another sad little Florida town. He started the engine, snicked the wiper blades once, twice, and lit another smoke. He pulled out of the parking lot and headed home.

All in all, not a bad gig tonight, he thought as he maneuvered through the swampy darkness. Not one of the all-time greats, but not bad, especially considering how often he'd gone off-script. *What the hell was that all about?* he asked, then answered himself. *Don't know, don't care.*

In general, he preferred not to over-analyze his work too much, particularly the improvisations. As a rule, he trusted his gut feelings. But he had to admit tonight had been extra-spooky, almost like he'd been channeling some careening and sentimental spirit. *Which was,* he chided himself, *pure nonsense. Also poppycock, balderdash, and one hundred percent undiluted donkey dung. Hmm, but maybe there's a bit in there.* He imagined a cast of potential characters consisting of ad-libbing ghosts, invisible oracles whispering off-the-wall jokes and insights into his ears, a mama's boy spirit perched on his right shoulder, an ectoplasmic evil genius on his left. He started to visualize it, could see the words and images meshing together.

He came to a red light. He hit the brakes and the car skidded to a reluctant halt. The route home was torture, a spaghetti of back roads engineered with a system of meticulously unsynchronized traffic lights. Each light seemed sentient, anticipating his approach and changing its lens to a burning red even if his was the only vehicle in sight. Red. Stop. Leaving his febrile imagination to conjure visions of nocturnal carjackers, man-eating alligators, the foreboding smells of mangrove and cypress, Cuban gangsters, sudden sinkholes. He tapped his steering wheel impatiently, clearly seeing the embryo of a vignette about municipal ineptitudes.

Green light and off he sped again. The bright green afterimage seemed to stay with him, behind his eyes. *A world of green.* He opened his mind and looked beyond the drizzly darkness to picture lush gardens, mountains of money, murderously jealous lovers, vaults of blazing emeralds. Subconsciously he filed it all away, the color green as a resource for future material. His mind never seemed to turn off.

As a boy growing up in Greenstone, he'd been fascinated by mazes and puzzles, kaleidoscopes, lighthouses, astrology and Greek myths, comic books, symbology, illusionists, and his own sepia-drenched dreams. His imagination was stoked by both the magnificently gargantuan and the perfectly miniaturized. His ambition was to witness new visions and to hear new songs that had nothing to do with the numbing normalcy of his hometown and his upbringing.

His father had been an icy oligarch and his mother a spunky do-gooder and a little bit of a dilettante. Tom often felt trapped in their strange and intense crossfires. Greenstone to him was a claustrophobic pit. Little wonder he took refuge in sarcasm and grew into a caustically observant teen. He learned to thrive on tweaking conventional thought, ruthlessly questioning authority, finding and exploiting the chinks in the armor of the arrogant. He took delight in kicking the Achilles heels of the indifferent and the supercilious. Early on he sensed that, when it came to most experts and pundits, the emperors often wore no clothes. He lampooned gossips, eviscerated meddlers, outraged teachers, and continually frustrated his parents.

"You're like a pygmy shooting arrows at giants," his father reprimanded him more than once. "If you ever put that energy into something constructive, son, you'd be unstoppable. You break my heart."

Well, that was Henry Demeter all right, quick to share his hard-won wisdom and judgment. All his free, unasked-for advice.

Tom shrugged it off. Hell, sometimes he broke his own heart. His outlook on the world was that eighty-five percent of the planet's inhabitants were stupid, rude, and selfish. "A complete and total waste of perfectly good protoplasm," as he often proclaimed in his stand-up act.

He got a lot of comedic mileage from this fatalistic stance, and yet he worked hard to offset it with an odd, kvetching optimism. Family, friends, and lovers shook their heads at this apparent contradiction. "Defense mechanisms," he'd say with a grin. "That's all."

Early on, he developed the ability to laugh at everything and everyone, himself included. The universe was a mess, his personal life a disaster. In his view, it was a world full of illusions and delusions. All Tom could do was poke fun at the absurdity of it all. His self-deprecation became a large part of his appeal.

Red light. He braked, and the car's slight slide before stopping reminded him he needed new tires. *Always something.*

The present, with all its passions and errors, was a painful place for him to occupy. Tom carried into his adult life the perception that things were always on the verge of looking up, and tomorrow could only be better than today. When he peered into his crystal ball, it was a comfort for him to see, next month or even next year, invigorating challenges and golden opportunities ahead. Peace for his vagabond soul. He was forty-three years old and still felt he was on his way to becoming the man he was intended to be.

For the time being, though, he got along all right. "You call that entertainment?" the execrable glob of phlegm named Ralph had challenged.

Why, as a matter of fact Ralph, I do. Tom had been lucky enough to cobble together a modest living from several different funding streams. Plus, he was forever tinkering with one screenplay or another. Sometimes his work life felt a little like being in a traveling freak show, but hey, whatever paid the bills. Also, whatever kept him far away from his personal idea of being buried alive, which was a desk job. Entombed like Poe's Montresor, brick by heavy brick…

He thought, *All right, enough of that. One more cigarette isn't going to kill me, right?*

Numerous red lights later, he pulled safely into the driveway of his rented house. The windows twinkled in welcome. Tom jogged from the car to the front door in a vain attempt to dodge the raindrops.

Donna waited for him inside. Her body language and the stricken look on her face telegraphed something gone wrong. He took a deep breath and prepared himself. With Donna, that 'something' could range from a broken garbage disposal to the outbreak of nuclear war. She was a nurse and saw the potential catastrophe in everything.

He kissed her cheek. He saw she'd been crying. "What?" he said. "What's the matter?"

She tilted her chin at the phone. "There's a message for you. From Robert." Tears formed in her eyes. "I'm sorry, honey. I'm really sorry."

Thomas nodded, going numb. He walked over to the phone, thinking this time Donna was probably right to catastrophize. With Robert, it was never good news.

Chapter Five

Violet stepped outdoors and her lungs filled instantly with thousands of ice-burning needles. The late afternoon was crystalline, with a high topaz sky and a jewel of a sun spiking over the ridgeline to the west. She stood on the frosted lawn of the two-story yellow house and completed her breathing exercises.

She decided to run uphill first, while her legs were fresh. She'd done her stretches and warm-ups inside, with the heater on and Mozart in the background. Her muscles were loose, her blood warm, her bones now singing with the cold. She jogged lightly across the whitened lawn. Green ice crackled underfoot. The streets and sidewalks were dusted with snow. Her cross-trainers gained traction and she headed north, straight up Sugarloaf Road.

Although she didn't live in this neighborhood, Violet was familiar with its hills and mazelike streets. In the sun and the snow and the cold, her body felt supremely alive. Everything was white, everything smelled clean. When the world was like this, without struggle or strife, what was there to trouble your mind? Running was therapeutic, inducing a kind of meditative state for her. She took a leisurely pace upslope, her arms and legs beginning to fall into an easy rhythm, her skin glowing pink. She breathed freely in the thin Colorado air.

She jogged in the direction of the church which was embedded a half-mile away inside this tidy, well-to-do neighborhood.

God, it was a gorgeous day. Inside the heated house, Violet's limbs had felt heavy, her thoughts sluggish. It was the familiar grogginess that reliably afflicted her after lovemaking. She'd forced herself to wake up, dress, and get moving. The cold helped shake some of her lethargy. A pleasant ache settled in her strong calves as she worked her way up a small incline to a higher patch of level ground. As she ran, she tried to center her emotions and energies. The sun's radiance, the crispness of the snow and the tendrils of the breeze blowing off the foothills became, she imagined, as one with her own heartbeat.

There was no sign of anybody out and about on the quiet serpentine streets. All the homes were well-tended and most of the cars parked in the wide driveways were late models. The neighborhood spoke of comfort and security. For Violet, the idea of a safe normalcy made it more delicious when she thought, *Each house hides its own dirty story, though. What lengths do people go to conceal their secrets behind these locked doors, those curtained windows?*

She'd grown up in a neighborhood not remotely like this one. Now she and Robert lived in a comfortable, upper middle-class area of Greenstone. It was a little slice of domestic utopia and she liked it. Her childhood had been a series of six-month rentals and fixer-uppers in one shabby suburb after another. She'd slept in off-white bedrooms with her telescope, her record collection, her acoustic guitar, her menagerie of stuffed monkeys, raccoons, and frogs. The bedrooms were in houses not like any of these homes. She'd been raised by dreamy and overmatched parents.

That's how she came to be an expert on stories and secrets, and how to become invisible even in plain sight.

Violet knew if she hadn't forced herself up and out of bed, she'd be pleasantly trapped in the house all day long. She couldn't risk that kind of a misstep. Sweet temptation was an awful thing. Strong arms held her close under the heavy quilts. The stereo issued soft jazzy instrumentals and the remains of a lovely fire sputtered in the hearth. It was dangerous to feel so lazy, so drugged. She easily could have whispered for him to bolt all the doors, unplug the phone, put on another pot of coffee, stay in bed, sleep and fuck till nightfall, and fall back asleep again. Easily. The vision thrilled her, then scared her out of her paralysis. The fear spurred her running out into the cold light of day.

The church came into view as she rounded a bend and navigated a path cutting through a small park with a frozen pond at its center. A flagpole stood in the middle of the pond. A frayed American flag rippled in the wind. School had let out and kids were ice-skating, arming themselves for epic snowball fights. Otherwise the park felt oddly still, a piece of a silent world Violet was passing through.

The church was built on top of a hill overlooking the park. It was a round building with thick white walls, vaguely modernist in design. A metal cross anchored in its parking lot towered thirty feet high. At night the cross was bathed in bronze light, making it visible for miles. The building sat squat and sturdy, looking as though it had risen as a natural outgrowth of the hilltop. Twelve slender rectangles of stained glass were set at irregular heights and intervals in the adobe walls. Lodgepole beams jutted from the circular roof in a pattern that suggested a sunburst. Here and there, the hillside was studded with greenery, firs and spruces.

It was a strangely peaceful spot and something in Violet resonated with its stillness. Which was odd because, given her upbringing, she tended to associate places of worship with guilt and sin. However, from the moment she'd accidentally discovered this church, jogging through the neighborhood when it had been new to her and when the affair had been new, she'd felt soothed by its presence.

The big sign out front proclaimed this was a United Methodist Episcopal church, with adult Sunday school held at nine a.m. and regular services at ten thirty a.m. and noon. Other announcements shared the billing. A Native American congregation met on Sundays at four thirty p.m., the Slavic Evangelical church gathered at seven p.m., and on Saturdays at seven a.m., the members of the Eritrean Orthodox Coptic church worshipped beneath the round roof. That was not the end of the listed activities. The Greenstone Nonprofit Interagency Council meeting was scheduled every other week on Wednesday afternoons at three. There was bingo every Thursday evening and a combination Scrabble fundraiser/bake sale planned for early January. For good measure, acoustic folk music concerts took place on selective Friday and Saturday nights. There was a contact number posted for upcoming shows and ticket information.

She'd never been inside, although once she'd gotten as far as the imposing ten-foot-tall double-doored entryway before whirling away and racing back down the hill.

What is sin, anyway? she thought now, standing at the edge of the parking lot, watching the flag whip over the icy pond. It seemed like a hell of a question for a thirty-eight-year-old woman to be asking herself. When she was younger, Vi thought for sure she'd have it all worked out by this time. These days it seemed like she couldn't help herself from asking the sin question, over and over again.

She supposed there were certain universals. Murder, for one. Theft. Blasphemy. Maybe even coveting. Beyond those, the definition seemed to be up for grabs. For instance, Vi's parents taught her that, in the eyes of God, divorce was a major transgression. Two people joined together to become one flesh, one spirit, so splitting them was the same as tearing a human being down the middle. The parents had been married thirty-four years before her mother succumbed to breast cancer at the age of fifty-three. In Violet's eyes, the real sin had been that they had *not* divorced, because if ever a couple should have avoided marriage in the first place, Hal and Jenny Inverce was that couple. How holy a union could it be when a marriage consisted of more than three decades of bickering, bad financial decisions, transience, spotty employment, and a steady diet of tranquilizers for Jenny and alcohol for Hal?

Murder, theft, blasphemy, coveting. Where on that spectrum, Vi pondered, was adultery? Her parents would say, on a scale of one to ten, adultery rated a twelve. Most people would be slightly more forgiving. Vi herself would say it deserved a six or a seven at most. There was no question infidelity was not a good thing. But what if you were no longer in love with your spouse? What if there were no children to complicate matters? What if you'd *never* loved your spouse, but only made a regrettable bargain? What if you coped well on a day-to-day basis, doing everything in your power to maintain a good public front, but a small private part of you, the best part of you, was withering to dust? What if, what if, what if?

She supposed she was only rationalizing. Standing in the church's parking lot with the wind picking up and the cold biting deep into her skin, Vi felt somehow virtuous. She approved of the stained-glass being muted, not gaudy, not too *religious*. There was just enough color there to suggest His glory. Growing up, she'd attended churches housed in everything from a converted tire warehouse to an abandoned storefront to a doublewide trailer. She'd been taught that material trappings were not important. A humble temple was every bit as much God's house as a glittering cathedral. But Lord, she'd prayed in some gloomy halls of worship. Although it wasn't supposed to matter, such places couldn't help but dampen the human spirit, mildew the soul.

Blank-faced, she stared at the church and thought about Robert. She thought about her lover. From inside the church, bells pealed the hour. The sudden sound made Vi jump.

In the following silence, shivering as a new wind cropped up, her feet growing numb in the snow, Violet pictured herself at age nine in an old trailer-church, chafing in her pink Sunday dress, the lingering taste of grape juice communion on her tongue, laughing like a jade-eyed devil with her sister in the back pews of the Glad Tidings congregation. Her father frowning, her mother glaring. The iron-haired pastor sayeth, "Children, there's a lot of *longing* in *belonging*." The trailer was gussied up with sandalwood candles, plaster Christ statuaries, and an elegant cherrywood cross. Alas, it was still a trailer.

Her parents were habitually poor. They thought of themselves as common folks filled with an uncommon love for God, and the family motto was, "There is no shame in honest poverty." *Whatever the hell that meant.* Hal and Jenny never beat her, or locked her in a dark closet, or tied her to a chair for hours on end, nothing like that. Somehow though, their stone piety resulted in Vi's neglect and what she would later hear diagnosed in others as "a failure to thrive."

Sabbath after Sabbath, she could feel the Holy Spirit being siphoned away by her parents' dry devotion. The years passed and, over time, Violet lost her faith in God.

Years later, she found it again as a young woman, one weekend while hot-air ballooning in the Sierras, wonderstruck by the gorgeous symmetries of the world floating by below her. She remembered shutting her eyes, lightheaded from lack of oxygen. When she opened them, the orange light of the new dawn spilled over her like a revelation. The balloon drifted over waterfalls and caves whose walls had metamorphosed from limestone to marble, above hundreds of square miles of moon-blessed forests. The cold air thrummed in her ears and Violet laughed at herself for ever doubting God was sovereign. She looked down and studied the glacier-cut valleys and the green-stoned rivers, and she knew this was no watered-down, Ansel Adams, weekend-with-nature kind of spirituality. No. It was God and God alone who had put the evangelical fire back in her gut. It was belief forged into matter while she was suspended joyfully between Heaven and Earth. She couldn't account for it, stronger than her love for her adventurous friends, hotter than the fire jets lifting her high above the sequoias and the canyons. The sky was a gold and purple frieze and the balloon juddered in the morning's wind and Vi swore she could hear a soft voice in the back of her head that sayeth, "There's a lot of *iron* in *irony*."

Now, here she was, an adulteress freezing on a Colorado hillside, standing outside an unfamiliar church. Why had she never gone inside? Was she afraid? No, fear wasn't quite the reason. Uncomfortable, yes. Scared, no. Her reaction stemmed from a briar patch of unworthiness and a dissociation from her own best self, from her hopelessly fettered faith and snarled emotions. She seemed to be at a juncture where she couldn't decode her own feelings. The wind gusted and her thoughts blew off like a spinning kite. Her past was a straitjacket and the future seemed unreal. All that mattered was the *now*.

The fringed flag blew straight out from its pole like a piece of sheet metal painted red, white, and blue. Now she felt the wind cutting through her clothes as the sun dropped and twilight crept in on long shadows. The church walls dulled in the antique light from the western sky, darkening from white to sandstone to an uninspiring mud-brown. She couldn't feel her toes inside her running shoes.

It was time for her to leave. It was time for her to return home.

Vi turned her back on the church and trotted downhill, past an old man in a frock coat strolling around the pond at a snail's pace, past a pair of high school sweethearts huddled against each other, past the kids and their newly-constructed snow forts amply stockpiled with pyramids of icy ammunition. Panting, the blood pulsing in her ears, she retraced her steps through the neighborhood. Her legs burned with a welcome fire, the church and the parking lot receded behind her, the white sun was a vanishing ghost. One by one, the streetlamps buzzed to life. Gray clouds scudded overhead.

From nowhere, the preacher's voice in her head proclaimed, "Mighty clouds of joy, dear Lord. Pure white clouds, blinding white as Heaven's holy train."

She stopped next to a silver Accord parked in front of the yellow house. Her key opened the door and fired up the engine. She gave one last glance at the house. Cautiously, she pulled away from the curb, executed a smooth U-turn, and drove out to the highway leading home.

As always, Vi's timing was flawless. An hour or so remained before Robert would return from work. In that hour, she showered away her sweat and the residue of sex and dressed for tonight's traditional visit with her mother-in-law.

Her husband came through the door at six-fifteen. She could set her watch by him. He brushed her lips hello with a dry kiss. Dutifully, Violet listened to the monotone account of his dull-as-dishwater day as he loosened his tie, said he was going to get in twenty minutes on the rowing machine, then take a shower before visiting Mother.

Violet nodded. "That would be fine, Rob."

She fixed herself a martini and switched on the stereo for some head-clearing jazz. Her body felt limber and strong. She reflected lazily on her busy day. Part of her purred with contentment, part burned in shame. She did believe Jesus was the son of God, so she considered herself a Christian, but what sort of Christian? She refused to follow those breadcrumbs down a philosophical rabbit hole. She'd almost convinced herself she was done with those useless, ethereal questions. Life had its own hard logic and unpredictable rhythms, and at the present time Vi was satisfied to be merely a rider on its wavelengths. Up and down, push and pull in ceaseless cycles. Experience taught her there was no point in fighting to get off the roller coaster.

The phone rang and she jumped at the abrupt sound. A little of her drink sloshed over and spilled to the carpet. She could hear Rob was out of the shower but, after fielding calls all day long at the firm, he rarely answered the phone at home. In no hurry, Violet glided across the room.

She picked up and said, "Hello, Demeter residence." She listened carefully to the voice through a mild gin fog. She nodded to herself and said, "I'll get him for you."

"Rob," she called down the hallway. "It's the agency. You'd better take it. It's about your mother."

Robert appeared and Vi surrendered the phone. She fell back into the living room's shadows and finished her martini. *There's no comprehending God's ways*, she thought, chewing on an olive, resisting the urge to mix another drink. *You simply have to trust in His purpose.* Sometimes it seemed to her the entire planet was just one gigantic, sacred experiment. Sometimes His mercy was a healing rain, and sometimes His justice engulfed you like white waters. Between the clay and the sky, between reason and fear, God walked somewhere in those in-between spaces.

She watched Robert's lips moving, his face stoic, his posture still, and she murmured a little prayer to herself.

Chapter Six

Flying into Denver, Tom could feel the dread gathering in his belly, weighing down his soul. He didn't think he was being melodramatic. The sky outside the jet's windows was a menacing gunmetal color. After hours of plains and prairies, the Rockies now loomed some miles ahead, jagged as shark teeth. The pilot breezily announced that, at three-thirty in the afternoon, it was twelve degrees in Denver with an excellent chance for snow tonight.

Though he'd been born and raised in Colorado, Tom never felt at home here. He wasn't much of a skier, didn't care for hiking or rock-climbing, always despised the cold weather. So really, what was there to embrace? Shortly after graduating from college, he'd moved to Florida and never looked back. The only times he'd returned to his native state before this trip had been for his father's funeral and for Rob's wedding, which for Tom had been like another funeral.

The flight attendant, he noted, was trim, chestnut-haired, with amazing chocolate-brown eyes. She asked Tom if he wanted something to drink. He said no, thanks. He was tired from not sleeping the night before. He was uncomfortable even in his aisle seat, where he could stretch his long legs, but the woman in the middle seat was a sprawler, intentionally crowding him. Long flights were not on his list of favorite activities, and he was so out of sorts he didn't bother to flirt. He tried to read part of a Julio Cortazar novella, but couldn't get past the first three pages without losing focus. Airplanes in general made him feel disoriented and venomous.

He silently decided to take out his poison on the man in the business suit sitting across the way from him. Joe Corporation, Tom dubbed him. Four hours in the air and the guy hadn't so much as loosened his conservative blue power tie. Evidently, he'd purchased tickets for his entire row. He sat by the window. On the seat next to his, he'd placed his briefcase, a laptop, a calculator, a pocket calendar, a cell phone, a Walkman and headphones. *What, no Swiss army knife?* On the aisle seat, Joe fanned out a complex arrangement of faxes, printed e-mails, spreadsheets, scribbled notes, numbers, and rubrics.

Tom noted Joe seemed oblivious to his surroundings, except when he was acting with imperious rudeness to the flight attendant. It also appeared he'd mastered the dark arts of time management and multi-tasking. Joe Corp could juggle eleven projects simultaneously, including the job of imbibing his third Tanqueray-and-tonic. *All work and no play, you know.*

He's a one-man turnkey operation, Thomas mused, unconsciously beginning the process of profiling and storing away for future reference. *Heading to some conference or seminar. Task force? Think tank? Focus group? Some shit like that. Wound tight as a three-dollar Mexican watch. You wouldn't want to be around him when he blew, a major fucking stroke in the making. Wife and three kids, maybe a honey waiting for him in Denver. Investment broker, software designer, information systems analyst run-of-the-mill salesman? His clothing is expensive-looking, so he's not your typical middle-management drone. Self-serving, self-indulgent. Poster boy for the coming Information Age, all statistics and zero insights. Lives by the gospel of situational ethics. Oh, and don't forget his devotions to demographics, the holiest of holies. A slave to longitudinal studies. Toady to gate-keepers and stakeholders everywhere.*

Thomas paused. *Too one-dimensional,* he reconsidered. *You want a villain, but not a straw man. Sure, he looks like a fucking robot, but is there anything human about him? Well, he drinks like a fish, that's something. What else? Maybe he cries or writes poetry when he's forced to fire someone? Maybe the Type A personality thing is a sham, maybe he really longs to get out of the rat race? It's just that he's just in too deep- mortgage, car payments, insurance, credit card bills, one kid in college, fancy toys, and hey, all those perks and bennies. Tough to give it all up just for peace of mind and a vow of poverty. What's he going to do, open a coffeehouse? A fucking bookstore? Get real. Does his wife still love him? Is he a stranger to his kids? Does he…?*

The plane began its gradual descent. Tom checked his seatbelt. He stole a glance at Joe, absorbed in his work, poring over portfolios mystic with colored pie charts and technobabble. It came to Tom the businessman was a dead ringer for his brother Robert. My God, Tom thought with a start, it's *déjà vu* all over again. Automatons with human likenesses doing as they're programmed, day in, day out, indefatigable, expressionless, goddamn spooky. Like twin sons of different mothers, they might have been.

Robert, the numbers cruncher, who had insisted on meeting him at the airport. Over Tom's protests, *no please, don't bother, I'll just rent a car, I'm a big boy now.* Rob would have none of it. It was his duty to take care of family. It was the right thing to do, especially in this time of bereavement.

Tom sighed. He would have much preferred the rental. A nice comfortable mid-sized sedan with a CD player, so he could blast music on the short drive to Greenstone. He could sing along to some favorite tunes and not have to think, and not have to try to make stilted conversation with his brother.

He gave in to the drowsy sensation of descent. He was happy to lose his thoughts in the Rorschach of cloud formations. There was a pair of a giant clown's outlandish floppy shoes. Over there were some lumpy white cows grazing in a broad rolling field of gray. To the south was a cluster of party balloons broken loose from the earth. Despite his discomfort with flying, Thomas was not phobic and did not fear crashing. He felt his body floating down, down. It was very pleasant, this soft little freefall, like a snowflake drifting on the eddies of the wind. He gladly slipped into a murky semi-consciousness until the plane touched down and taxied toward the terminal. He was jolted awake again by his fellow passengers' bovine scramble to gather their carry-ons and pop open the overhead bins.

Joe Corporation was one of the first to collect his flowcharts, equipment and garment bag, and elbow his way off the plane to whatever destination desperately awaited his presence. Thomas beamed him a telepathic congratulations. *You win, asshole. You got off the plane before most everyone else. Nice going and many happy returns.*

Denver being Denver, he couldn't find Rob at the gate's reception area. He waited a few minutes, watching families smile and hug, watching lovers re-unite. Finally he told himself *screw it,* proceeded to the baggage claim where his flight's carousel was experiencing mechanical trouble. He sighed and decided to visit the men's room. A man at a urinal was talking to himself in a matter-of-fact tone. "Yeah, just got in. I'll grab a cab to the Radisson, then there's dinner with Calloway tonight at eight…" It took Tom a split second to realize the man wasn't delusional but talking on a hands-free phone while peeing. *Welcome back to the Mile-High City, baby.* Plus, there were no paper towels in the dispensers.

When he left the restroom, shaking his dripping hands, he spotted Rob over by baggage. The carousel was now spinning. Rob craned his neck, searching the crowd for his brother. Tom held back a few moments, stifling a laugh at the sight of Rob tapping his foot, consulting his watch. A small crease of impatience zigzagged across his forehead. All was not according to plan. Tom decided to show some mercy and circled around to Rob's back.

"Dude, what's happening?" he said, touching Rob's shoulder.

His brother spun and his face broke out in a tight grin of half relief, half annoyance.

"There you are." Rob extended his hand.

Thomas took it and shook solemnly, remembering his brother was not a hugger.

"I was just starting to get worried. Your flight was a few minutes early, so I came straight down here to baggage and…where have you been?"

"Nature called, man. Nice to see you, too, by the way. Hey, there's my bag. Let's get the hell out of here."

Tom snatched his suitcase and followed a step or two behind Rob through the airport. Neither spoke. Rob was focused on his responsibilities as guide and driver. Tom was too jetlagged to attempt words with his brother just yet. They walked briskly to the parking structure.

Tom stared at the back of Rob's neck and thought, *Wow, he hasn't changed, not one iota.* While Tom was dressed in what might be termed 'tennis bum chic', his brother was business casual. Tom thought of him as a man out of time, frozen somewhere back in the worst years of the Eisenhower era. Not so much in appearance as in mindset. The events which had been so crucial to shaping Tom were rock-&-roll, the civil rights movement, the assassinations, Vietnam. All seemed to have been incidental to Robert. He might have been born a boy in a bubble, thrust into a twentieth-century vacuum. In Rob's buttoned-down world, it was best to be conservative in dress, demeanor, finances, and politics.

Also love, Tom thought, a little bitterly. He wondered how Violet was doing.

"It's good of you to come," Rob said as they reached his car, a Lincoln Continental, brand-new and blue/black. "I wasn't sure if you would."

Tom tossed his suitcase in the huge trunk and settled into the passenger seat. It was leather, very plush. He flashbacked to his father declaring, "those new Asian cars are deathtraps", and that he, H.D. the staunch patriot, would always, always buy American, even if it cost him a few dollars more. It didn't surprise Tom to see Rob following suit.

"Hey, I couldn't not come. How are you holding up?"

"I'm fine. There's a lot to do. I guess I lose myself in all the busyness." Rob managed a wry, self-conscious grin.

He started the car and began navigating his way out of the airport.

Tom coughed into his fist, and said, "I suppose I shouldn't smoke in your fancy ride, huh?" He noticed the interior was spotless and there were no ashtrays.

"I'd prefer that," Rob told him. "We'll be at the house in no time. You can smoke on the deck out back."

It was about a forty-five-minute drive to Greenstone. As predicted, snow flurries tumbled from the dark gray skies. Once out of the parking structure, the car was buffeted by high winds. Thomas tried to orient himself by the foothills but found them obscured by low-hanging storm clouds.

He knew he was probably exaggerating, but it seemed to take an infinite number of intricate and unnecessary maneuvers to escape the airport vicinity. He could have sworn Rob had to decipher cloverleafs, figure eights, and dangerous s-curves just to reach the straightaway leading to Greenstone. As they drove out of the Denver city limits, the snow fell heavier, wetter.

"You know, that last winter I lived here, it snowed every goddamn Monday, Wednesday, and Friday, not to mention a few weekends in between. All the way from late September to early May. I thought I was going to go out of my mind. Felt like Dr. Fucking Zhivago."

"That's pretty unusual, even for Colorado," Rob said mildly. "Normally, even when it snows hard, the sun's out next day to melt most of it away."

"Yeah, well, that was the last straw. I finally thawed out by spring and said, 'Florida, here I come.'. Hurricanes, June bugs, humidity, and all. Those I can deal with."

"No second thoughts?"

"None."

A silence fell. It was late afternoon, but it already felt like dusk. Traffic moved cautiously but steadily.

Rob cleared his throat. "So what are you doing these days?"

Tom half-smiled to himself. In Rob-speak, the question was really, "What are you doing for work?"

He said, "Oh, a little of this and a little of that. It's like it's always been with me, Rob. My life's a hodgepodge. Look up 'chaos' in the dictionary, and there's my picture alongside the definition. It all seems to work out, though. I make ends meet, anyway."

"Huh. What are you doing for health insurance?"

"I try real hard not to get sick," Tom replied with a grin.

"Do you like living that way?"

There was just a dash of incredulity in Rob's tone, just a trace of condescension. Tom decided to let it pass.

"It's not so much about liking it," he said. "It's what I'm used to and I really don't know any other way. I do seem to thrive on the pressure. Half the time I'm running crazy, the other half I'm zoned out."

"All or nothing."

Thomas shrugged. "Works for me."

"Last I heard you were...doing standup? Is that right?"

"Not exactly."

Tom thought, *no, I'm not a comedian, nor a social commentator, nor a political pundit. I wouldn't call myself a psychosocial voyeur, or a reporter. Kind of a gumbo of all the above.*

Aloud, he said, "I have a one-man show that's pretty popular regionally. Get to travel a lot, get to make people laugh and think about their lives. I've also got a morning radio show where I can play some eclectic music and I'm on display as the station's token liberal. That gig's pretty secure as long as I stay funny and don't get too political. Oh, and I write a little newspaper column twice a week. Looks like it may be picked up soon for some limited syndication. The column's pretty much just a printed version of my radio show, which is really a distilled version of my one-man performance. Basically, I get paid to be a smartass and to spout my leftist opinions. What a stretch, huh?"

"Nice work if you can get it."

"Yeah, well, it all sounds like fun-and-games. Believe it or not, I do work my ass off juggling everything."

"Jeez, it's really starting to come down, isn't it?"

Rob stared intently through the windshield at the swirling whiteness. His hand moved to crank the Lincoln's heater up a notch.

"I always wondered how people got jobs like yours. Film critics, restaurant reviewers. You have to be a little lucky, I would guess."

"Yeah, dirty jobs but somebody has to do 'em. Anything to keep me out of a cubicle." He caught himself and winced.

To bridge the sudden awkward silence, he said in his best Jimmy Stewart voice, "So, how's things at the old Bailey Building and Loan? Thrown any widows out in the cold lately?"

"The firm's fine. A lot of hours, but I shouldn't complain. I knew what I was getting into, and so many people are out of work these days." Rob's voice trailed away as it often did when he talked about himself. All at once he brightened. "Ben's got work. I didn't know if you'd heard."

"I hadn't. That's terrific. How's he doing?"

"Good, good. He's at a little Italian restaurant clearing tables, prepping salads, cleaning up, that sort of thing. I know the owner from the Chamber lunches. He's a friend and he was willing to help out. I think Ben's almost up to thirty hours a week, which is pretty good for restaurant work."

"Sure is. God, I remember working three days in an IHOP when I was a kid. I thought I was going to blow my brains out." Thomas shook his head and gave in to a little shudder. "I guess I meant more like, how is Ben?"

Rob's eyes remained flat and unblinking, but Tom could almost hear the circuits buzzing in his head as he calculated his response. "Oh, he's doing well. I mean, he's doing the best he can, considering his condition." He paused.

For a moment, Tom thought he might not continue, then reconsidered. "Tom, you know Ben's never going to be one hundred percent again. Don't you?"

Tom nodded. "Yeah. Yeah, I do. I just remember him so clearly the way he was, and I just wish he could be right again. Maybe ninety percent of what he was. Is that too much to hope for? For him to be more like his old self?"

"Maybe seventy percent. What's done is done, Tom. There's nothing we can do about the past, can we? Believe me, if I had a time machine…"

Rob's lips were compressed, a sure sign since childhood that irritation was starting to set in. "Well, that's a waste of time, isn't it? Might as well wish for a magic wand. Stupid. He's got to play the hand he's dealt, the same as anyone."

He snuck a sideways look at Tom and there was something there that Tom couldn't decode.

"You don't see him day to day like we do. With a head injury, any progress is going to be slow and unpredictable. There's a big frustration factor involved. A lot of three steps forward, two steps back. Good days and bad days. Remember, at first the doctors didn't even expect him to live."

"I remember."

"Ben's lucky in the sense that he doesn't have a lot of anger. Most of the time, his impulse control is pretty good. He has trouble concentrating on anything, and he'll always have problems with his memory. His therapist says the job is a major positive step, because structure is very important. The little paycheck gives him some sense of being independent."

"He's still living on his own?"

"Yes, that seems to be working out. So far."

"And he still has his faith. The accident didn't wipe that out?"

"Yes, he still has his faith." It was subtle, but Rob had shifted to a slightly patronizing tone. "Also, a case worker, a trainer, and his advocacy group. I really think he's in pretty good shape, all things considered. He's just never..." Rob drove at a steady speed and maintained a textbook distance from the taillights in front of him. "You haven't said a word about mother, Tom."

"Ah." Tom thought, *smooth change of topic, lightly accusing tone, and away we go.* He reminded himself to skate the surface with his brother, to avoid the landmines as much as possible. "Well, we've known it was coming, haven't we? Her health hasn't been good since Dad died. Although, nobody expected this." Again, there was a brief heavy silence between them. "I'm guessing you've made all the arrangements?"

Rob's voice was deadpan. "Yes, pretty much. I've taken care of all the hospital paperwork and chosen the mortuary. Oh, I need to get your signature on the authorization to cremate. Grace is a nervous wreck, so it's taking a lot of energy to keep her calm. Remember how she was with Father? Same reaction, only doubled."

Without any particular affection, Thomas remembered the homecare worker as a spindly, anxiety-ridden woman who had always seemed to be vaguely middle-aged. Constantly humming those damn showtunes.

"The memorial service is the day after tomorrow," Rob went on. "The sooner the better, I figured. Maybe we'll scatter the ashes up at the shelter on Thursday. As I said on the phone, Mother made me the trustee, but naturally I haven't had time yet to review her estate. Give me a week or so to plow through her bills and assets so I can make the disbursements according to her wishes. One thing we'll need to decide together is whether or not to sell the house. Sentimentally, I'd like to keep it, but the practical thing, really, is to unload it while the market favors sellers. Oh, then there's her stocks, her annuities, the life insurance…"

"Well, the old lady knew what she was doing, all right. You're definitely the money guy." Tom grinned at Rob retreating to his comfort zone, shifting to financial advisor mode. "I'm assuming Dad left her in decent shape. He always was a good provider."

"As it turns out, he left us all in decent shape. Listen, Tom, I hope that once this part is over, you won't hesitate to ask for some guidance if you need it. With this kind of money, financial planning is key to ensuring…"

"Thanks, Rob. I wasn't asking about the inheritance, but I appreciate the offer."

Comfort zone or not, the drift of the conversation was starting to feel a bit ghoulish. Tom couldn't help noticing both of them were avoiding any talk of Rachel's cause of death. A little meanly, Tom said, "You haven't said a word about Violet."

"She's fine," came the clipped response.

It's probably my imagination, Tom thought, *but it sure feels like the temperature in the car just dropped twenty degrees.*

Rob continued, "She keeps herself busy. She's been a huge help dealing with all Rachel's friends. I'm a little surprised your girlfriend didn't come out with you, Tom. What's this one's name again?"

"Donna."

He had to make a conscious effort to wring the emotion out of his own response. Too many embattled memories of Tom shouting senselessly, lashing out, a raving lunatic versus the implacable Rob.

"Her name's Donna. She works and she couldn't get the time off on such short notice. Anyway, I'm not sure it would've been appropriate. We've only been seeing each other a few months. We're living together, but this is really for family, I think."

"Hmm, sure," Rob said in his maddeningly neutral tone.

Tom realized his tactical mistake. *I forgot, I'm not a serious person, never have been. I'm especially never serious about relationships or commitments, nothing ever changes, I'll never grow up, I'm like some sunbelt Peter Pan, etc.*

Robert, now, he was the serious brother. The responsible one. Always was, and forever would be. Trouble was, he carried that seriousness on his back like it was a fucking cross. "Tom?"

"Hmm?" Viciously mimicking Rob's colorless inflection.

"About the inheritance. I mean, when this is all said and done, and we get back to the business of living our regular lives, well. I don't mean to be insensitive, but I know you don't have much experience with this amount of money, how to invest it all properly and whatnot. I want to help, if you'll let me. See, you have to play your cards right. This is going to sound funny, but you'll almost have more problems with money than without."

"Nice problems to have though, Rob, don't you think? Tell you what, let me know how you and Vi invest your chunk of the estate, I'll just copycat you. Monkey-see, monkey-do. Keep it simple. On account of my lack of experience and all. How does that sound?"

Besides petty and childish, that is. I just can't keep my mouth shut, can I? I've barely touched down in Denver with its rotten weather and rotten vibes and I'm already spouting off. So much for keeping the goddamn peace this time around.

The silence that followed this exchange was deafening. When Rob did speak, his words were edged and measured. "It's just a fact of human nature to fight for what's yours, Tom. To protect your territory. Do you understand what I mean?"

Tom ignored the question and turned his face to the passenger window. It was fogged up. He wiped at it with his hand and could make out the fuzzy lights of Greenstone down in the long valley stretching ahead. The brothers rode the rest of the way through the snowy twilight in silence, each lost in the roar of his own thoughts.

Chapter Seven

At first, Violet disagreed with Ben when he said it was, "the best idea in the world" to drive up to the shelter. True, it had been a full month since their last visit. Now, Ben had the day off and Rob had gone to meet Thomas at the airport. The afternoon was gusty, and a cold mist clung to the foothills as a premonition of storms later in the day. Anemic sunlight stained the sky mustard-yellow and formed a faint rainbow over Greeley Lake and the alfalfa fields north of Greenstone. Even on clear sunny days, Violet never looked forward to the snaky drive up Arapaho Avenue. Today, she dreaded the thought of getting marooned in the mountains if the snow started falling and the roads iced up.

Ben pleaded in his sweet, convincing way, and he so rarely asked for anything anymore. Her resolve melted. She advised him it would have to be a fast trip there and back, leaving maybe half-an-hour to pay respects to his father. Ben insisted on stopping at Mountain High Donuts before heading out. There he purchased two coffees, one hot chocolate, and three plump cinnamon rolls, warm and sticky from the oven.

The woman at the counter recognized him and broke into a broad smile. "How's my best customer today?" she boomed.

"Ben is good," said Ben. "How are you, Betty?"

"Betty is good," she grinned. "You have a beautiful day, Ben."

From downtown, it was a twenty-minute drive to the shelter. The two-lane road was well-maintained by the county, but was also a natural twisty nightmare, loosely following the meanderings of a mountain creek. There were three or four hairpin turns and, on an average trip, a half-dozen or so harebrained motorists. Woods of pine and spruce flanked the road, but in some areas the trees fell away and suddenly there'd be a narrow gravel shoulder beyond which the mountain angled sharply down into rocky canyons. Along with plenty of routine fender-benders, this road spawned a few spectacular and legendary accidents. Once, Vi saw a red pickup truck out in the middle of the frozen creek, spinning in slow circles, its driver looking forlorn and disoriented. Another time, in the middle of the night, a car carrying four teen-aged girls hit a patch of black ice and went sailing off the mountainside. The vehicle landed upside-down in a y-shaped branch of a tremendous Ponderosa pine, where the girls passed the evening weeping for their lives and screaming for help. They were pulled to safety in an intricate early morning rescue effort. One girl suffered a broken pelvis, but otherwise the group survived its ordeal with superficial cuts and bruises, and a tale to tell their children's children.

Violet didn't know which was worse, crawling up the hill or hurtling back down. She white-knuckled her way along the narrow road, headlights blazing. Beside her, Ben didn't say a word, lost in his own unreadable thoughts. When a tank-like SUV raced up behind her and began tailgating, she pulled over at the first available turnoff. Once the fool passed, she continued trawling through the light fog, driving a few miles under the speed limit, fighting episodes of shooting pain in her lower back.

Another plausible reason for not wanting to go to the shelter today was Violet experiencing killer cramps. She'd downed a couple caplets of Midol after breakfast, but they'd provided only temporary relief. Since junior high, she'd been afflicted with these crippling monthly attacks. As a teenager and later as a younger woman, her mind escaped the pain by blacking out for up to thirty-six blissful hours at a time, leaving her wracked body behind. Unfortunately, by her late twenties she'd lost that talent and now had to suffer through the spasms which shot through her like little earthquakes. Today, the cramps were not the worst they'd ever been, but they were bad enough to be a serious distraction. She bit her lower lip and tried to keep her focus on the demon road, pondering God's mysterious sense of humor.

What was Ben thinking, cocooned in his silent world? He sat placidly in the passenger seat, his face serene, his thoughts tuned to his own private radio station no one else could hear. The white bag of cinnamon buns rested on the floor between his feet, and he cradled the coffee and hot chocolate in the cardboard carrier on his lap. He didn't offer Vi her coffee because the ritual was nobody ate or drank until they'd reached the shelter. She would not have accepted it, anyway. She was intent on keeping both hands welded to the steering wheel, no matter what.

It amazed her whenever Ben wanted to go anywhere near the shelter. Henry Demeter's ashes had been scattered there as a sentimental, if illegal gesture. Later, Vi and Rob chose the location for their modest wedding.

Small and rustic, the shelter was constructed of rough timber, slate, and river rock. Situated across the road stood the very tony Sugarloaf Inn where, Vi often observed, you could enjoy a sumptuous Sunday champagne brunch for four if you were willing to take out a second mortgage to pay for it. A dirt path led slightly downslope to the shelter, maybe fifty feet or so, A crude slate apron led out from the shelter's entranceway, and the structure was ringed by a half-moon, slumpstone wall, perhaps three feet high. It sat atop a ridge overlooking a deep valley green with pine, spruce and an occasional oak. It was a scenic spot, particularly in springtime and autumn.

Nearly four years earlier, it was also the site of Ben's accident.

Still, he seemed to hold no bad associations with the shelter. To the contrary, he was often eager to ride up and visit his father's ashes. Before Rachel Demeter fell ill, she and Ben had frequently come up together to commune with Henry's spirit. It was pagan, Violet believed, but it was also very touching.

"There it is! Turn here!" Ben cried as was his custom, trying to be helpful.

Vi braked and made the slow left turn into a gravel parking lot. There were no other cars in sight. It would make Ben happy, having the place all to themselves. They parked, got out of the car, and hiked cautiously down the slight slope, sidestepping the random beer cans and sprays of broken glass. Ben carried the cardboard tray of hot drinks and Vi handled the bag of cinnamon rolls.

Ben went to the wall and set down the drinks. He stared out over the valley, breathing in the fog and cold drizzle. He shut his eyes and whispered something Violet couldn't hear. He handed Vi her coffee, popping the lid on the other cup. He placed it on a nearby picnic table where the coffee steam rose up and merged with the mist. Again, he whispered a few words and, although Violet still couldn't hear him clearly, this time she knew what he'd said.

"There you go, Dad. Cream, no sugar."

Violet's coffee was exactly the reverse, very black and very sweet. To her, the contrast made perfect sense, since she and Henry Demeter had been complete opposites in temperament. The old man disliked her from the start, never so much as bothering to modify or conceal his feelings. What was it he'd seen in her that had pinged his radar? She'd never known and, over time, she'd learned not to care. He'd died three weeks after the "draft-dodging, tomcatting, tree-hugging son-of-a-bitch" was inaugurated, just after Ben's accident and just before Rob and Violet's wedding.

The coffee spread in a warm and welcome pattern through Vi's chest. Her back still hurt like hell. No matter her position, she couldn't get comfortable. She tried to take her mind off the cramps by studying the sky and the trees and by willing herself into a meditative silence. A dry streambed ran adjacent to the shelter, cut sharply to the right, and vanished into the woods. Violet knew it continued on, hidden from view for miles, only to re-emerge on the western fringe of downtown as Greenstone Creek. In springtime, the snowmelt turned it into an inner-tuber's paradise. The teenaged Demeter boys spent many long summer afternoons tumbling through its waters. There were also several good restaurants along its banks where, during happy hour, you could watch the creek flow by from overhanging wooden decks, enjoying potent daiquiris and margaritas. Sweet college drinks, Vi thought, from their sweet days of youth. Her own favorite? Tequila sunrises, hands down.

There was nary a sign Henry Demeter was responding to Ben's offer of coffee and a sweet roll. No angry fire from the mountains, no breath of wind knifing its way over the hills, no impatient cough of thunder. Just black skies and the promise of snow later in the day.

Ben was content to perch on the wall and aim his gaze into the woods. He slurped his chocolate and licked cinnamon glaze from his lips.

"Hey, Ben?"

"Mmm?"

"Tell me what you're thinking."

"Oh, nothing, Vi."

Violet nodded to herself. With those vacant eyes and flat affect, he might truly be a blank slate of a man child. She tried again. "When we come up here, what is it that you think happens?"

Now his face turned to hers in mild bemusement.

"What do you feel?" she asked.

Ben's lips parted slightly as the light bulb went on for him. He frowned. "Hard to explain, Vi."

"Can you try?" She shifted her weight from one foot to the other, seeking distraction from the cramps.

"I feel." He looked off again into the hills.

Vi followed his stare and saw nothing but another overcast Colorado afternoon.

"It's confusing," he said, and his eyes turned downward. "I feel confused. Sometimes, I swear I can feel Dad up here. In the rocks, or maybe in the weather. But I can't tell if he's really here or if I'm just remembering things…"

"What kinds of things, Ben?" Violet asked, keeping her voice neutral.

He looked up again and his eyes met hers. "I'm not sure. He's hard to picture any more. I'm starting to forget what he looked like. I know he didn't smile much. He was mad a lot, too. I've heard Tom and Rob talk about his temper. And I know you didn't like him, Vi."

Vi started to protest, then shrugged. *We're all adults now*, she thought. *We can be relatively honest.* She coaxed him, "You feel something different up here?"

Ben flashed a half-smile. "I feel like he was sad all the time," he said. "Maybe disappointed. Yeah, that's it. A lot of heavy disappointment."

"Your father was a perfectionist, Ben. He allowed himself to be easily disappointed in people."

"You mean, in us?"

She went to deny it and again caught herself. Her shoulders sagged. "He seemed to be extra hard on his family, yes. He had high expectations, Ben. Nobody could measure up to what he wanted for you guys."

Ben didn't answer. He sipped his chocolate. His face assumed the bland, faraway expression signaling he was lost in his thoughts. Once more, Vi wondered what he was thinking. What he was *remembering*. Was it possible that, at some point, he might recover bits and pieces of his memory? Anything was *possible*, the doctors conceded, though not with much hope. Ben said he'd been dreaming a lot lately too, 'crazy dreams', and Vi considered the plausibility of those new dreams containing shards of memory as well. *If so*, she thought darkly, *then what*?

If Ben had the vocabulary to describe his jagged thoughts and disjointed dreams, he might have used words like 'surreal', 'hallucinatory', 'visceral', 'hypnotic', and 'disturbing'. Without an adequate vocabulary, he felt only confused and frightened by the images in his own head. *Green ice cracking. Blue slate all around, and twilight. Rock and stone, a howling wind, wild skies.* On many nights the pictures cascaded through his poor brain. *Black snow and liquid music. Tornadoes of ash, the hills rippling.* He'd bolt awake in a cold sweat. What did it mean, what did it mean? Ben was afraid he was losing his mind, meaning he might lose his independence, which he was not about to let happen. So he kept mum, leaving Vi and Rob to guess at his thoughts. Especially Rob. Ben knew his brother would have him back to the doctors for a series of MRIs, then placed in some group home at the first tiny sign of instability. He regretted keeping things from Vi, but she would worry, run to Rob and that would be the end of Ben's freedom. Sorry, not happening. *A vortex of voices pouring forth, no, no, no. no. Falling and blackness. Awareness, then not-awareness. Wood beams, stone benches. A wind which was not a wind. An animal crying out, and long spaces between sounds.*

"Oh!" he cried out. Violet jumped, nearly spilling her coffee.

"Ben, are you all right?"

"Why can't I remember?" He wore the lost expression which

made him look savant-like, and it scared her. "Why can't they fix me?"

Vi took him by his shoulders. He wouldn't look at her. "You have a head injury, Ben. The doctors don't know enough to help you as much as we'd all like them to. They do say your memory *might* come back in stages, bit by bit. But there's no guarantee. Even if you do start remembering, maybe none of it would make sense to you."

"They're right about that part."

She smiled. "So the story of your life before, y'know, what happened? It may not fall together the way you think it would. Your emotions may be stronger and come through more clearly than the pictures. Like when a TV screen is scrambled but the sound is just fine? The signal may never become completely clear, but you'll hear enough to get a feel for what's playing. That *feeling* could be sharp and confusing."

Ben took a minute to drink his chocolate and digest Vi's words. His eyes wandered over the overcast sky, the fog, the creek, the rocks all around. In a dim corner of his mind, he found it interesting that his accident was often characterized as What Happened or That Awful Time.

"When I'm up here," he said, "I feel mixed up, it's true. It's a good place, I think. Good vibrations, with all the history. Dad's ashes and your wedding. Tom says the shelter is like church for him. He says he came up here a lot in high school, for parties or by himself, when he wanted to be alone. I think I did, too. Sometimes I can catch a memory of crowds, dancing and music. Beer. It's more like a movie than something that actually happened to me."

"I don't think it's like church at all," Vi said.

She turned her back to Ben and raised her cup to her lips but didn't drink.

Ben sensed her disquiet and fell into his own silent mode. They sat that way for several long minutes, quiet and still, watching the sky grow dark. When the first flurries appeared, Ben knew Vi would want to leave soon. He noticed she hadn't touched her cinnamon roll. She seemed lost in her own thoughts, which was mostly all right with Ben. He had some sorting out to do himself. For instance, he wondered about the disturbing, conflicted feelings he had when he was around Vi. Especially here at the shelter. It almost felt as if there was a shared history between them, something beyond the stories he'd been told and the obvious natural rapport they shared with one another.

My sister-in-law, he chanted to himself. *Rob's wife. My brother's wife.* That was right, but somehow not right. Not *completely* right. Something important was missing, but what? He searched his memory, but it was hopeless. He could recall scraps of his childhood, his school days, but hardly anything of his late teens or adulthood leading up to his fall.

He'd been told that, prior to the accident, he and Violet were close friends. He also knew Tom dated her in high school and college. He'd been told she'd left Greenstone in the early Eighties, returning for his father's funeral in spring, 1993. Where was she all that time? What was she doing? Vi never explained her missing decade, at least not to Ben's knowledge. His own memory of the time was a blur. Try as he might, he couldn't recall details from those years.

She spoke again, startling him. "Ben, do you remember the amphitheater?" she asked gently. "It's a little further up the road, about ten minutes more into the mountains. During the summer, they used to have concerts under the stars. Jazz mostly, sometimes classical. People would bring picnic dinners, cheese plates and fruit and summer sausage. They'd even let you bring wine. Hardly anyone ever got drunk or stupid. It was just music, and good food, people having a grand time."

"I don't remember, Vi."

She nodded. She turned to face him. There was something in her eyes Ben couldn't read. Snowflakes landed in her hair; her face was moist in the mist. "Of course you don't, sweetie," she said with a sad smile. "Now that place…*that* was more like church for me."

"I'm sorry. I don't remember."

Violet swung her gaze away and took a sip from her cup. "Ugggh," she said. "Cold." She tossed the black liquid over the stone wall, and in a flash, Ben remembered the day the family scattered his father's ashes. It was windy, and Rob opened the box to fling its contents over the wall, expecting a gust to carry its contents into the knapweed and thistle. Instead, the wind chose that precise moment to lull, so the ashes and bits of bone plummeted straight to the ground in a gray mound.

Ben recalled the look on Violet's face then and now stared at her, trying to piece together the rest of the memory. It eluded him, and he uttered a frustrated sound. His groan drew Vi's attention and seemed to alert her to the changing weather.

She stood, tossing her cup and pastry into the shelter's one trashcan.

"Ready?" she said.

"I guess." The snow wasn't dangerous yet, but it soon would be. Still, Ben was always reluctant to leave.

"Ben." She softened her tone and waited for him to meet her eyes.

Her cramps were getting worse by the minute, but she forced herself to smile at him. "I'm sorry we can't stay longer. Next time, we'll plan a little better. We really have to go now."

"I know."

He swallowed the rest of his chocolate and gobbled the last of the cinnamon roll. They walked back to the car, Ben licking his sticky fingers, Violet lost in her own thoughts.

The windshield was starred with hundreds of water beads. She backed out of the parking area and cautiously pulled onto Arapaho. The snow was already sticking to the road. From the corner of her eye, she saw Ben's lips moving and knew what he was whispering without hearing his words.

"Bye, Dad. See you soon."

Chapter Eight

The original plan had been for dinner up at the Wonderview Lodge, a faux-alpine restaurant in the mountains specializing in wild boar soup, elk steaks, and ostrich burgers. By evening, snow made the trip impossible, even with chains. Everyone seemed tired anyway, so Violet suggested they order Chinese, home-delivered.

"The path of least resistance," she said. "Lots of kung pao chicken, beef with green peppers, pork - Szechuan style, a veggie stir-fry, shrimp egg fu yung, potstickers, and spring rolls. Hope nobody minds, I decided for everyone."

Past experience with the Demeter clan taught her it would be another hour before they'd make up their minds on the menu, and she was too hungry to wait.

"You sure they can make it through this weather?" Tom asked.

"You've been in Florida too long. The guy on the phone said they were running about thirty minutes behind on deliveries, but they'll make it. It's just snow, not an ice storm."

"Sounds excellent, honey." Rob kissed her cheek. "Beer, anybody? I've got a pretty interesting collection downstairs from the local microbrewery."

"Beer, hm. What an interesting and quaint proposal." Tom grinned and dragged his fingers through his longish brown hair.

"I'll take that as a yes. Ben?"

Ben looked glum and shook his head reluctantly. "My meds," he said. "I better not."

Rob nodded. "You know," he said gently, "I don't think one would hurt, Ben."

"No?" Ben glanced at Tom for reassurance.

"Hell, no," Thomas laughed. "Sometimes a cold one is the best medicine there is."

"Okay." Ben seemed relieved. "I will have a beer tonight, then. Just one."

"Good choice."

"One's not going to hurt, right?"

"That's right, Ben. I'll be right back." Rob started down the stairs to the finished basement.

Vi called after him, "Don't forget one for Mom."

"Got it."

As Vi buzzed and fussed over the various preparations of a meal she was not cooking, it struck her the house had shrunk into itself with the four of them here together again. Her home was three levels and normally roomy, but the Demeter brothers had a way of turning it into a cluttered dollhouse. There was a weight in the air, as if they were all auditioning at being adults and doing an unconvincing job of it. Vi folded her arms against her chest. She disliked being made to feel like a child. It raised all sorts of unpleasant memories for her. It made her feel ridiculous.

"Cold?" There was Tom standing in the kitchen entry and Vi thought how much she'd missed him these past years. *We all missed him,* she corrected herself. He looked as he'd always looked, tall, rangy, and shaggy, with laughing blue eyes. The perpetual teenager. He could be intelligent, ironic, immature, maddening, and bemused all at the same time.

"No. Yes. Well, yes, a little. It's this damn house. It's so damn drafty."

"Well, damn it," he said lightly. "Do you want a damn sweater?"

She laughed. "No, it's probably just me. Are you chilly at all?"

"Nope, I'm comfortable. I'm pretty warm-blooded, though. So maybe it is you?"

"I'm not cold either, Vi," Ben volunteered from somewhere out in the living room.

"Guess it's me." She smiled. "I'll warm up once I've had some wine and hot food." Right on cue, the doorbell chimed and Rob reappeared from the basement clutching four brown, long-necked bottles in his fist. "Oh, the delivery guy. Tom, could you get the door? Wait, here's the money and a coupon."

"It's all right, Vi, let me get this."

"You don't have to…well, take the coupon anyway. And give him a nice tip, please. He's earned it tonight; the roads are just horrible. Honey," to Rob, "let me help you."

Rob placed the bottles on the counter while Vi rummaged through a drawer for an opener. After some deliberation, he'd chosen a pale ale brewed in Estes Park. The bottles were dark brown and their labels featured a cartoon elk wearing a quizzical expression.

"Can I help, too?"

"Not right now, Ben. You can help clean up later, though, if you like."

Tom came into the kitchen carrying two large white plastic bags of food. "This smells delicious," he announced. "All of a sudden, I'm starving."

"How was the driver? Was he holding up okay?" Vi was concerned.

"She," Thomas corrected her, then laughed at Violet's look of mild disbelief. In a mock anchorman's voice, he intoned, "Shattering all stereotypes and defying common wisdom, the Chinese food delivery driver was…a woman." In his normal voice he mused, "Funny. They hire a Mexican girl to deliver Chinese food to a white bread neighborhood on a night fit for Eskimos. It's all Greek to me." He shook his head. "Did I mention she was driving a Japanese car?"

"Stop it," Vi commanded.

"Probably lives in Koreatown. Or Little Italy, maybe?"

"Let's eat before the food gets cold," suggested Rob.

Vi set a table for five while Robert distributed the beer to his brothers and himself. He placed the final bottle at the head of the table in front of an empty chair. Everyone was seated and Rob raised his bottle.

"To Rachel," he toasted.

"To Rachel. To Mom." The bottles clinked together solemnly, with Vi's wine glass ringing in.

"Now dig in," she ordered. "Let's not be morose. You know Mom would want a lot of laughs and food and booze and family stories. No tears, though. Right, Ben?"

Ben nodded, his round blue eyes moist. "No tears," he said obediently.

"Let us hereby concur and abide by the No Tears resolution, shall we?" said Tom, helping himself to the lo mein noodles. "Motioned, seconded, and carried. Yow! This shit is hot. Did you nuke it, Vi?"

"No, it just came that way. Be careful."

"Maybe if you'd wait a minute and let it cool off a bit," Rob scolded him mildly. "Even when you were a kid, you gulped your food like a jackal. Are you all right?"

"Yeah, except for my tongue getting steam-cleaned. Ouch."

"Well," Rob cleared his throat, just a little theatrically. "The funeral home arrangements have been taken care of. Mother will be cremated in," he consulted his watch, "about twelve hours. Visiting hours are for family only tomorrow. There'll be a small memorial service the next day. Afterward, we'll take her ashes and scatter them up at the shelter early Thursday morning."

"Did they give you much trouble about the ashes?"

"It's not legal to spread them up in the mountains, if that's what you're asking. Trust me, it's best to do the don't-ask-don't-tell thing. They'll box up the ashes for us and discreetly look the other way. For our part, we won't volunteer any information."

"They can just assume Mom will be resting in peace on the fireplace mantel for all eternity." Tom nodded. "What about this memorial service? Mom wasn't the most religious person in the world. She wouldn't want some phony-baloney preacher man she never knew talking about her soul being in a better place."

"Right. It'll just be friends and community figures coming by to pay their respects. If family wants to make some remarks, that would be fine. We'll fill the room with old photographs, flowers, her favorite music, candles. Don't worry, it'll be classy and understated. The mayor will be there, I think."

"Yes, as long as the mayor shows, that's the important thing." Vi immediately regretted her words. She poured herself another glass of red wine. "No, I guess the important thing is it'll be the way Mom would want it. A little bit of a party, and a tribute to her place in this town. You've done a fine job, Rob."

Robert gave her a thin smile.

"Well, I approve, for what it's worth," Tom said. "It sounds like it'll be very respectful and a tad bit heathen. Classic Mom."

A silence fell upon them then, and the four greedily attacked the feast before them. They filled their plates with a cornucopia of chicken, noodles, baby corn, pork, snow peas, watercress, rice, peppers, onions and mountains more of food because Vi always over-ordered, she couldn't stand the thought of company leaving the table wanting more. They were hungry in many ways and they couldn't help being reminded of the countless Sunday and holiday meals at the gigantic Demeter dinner table which Tom famously described as "a football field long." Rachel usually prepared a roast of some variety and taciturn Henry was coerced into mumbling a few words of grace. Then they'd devour the food with gusto.

"Like a pride of lions on a gazelle," Tom recalled for them.

"Like piranhas," laughed Ben.

"Like buzzards." Even Rob was smiling. "Like sharks."

Vi rolled her eyes and took another swallow of wine. "Just like old times," she remarked. "The more things change, the more they stay the same. You know, I miss it sometimes. Those marathon conversations."

Tom grimaced. "Those arguments, you mean. Those battles. Oh, my God."

"Let's call them debates. You guys were pretty civil most of the time. My first time, though, I thought, these people are crazy. Passionate, yes. Opinionated, for sure. But crazy."

"Which, of course, was a highly inaccurate diagnosis." Tom crossed his eyes and stuck out his tongue. Ben giggled, then gagged a little on his beer.

"Long time ago," Rob said dreamily. "It all started with Tricky Dick, didn't it?"

"Oh, Christ, fucking Nixon. Did you guys want to puke when they eulogized that sinister shit as a Great Statesman? That sneaky, conniving, slope-nosed bastard…"

"My, the language," Vi scolded gently.

"Father thought the man could do no wrong," Rob recalled. He deepened his voice and orated, "The GOP is the political party for grown-ups in this country. They understand fiscal responsibility, goddamnit, and old-fashioned Main Street values. Richard Nixon is a strong leader and a decent man. I never thought I'd see the day when strength and decency came under attack in America."

"Hey Dad," Tom piped up in a fair impersonation of his own sixteen-year-old voice. "What have you been smoking? What about Watergate, huh? Huh, Dad? What about that?"

"What about it?" Robert-as-Henry spluttered. "A third-rate break-in…an error in judgment…the media blew it all out of proportion, goddamn them. Brought down a great man because of their unpatriotic, narrow-minded, cowardly agenda."

There was no doubt Nixon was the turning point. Prior to the disgraced president, the dinnertime discussions revolved around sports, homework, weekend plans, and what was showing at the movies. By far the worst and most soul-deadening of all topics was Father's Day at the Firm. This last subject was broached in a baritone drone which induced yawns and heavy eyelids. The report fell into several distinct categories, such as how stupid and careless people could be with their money, or how Father courageously stood up to So-And-So or put that self-righteous What's-His-Name in his place. Worst of all was a numbing, blow-by-blow recital of Henry's mundane workday activities.

Ah, but after Nixon there were suddenly, gloriously, no boundaries for talk at the table. King Richard's outrageous polemics and proclamations shattered the old convention, the unwritten code of speaking only in a 'positive' manner, unfailingly cheery, non-controversial and totally mind-numbing. The food fueled heated discussions of new literature and modern films featuring a great wave of anti-heroes, Vietnam, ecological concerns, racial volatility, rock-and-roll. "That's not music," tormented Henry, his own tastes running to Ella Fitzgerald and Tony Bennett, would protest, close to tears. "How can you think that's music? It all sounds like a terrible car wreck." They argued over politics and religion, abortion and the welfare state. Over beef brisket, they shouted at each other about vegetarianism. Over pork, the talk was congressional malfeasance and misappropriations, gerrymandering and filibustering. Over chicken, it was Nixon. Nixon and his baleful television presence, his evil-looking five o'clock shadow. Nixon and his dreadful miscreant apprentice Spiro.

The tinderbox atmosphere at suppertime began in the 1970's, when the boys were in their teens, and continued through their young adulthoods. If Vi was honest with herself, she'd admit the dinner diatribes were a substantial part of her original attraction to Tom. Her conservative upbringing spawned a natural youthful rebelliousness of her own. Once exposed to the Demeters, she had no inhibitions about jumping into the fray, usually disagreeing with Henry and forging an early kinship with Rachel.

Now she said, "Remember when Mom voted for Carter? That was a dagger in his heart, wasn't it?"

"Yes, but how did that turn out?" Rob interjected. "American hostages, oil prices through the roof, the Democrats in shambles. Thank goodness for Reagan."

"Oh, oh, oh." Tom stopped chewing and brandished his chopsticks at his brother. "Fair warning, do not go there, Rob. Do not go all 'Morning in America' on me."

Rob started to reply, thought better of it. Just then, Ben said, "I like President Clinton. I think he's doing a good job."

Everybody laughed and Ben reddened. Vi reached over and took his hand. "I think so, too, Ben."

"He's doing a good job if you think…" Rob said. "Oh, forget it. I think this might be a good time to bring up some more beer."

"Fantastic idea," Thomas agreed, blowing a tuneless whistle into his bottleneck.

While Rob clambered down to the basement, Vi and Ben cleared the table. Tom had a few moments alone in the dining room with Rachel's empty chair. For the first time since he'd touched down in Denver, he thought about his mother being gone forever. At one time or another, they'd all claimed Rachel would outlive everyone. Even when she became ill, it had been inconceivable to think in terms of her possible death.

"It's good that H.D. went before Rachel," he called out to no one in particular. "He never would have survived this. She was always the stronger one. He liked to brag about being a self-made man, but he could barely tie his shoelaces without her."

For replies, he heard only the clinking of the dishwasher being loaded and the creaking of the basement steps from Rob's weight.

"That's okay. I'll just sit here and talk to myself like a loon," he told the empty dining area. Then, softer, "I miss you, Mom."

"Did you say something?" asked Rob, materializing with an assortment of beers.

"Yes. I was saying that I really need much more alcohol to get through tonight."

"Glad to oblige."

"Anybody ready for dessert?" Vi called from the kitchen. "We've got ice cream, German chocolate cake, and some cheesecake left over from the weekend."

Both Tom and Rob groaned. "Maybe later, honey," Rob said. "Let's take a little break. We can have coffee in a bit."

"Sure thing," Thomas agreed. "We'll be hungry in an hour anyway, right?"

"That's really stupid," Vi told him, emerging from the kitchen with a replenished glass of wine. Ben followed, holding a cup of orange tea sweetened with honey. They sat down again, and after a brief period of quiet the talk turned to Rachel's long years of community service. She'd been a walking, talking paradox, a woman who'd been a champion volunteer, who'd believed deeply in the value of volunteerism, but who'd also been irked by the lackluster efforts given by some of her fellow volunteers.

Henry had not been as ambivalent in his criticisms. "Anything worth doing right is worth getting paid for. If you have to rely on volunteers, you're just asking for trouble." He wondered why his wife wasted her time and talents with some of her 'half-baked' projects. When one of Rachel's co-volunteers botched an assignment, he'd be quick to gloat. "That's what you get when you recruit your workers from the Pennysaver."

Rachel was less sardonic but could be just as savage in her assessments. "Some of these people," she'd fume. "They think they can just show up when they please and everyone should bend over backward with gratitude. They're in love with the idea of helping because it makes them feel better about themselves. They don't seem to understand that volunteering is a job, only without pay. A job," she'd add for emphasis. She reserved a special disdain for those people who volunteered mainly to escape their personal problems, to pad their resumes, or, worst of all, to 'find themselves'. She could tick off a checklist of such disasters. "Recently divorced women who want to weep and jabber instead of work. Men in recovery who have seen the light and now want to save everyone else's souls. Retired geniuses who want to run things rather than fill a niche. Young do-gooders with no work ethic and poor communication skills. People who need more help for themselves than they can ever give to others."

"Jesus, I thought I was jaded," Tom would cry in mock horror. "You must be a laugh riot to work with, Mom. Aren't you being a little harsh?"

"I don't think so. I've watched too many managers and coordinators bend over backward to please a rogue volunteer. It almost never turns out well. It's a waste of time, I tell you, putting eighty percent of your energy into the twenty percent of folks who cause nothing but grief. Goodness, you're supposed to be volunteering to fill a need or to help people less fortunate, not because *you're* the needy one."

When all was said and done, Rachel was, in Thomas' words, "the poster child for volunteerism."

She threw herself into worthy causes like a boxer rising to meet the next punishing round. She worked odd shifts and special events. She baked, she worked phone trees, she wrote grants, she schmoozed with Greenstone's high-and-mighty, she sold raffle tickets, she developed a media contact list, she mopped floors when necessary, she donated money to nonprofit organizations great and small. Her motives were pure and tender-hearted, whether she got involved in casino nights to benefit meals-on-wheels, galas to help abused children, jazz concerts at the local winery to keep the doors of the women's shelter open, or silent auctions to buy food for the homeless. Greenstone's most active volunteers were her best friends and the people she most respected. She'd been fond of saying, "This is still a small town. The same two hundred people do *everything*."

"And now she's gone," Ben sighed, stirring his tea.

With that, the table fell into a heavy silence for another ten or fifteen seconds as each Demeter pondered what it meant to be 'gone'.

Tom swooped to the rescue. "The time has now come," he rumbled. "We can delay it no longer. This evening will not be complete without the solemn reading of the fortune cookies."

Rob said stiffly, "It's late, Tom. There's lots to do tomorrow."

"If you're tired, you should read yours first, then." Vi fixed her husband with a stare.

Rob recognized the look and calculated it wasn't worth arguing. Reluctantly, he cracked open his cookie. "'Great fortune awaits you,'" he read. "'But beware, too, of great sorrow.' Now that makes perfect sense," he said irritably. "Does it mean I should go to Vegas or not?"

Tom laughed. "Grasshopper," he intoned, "one must cultivate patience for the mists of the future to part."

"Yeah, whatever. Somebody else go, I need to get some sleep."

"Ben, what's yours say?"

Ben didn't have to be asked twice. Like a kid, he split his cookie with a look of glee. He read slowly. "'You may dive for and find pearls in the deep pools of the past.'"

"Hmm. Well, honey, they don't always make sense," Vi said quickly at Ben's deep scowl. "Remember, it's just for fun. Who's next?"

"Let's open Mom's," Tom suggested.

"Good idea." Violet did the honors. "'Yours is the green harvest and the barren earth.' Isn't that a contradiction?"

"Fortune cookie, make up your mind!"

"I think we've got a bored fortune writer," said Rob. "Tom, you're up."

"Too bad we're all too tired to interpret some of these profound prophecies and prognostications," Tom slurred grandly. His fingers cracked open the little shell and unfurled the strip of paper. His expression darkened. "Hey, I've been gypped!" he complained. He held up the paper for all to see. It was blank.

"Factory error," Vi said with a smile.

"Or, you have no future," Rob said with a touch of smugness.

"I was hoping to get one of those nice, generic, uplifting fortunes," Tom said wistfully. "You know, like the ones you can add 'in bed' to. Something to the effect of, 'You are meant to find joy and pleasure.' 'In bed.'"

"I don't get it," Ben said, looking around.

"Evidently, neither will I. All right, enough of this pity party! Vi, I believe we've saved the best for last."

Vi opened her cookie. She read her fortune first and shook her head with a little smile. She read, "'The juggler eventually grows weary and inevitably drops a pin.'"

"Okay." Rob stood up. "With that, I say goodnight everyone. See you in the morning. Ben, you'll spend the night. I know you don't like to be away from home long, but nobody should be out driving on a night like this. Mr. Whiskers should be all right till tomorrow. I'll swing you home before the viewing, okay?"

"Yes, Rob."

"Wait a minute," Tom protested. "What the hell does Vi's fortune mean?"

Robert yawned. "What did any of them mean? Good night."

Vi waited until Rob had left the room, then said, "He's right. It's all just silliness. Ben, will you help me clean up? Tom, if you can get the trash that would be great. No dessert, anyone? Coffee? You're sure?"

Classic Violet, Tom thought. Food was a comfort and an intimacy with her. When everyone was eating and drinking, all was right with the world.

"All right, then. Kitchen's closed. Jesus," she said under her breath. "What a day."

"Amen," said Ben.

Chapter Nine

Out on the back deck, Violet watched the bats soar through the tumbling snow, their wings silhouetted and magnified against the red moon. The night was redolent with the smell of pine trees and burning firewood. Houses glowed with Christmas lights. It was late, or rather, early in the morning. There were no headlights moving through the streets, no music blaring, no strands of conversation echoing in the weird acoustics of the neighborhood.

The air was bone-cold, but the world felt clean. Vi refused to wear a coat. She wanted the cold to pierce her and work its numbing power on her skin cells and nerve endings. When the glass door slid open behind her, she tensed but otherwise showed no sign of reacting. Tom stepped out on the deck.

"Beautiful night," he breathed. "Mind if I join you?"

"No, that's fine."

"If you came out here to be alone…"

"It's okay, Tom. Really."

"Will it bother you if I smoke?"

She shook her head and lifted her face to the stars.

Tom followed her gaze. His slight astigmatism rendered the starlight glittery as diamond shine. The sky was pearl-gray, the clouds a deep vermilion. He blew a plume of blue smoke into the freezing air. "It's never enough, is it?"

"Excuse me?"

"All this." Like a magician, he waved his free hand at the cosmos. "Peaceful snowy night. Gorgeous sky. The splendor and the majesty of the universe at our finger-tips."

"God's work."

"Could be. Fantastic, whatever its source." He fell silent for one heartbeat, two. "Too bad it's never enough for us."

Vi allowed herself a wan smile. "Oh, boy, here we go."

That brought a snort of laughter from Tom. "You bet," he said. "Climb aboard, buckle up, and hang tight. It's Mr. Tom's Wild Ride. Hey, I'm jetlagged and my mother's dead. I'm not allowed to be a little melancholy?" Before she could answer, he aimed his cigarette at her. "Don't say a word. Let me finish my morose thought. They say that pain reminds us we're alive, right? Mom doesn't have that luxury any more. Therefore, as the comic book heroes say, permit me to elaborately elucidate."

"Don't let me stop you."

"It seems to me," Tom continued in a tone of mock-grandeur, "that it can't stay like this, natural and pure. It never does. People can't leave paradise alone, right? We have to bite the apple; we can't help ourselves. Original sin is all tangled up in the strands of our DNA. You can say oh, that'll never happen in outer space. But believe me, it'll be exactly like the condos, casinos and shopping malls covering every square foot of shoreline. Or how if we ever find Atlantis, we'll plaster it with billboards and stick a Burger King at the bottom of the sea."

"Might make more sense to make it a Long John Silver's," Violet noted.

His eyes took on a thoughtful and slightly demented sheen. Vi knew he was off on a tear, and there would be no muzzling him now.

"What I'll bet will happen is, first we'll colonize the moon and use it as our staging area. We'll build a fleet of solar-powered flying wings to annex the planets. Then it's just a matter of time before Exxon has space freighters chugging between Mars and the moons of Jupiter. They'll stop only for potty breaks and Frappuccino's at a Starbucks kiosk in the asteroid belt."

He stopped to take a deep drag off his cigarette. Vi indulged him. "Sounds like the stuff of a new monologue."

"The start of one, maybe." He shut his eyes, visualizing it. "Although, lately I feel more like I'm an old storyteller who's just sick to death of other people's stories. Christ." He squinted into the murk of the backyard as if he had spied something without shape, dark-on-dark. The cigarette glowed like a hovering firefly. "Why do you suppose we think of ourselves as unique? Here we are, standing outdoors on this beautiful crystalline night, beneath a zillion stars and satellites. We're totally insignificant, with all our petty problems and trivial concerns. Almost insects."

"Is this what you came out here for?" said Vi, her voice unintentionally edged. "You know all that nonsense isn't true, Tom. I know you're not a believer, but even some atheists can feel that life is sacred. What about the soul? That's what makes us unique. Think about Rachel's spirit…"

"Wait, what's that?" Tom cupped a hand to his ear. "Oh, right, it's just my bullshit detector going wild. Vi, I'm sorry. You know I don't think the way you do. I wish I did. It must be a comfort to be so certain all the time, to know there's a plan and a purpose to this shithole planet. Life being sacred? That's a fairy tale. Look around you. Read your history books. Real American fairy tales, everywhere you go. Just like liberty and justice for all. Like money can't buy you happiness. Like Oswald acted alone." He heard himself becoming strident and modulated his voice. "Look, I'm sorry. You came out here for some peace and quiet, I'm sure. And here I am in my funky fucking mood. Tell me to piss off, if it'll make you feel better."

"It's okay, just stop apologizing for being yourself. I know you can't have a simple conversation without turning it into a speech or a lecture." She grinned to take the sting out of her words. "You can't fool me, Tom. You're a cynical idealist. Always have been, always will be."

"As opposed to being an idealistic cynic?"

"I suppose that's what makes you a good tortured artist. All I mean is, you don't have to be so hard on yourself, and on everybody else."

"Yes, yes, I see," he said, rubbing his chin in the fashion of a cartoon therapist. "My mother just died, after all. So I can be forgiven my crude and boorish tirades. Let's also not forget the ancient Demeter family curse of mood swings and melancholia. Then there's the sorry random unfairness of the world at large to consider. No wonder I'm a mess. Thank

God for armchair psychoanalysis."

Violet sighed. "It rains on everyone, Tom."

He surprised her by giving a bitter laugh. "Yeah, but there's them that's got umbrellas and them that ain't. Shit, is that supposed to make me feel better? Come on, Vi, you know me better than that. I'm your classic glass-is-half-empty kind of guy."

"I remember that." She turned to look at him directly. "That's probably why it never worked between us."

"One reason, anyhow," he agreed. "Maybe one of many."

An awkward silence fell between them. The light snow dusted their hair. The red moon seemed to inhale and exhale in a series of long sighs.

Violet held his eyes for a long minute before letting him off the hook. "What're the boys doing?" she asked with a nonchalance she didn't feel.

"Ben's downstairs watching TV, or maybe playing a video game. I think Rob's turned in." He watched her face carefully. "He's been running crazy, taking care of everything. He's got to be pretty tired."

"He's always tired." She hadn't meant to say it so sharply, or even say it at all, but there it was, out in the open. "Tell me, how's your new girlfriend? Is it…Deborah?"

"Donna."

"Oh, sorry. I can't keep up with all your romantic escapades. You've been together, what? Three months now?"

"Almost four. Things are good, for the most part. They feel good to me, anyhow." He noted her crooked grin and added, "Mind you, that doesn't mean wedding bells are in the air. It just means I'm not feeling too bad about this one, y'know?"

"Now there's a real declaration of head-over-heels romantic love," she chided. "She must be something special to put up with you. She's a nurse, isn't she?"

"Yep. And trust me on this," giving Vi an exaggerated leer, "everything they say about nurses and their lack of inhibition is one hundred percent true."

"Spare me, stud. It's all one big anatomy lesson to them, I

suppose. I'll bet she wears you out."

"You've got that right. I just do my best to keep up with her." He uttered a little laugh, but his eyes were serious. "She's very independent. I like that about her. She's not the possessive type, which is a real switch for me. Usually I'm dating the insanely jealous, potentially violent ones. If I get hit by a truck tomorrow, Donna would miss me, sure, and grieve for a little while. But she'd get on with her life sooner than later. Find another man, and all that happy ending crap."

"Sounds like she has a good head on her shoulders."

"Yeah. She's got her priorities straight, all right. It's pretty weird being involved with a girl like her. Almost normal, I mean."

"Wow. Don't tell me this is maturity I'm hearing?"

Tom didn't answer. Instead he cocked his head as if he was listening to radio signals being transmitted from a far-flung galaxy. Vi was speaking in a soft voice, but he couldn't decode her words. He stood stock-still and contemplated the red moonlight tinting the snow pink, painting purple shadow. He pondered the background buzzing of quasars and interstellar extinction, ruminated on wormholes and the enigmatic nature of neutron stars. He also wondered how, in a single night, without saying anything seductive or spectacular, Vi managed to make him fall for her all over again. A sudden yearning for her went through him like a bolt. It had been nearly twenty years, and all she had to do was stand in what seemed to be her own cylinder of polar light and everything about her was capable of rekindling old feelings. The slightest lift of her chin, the cut of her hair, the way her jeans rode her hips, all roused tender memories. *Robert's wife*, he reminded himself. Again, moving his lips. *Your brother's wife.*

She noticed his faraway look and misread it. "It's incredible, isn't it?" she whispered, nodding to the firmament. "So vast and yet... Have you ever heard the expression, that all the world's dreams can be held in the seed of a single gourd? That's the glory of it, Tom."

"Whatever happened to us, Vi?" he blurted.

It was like suddenly he'd been afflicted with Tourette's, the physical pressure to say the unsayable building up and building up inside, growing unbearable, finally spewing forth. It was unedited and too late to pull back and, embarrassed, Tom launched into a self-deprecating, seriocomic rant about unrequited love.

Violet drowned out the sound of his voice by focusing on the dull metronome of her own blood beating in her temples. For a host of reasons, she didn't respond at once. His question had been so unexpected, she'd been caught totally off-guard. More, she didn't want to give him the satisfaction of hearing the tears in her reply, or the anger, or the numbness. Through the snow flurries she spied a shooting star and, for the briefest of instants, flashed on all her missed opportunities and lost possibilities. She remembered her fortune cookie and pictured herself juggling alternate endings. For just an eyeblink, Vi entertained the atheistic idea that life might be pointless.

Finally she said, "Don't you dare get sentimental on me now, Tom. That was a long time ago. What happened to us is what happens to most young couples. We tried it, it worked for a while, then after a time it didn't work so well any more. So we broke it off and moved on. End of story." She did a masterful job of keeping her features blank, hoping she'd been successful at keeping her tone level and conversational.

"That's it, huh?" Tom stared out into the snow. She observed his fingers tightening on the railing.

"That's it, darlin'. So sad and too bad."

"Don't you mean, so much denial and rationalization? That's it? That's *it*? You took your broken little heart, went underground for a dozen years or so, resurfaced, and what happened then? Oh, that's right," bitterly, "then you married my brother."

"Tom, we really don't need to…"

"Ah. Ah. Ah." He cut her off, the flat of his hand slicing the air in a silencing judo chop. "Don't bullshit a professional bullshitter, Vi. Give me some credit, okay?" He hung his head. "I'm an idiot, I know. Sorry. Should know better than to dredge this up again. Especially now, when everybody's feeling so raw…"

"Shh," said Violet. "Shh. It's all right."

Tom felt a rush of coldness on his face. "No," he told her. "That's one thing it definitely is not. Not by any stretch of the imagination is anything all right. Sorry, I know I'm being shitty. But let's not make things worse by lying about them."

"Tom, I'm not…"

"No, of course you're not lying. That was coarse of me. Sugarcoating, then." He shook his head. "Jesus, Vi. He's a *broker*, for Christ's sake. A numbers-cruncher with a fucking database for feelings. I *know* you can't be in love with Robert. He's my brother, but goddamnit…"

"You can stop right there." It was Vi's turn to be angry. "First, Rob is my husband. What that means is that I can complain about him all I want, but nobody else can. Not even his brother. I'm the first to admit things between us aren't always perfect. We're a team, though. We've gone through a lot of ups and downs together and we've made this marriage work. There are depths to Robert a clod like you can't understand. Secondly, this is my house. You're welcome to be here, Tom, but I will not tolerate your negativity or your blaspheming. Are you hearing this?"

Her eyes burned at him. Her hair, always a little unruly, was starting to frizz out from the wet snow and from her anger. Tom nodded slowly. "Third, you had your fucking chance, you jerk. You had me hooked heart and soul, and you threw it all away. Now you have no rights, no say, no nothing. You careless, childish, insecure…"

Vi ran out of fuel. She stopped and simply glared at him. For a long couple of minutes, the night turned dead quiet, as if her diatribe stilled the entire neighborhood. Tom looked so hangdog she almost said something to take the sting from her harsh words.

He lit another cigarette, took a puff with a distracted air. Then he said, "Man. That was pretty articulate. Plus, you're a Christian and you said 'fuck.'"

"Yeah, I'm a bad girl," she said with a laugh.

"What you are is a seeker, Vi." Thomas compressed his lips, blew his cheeks out, hesitated, then decided to say it all. "What I don't get is, how do you stand it? How did you of all people turn into a suburban Stepford soccer mom zombie? Well, you're not a mom, but you get the idea."

"Tom, why are you rehashing this? What does it prove? What are you trying to accomplish? Are you offering to rescue me? Turn the clock back and pretend you'll carry me away from this life of dreariness and drudgery? You need to grow up."

"Be honest, now. Do you have any feelings left for me?"

"No," she told him. "No, not like you mean. Even if I did, it wouldn't matter. The past is gone, and we've both made our beds, haven't we?"

"Interesting metaphor. Speaking of which are you sleeping with anybody? Please tell me if this is none of my business."

When Violet blushed, her face became a smaller version of the moon. "That's none of your business, is right."

"Oh, that's a yes. Makes sense. How else could you survive being married to…"

"Keep your voice down, please." She wanted to scream at him, so her words were a caution to herself as well as Tom. "You know what Rob would say to you right now? That you always wanted to be Bob Dylan or Richard Pryor or Ralph Nader, or name your own stupid crusader. Because normal was never good enough for you." She took in a breath, then hissed, "Not everybody can play the privileged artist game, Tom. We can't all afford to be so self-indulgent."

"Oh, why not just say 'selfish?'"

She held his gaze. "Well, if the shoe fits…"

"That's what Robert *would* say," he agreed softly, leaning in towards her. "That's because 'good enough' defines his whole life. What does Violet say, I wonder?" He placed a finger gently on her forehead. "Is she still up here?"

At his touch, Vi's face grew warm. Just as gently, she pushed away his hand. "I don't know if the Violet you want me to be is still here," she said slowly. "People change, don't they? Just because your brother is conservative, just because he's a responsible man, that doesn't automatically make him a bad guy. You have no idea how big a heart he has." Thomas barked a short laugh, but Vi repeated fiercely, "No idea. How do you think the world would look if everyone decided to sing protest songs? Or mocked the government, or made fun of other people's attitudes and beliefs? Who would be the builders, Tom? You know who

I'm talking about, don't you? The ones who help keep you warm and fed, mobile and safe. The ones who fix the plumbing, purify the water, haul away your trash, repair the cars. Those people."

"Come on, Vi…"

"The ones who learn useful skills and keep the world moving forward," she said evenly, but with a slight lupine smile, "while clowns like you flap your lips about politicians and do your dog-and-pony shows about how superior you are to everyone else."

Tom didn't answer right away. His dismay was so great, he was struck with a rare bout of speechlessness. This was definitely Robert talking, not Violet. Tom would have bet his life their marriage would have made Vi the ventriloquist and Rob the dummy, not vice versa. Rob's stodginess seemed to have swallowed whole the free-spirited Vi. This was like listening to a slightly imperfect and much duller clone of Violet. And *still* she had the power to hex and vex his heart.

Choosing his words with care, he said, "Look, Vi. I don't want to fight. You're right and I apologize. All this stuff is ancient history. Can we put it behind us? I don't know what I was thinking. Between lack of sleep and all those microbrews, my brain is fried."

For her part, Vi felt drained, and her exhaustion made her more forgiving than she normally might have been. The snarky look fled her face. She stretched her arms and observed that her skin was prickled with gooseflesh. Without thinking, she reached her palm to Tom's cheek and let it rest there for a long moment. Without being aware of it, Tom held his breath. Her hand was so warm.

"I'm going in," she said gently, with no rancor. "It's been a marathon day and we're both wiped out. But I can't deal with Memory Lane anymore. Do you understand? It's good to see you again, Tom. You make me laugh. There's just no point in digging up the past." She yawned "We have a lot to get through in these next few days. Get some sleep, okay?"

Tom nodded. "Sure. Good night, Vi. It's good seeing you, too. Don't forget, say your prayers."

She searched his face for the sarcasm but didn't see it there. "I always do," she told him. "See you in the a.m."

Chapter Ten

Tom got up early. He never slept well in strange beds. He didn't feel rested, but he knew it was futile to lay back down. He remembered that, at best, Colorado weather was freaky, and so was not surprised when the morning unveiled hard yellow sunshine which already was thawing the icicles outside the guest room windows. By noon, the unseasonable warmth would clear the main roads of ice. Which was good, because every year the city of Greenstone reacted to snow as if it was the rarest of occurrences. Imagine, snow, in winter, in the Rocky Mountains. The workers moved like tranquilized turtles to clear the streets.

He owned a lightweight hangover and a wicked case of dry mouth. He sipped at the cup of water he'd carried to the bedroom after saying good night to Vi. He wondered how *she'd* slept. There was no use going down that road, so Tom turned on the room's little radio and surfed until he found a news channel. Predictably, the news was all bad. The airport was shut down, terrorists had blown up part of an embassy somewhere in the Middle East, energy costs were in the stratosphere, a little girl had been kidnapped outside of Denver, the body of a young woman who'd been missing for weeks had been found in a park in Arvada, morning rush hour traffic was snarled in all directions. Unemployment was up and the stock market was down. The Nuggets lost last night. In the White House, a sex scandal was brewing.

Enough of this, he decided and switched off the miserable radio. He moved slowly in the morning chill. He dressed and made the bed. The room's décor brought a small smile to his lips. It was no trick differentiating Rob's influence from Vi's tastes. The walls and themes of the room of the entire house were done in various shades of brown.

Robert-browns. Beige, sandstone, tan, ecru, terra cotta, everything inoffensive and easy to match. To all the drabness, Vi introduced subversive bursts of color. The comforter Tom yanked up over the pillows was stitched into a crisscrossing diamond pattern, the diamonds dyed in rich reds, greens, and blues. A Paul Klee calendar hung on the back of the bedroom door, and there were several Peruvian masks displayed above the headboard. A good imitation of an Oriental rug, all red-and-gold abstract designs, lay at the foot of the bed. On the windowsills were candles, on the dresser a Navajo runner, on the small writing desk a pale green Tiffany lamp. It was a hodgepodge, but Vi had made it work somehow.

Throughout the rest of the house, everyone else dozed on. Tom decided to brave the slushy sidewalks for a little walk. He pulled on his seen-better-days FSU sweatshirt, black jeans, and battered cross-trainers. For one insane moment, he considered waking Vi and asking her to join him, like in the old days.

He snapped to his senses and without making a sound slid outside. The cold stung his eyes to tears. He lit a cigarette and drew the smoke deep into his lungs. *Nothing like that first nicotine hit,* he thought.

Gingerly, he started down the hill, through the grid of streets and split-levels. It was the type of neighborhood where there were countless sightings of snowmen, plastic reindeer, mangers of myriad sizes, blow-up Santa's, wreaths, electric stars, cardboard magi, and a rare menorah or two. Some folks left their lights on all night and they glimmered weakly in the gray-and-salmon dawn. The scaffolding of a story started taking shape in Tom's imagination. He let it sit there awhile. Experience taught him it did no good to force the ideas to come together. More often than not, they amassed on their own, given sufficient time and patience.

Tom loathed his memories of a Colorado boyhood fraught with head colds, bronchitis, nasty allergies, and sinus infections. His nose ran constantly and the snot would freeze solid beneath his nostrils in tiny green stalactites. He'd hated winters for as long as he could remember. Sometimes, Henry held lit matches to the keyhole of his Lincoln, thawing it enough to enable his key to work open the lock. He loved to tell the tale, surely an urban legend, of the morons who used the match trick to peer into the murk of their gas tanks, when *ker-bloom*! Their garages blew apart like fiery houses of straw and the explosions scattered their sorry asses to the four winds. *Fucking Colorado.* Icy fleur-de-lis crusted every exposed glass surface, and there was never any hot water when it was most needed because the pipes froze and cracked at the very worst times. After college, Tom couldn't flee fast enough to the endless summers of Florida.

In his acts, he frequently introduced his hometown stories by beginning, "Greenstone made Kings Row look like Bedford Falls."

He'd left Greenstone as a young man and returned only a few times since. Each time he'd been stupefied by the growth. Developers discovered the pristine foothill town, and once the secret was out there was no stopping the sprawl. Zero population growth was a bump in the road to progress, as were the protests of the greenbelters, the conservationists, and the most vocal of the longtime residents.

The weapons were big money and eminent domain. The city leaders took part in the backstabbing, gleefully lining their pockets with each new bridge built, shopping center contract signed, and condo complex erected. The population had tripled since Tom's school days, and gentrification had crept in. While the town now boasted an abundance of specialty marketplaces, upscale boutiques, bodegas and bistros, the infrastructure had not kept pace.

Now he emerged from suburbia to a major intersection buzzing with rush hour traffic. Across the way was a shopping mini-mall utterly without character. It featured a laundromat, liquor store, a storefront taekwondo studio, a grungy Thai restaurant, and a video mart. Tom crossed and stepped into a generic doughnut joint that was open twenty-four/seven for no discernible reason. It might have done a fair-to-middling business, but nothing to warrant round-the-clock service. He speculated it might be a front for a small potatoes bookie or a drug distributor. Cheesy holiday muzak poured from hidden speakers behind the counter. Undaunted, he ordered a bear claw and a small coffee from the unhappy Latina teenager working the cash register. The tab was a dollar-forty-nine. He thought she was going to burst into tears when he presented her with a ten and two quarters. He might as well have asked her to solve a quadratic equation in her head.

"Just give me nine dollars in change," he instructed. He promised he wasn't trying to cheat her. "Keep the penny. Someone else might need it." *Or*, he thought meanly, *add it to your college fund so you don't have to work here the rest of your life.*

He carried his coffee and pastry to a dingy plastic table the size of a postage stamp where, for no apparent reason, he heard the phrase, "There's still no room at the inn" loud and clear inside his head. Amused, he sat down and watched the traffic stream by. Except for the cashier, he had the place to himself. It was lovely to be so lazy, he thought. Tom thoroughly enjoyed the slow pleasures of walking, rather than jogging's grim need for discipline and pacing. Perhaps that was another reason why things had never worked out with Vi. She was restless, always seeming to need to aspire to some new task or activity. Whereas for Tom, leisure provided time for introspection, cultivated peace of mind, and prompted left-brain activity. Outside, commuters rushed to their jobs and a group of homeless men waited at the corner, probably for day labor. Between the caffeine and the sugar-rush, Tom's imagination was able to sift through five new ideas for possible sketches, travelogues, and polemics which finally coalesced into a rough draft for a Christmas parable.

"Hmm," he said to himself, just loud enough to catch the ears of the clerk and to further spook her. She seemed relieved when Tom stood up and told her goodbye, have a nice day.

It was slower going back up the hill to his brother's house, but he was in no hurry. He took out another cigarette, but halfway through he was seized by a violent coughing fit and put it out. Along the way, he added to his little story, then deleted some parts. Tinkering with a piece always brought him great pleasure, almost more than completing or performing it. He passed a couple moseying arm-in-arm down the sidewalk opposite him, early risers like himself, and made a mental note to call Donna before leaving for the service.

When he arrived back at the house, he found Ben up and making coffee.

"Morning, bro."

"Hi, Tom." Ben looked befuddled, but otherwise awake.

"Thanks for making coffee. Sleep good?"

Ben stopped what he was doing and considered the question. "Lots of dreams," he said finally.

"Huh." Tom came around to the kitchen and rummaged in the refrigerator. He found a bowl of red grapes and scooped out a handful. "What kind of dreams?"

"I dunno. All jumbled. Didn't make much sense. I hate bad dreams." He squinted peevishly at the coffeemaker. "Tom?"

"Yeah?"

"Why do you think Mom killed herself?"

Tom coughed, almost choking on a grape. Why indeed? Wasn't that the six-million-dollar question everyone had tap-danced around since learning of Rachel's death? Cautiously, he said, "I don't know, Ben. Maybe she didn't. We don't know for sure."

"She did," Ben told him flatly. His eyes wouldn't meet Tom's, but his certainty reminded his brother Ben was only handicapped, not stupid. "We know."

"Guess we do," Tom admitted. "Well, she was in terrible pain, Ben. I had the impression she wasn't very happy, being in bed all the time, depending on Grace for everything. That wasn't Mom."

He searched for a coffee cup. He bypassed the homely set of four, off-white cups with thin brown bands painted around the rims. Rob's, no doubt. He favored one which had to be Violet's, fresh off a potter's wheel, glazed a beautiful green, adorned with a hand-painted red-and-blue tiger lily, part of which swooped up the curve of the cup's handle. "She didn't have much time left, you know."

Ben stared trancelike at his blurred reflection in the stainless-steel kitchen sink. He'd always looked more like Rachel than Henry. "Happy," he repeated dully. He scratched his ear. "Tom, do you think that suicide...do you think it's a sin?"

"No," Tom answered without hesitation, but thinking, *why do I get all the tough fucking questions? Where the hell is Rob, or Vi? Are they going to sleep till the crack of noon?* "No," he said again. "I think suicide is sad, and it's a shame to lose Mom this way. We're all going to miss her terribly. But it's not a sin to want to be free of pain, Ben." He did not add he'd been tempted to send Rachel materials from the Hemlock Society and let her make up her own mind about her options.

"I heard it was a mortal sin," Ben persisted. "Do you believe in sin, Tom?"

"Not sure I even believe in God, Ben. Is there any o.j. around here?" He ducked his head into the fridge. "You have some big questions, Ben. You're probably better off asking Vi those types of things, y'know?" There didn't seem to be any orange juice. Thomas returned to his coffee.

"I'm just trying to figure a few things out. I want to understand about Mom. About her being a good person and doing this bad thing. I know she had this bad pain that hurt all the time and she couldn't stand it anymore. I could see that. But what the church says…" Here, his voice broke off. He even looked a little desperate. "I don't want to be a bad person. Mom wasn't bad, either, so… I'm just really confused."

"You and everybody else," Tom told him, not unkindly.

"Tom?"

"Yeah?"

"You feel like some waffles?"

"Uh, no."

"I do. I think Vi has some blueberry waffles stashed in here." He was peering into the freezer. "Sure you don't want any?"

"No, thanks. You go ahead, though."

Ben didn't need any encouragement. While Ben was placing the waffles in the toaster oven and trying to locate the maple syrup, Tom realized his brother made the perfect captive audience. "Hey," he said brightly. "Want to hear a story, Ben?"

"A new one?"

"Yeah. I don't know if it's very good yet. You can help me decide that."

"Let's hear it."

Let me tell you about the office Christmas party.

After a year of blue-sky concepts, greenlighted projects, golden parachutes, and a tsunami of red ink from the latest paradigm shift, the lions were expected to lay aside their aggressions and make nice with the lambs for a day. Naturally, they resisted.

So, Quotations and Sales together lamented the lack of alcohol and dreaded the tedious luncheon, the horrible gift exchange, the headaches from all the feigned goodwill. I headed home at last, with "Merry Christmas, Baby" on my car radio. The village sheened silver with cool counterfeit cheer. Shop windows glowed warm and gemlike under marquee lights. In my neighborhood, the kids played basketball in their driveways and acted out the holiday fantasy that, for one day, they were sweet as marzipan and pfefferneuse cookies.

Inside my house, there was a fire, and the hearth was done up in garlands, diminutive nutcrackers, tiny sleighs hand-painted red and green, cranberry candles. My wife doled out Baileys in etched crystal cordials that once belonged to her grandparents. She kissed me, we sat together on the sofa, we watched a Christmas movie on the tube, we were warm and content together. I imagined this quiet joy was Xeroxed up and down the avenues in little stucco houses with red-tiled roofs and small green lawns exactly like ours.

The night smelled like rain. It wasn't cold enough to snow, but when I stepped outdoors later on, the kids asleep, my wife reading and relaxing in a hot bath, there was a definite dark vault of a winter sky, black as ravens, onion-skinned, weird to behold. Starlight arrowed down and the evening wind vibrated eerily like a harp, or like a premonition in the branches of the honey locusts.

Hours went by. We were asleep, then awakened by a sound like the ripping of silk, like a sonic boom, like a hell bound meteor screaming through the excellent acoustics of the thin winter air. We flowed out of our beds and into the wet purple-gray streets where our neighbors joined us in a pod-people shuffle through morgue-like cold. We arrived at a catch-basin ringed with pampas grass, a wrought-iron fence and swampy green midnight vapors. In this basin was a crater which had not existed the day before, and in this new hole in the ground lay a naked child. In its hand, it grasped a stick. It appeared uninjured, though the babe's fine brown hair was beaded with frost and its skin was starting to turn blue It waved its stick comically, like a toy scepter.

Gertie Culpepper, who lived down the street, was sexy at sixty, and was a champion fundraiser for Our Lady of Perpetual Grace, cried,

"Oh, it's one of God's smallest sparrows, fallen out from under His hundred-mile wings."

Nobody disputed this. But neither did anyone step forward to touch the frozen child.

Now, we're good people, and we live in enlightened times. We love our children. We know their need for shelter and for protection. In this age of reason, surely someone would care for this child. Someone, some law, some church, or some agent. One by one, though, we filed away, turned up our collars, and, because the infant shivered in the cold gathering mist, we avoided one another's eyes. We all trudged home to our tannenbaums and gold foil boxes only to find, cozy on throw rugs before dying Duraflames, all of our cats and dogs, knees buckled, forepaws folded left across right, eyes closed and ears tuned to chimes inaudible to us human masters. The animals lay there like the brute spirits of old who, in the presence of light, had possessed the grace to hunker down in beds of fresh hay.

Over our rooftops, the zodiac exhaled fearsome chinooks and the millennial freeze got underway.

As Tom finished his tale of the frozen child, he noticed Violet out of the corner of his eye. She was standing under the kitchen archway and was regarding him with a slight enigmatic smile. Warily, he nodded back. "Morning."

"Good morning. Sleep well?"

"Ah, never do any more. Especially when I'm away from home. No offense, I appreciate you and Rob saving me the cost of a hotel room."

"None taken. So, was that supposed to be a Christmas story?"

Tom smiled slightly. "Yeah, kind of. I don't know how much you heard. I was test-driving it on Ben."

"Sort of a Christian message in there. Lots of religious imagery. Am I misunderstanding?"

She grinned and he was glad last night hadn't made her awkward with him.

"Go figure. I've always liked Christmas time. Thought it might be appropriate to write something about the season. Rob still sleeping?"

"He went into the office for a few hours," she said, her face tight.

She turned to Ben. "Did you like Tom's story?"

Ben beamed. "It was great," he assured her. "I didn't understand all of it, though. I need to hear it a couple more times, Tom."

"Glad to oblige, Ben. The more I can practice, the more natural it'll sound. Thanks for the offer." He glanced at his watch. "Listen, I should call Donna before it gets too late. Excuse me a minute. Ben's making waffles, by the way."

"They got a little burnt," Ben said ruefully.

"Those are the best," Vi told him. "Come on, let's eat. I'll bet Tom really wants to sneak off and listen to some old Christmas albums. Johnny Mathis and Andy Williams, right?"

"He said he was going to call Donna."

"Oh, he just doesn't want us to know how sentimental he really is. How about some cold milk with those waffles?"

"Hilarious," Tom told her. "I'm borrowing your phone and running up your long-distance bill."

Tom found himself pleased with their bantering. It felt normal, like old times. He dialed Donna's number at the clinic and had her paged.

"Hey, good looking," he said when he heard her voice. "You busy?"

"Hey yourself. I can take a few minutes. How's Colorado?"

"Same as always. Cold, snowy and miserable. I miss Florida. I miss you."

"That's sweet. How's the family?"

"They're psychotic. Which as you know means everything's normal."

"Tell them we have a pretty good mental health ward out here. So, what's on your schedule for today?"

"I had a nice morning walk already. Cleared my head. We have the viewing in a little while, and I thought I'd better call while I had a few free minutes. Tonight, I'm not sure what's happening. I'll tell you one thing, though. I'll go batshit if I have to stay here and make small talk. My plan is to escape, weather permitting."

"With an old flame?"

She was kidding, but Tom could hear the hint of strain in her voice.

"Yeah, you busted me. Well, actually with two of them. Nothing like a nice warm *ménage a trois* on a cold night in the Rockies. That's what John Denver should've been singing about all those years instead of…"

"Never mind, sorry I asked. It's a little insane here, to tell you the truth. There's a case of the creeping crud going around that seems to be hitting everybody and his brother. I should go."

"Wait, wait. What about me? What about my medical needs?"

She gave a short laugh. "What needs? Is it an emergency?"

"Yes, nurse," he said solemnly. "I have a bad, bad case of homesickness. The miss-my-girlfriend blues, you know."

"Oh," she said. "I'm not sure your insurance covers that, Mr. Demeter. Especially being out of state and all."

"Plus, I think my heart might be broken."

"That may be considered a pre-existing condition. I'll have to check and get back with you. Seriously, I need to go."

"You sure you're not rushing off to play tonsil hockey with some handsome doctor?"

"Mm, I wish. You'll call later?"

"Depends on what time I get in tonight. Don't wait up, okay? I'll call again in the morning."

"All right, honey. Good luck today, and give everybody my condolences. I love you."

"Love you, too. You know that, right?"

"I have to go. Kisses. Talk to you tomorrow."

Tom hung up. He went outside on the deck and lit up a cigarette. He spent some time sorting through his thoughts, replaying parts of the conversation with Donna in his head. For some reason, the cigarette tasted stale, unsatisfying.

Chapter Eleven

The memorial was to be held at the Helms Brothers Mortuary, an elegant brick building several blocks off Canyon Creek Boulevard, one of the town's main drags. It was wedged between a landmarked art gallery and a shop which sold baseball cards and comic books. The mortuary's interior was musty and solemn, though no more so than a country club or private lodge. Patterned mauve wallpaper, dim lighting, and dark gray carpets all conveyed a properly somber mood. Rachel's urn had been placed in one of the larger rooms near the back of the building. It was slender and deep blue, surrounded by photos and memorabilia accreted from her lifetime.

Tom didn't care for the looks of the funeral director. Her nametag identified her as Harriett Ichthy and, while the mortuary was family-owned and enjoyed a venerable reputation, Ms. Ichthy was not a Helm. She was an outsider and gave off the vibes of a hired gun. With her cavalier attitude and her dumpy purple pantsuit, she might have been a harried administrative assistant or a real estate flunky. *Nothing matters to her,* Tom thought, *she's only here for the paycheck.* She had no passion for the work and no real feel for comforting people.

Rob approached her with his businesslike persona, and Tom was grateful for that. Ms. Ichthy had long lank black hair and a lean predatory face. Her eyes held a dead, just-another-day-at-the-office glaze. When she reached out to shake Rob's hand and wave him toward her desk, Tom couldn't help noticing her scaly knuckles and long hooking fingernails. Repulsive, but not the worst of it. The worst was that *she was eating a sandwich* while she and Rob reviewed the paperwork. It didn't seem to ruffle Rob, but Tom found it not only inappropriate but having to fight his gag reflex. It seemed to be the soggy remains of a meat-and-cheese deli style sub. She snapped at it like a barracuda. A dollop of mayo smeared her cheek. Ms. Ichthy didn't seem to be aware of it. Rob, always self-conscious of the line between good manners and embarrassment, didn't mention it. The white blob remained in place while they pored over the contracts. Tom turned away when the woman began tapping her fingernails on the desk's glass top. Her scaly hand and clacking fingers reminded him of a hungry crab about to pounce on its prey.

They were there to sign the final contracts and pay quiet respects to Rachel, prior to the public memorial. Tom predicted the whole affair was likely to turn into a noisy circus, but he had enough sense to keep his opinion to himself.

Vi and Ben were also in the room, remaining quiet. Rob was in his element here, reviewing the paperwork, ensuring that all the agreements had been formally captured in black-and-white. The family was there to provide moral support, but Tom soon found himself impatient to escape Ms. Ichthy's presence.

There seemed to be some sort of a disturbance up front. Ms. Ichthy frowned, muttered an insincere apology at the interruption, and stomped her way to the lobby to investigate. Moments later, they heard her half-bossy, half-bargaining voice addressing the situation. "I'm sorry, sir, I'll have to ask you to come back tomorrow. Only family is permitted today. Well, I don't know about that. I must insist. I'm afraid I *must* insist. Oh. Well then. I suppose I could check with Mr. Demeter. If you'll be good enough to wait here in the lobby just a moment…"

Ms. Ichthy swam into the room. A gigantic black man lumbered in behind her. She heard his heavy footsteps and spun, astonished that she'd been disobeyed. "Sir, I asked you to wait until…"

"It's all right, Ms. Ichthy," Rob told her with a smile. "He's family."

Her astonishment migrated from the giant to Rob. She sputtered, "But he's… You can't mean…" She fought to regain her professional composure. "I suppose if you say it's all right, Mr. Demeter…"

"It's all right," Rob confirmed softly. "How are you, Cliff?"

Clifton Parker grinned and eased past the mortified Ms. Ichthy.

Tom couldn't suppress a bark of laughter. He hadn't seen Clifton in at least a decade. The big man's fingers engulfed Rob's hand and shook it hard. He then gave Vi a gentle brotherly hug and playfully messed with Ben's hair. Finally, he made a beeline for Tom with all the grace of a marauding ox.

"So sorry about your Mom," he rumbled. He took Tom's hand and pulled him close. Clifton locked his old friend in a fearsome bearhug. "You sorry sack of shit," he whispered. "You don't call, you don't write…"

"Cliff, right now I can't breathe," Tom wheezed. Clifton showed mercy and eased off some. Tom gulped in air gratefully. "That's better. Much better. Oxygen is good." He took half-a-step backward and regarded his assailant. "I think you might have cracked a rib, you animal."

Clifton Parker's chuckle was a slow roll of thunder. He was a huge man, six-five and in the zip code of three hundred fifty pounds. Everything about him was gargantuan, from his broad, affable face to his size sixteen brogans. He was almost, but not quite, obese. In his athletic prime, he'd been a star first baseman, weightlifter, and third-string offensive lineman for the University of Nebraska. He wore glasses that were too small for his face and gave him an odd feline appearance. Injuries had cut short a promising career in baseball, but Tom considered Cliff hadn't lost an iota of his impressive strength.

They'd been friends since high school. They hadn't talked in years. Clifton remained in touch with Rob and Ben. He'd also been fond of Rachel Demeter, who'd treated him as a fourth son.

"Smartass," he said sadly. Clifton gazed up at the ceiling and addressed an unseen being there. "The boy never changes."

"Thanks for coming, Cliff. It's great to see you." Tom grinned. "We'll have to find some time to get together while I'm out here."

"Sounds like a plan," agreed the big man. "Maybe a buffet dinner followed by a night carousing on the town."

The old in-jokes. Clifton liked boasting about the days when he and his college jock cronies bankrupted several Nebraska steakhouses on their all-you-can-eat nights. He also fancied himself a champion party-hearty kind of guy, "Any excuse", willing and able to pub-crawl into the wee hours at the drop of a hat. Tom had pleasant memories of them playing ball alongside one another, tailgate parties fueled by monstrous meat sandwiches and potent daiquiris, semi-coherent philosophic conversations lasting deep into the evening.

"I don't know that I can keep up with you anymore, but sure, let's make it a date. Say, are you still working at…oh, what the hell's the name of that company?"

"P & C Carpet Cleaning. It's a living," he shrugged.

"Whatever happened to going back to school for…what was it? Chemistry?"

"Yeah, biochemistry." Clifton had often talked about working for a pharmaceutical mega-corporation based in Denver, doing research and development, becoming deeply involved with developing some of the marketplace's better-known medications. "Treatments for depression and social anxiety, hypertension, diabetes, rheumatoid arthritis, you name it. Saving-the-world stuff, you know." He flashed a small self-mocking smile. "Well, that was the dream once. We all grow up, right? How about yourself?"

Tom brought him up to speed on his myriad projects and revenue streams. Just as he was finishing, he heard Rob calling for everyone to reconvene for the final contract signings. "Scuze me a sec, Cliff. Conversation to be continued."

The family gathered around Ms. Ichthy's big reef of a desk while she and Rob agreed on some final details and arrangements. With Ms. Ichthy overseeing the signature process without, Tom noted with a shudder, once blinking her eyes, Rob signed the sheaf of official paperwork. Sale secured, the woman presented them all with a slow smile as wide and mirthless as a shark's. She folded her scaly hands in satisfaction.

"It'll be a beautiful memorial, Mr. Demeter," she assured Rob in her apathetic monotone. "Thank you for trusting Helms Mortuary with your business."

Rob turned to face the family, one hand smoothing back his hair, the other dangling at his side, still gripping the pen. "Yes. Well that's that," he said briskly. "Now we're all set for tomorrow. Want to check in with Mother before we leave?"

They followed one another down a glum corridor fitted with fake scones emitting the dimmest of lights. They walked in silence till they reached the memorial room.

"Hey Mom," Tom addressed the vase set on a glass table to the immediate right of the speaker's podium. "You always did look good in blue." The room seemed cavernous without all the folding chairs, floral displays, and refreshment tables due to be set up for tomorrow's service.

Several long moments passed without anyone saying anything more. At last, Vi spoke up. "Ready to go? We have a big day tomorrow, maybe we should all get some rest before then."

Rob nodded and flashed the thumb's-up sign.

Vi smiled wanly and turned her attention to Clifton. "It's nice seeing you again, Cliff."

"Been a long time," he mumbled.

"Can you come tomorrow? To the service, I mean?"

"Count on it," the big man said.

"Okay, people, I think we're pretty well wrapped up here," Rob interjected, tugging at one sleeve. He realized he still held Ms. Ichthy's pen and gave a start, as if he'd discovered he was hanging onto a tiny electric eel. He placed it on the podium and wiped his hands together. He glanced meaningfully at the exit. "Shall we? I know I for one have a ton to do before the service. Ben, you're going to want to make sure you get a good night's sleep, hear?"

On cue, Ben let loose with a dramatic yawn. Rob smiled and signaled everybody to head for the exit. Once out in the mortuary's small parking lot, the Demeters said goodbye to Clifton and started piling into Rob's long black Lincoln. Tom waited for Clifton to wedge himself into his own ridiculously miniscule sports car, a 1972 canary-yellow Karmann Ghia coupe. It was the same car Cliff had driven since college. Tom leaned down to say goodbye. Through the window, Clifton jabbed his fat index finger into Tom's chest.

"Ow! Goddamnit it, that'll leave a bruise."

"Tonight," growled the big man, making the single word sound threatening.

"Tonight? What do you have in mind?"

"Don't know and don't care, as long as food and alcohol are included in the package," said Clifton. "Make the plans. No argument. I know you; you'll procrastinate and procrastinate. Next thing you'll be back on that plane to Florida and we won't see each other again till God-knows-when."

"All right, all right, I'll think of something," Tom promised. "Around seven?"

"Make it six. I'll pick you up. Let the debauchery begin early."

"Can two of us fit in that toy?" Clifton's features settled into a glower, so Tom hurriedly confirmed, "Six o'clock. See you then."

Clifton growled something inaudible. He somehow crammed his bulk behind the steering wheel of the Karmann Ghia, started the car, and pulled away with a whoop and a wave. Tom shook his head and trooped back to the Lincoln where his family waited impatiently. *Tonight, at six. I'll figure something out. No pressure.*

Chapter Twelve

"Let me get this straight," Clifton said slowly over the phone. "You want me to go to a *folk* concert with you? Dude, I'll be the only black guy in the theater."

"Dude, you're practically the only black guy in Greenstone," Tom reminded him patiently. "C'mon, be a pal. It's a good chance for you to broaden your horizons. Besides, it's not exactly what you're thinking. You'll love it, I promise."

Despite his negative outlook on the City of Greenstone, Tom would admit missing two features of his yuppified hometown. The first was the sheer number and variety of restaurants and bars. Many were locally owned, although the chains had started creeping in during the past decade.

The second was the Greenstone Bijou. The theater had been built in the 1930's, then reworked with an art deco façade in the fifties. Its original purpose had been to house first-run films in a lush atmosphere of fresco ceilings, state-of-the-art sound, thick velvet curtains, wood paneling, colored glass tiles, and towering murals. Tom loved the spacious balcony, which seated about two hundred people. Through the years, the theater had enjoyed its glory days, then suffered a period of run-down splendor in the sixties and seventies. This was followed by a buyout bid with the intent of it being shut down and razed in order to build luxury apartments on its site. To its credit, the community responded with a vigorous protest that resulted in the Bijou being preserved as a state landmark. A local nonprofit wrote some grants and raised funds for the theater's renovation. Rachel had been involved with the group, Tom recalled. By the early nineties it had been transformed into a jewel of the revitalized downtown outdoor mall. Its mission changed with the times, also. The Bijou still debuted important films deemed worthy of its majestic reputation, and even hosted Greenstone's own independent film festival in the springtime. It also added plays and concerts to its lineup, notably showcasing blues, jazz, and folk music.

Although the holiday season necessitated the booking of the obligatory Christmas shows, Chanukah pageants and singalongs, Tom saw that, just the week before, Bela Fleck performed. Next week, when he'd be back in Florida, Chris Smither and Lucinda Williams were both scheduled. As luck would have it, though, David Lindley was playing two shows tonight.

After some dickering, Tom and Clifton decided on going to the early show. Dinner and drinks could follow afterward.

"Especially drinks," Clifton growled. "All right. I should have my head examined, but what the hell. See you at six." Tom called and had no trouble purchasing tickets to be held for him at will call.

Clifton picked him up as promised. Then and now, it amazed Tom the big man could squeeze his abominable snowman body behind the steering wheel.

"I can't believe you're still driving this thing," Tom said, wriggling into the passenger side. "I remember it being a maintenance nightmare."

"Yeah, but it's a Veedub and a classic," Clifton beamed. "Gotta love it."

"So it's a bug. There's no legroom," Tom complained.

"Shh, you'll hurt its little feelings."

They arrived early, got their tickets, and ordered drinks at the theater bar. They sat in the front row of the balcony. Clifton had been wrong. There were four other African–Americans in attendance. A young well-dressed couple, either dating or newly married, sat third row center, radiating the superior give-a-damn vibes of the true aesthetes. There were two black guys who looked like they'd accidentally wandered into a lecture on astrophysics delivered in Farsi. They had no idea what they were doing in the audience. Tom made sure he pointed them out to Clifton.

"Clueless," the big man said glumly. "That makes three of us." His mind was already on the steak and beer he would devour after the concert.

"You're in for a treat," Tom advised him. "Listen and learn."

As always, Lindley was incredible. The man could play anything with strings, and his demented clowning kept the show moving. Throughout the performance, he played his trademark lap steel guitar, plus banjo, mandolin, fiddle, ukulele, oud, bouzouki, and saw. For Clifton's benefit, Tom catalogued the homages to Browne, Zevon, Ronstadt, Cooder, Springsteen, and CSN. When Lindley played two indigenous Malagasy songs, Clifton, bored, leaned over and whispered in Tom's ear:

"What in the world is he wearing?"

Thomas explained the musician's outrageous duds were part of the show. His suit was a black-and-green checked atrocity. His shirt was electric blue, and his raggedy neckerchief appeared to be cut from a red bath towel. The pants were rust-colored, the socks neon green. Lindley's boots were the *coup de grace*. They were made of some supple, synthetic material that resembled blue alligator skin.

Clifton listened to Tom without expression. "Yeah, whatever," he remarked. Lindley closed with a Turkish folk song and a short reggae-flavored encore.

After the show, they trolled the mall's restaurant row. The sidewalks were clean and inlaid with tile mosaics and brick designs. All the trees were adorned with white Christmas lights. They found a chophouse, pleasantly dark inside and not too crowded. A college-aged waitress, cute, with short blonde hair, led them to a table and handed them menus. They ordered Mexican beer and sirloins for dinner. They talked.

Sports fans in Greenstone remembered Clifton Parker as a can't-miss, homegrown baseball phenom, the scourge of Colorado's Mountain Valley high school league and later a terror with the Cornhuskers in the Big Eight. His girth suggested he'd become a monster football star, but baseball was his real gift. He'd been a behemoth at the plate and, despite his size, a cheetah on the base paths. He'd had the oddly dainty physical grace that big men often display, and played first base with a ballerina's finesse. His home runs had been legendary, genuine tape measure shots. He'd been something to see in his pinstripes, stirrups, cap, and cleats.

One night in Norman, Oklahoma, Cliff caught his spikes in soft dirt while rounding third, hustling to score from second on a bloop single. His ankle twisted, he fell hard to the grass, and his knee shredded. That was all she wrote. There were two operations, eighteen months of painful rehab, then surrender. Surgery could reconstruct the leg so he could walk without much of a limp, but his life in competitive baseball was over. No more running the leading edge of a double steal. No more scooping out wild throws at first or throwing a laser beam home to gun down a runner. No more legging out seeing-eye grounders to the hole, no more knocking in the winning run, no more late inning heroics.

So what happened since? Rob and Vi provided brief updates on Clifton over the years. Now Tom listened as the big man chronicled his life-after-baseball over a thick porterhouse and a massive mug of Dos Equis.

"I had a buddy, Phil Jurgenson, everybody called him Philly. You might remember him from high school."

Tom had a fuzzy recollection of a wiry little guy with the face of a nutria.

"Anyway, we lost touch when I moved up to Lincoln to play ball. He read about my injury, how I wanted to come home to Greenstone and stay connected with sports somehow. When I got back, he gave me a buzz. Said he had a business proposition." He paused long enough to suck on a lime wedge and glug down some brew. He laughed softly. "Said he had a five-year plan for me. Philly said, 'Let's be partners, Cliff, you and me.' I thought, what the hell, it can't hurt to listen. I had a blown knee, I was pissed off and full of resentment, I had no plan for the rest of my life. So I listened. Philly said he wanted to open up a carpet cleaning business."

"Carpet cleaning," Tom repeated, nodding. He swallowed some of his own beer.

"Yeah, carpet cleaning. About the furthest thing from my mind was starting a career in carpet cleaning. I knew it was backbreaking work, and I reminded Philly about my knee. He brushed me off and said I'd be part-owner and manager, not one of the grunts. My job would be to supply a little capital, learn the trade, get certified, and do some marketing. Some hiring and firing. His idea was that I was still a local hero and my name would get us some business right off the bat.

"I had some money saved, and it wasn't like I had a shitload of other options. Still, I wasn't convinced. I mean, who dreams of growing up to become a carpet cleaner? I was going to be the next Willie McCovey, y'know? I was reluctant, to say the least. Philly then brought out his secret weapon, the one he knew I wouldn't be able to resist.

"He says, 'Cliff, you want to stay in sports, right? I understand, it's what you love. Here's my proposal, and all I ask is that you think about it. No pressure, no hard feelings if you say no. Think it over first.' He says, 'Five years, Cliff. Five years, tops. Do you know how much money you can make in this business if you work hard and play it smart? In five years, you'll be able to save enough to get out of the rat race for good and to set up your own baseball clinic, free and clear. Batting cage, hitting instructors, celebrity seminars, the whole works. Think about that. You can't play anymore, okay, but you can still leave a hell of a legacy.'

"That got into my head, Tom. I had no desire to get into the carpet cleaning business, but as a means to an end where maybe I could stay connected to the sport? That I could definitely get behind. I started picturing my own clinic, with a shiny, state-of-the-art batting cage. Teach kids how to develop patience at the plate. Wait for your pitch. Keep your knees bent and your swing level." Clifton's eyes were damp and his gaze fell somewhere over Tom's right shoulder.

Maybe it's the alcohol talking, Thomas thought.

"I could show them how to shift your weight at bat, teach them that all your power comes up from your legs. Keep your eye on the ball from the minute it leaves the pitcher's hand. Don't try to overpower the pitch, just make sure to make contact. Then drive the son-of-a-bitch and hope it finds an alley."

He paused again and motioned to the waitress to bring more beer. "Dos Dos Equis, por favor," he bellowed, drawing stares from other customers. Clifton mad-dogged them They quickly turned away.

"Tom, I remember one pitch in particular," he went on with just a trace of a slur. "Clear as glass, like it happened yesterday. It was a shitty little curveball that barely wrinkled when it got to the plate. Low and inside, a lefty's sweet spot. Oh man, I was all *over* that baby. I can still feel my legs and hips unwinding, my textbook swing, my smooth follow-through. The ball *whistled* past the first baseman, just inside the right field line, fair by inches, a *screaming* double. Damn." His eyes looked beyond Tom again.

What's he looking at? Thomas wondered. *His past self standing triumphantly at second base, admiring the power in his own wrists and muscles? A vision of his longed-for batting cage like a castle on a hill?*

Clifton crumpled his napkin, gave a rueful grin. "Tom, you can't imagine," he said with a calmness that was somehow more worrisome than all his agitation. "Ten thousand people cheering for you, yelling your name. I could get drunk on all that applause." The waitress appeared with the beers. Clifton downed half of his in a single swallow. "Isn't it funny, the thing I'd remember most is that double? Not any of the home runs I hit, but that damn double."

Tom nodded. "So what happened?" he asked gently, although he already knew how the story went.

The big man couldn't come straight to the point. He had a tale to tell, and his style was to chronicle it in a series of mundane episodes. Perhaps it was the only way he could rationalize how things unraveled. He told Tom he finally committed to Philly and together they opened P & C Carpet Cleaning. It soon became obvious they had underestimated start-up costs. Clifton found he had no choice but to pitch in with the crews in addition to his administrative and marketing duties. He was putting in sixteen, eighteen-hour workdays, six days a week. He told himself it was just temporary, until he and Philly could establish a customer base, maybe hire another guy. Besides, he reasoned, it wasn't a bad idea to get to know the business from the ground level up. He'd always disdained coaches who never played the game, and figured it wouldn't hurt for him to get his hands a little dirty.

Clifton described his carpet cleaning life in such painstaking detail, Tom thought his head was going to explode. The big man spoke of P & C's clean white van jampacked with optic brighteners, pet deodorizers, spot removers, Scotchgard, and a sargasso of pungent chemicals guaranteed to leave a carpet pristine and fragrant. Philly drove it like a limo and flirted with all the myopic housewives, the housewives with tinted hair, the randy, high-toned housewives. Many of them would brandish a coupon, but Philly was the king of the plus-sell. "Now sure," Clifton mimicked Philly's buttery delivery, "three rooms for thirty-nine-ninety-five *seems* like a good deal. That's for a basic service, though. It won't get rid of those dust mites encamped in your fibers, or erase that cherry Kool-Aid stain."

The more Clifton talked about Phil Jurgenson, the less Tom liked the man. Clifton told a story about one morning at breakfast while they were between jobs. Philly was scanning the newspaper and a headline on page three caught his eye. A man had killed his wife and himself in a nice neighborhood on the west side of town. The report was on page three because the Greenstone Gazette never printed bad news on its front page. The publishers did not want to depress its readership and thought by running only upbeat lead stories, circulation would steadily increase. Not to mention advertising dollars. They were mistaken, but it wouldn't become obvious for another ten years. At any rate, this sordid suburban saga was shocking for a number of reasons. One, the west side had the lowest crime rate in all of Greenstone. Two, it was the city's first recorded murder-suicide ever. Three, the killer was the high-profile owner of a large car dealership, well-known for his philanthropy, his political ambitions, and his work on the advisory board for a bureau dealing with at-risk children. He was fifty, his wife forty-eight. There'd been no reported history of illness or trouble between them. He'd shot her in the head while she slept. Next, he placed the gun against his own right eye and pulled the trigger.

As reported by Clifton, Philly's take was purely businesslike. "Tragic," he'd said while shoveling scrambled eggs down his throat. "But y'know, Cliff, the realtor's gonna have to hire *somebody* to get the blood out of those carpets."

After that anecdote, Tom tuned out and only half-listened to Clifton's drone. He nodded here and there to indicate he wasn't totally asleep. He remembered this about Cliff, the steady buzz of his voice so much like the monotonous engine hum of small, low-flying aircraft.

Words, words and more words. It didn't matter whether they were about baseball, carpet cleaning or Clifton's bad luck with women. After a while, they all bled into one solid din. The cute waitress was back, not as friendly as before. Tom ordered two more beers. She shot a meaningful look at Clifton and arched an eyebrow. The big man's eyes were glazed and watery, like buckshot behind his tiny glasses. He was getting louder. Tom waved her an it's-all-right-he's-with-me gesture, and she disappeared back behind the bar.

"More brews coming," Tom said mildly when Clifton paused for air. "Maybe this should be last call. We can go somewhere and get some coffee, huh?"

"What time is it?" Clifton demanded, and looked at his wrist where there was no watch. He squinted, swiveled, and shouted at the couple behind him, "Do you have the time?" The woman gave him a frozen smile and said about eleven-fifteen.

"Thanks!" he roared. To Tom he hollered, "Suddenly you're the world's biggest pussy? You can't even drink till midnight anymore? We're just getting started."

Tom nodded wearily. Even in their carousing days, Clifton never could hold his liquor. Tom held up a single finger. "One more round, dude. You're right, I can't drink for shit any more. You have to promise me to lower your volume a bit. The natives are freaking out."

"I have more to tell you."

"I know you do. I'm listening. But take it down a notch, okay?"

Clifton shook his massive head. He wasn't saying no, only trying to clear his mind. There was so much to say to Tom, he had things to describe and explain. He was afraid he didn't have the time or vocabulary to do justice to his stories. When the beer arrived, Clifton took a healthy swallow and started talking again, taking pains to keep his voice low.

Tom had heard this sad tale's ending before from Rob and Vi. He wasn't particularly riveted by Clifton's rambling version, which included numbingly detailed vignettes of his busy days making humdrum house calls for various carpet cleaning emergencies such as lifting greasy footprints from an ecru berber, or removing Junior's chewing gum without destroying a high-traffic section of deep-pile shag. Equally tedious was the recounting of Philly's umpteenth gimmick for broadening his profit margin.

Look here, ma'am. Behold this bucket of black, nasty water. This is just a sample of the filth to be found in your carpet fibers. Might you be interested in purchasing a special, all-natural cleaning product? No chemicals, no toxins. It'll ensure your carpet never becomes this soiled again. I'm talking about your carpet, where you walk barefoot every morning. Where your toddler crawls.

One Indian summer morning, brass bright and September warm, Clifton had slept through his alarm, and when he arrived at the office, he was forty-five minutes late. Thinking back, he thought he must've had an early premonition of disaster, because the first thing he'd looked for was Philly's Chevy Nova in the parking lot. There was no sign of it. Clifton strolled into a roomful of long faces. All the staff was there, the receptionist, the techs, the bookkeeper, one person who he recognized but wasn't sure what she did. The heaviness in the room was suffocating.

"Where is he?" he demanded.

"We don't know, Mr. Parker," Bonnie the receptionist told him unhappily.

It was as if the staff had drawn straws for the job of breaking the bad news to the boss, and Bonnie lost. "There was a message on the answering machine from late last night, Mr. Jurgenson saying he wouldn't be in."

"For how long?"

Bonnie swallowed hard. "Forever, I guess," she said in a tiny voice. "Looks like he left this for you." She handed him a large manila envelope marked CONFIDENTIAL. Dazed, he took it and plodded to his office.

The letter inside was full of apologies, rationalizations, remorse, and countless misspellings. Cutting through the crap wasn't easy, but the gist of the message was an old one, a petty one and, in retrospect, not all that shocking. There were bad gambling debts, embezzlements and cash skimming. The tipping point was where it made more sense for Philly to go into hiding than to pay off his bookie and the loan sharks from Denver.

"I'm sorry, Cliff. I never meant to screw you like this. Things just got out of control, and now I'm in a talespin. I hope you know there's nothing personal in all this. But if I stay, I ether go to jail or will be in danger. I can't win for loosing. Anyway, that's not your concern. I'm just sorry I left you holding the bag. I feel like a weesul. Forgiv me. Your frend, Phil."

As he read the note, Clifton knew that all of Philly's dodging and squirming would be futile and he'd be caught, probably sooner than later. His capture was inevitable because he was not smart enough to elude both the law and the small-time hoods who wanted to have a little dialogue with him about the money he owed. Luckily for Phil, the cops located him first. He'd been trying to blend in with the natives in Gallup, New Mexico, and had even opened a new carpet cleaning business in town. When Clifton heard that, the last of his good will for his former partner evaporated. The bad news for Philly was that he was going to spend the next eight years behind bars. The good news? He would get to keep all his fingers, not having to face his disappointed lenders and their tin snips for at least another eight years.

None of this was much comfort to Clifton. As Philly's business partner, it was left up to him to try to repair the damages to P & C Carpet Cleaning's finances and reputation. The employees turned to him for leadership and reassurances of job security. The banks holding loans for P & C's vehicles and equipment had questions about the company's fiscal solvency. More importantly, they were leery about Clifton's intentions. The customers looked for signs that Philly's malfeasance and ethical lapses had been confined to the man, and had not corrupted the company itself.

It would have been easy for Clifton to fold his tents and declare bankruptcy. He had his own good name to consider and besides, he couldn't face the thought of putting people out of work. So the dream of the batting cages was placed on indefinite hold while Clifton figured how best to deal with the fiasco, and pondered over how he had gotten himself trapped into caretaking a business he'd really wanted no part of from the beginning.

"The books were cooked and I found out our credit line had been maxed out. Rob helped me through so much of the financial bullshit. The hardest part is to keep on running the office, going out on calls when we're short-handed, working till midnight knowing it'll be years before I see any daylight for myself. And waking up every day to do a job I hate, because I got myself in a bind and it's the right thing to do, y'know?"

"Cliff, we don't have to stay here," Tom said again.

"Let's stay, Tom. It's good for me to talk, and it's good to see you again. Look," he held up two thick fingers, Scout's honor. "I'll behave. No blubbering, no screaming, okay?"

Tom weighed the pros and cons. He nodded. He ordered two coffees and a raspberry cheesecake with a couple of forks.

Clifton watched the waitress walk back into the kitchen. He shook his head appreciatively and breathed, "I am so disappointed in you, Thomas. You're slipping."

"Why's that?"

"I thought by now you'd have charmed the pants off that little darling. She's just your type."

"Maybe I'm not *her* type."

"Oh, she likes you, all right," Clifton assured him. "She's not crazy about me, but she's very interested in you."

"Well, I guess I'm not interested, okay? Not tonight, anyhow."

Clifton blinked, indicating disbelief. "Who are you, and what have you done with my friend Tom?" he demanded. "This is not you. Thomas Demeter would die before passing up a golden opportunity like this."

Tom sighed. "Listen, Cliff. If you'll search your remaining brain cells, you'll recall that I am in town for my mother's funeral. Not exactly the greatest aphrodisiac in the world, you know?"

Clifton stared at him, stone-faced. "Uh-huh."

"Besides, where am I supposed to take her? Back to my brother's place? Yeah, that would be real romantic."

"I don't know if you've heard, but there's this new thing out, it's called a motel? I'm not sure if they have those in Florida yet, but I know for a fact that Greenstone has several fine ones."

Tom waved him off. "Not tonight. I'm worn out. Besides, you and I haven't seen each other in forever. What kind of a friend would I be if I abandoned you right this minute, just because I have an excellent chance of getting laid?"

"Oh, now I know you're bullshitting me," Clifton laughed. "How many times did you drop me like a bad habit in your horny college days? Who was it that taught me a hard dick has no conscience?"

"Well, now…"

"Don't be modest, Tom. Do you remember the time we were at that club over on Canyon Street? It was a tri-level place, restaurant on the ground floor, a big bar on the second level, disco on top? They had the big mirrored balls and the thumping dance music and all kinds of drugs floating around? Lasted only six months, if I remember right. Now it's a consortium of medical offices. Anyway, there was one poor bastard, he was so sick, he threw up over the disco's railing, and the puke sailed past us at the bar and landed in someone's salad down below."

"If your intention was to jog my memory, then you've succeeded gloriously. We were lucky it was projectile vomiting, as I recall. It had the necessary arc to make it all the way to the ground floor."

"What else do you remember about that night?" When Tom looked blank, Clifton provided helpful clues. "We'd been bar-hopping? There was a group of co-eds partying in a booth by the dancefloor? You took a fancy to one of them, a cute redhead. I went to the restroom for a minute, and when I came back…"

Tom's face lit up. "Oh, yeah."

"Oh, yeah. When I came back, you mysteriously disappeared. Oh yeah, and the redhead was gone, too."

"I do remember, now," Tom said, grinning. "She was something else."

"Uh-huh. I had just enough cash left for the taxi home. Oh, and how about the night you were supposed to help me move my stuff to some new apartment and decided to go skinny-dipping with Lisa and Beth up at Crystal Lake instead? And don't forget the weekend…"

"Okay, okay, point taken." Tom was relieved Clifton seemed to be sobering up some. "I'm a scurrilous skunk. A fickle, feckless, and fair-weather friend. A lascivious louse."

"All that, and more," Clifton agreed mildly.

The coffee and cheesecake arrived, along with a dirty look for

Cliff. He spread his hands apologetically, but the waitress was already off to another table.

"Unforgiving. Hey, do you remember that time when…hey, wait a minute. Are you seeing somebody in Florida?"

Tom nodded and mumbled a reply.

"What? Is it serious? Are you shacking up?"

Again, a mumble.

"You have got to be kidding me, man. You're living with someone, for real? And you're being…faithful?" He pronounced the word distastefully, as if he'd suddenly found black mold growing inside his mouth.

This surprised Tom. He hadn't thought of Donna in terms of fidelity. It was true, he hadn't strayed since being with her. Thought about it a few times. Tempted by the fruit of another, and all that. Nevertheless, he hadn't acted on those impulses.

When he remained silent, Clifton leaned forward, disbelief written across his face. "Are you in love?"

"I don't know," Tom said, bemused at his own honesty.

Clifton slurped his coffee and stared at his old friend.

"I hadn't really given deep thought to the faithfulness issue. That's interesting, huh? I'm either getting old or this is something different for me. I'll tell you, though, this Donna, she's pretty special."

"Aw, you're lovesick, all right. When you set up housekeeping with a woman and don't cheat on her even when you're two thousand miles away, you've got it bad. And that ain't good," Clifton sang. "I'm in shock, baby, I truly am. Never thought I'd live to see the day. I figured you to be a lifelong ramblin' man. So, when's the wedding?"

Tom laughed. "Christ, not so fast. I said she was special, not necessarily death-do-us-part material."

"You'd look good in a tux, man. And a ball-and-chain."

"I don't know, Cliff. I can't imagine myself sleeping with the same woman for the rest of my life. Settling down scares me. Donna's great, though. It's working out, for the time being." Tom picked up his fork, intending to try the cheesecake. It was gone, except for a few crumbs and a line of raspberry drizzle. "Weren't we supposed to share this? I thought that was the idea behind the two forks and all?" Clifton shrugged and dabbed the corners of his mouth with his napkin. "Glad you enjoyed it. How about yourself? You were always so picky about your women. You seeing anyone?"

"The word is 'discriminating,' not 'picky.' Yeah, I'm kinda seeing someone."

"Good. Because you're no fun at all when you're not getting any. So let's have it. Who is she, what's she like, and what the hell does she see in you?"

The big man winced, and for a split-second Tom sensed his hesitation. "What is this, an interrogation?" Clifton said, half-kidding, half-defensive.

Tom waited patiently.

"She's just this girl. She's fun to be with, and bright, and serious, pretty good-looking. What else is there to tell?"

"How long has this been going on?"

"We've known each other for years. We've been friends, and now we're just experimenting with a new phase. That's all. Just letting things happen and seeing where it all goes. I don't really like talking about it."

"Oh, you don't? You just enjoy badgering me about my love life. Come on, tell me more. How's the sex?"

Despite his reluctance to talk, Clifton had to smile. That was vintage Tom, cutting right to the chase. "It's pretty mind-blowing, I have to admit." His smile faded and his feline face turned somber. "You're right about one thing, Tom. I *am* discriminating. I don't enter any relationship lightly. That's important to understand. This time, it just feels right. Although who knows how it'll turn out. But she seems to be worth the risk."

"Risk? What, is she on the bomb squad or something?"

Clifton shrugged, and took a moment to choose his words. "You know, man. The risk you take getting close to anybody. The whole helpless tightrope-walk of falling in love, even when common sense tells you to go slow."

"Or run the other way. Sure, I get it." Tom finished off his coffee. "Listen, maybe I can meet this mystery woman before I leave, huh?"

"Maybe."

"That didn't sound too enthusiastic, dude."

"I'd love to introduce you, but I don't see where you'll have the time and all. You have the service tomorrow, and you know that'll take up most of your day. Thursday, you guys are up at the shelter with Rachel's ashes, right?"

"Yeah, but that won't take all day. Why don't we hook up for an early dinner? I mean, who knows when we'll see each other again, right?"

"Right," Clifton agreed, but looked doubtful. "Listen, I don't think it's going to work. I'll have to check my schedule, but I may have a late job tomorrow. Oh, and I think that's her 'girls' night out,' anyway. She and some friends usually go to the movies on Thursdays."

"Okay. Sure." *Was it possible to invent excuses that were any lamer?* Tom thought. *So he doesn't want me to meet her, whoever 'her' is. What's that all about?* "What's her name, anyhow?"

Behind his glasses, Clifton's eyes performed two or three rapid cat-blinks. "Name?" he repeated dully.

"Yeah, your girlfriend's name?"

For a half-second, Clifton's face went blank, the blankness of the total brain-freeze. He finally murmured, "Vera. Veronica, I mean."

"Veronica, okay." Tom wondered if Clifton was drunker than he'd guessed or, for his own reasons, just lying about the girlfriend. "You call her Vera for short?"

"What?"

"Because in the *Archie* comics, Veronica's nickname is Ronnie. Not Vera." Tom leaned forward on the table and gave his friend a grin and a searching look. "Of course, your Veronica is real life, not someone made up from a comic book. She can call herself whatever she likes, right?"

Clifton appeared too flustered for words, so he nodded his big head and smiled thinly. He dropped his eyes and developed a keen interest in the bottom of his coffee cup.

"Well, best of luck to you and Veronica, my friend. Me, I always preferred Betty. Never understood why she played second fiddle with Archie. Thought blondes were supposed to have more fun." Tom stretched and gave an exaggerated yawn. "Well, I'm beat. You about ready to call it a night, Cliff?"

"I am," the big man said, looking relieved, quickly snapping back to himself. "Let me get the check and we'll scram. No, don't argue. Like you said, I don't know if we'll ever see each other again. Also I talked your ears off all night with my carpet cleaning woes. You earned a free dinner."

"I wasn't going to argue," Tom told him. "Speaking of earning something, leave the waitress a generous tip, will you? She had to put up with your bad and bodacious self tonight. I'm going to catch a smoke. I'll meet you outside."

While Clifton settled the bill, Tom waited out on the steakhouse porch where the air was so cold it instantly brought tears to his eyes. He lit a cigarette, inhaled, and held the smoke there a moment before exhaling. *Cancer sticks*, Donna lectured him constantly. *Coffin nails*. He missed her and wondered which side of her worried the most about his atrocious habits, the lover or the nurse? If she were here with him, he'd tell her nonchalantly he'd rather know his poison and ingest it rather than live in denial. She would narrow her eyes and compress her lips. To deflect her displeasure, he'd recount or fabricate a cautionary tale about a fitness buff who'd been killed by a freak accident, a horse's kick to the heart. Or maybe the one about the health food fanatic who'd gotten run over by a truck while jogging. "Honey," he'd tell her gently, "when your time's up, it's up. There's no reprieve from the governor and no deals to be made with the devil. So why give up the few pleasures we have?" The cigarette tasted wonderful. Tom savored the way the tobacco cleared a path through his sluggish mind, counteracting the dulling effects of alcohol and heavy food.

"Get your nicotine fix?" asked Clifton as he barreled out the restaurant's door. "Let's roll, then. It's late and it's fucking freezing."

Clifton drove slowly through the early morning streets. The Karmann Ghia was not built for winter traveling in Greenstone, but he was more worried about attracting a cop's attention than in practicing defensive driving. The two men rode mostly in silence. They were tired, talked-out, and distracted by their own thoughts. Clifton coasted into

Rob's driveway and said good night. Tom nodded and had one foot out the car door when Clifton said lowly, "It's good to see you again, you silly son-of-a-bitch. Tonight makes me remember what I miss about you not being around. I'm sorry I'm not better at staying in touch, man."

"Listen, that's a two-way street. No regrets, baby. This was a good night."

"One thing."

"Yeah? What's that?"

Clifton's hand slid along the steering wheel. "Next time," he rumbled, "I get to pick the show. Drag your white ass to some all-soul revue, see how you like being the token minority in the audience."

Clifton was still laughing as he backed down the driveway and gunned the sports car up the road, over a hill and out of sight.

Chapter Thirteen

Since childhood, Violet imagined the afterlife might resemble a wild river flowing in the confounding shape of a Moebius strip. There would be no clocks or calendars, maybe no Heaven or Hell. Only a sort of liquid looping of the space-time continuum. Its currents would roil and curlicue. Pasts and futures would cascade violently through a series of rapids, cataracts, waterfalls. In her mind's eye, Vi watched dispassionately as the soul of Henry Demeter bobbed up and down in a tiny kayak among the turbulent eddies. *Well, assuming the old man possessed a soul,* she thought darkly. The river veered through sheer canyon walls and deep forests, twisting like taffy, like a distended rubber band.

She pictured the river *becoming* a rubber band. It stretched to its outer limits, then snapped back upon itself. The letters WWHD appeared to her like waves along its great elastic length.

What Would Henry Do?

What *could* he do? Vi asked herself with some satisfaction. She had no doubt Henry probably resented the hell out of being dead. He wouldn't have much patience for the afterlife, she knew. He'd be thinking he had too much left to do. It would rankle him to know he no longer could control events, his surroundings, or his own fate. He would drift helplessly, borne along by rough waters. Round and round in an eternal loop. No headwaters, no deltas. No Heaven, no Hell. These images brought a smile to Vi's face, despite the cramps which seemed especially crippling today.

What did the dead want? To be alive again, Vi supposed, but what else? What would the dead miss? In Henry's case it would be a concise list. Fifty-year-old bourbon, the carnal charms of the flesh, golf and poker, the chase for the almighty dollar, porterhouse steaks, his properties, his holdings, the satisfaction of besting his rivals, the admiration and respect of his peers, the pride he felt in his beautiful, stylish wife. Vi liked to think Henry's ghost would be burdened by these memories and by whatever few emotions he might still possess. She hoped the old man would remember and suffer, preferably for all eternity.

~ * ~

WWHT. What Would Henry Think?

That was the question nagging Rob. In fact, it had *always* nagged Rob. What was his father's opinion? Henry had been fond of boasting how proud he was to be a Demeter, the mythological name associated with growth and fertility. He could've cared less about bounties of vegetables and fruits and grain. Henry's favored crop was money. He'd spent years building a business with his own two hands and with the force of his considerable will. Why? To provide for his family, sure, but also to satisfy the primal urge of becoming the architect of his own destiny. His expectations for himself and others were high. When his objectives were met, he doled out riches and rewards accordingly. When he was disappointed or angered, his response was a withering neglect that dried up everything in his orbit.

As a young man, he'd been all about hungering, striving, compulsively working and obsessively producing. In his middle years, with his family secure and his reputation golden, his thoughts turned to his legacy. He took to heart Andrew Carnegie's warning that "a kept dollar is a stinking fish," and John D. Rockefeller's retort that "the man who dies rich dies disgraced." H.D. wouldn't go quite *that* far, but he was serious about emulating those great men and their teachings. Great men displayed exceptional courage and superior wisdom. They were subject to a far different set of standards than was the common worker. In fact, H.D. might have gone so far as to say that, to men like Carnegie and Rockefeller, rules were made for other people.

"Mere money-making was never my goal. I had an ambition to

build." John D. again.

With dear Rachel to guide him, Henry became a benefactor, contributing to more noble causes than he had fingers and toes. He was a platinum donor to the performing arts center, gave money to the hospital, established a college scholarship fund, funded soup kitchens, patronized the local history museum, spearheaded charitable golf tournaments to benefit cancer research, sat on five nonprofit boards, consulted seven community action committees, and the list went on and on. Rob had long ago lost count of his father's endless commitments, memberships, philanthropic projects. It made his head swim to dwell on Henry's widespread influences, as well as his sheer stamina. When had the man slept?

By the time he'd reached sixty, H.D. was thinking about his successor. Naturally, it would have to be one of the boys. He'd never groomed any of his sons for the investment business, had not felt the need to take them 'under his wing'. After all, no one had done so for him. Their blood was his blood and, he assumed, his wants were also their wants. Not until his later years did he start having reservations about the suitability of his sons to step into his position.

Robert was firstborn, and so first entitled. He both admired and feared his father. As a young man he wanted nothing more than to emulate him. Rob knew Henry considered him an inoffensive, muddling and unimaginative dullard. The knowledge stung, but Rob told himself it was better to take a realistic view of his prospects than to romanticize them.

When all was said and done, Thomas was really H.D.'s first choice as a protégé. He had the brains and the aptitude for the business. Alas, though, not the drive. No, it was more than that, Rob thought. Tom outright rejected his father's life. He made no bones about renouncing his father's vocation. Driving home his disdain, he turned tail and fled to Florida to indulge his pathetic gypsy existence. *Quitter*, thought Rob. *Bellyacher. Typical Tom.*

That left Benjamin, who had always been something of a cipher to his father. There was never any doubt about his abilities. However, the youngest son had a clandestine and furtive nature H.D. could not apprehend. More importantly, he didn't trust Ben. The boy presented with a broad open smile and an honest grip when he shook hands. Still, Henry couldn't shake the image of his son's free hand hidden behind his back, gripping a dagger.

Rob couldn't picture Henry looping around Rachel's river of infinity. He figured H.D.'s Heaven was confined to the shelter where his ashes lay. Up there, frost streaked the tips of the long wild grasses, and the polyrhythms of fifty thousand insects paid homage to the cold and the everlasting darkness. The night sky glowed green and gold with shooting stars. Barn swallows and mountain bluebirds rested, conserving their strength for a daybreak which seemed almost as gloomy as the black evenings. It was a lonely, icy paradise. Rob guessed it suited his father's lingering spirit just fine.

~ * ~

WWHS: What Would Henry Say?

In Ben's more lucid moments, he sometimes wondered how his father would describe his own final days. Near the end, H.D.'s flesh had become a torment and a burden to him. For sixty years, he'd been 'healthy as a goddamn horse'. He didn't know how to react when his body started feeling picked apart by the sharp beaks of buzzards and vultures, piece by bloody piece. Twinges in his chest. Spells of dizziness and nausea. Humiliating digestive issues. Fire in his feet and legs. In the wee early hours, a new heaviness in his limbs. By mid-afternoon, a strange debilitating lethargy. Colleagues and friends assured him his symptoms were all normal, if unpleasant, parts of the aging process. His doctor pronounced him in good shape and provided pedestrian advice for his continued well-being. Mild exercise, sensible diet, all things in moderation.

"Is this what I pay you good money for?" H.D. snapped at the sawbones during one such visit, irritated by his cheeriness. "To tell me things any idiot would know?"

"Haw, haw," said the doctor. "You'll live to be a hundred, Henry."

Instead, lightning struck at sixty-five. There was no warning, no chance to cry out for help. One spike of pain in his chest, a torch in his skull, and H.D. died in his office at work. His body slumped forward onto his broad teak desk. His head came to rest on the blotter. His eyes remained open, his glasses knocked askew. The green shade from his banker's light cast his skin in a ghoulish pallor. One arm rested outstretched atop the desk, the other dangled straight down. His Cross pen fell to the floor. The wheels on his oxblood executive's chair rolled slightly backward, creating the illusion of Henry merely deciding to kick back and take an afternoon nap. His office was furnished with polished brass railings and warm wood molding and hunter-green wallpaper. "A man's office," Rachel observed, not altogether as a compliment. None of it mattered to Henry now. His one window looked out at the impassive foothills built up with shale and sandstone, as well as millions of dead rocks like feldspars, quartzites, hornfels, green schists. Henry could no longer appreciate the view. Photos of Rachel and his boys stared at his body with eyes bright for the camera, beaming artificial say-cheese smiles.

Above and behind him, fixed to the wall, was an ornate plaque which was inscribed with a quotation. "Coming together is a beginning," it read, "staying together is progress, and working together is success." Those were pearls from Mr. Henry Ford. They'd been a philosophy and guiding star for H.D. throughout his long life in business.

Not so much in family life, though. Ben remembered that much about his father.

Ben also believed with all his heart in Heaven, but not as a river or within the confines of the shelter. He hoped H.D. had found peace in his own Heaven, assuming his soul had risen and not been designated for descent.

~ * ~

WWHJ: What Would Henry Judge?

Thomas knew all about Henry's judgment, particularly regarding his offspring. The old man had three sons whom he'd looked upon as a trio of supreme disappointments. One was a colorless mediocrity, another wasted his natural gifts and potential. The third sabotaged himself and had fallen on the sword of his own flawed nature. All three, in H.D.'s jaundiced view, had been undermined by a viper in female form.

His passing brought them all back together in Greenstone. The funeral lured Rob back from his commonplace, stuck-in-neutral military career. It roped in Tom, the journeyman clown who'd sneezed at success and scoffed away the chance to become H.D.'s successor. It brought back the hellcat, the she-devil, the hypocritical churchgoer who'd cast her carnal spells on H.D.'s progeny and, in doing so, ruined them all. H.D.'s death even brought back Ben, the lost and tragic son, who appeared in town several weeks after his father was gone.

Tom recalled he, Rob and Rachel seeing to the cremation and, in accordance with Henry's wishes, transporting the remains to the little shelter in the foothills where he'd first proposed to his young Rachel. His will instructed his family to scatter the ashes with the help of the mountain wind and to consecrate the remains to the goat's head and chokecherry bordering the creek, to the white phlox and white campion stippling the hillsides. H.D. imagined cinders of himself coming to rest in the Rockies' old gravel pits and tungsten mines, maybe borne away on the wings of a grackle. He was at peace with becoming one with the food chain and eco-system. It seemed a grand way to glorify his human life, a bit of immortality in the world he'd left behind.

Except they'd botched it. Henry's lunkhead eldest had been selected for the honor of launching H.D.'s dust and minerals to the wind. Whether it was Rob's scaredy-cat caution or his unfailing talent for lowering the bar on the expectations that he might do *anything* better than half-ass, the bumpkin managed to toss the ashes in the singular moment when not the slightest breeze was blowing among the foothills, when the world was hushed. Therefore, H.D.'s remains were *dumped* rather than majestically cast aloft. They plunged to the dirt in a powdery gray clump, a testament to slipshod Rob's good-enough-for-government-work approach to the simplest of tasks. The mound of ashes sat protected by the shelter's stone wall when, two seconds later, the air started gusting again. Tom reckoned if H.D. had been able to attend his own funeral, he would have been highly pissed.

To complicate matters, the family then brainstormed ways to

repair the damage, one suggestion worse than the next. Scoop up the ashes and try again. Go home, bring back a rake, and spread H.D. around as best as possible. Pour water on the mound of ashes and watch the resulting oatmeal slowly ooze its way down the mountain. In the end, they voted to let nature take its slow-but-steady course, the best of many bad solutions.

In life, Henry had been high-minded about the Demeter name. He'd wanted to pass it along to his three strong sons, and in turn have them transmit it to the generations which would naturally follow. The ultimate irony, thought Violet, was to own a surname synonymous with fertility and to stand by helpless as the bloodline ended. From beyond the grave, H.D.'s harsh judgment might sound like, "Benjamin will remain childless, obviously. If Thomas wasn't shooting blanks, any children he might father would likely be bastards, anyhow. Robert longs to be a father, but the spiteful bitch won't oblige him."

~ * ~

Vi stood off to one side while the brothers and Rachel debated the fate of the ashes, a bored half-smirk of victory on her face. What H.D. detested most about her were not what he considered her many sins. No, what he loathed was her naked insolence and false piety. She was all God-this and Christ-that to rationalize and excuse her most egregious behaviors. He'd found it despicable the way she used her religion as a get-out-of-jail-free card.

Yes, WWHJ? No question, he'd fault Violet for there being no further descendants to carry on the dignified Demeter name. *Damn you,* she heard his jeering voice, accusing her even in death. *Damn you for all time.*

Chapter Fourteen

Rob's favorite time of the work day was the two hours before the firm opened its doors to the public. The phones were quiet. Clerks and salespeople were busy with their own paperwork and preparations. Few employees intruded on his time. He could get a lot of work done here in his father's old office.

Some colleagues advised Rob against working at the same desk where his father once collapsed and died. It was a little morbid, they whispered. It was bizarre. Rob dismissed the talk as superstitious bunk. It was an office filled with furniture, that's all, not a haunted house. He didn't believe in ghosts and considered such nonsense a sign of silliness in others. The office gossips interpreted Henry's death as an analogy for the consequences of an unbalanced life. 'All work and no play.' Robert waved off that sort of talk. Above all else, his father had been a man of moderation. Rob regarded as sheer coincidence the fact of H.D.'s body giving out at that particular time, in this particular room. Henry spent most of his waking hours at the investment company, so it was hardly a shock when his brain chose to short out right there at his desk.

Rob stared out his one window at the foothills. The landscape was bleak, all browns and whites. Rocks and trees filled his view but barely registered. Violet would know their names and could describe them for him if he was interested. There was some snow remaining up there, but in town the streets were clear. The forecast today was for sunshine and temperatures in the sixties. Most days, he was indifferent to snow and ice, except for the inconveniences of shoveling the driveway, warming the car, scraping the windshield, and driving along Greenstone's hilly streets. Like they said, if you didn't like the weather in Colorado, stick around another five minutes and it would change. Vi didn't care for the winter months. She often said her dream house would be in the desert, New Mexico or Arizona. She loved the dry heat, and often talked about retiring in a little adobe house somewhere in the southwest. That was pleasant to chat about, but realistically Robert knew those days were a long way off.

Tom, too, hated the cold and snow. "I have to get the hell out of here," he declared shortly after graduating college. "I'll go fucking insane if I stay. I need to be by an ocean." *Have to. Need to.* That was Tom in a nutshell, all right. Dramatizing his feelings at every opportunity, turning preferences into principles.

As always, a mountain of work awaited Rob. He attacked it with gusto. There were phone messages and emails to be returned, small business loans to review, an audit to prepare for, a meeting with his admin assistant to update his calendar. His signature was required here, his presence requested there. It was a high-stress job and the routine could be jangling. Today, though, Rob welcomed the distractions. He had four hours to get caught up and he was determined to make a dent in his work piles.

Rachel's memorial service was at two o'clock. Several hundred people were expected to pay their respects. About a dozen asked for a few minutes each to recount their touching and amusing memories of his mother. Rob calculated he himself would only have to say a few words. He had a dry public speaking style and, while he could address a crowd competently, he never enjoyed doing so. This, he acknowledged, might become a liability once he started his run for public office. *For now, though, leave the theatrics to Tom,* he thought acidly. Light refreshments would follow, people would mingle, talk and eventually disperse. At that time, the Demeter family would go out for dinner. Rachel's ashes could be scattered at the shelter tomorrow afternoon. At last, she and Henry would be together again.

Rob would be relieved when it was all over and done. The investment company offered a week's grief leave and he intended to take at least a few days afterward. His plan was to sleep and vegetate, nothing more.

It was tiresome being the one who had to think of all the details, deal with all the necessary arrangements, plus do his job at the firm, plus cater to Ben's needs and Vi's emotions, plus, worst of all, welcome Tom into his house. Whenever Tom was involved, the dynamics were bound to go all out of whack, especially between Tom and Vi.

Tom's nature was to yak on about everything and anything on his mind. It drove Rob absolutely berserk. What point was there in analyzing things to death? Tom claimed to seek truth, mining for deep meaning, but he also craved attention. He often acted as if grieving was an Olympic competition. His actions and speech were designed to wring the juice out of any situation implying, *I care more. No one hurts like I do.*

"People can change," Vi suggested last night when Rob tried to put his frustration into words. Well, of course she would defend Tom. They shared a history, after all. They'd had seven years together through high school and college. By all accounts, they'd appeared to be a happy couple, with the family anticipating a wedding shortly after graduation.

Rob remembered envying Tom's luck, but the stupid son-of-a-bitch didn't seem to realize or appreciate his good fortune. Rob supposed he'd been in love with Violet back then, maybe even from the first time Tom brought her to the house to meet the Demeters. Rachel adored her at once, while Henry glowered at the poor girl all through dinner. Rob never would have thought about trying to win Vi away from his brother, because, as Henry's all-purpose advice would have it, "Gentlemen don't behave in that unseemly manner." Tom always sneered at their father's axioms. "Guess I'm no gentlemen, then," he'd laugh. Rob, on the other hand, readily accepted H.D.'s word as law. He'd sooner stick his hand in a furnace than chase after his brother's girl. Another of Henry's decrees helped him through his lovesick period. "A man cannot help what he thinks or feels. What he can and should control are his actions." This gave Rob permission to secretly yearn for Vi and to freely direct venomous thoughts at Tom, while taking a small measure of comfort in acting like an honorable and civilized man. Like a gentleman.

With a start, he realized he'd tried to read the document in his hands three times without comprehension. It bothered him that he was letting these memories distract him from his work, but he couldn't seem to shake them off. He was surprised at himself for feeling a little taken for granted. Ben and Tom would have their moments in the spotlight, but no one ever asked how Rob was doing. What was he, a robot? Did people really look at him as having no emotions whatsoever? More importantly, did his wife see him that way?

On impulse, he picked up the phone and called the house. Tom and Ben planned to go into town this morning, have breakfast together, maybe browse through a record store afterward. It was nice having Tom gone with Clifton last night, and also Ben was whiny, deciding not to stay over another night. With the house to themselves, Rob thought this might be a chance to talk with Vi alone for a while. He'd say things she needed to hear and he needed to say. Before he could approach her, though, she snapped on the television and made it plain she was not receptive to conversation.

The phone rang and rang, and finally the answering machine clicked on. Rob didn't bother to leave a message. So she was out, too, shopping or jogging or running an errand before the day got too far along. He told himself, *okay, that's normal.*

Still, he couldn't help wondering where Vi had gone, and he hated himself for his suspicions.

By and large, Rob regarded himself as a contented man. He scrupulously worked to the best of his abilities and limitations. In sports jargon, he 'played within himself', a phrase his high school coaches often used to describe him. He described himself as 'happy enough'. He knew he was considered a kind of a throwback, a nose-to-the-grindstone sort of boss and a taciturn husband, not too exciting but steady and stable. Most of the time, he accepted those characterizations as compliments.

Lately, though, it galled him to admit he was not more naturally outgoing and carefree. Fair or not, he blamed Tom for this. Watching his brother interact with Vi, their easy laughter with one another, the way she lit up around him, Rob felt like he suffered severely by comparison. Try as he might, he never seemed to remember to bring home flowers or arrange spontaneous dates with Vi. She'd been after him for years to take yoga lessons with her, learn how to slow dance. He always came up with an excuse. Part of him knew he should pay closer attention, rub her back more often, massage her shoulders and feet, make love with her at other times than the occasional Sunday morning. It seemed he always had serious matters on his mind, the world never seemed to let up, there were always work-related crises, maintenance around the house, or Ben needed looking in on. Recently Rob's tank had been running on fumes. The least little occurrence seemed to tucker him out, draining him entirely. He had nothing extra to give anyone, not himself and not Vi.

He never kidded himself that theirs was one of the great romances. From the start, she'd been coolly polite with him. Standoffish. Looking back, Rob was sure she must have sensed his feelings for her from the start. She had to have felt his great conflict, smitten with his brother's long-time girlfriend. When he finally began courting her, he did so carefully, terrified of doing something to scare her off or saying something to invite rejection. Steadily, he chipped away at her resistance. Slowly, she lowered her defenses and became cautiously receptive to his advances.

In the first year of their marriage, Rob hoped to give her children. When customers filed in and talked about opening college savings accounts for their sons and daughters, Rob experienced hot pangs of envy. These parents complained about behavioral challenges, raging hormones, grades at school, but behind their bitching was an undeniable pride he could only admire and covet. Henry contended, "Having children makes a man less selfish. Helps him develop purpose." Rob knew he'd make a decent father. He believed a child might help strengthen his marriage. Also he wanted an heir.

At any mention of babies, however, Vi grew agitated. She was adamant about not being saddled with a litter of rugrats. "Are you crazy?" she groaned whenever he tried in vain to convince her. "Me, as a mommy? I'd be hopeless, Rob. I'd go out of my mind. Besides, I'm too old. It would be too dangerous for me, and for the baby. Anyway, who would my role models be? My parents? Yours? No, thank you. The world doesn't need one more screwed-up human being. No, I'm not talking about this anymore."

It remained a sore spot in their marriage. What hurt him was she'd never once considered his feelings or desires about children. For Vi, it was case closed, as so many subjects were for her. Sometimes it seemed like their entire relationship was built on a shaky framework of silences and secrets. Rob would have to remind himself he was a lucky man to be her husband, going on four years now. He still marveled, recalling her acceptance of his clumsy proposal eighteen months after H.D. passed on, half-a-year after Ben's accident. Funny how life worked out, sometimes. The stars somehow aligned and there they stood at the shelter, beautiful bride and nervous groom.

Maybe Vi decided to tag along with Tom and Ben this morning. No, thought Rob, she'd been the one to insist it was important for the brothers to spend time together. Ben needed Tom's support, and Tom needed to bond a bit with Ben.

Greenstone had its share of magpies and tongue-waggers who never cared for Violet Demeter. These were mostly dowagers and young professional women who made it their mission to keep the grapevine humming about Vi's unsuitability as the spouse of the president of the town's biggest investment company. These esteemed arbiters of taste and judgment gathered at lunches, teas, baby showers and fundraising events where they complained Vi was altogether too high-spirited to properly represent the town's most distinguished and venerated financial institution. Too wild. Too independent. Some memories went back twenty-five years, to Vi's school days, to her love affair with Thomas Demeter, and to her sudden disappearance. One biddy declared Vi had never been trustworthy, and one crone proclaimed that a respectable marriage late in life couldn't rectify all the sins of a promiscuous youth. Shops, bistros and meeting halls buzzed with chitchat about leopards and their unchangeable spots, scorpions and their true natures.

She didn't have many female friends. Women weren't fascinated by her or drawn to her as men were. They viewed Vi either as a threat, too much of a maverick for her own good, or simply as cold and unlikable. Her Christianity was steel-belted, not the socially acceptable old-time religion which was Greenstone's staple. Her faith did nothing to soften her edges or endear her to her peers. She was not exactly shunned by polite society, but neither was she warmly embraced. Vi was a loner, not by nature a joiner of clubs or committees, definitely not a do-gooder like Rachel. "The gates of Heaven are open to all who have faith," she'd been overheard saying, "regardless of their good earthly deeds."

Most women viewed her as haughty and self-involved. Rob knew it was only Vi being Vi, authentic and genuine. He was as conservative as anyone, but he didn't give credence to empty-headed gossips living in a nineteenth-century fantasy world. He knew his life would have been easier had he married a respectable daughter of Greenstone, one with good bloodlines, weak charm, and exquisite fashion sense, along with tired eyes, old money and maybe a numbing Valium addiction. More than anyone, he was aware of Vi's flaws and excesses. Rob didn't care. He loved Violet. He flat-out loved her. Sometimes she was a silver bullet to his poor heart, but he loved her all the same. She couldn't be anyone else, even if she wanted to, even if she tried.

"Mr. Demeter?"

Until he heard his name spoken, Robert hadn't realized how far he'd sunk into his own reveries. Patty Zimmer was birdlike and competent. She'd been his father's secretary for thirty years and Robert kept her on as his administrative assistant. Now she fluttered nervously in his office doorway. "Is everything all right, sir?"

He blinked and smiled at her, beaming what he thought of as his don't-panic-everything's-perfectly-normal smile. His leadership smile, acquired and honed while in the military. "I'm fine, Mrs. Zimmer."

His first day at the helm of the firm, Rob tried to penetrate Patty Zimmer's air of unctuous formality. "Call me Rob, please. Mr. Demeter was my father. I'd like everyone to feel a bit more relaxed around me."

"Sir?" She'd gaped at him as if he'd just arrived from Jupiter. With her snow-white hair, outsized glasses, and black business suits, Mrs. Zimmer resembled a worried, underfed egret. Her high metabolism made her an efficient assistant and a poster child for anxiety attacks. She chirped, "Sir, with all due respect, I would find that level of familiarity very…challenging. Of course, I'll make the effort, if you insist. But your father, may he rest in peace, he was a stickler for proper decorum, sir. He would have thought it unprofessional and…well, vulgar…to be addressed by the first name in the workplace. Speaking for myself, it will be a difficult habit to break. I believe I speak for the rest of the staff, as well."

So Henry continued to cast his long shadow here at the firm he'd built, somehow enforcing a 1950ish work culture well into the 1990's, and now beyond the pale. Not for him any touchy-feely management fads, generous attaboys, office retreats to boost morale, casual Fridays, and the like. If an employee ever expressed feeling underappreciated, H.D. offered succinct advice. "Consider your paycheck your thanks." If a worker's feelings got hurt, he was encouraged to resign and find a more fulfilling job. There were usually ten applicants waiting in the wings to replace the departed, soul-searching employee.

Henry Demeter made it clear it was the worker's job to please him, not the other way around.

It became easier for Rob to fit into the existing workplace culture rather than try implementing one of his own. With that, every day became a reminder that Foothills Investment Services of Greenstone was, indisputably, the house which Henry Demeter, the *original* Mr. Demeter, had built. Rob might never rise to equal H.D.'s legendary stature, but once he'd accepted the offer to step in as president in the summer of '93, he was determined to give it his bulldog best.

Now Patty Zimmer cocked her head and with one eye searched his face in keen appraisal. "Pardon me for saying, sir," she twittered, "but you ought to go home."

"Thank you. I'm almost finished with what I came in to do."

"Everything's under control here, Mr. Demeter. You don't need to worry about the office. Go home. Your family needs you right now."

Mrs. Zimmer had a long history of loyalty and compliance. In that context her comments were extraordinary, bordering on insubordination. Robert understood it took courage for her to speak up, and for that he admired her. He said, "You're right, Mrs. Zimmer. I said thank you. That will be all."

She nodded stiffly and backed out of his doorway. She was chastened and a little miffed, but too polished to show it. The son was not the natural leader his father had been. H.D. had not been a 'people person', but he'd had an instinct for basic psychology. He understood cause-and-effect, actions-and-rewards, the pleasure principle, and so on. He knew how to wield authority. It was none of Mrs. Zimmer's business, but in her humble opinion, when Robert Demeter agreed to step into

Henry's large shoes, he'd had no idea how far out of his league he was roaming.

Patty Zimmer might have been surprised to learn that Rob would have concurred with her assessment. Take golf, for one small, ludicrous example. The city's business community widely assumed Rob would be joining the Greenstone Country Club, skirting the two-year waiting list because, according to 'gentlemen's rules', he was eligible to inherit Henry's lifetime membership. For a hefty, one-time transfer fee and an annual 'contribution', Rob was made a member in good standing, and he quickly learned that golf was practically a cult among the business elite. Sure, he'd played once or twice in his youth. However, nothing prepared him for the zealousness of the competition, or the importance golf played in forming professional alliances. Deals were brokered on tees and greens. Coalitions were forged on the famed nineteenth hole over martinis and steak sandwiches. A handshake with a councilman in the clubhouse on Sunday afternoon might translate into a favorable zoning vote by Tuesday evening. There seemed to be a charity golf tournament for worthy causes every other weekend.

To his dismay, Rob was terrible at the sport. He could drive a ball long and with fair accuracy, but he lacked finesse with his irons. Also, his putting was hopeless. His reputation as a hacker quickly mushroomed, and he was subjected to a great deal of good-natured ribbing from his fellow players. In vain, he took lessons, got up early on Saturday mornings to practice hitting irons at the municipal driving range, learned that, originally, golf was an anagram for 'gentlemen only, ladies forbidden', and memorized the lingo of doglegs, eagles, pin placement, slices versus hooks. Nothing helped. The best score he could coax out of his abilities was in the low nineties. Golf was a mental game like no other and it messed with his head. His short game remained abysmal. He'd hit one spectacular shot to elevate his confidence, then blow a sixteen-inch putt to torpedo himself. He couldn't read greens at all. He had a talent for landing in the worst bunkers with alarming regularity. On average, he lost six balls per round in the rough or in water hazards.

Fortunately, he was accepted in the clubhouse and at the Chamber of Commerce because he was a 'good sport'. Aside from golf, he kept himself fit on the treadmill and the rowing machine. Vi, too, became a fixture at the country club. Not because she was agog over the chances for social networking, but because she enjoyed swimming in the club's enormous pool during adults-only hours. Her presence also helped pave the way for Rob's acceptance.

Maybe that's where she is now, Rob pondered. *At the club, swimming. Or shopping. Maybe jogging.*

He called home again, and again the answering machine responded. This time he left a message. "Hi honey, it's me. Just calling to check in, see if you need anything while I'm out and about. I'll be here till about noon, then I've got one stop to make before I head home. Call me if you need anything." He was ninety-nine percent sure she would not return his call, but his way was to leave options, just in case.

He shuffled papers, rearranged piles around his desk, fiddled with his calculator. Strange, how life worked out. He'd enlisted in the Army shortly after college, right after a brief stint under Henry's auspices at the firm. What a disaster that had been. The old man took on Rob as an entry level clerk and vowed to teach his son the inner workings of the institution from the ground up. H.D.'s ideal plan had been to groom Tom as his protégé, but Tom was outspoken about wanting nothing to do with a career in investment services. 'Zzzzz', had been his original response. He had Henry's brains and entrepreneurial spirit, but nothing of the old man's drive, or his persistence. "Oh no, thank you," he'd shuddered. "Cooped up all day long like a farm animal? Answering phone calls, one after the other? Acting nice to asshole customers? Just stick a knife in my heart now, Dad. Get it over with."

Ever the oracle, Tom had even said, "Yeah, sounds like my dream job, all right. Work like a horse for forty years only to wind up keeling over at my desk."

Rob wondered if Tom remembered saying that and, if so, if he'd ever felt a stab of remorse over it. Henry had guffawed because Tom could always make him laugh. It was obvious, though, the old man felt let down. Heartbroken, no. Disappointed, most assuredly.

So, Rob became Plan B. Because he idolized Henry, he was thrilled to be selected, even as a second choice. Above all else, Henry was a practical man and he reckoned, between Robert's business education and his bulldog approach to tasks, his second son might just work out. Unhappily, while Rob possessed some of Henry's ambition and, unlike Tom, had no objections to working in a cubicle for forty years, he had little aptitude for the finer points of management. Oh, there was no question he could work himself cross-eyed over contracts and columns of numbers. He was superb at mechanical projects like deconstructing business plans, interpreting architectural drawings, calculating projected profit-and-loss scenarios. He simply wasn't an outside-the-box thinker. He had no feel for a client's risk tolerance, and the art of creative deal-making was lost on him. Anticipating industry trends, decoding social cues, recognizing when to cut loose from an outmoded paradigm... all those scenarios perplexed him.

Add the fact that Henry was a relentless taskmaster. He bore down hard on Rob, cruelly, unreasonably. He worked him tougher than any three other employees. Trying to force the square peg into the round hole. Trying to turn Rob into Tom.

True to form, Rob gave his decision to join the Army serious and thorough thought. He was smart enough to recognize he and Henry could not work together under the same roof. It was obvious Rob's best would never be good enough for his father. In fact, the time had come when perhaps Greenstone itself was not big enough for the two of them. Coolly, Rob evaluated his options, concluding the military might be a temporary but tailor-made solution for him. He thought his father might be pleased. Rob typed his thirty-day notice and handed it to Henry in his office.

As his father read the letter, Rob noted, for the hundredth time, a framed Henry Ford quote on the wall behind H.D.'s desk. "Thinking is the hardest work there is, which is probably the reason why so few engage in it."

Henry pushed aside the letter. "The Army, eh?" he said gruffly. "Why not the Navy, or the Air Force? The Army is for eighteen-year-old mediocrities with no future. Cannon fodder." He snorted, removed his glasses, closed his eyes painfully. "Well, what's done is done, I suppose. It wasn't working out so well here."

"Dad," Rob said, "I don't want to spend the rest of my life battling with you."

"I don't need thirty days," Henry snapped, refusing to look at him. "You can clean out your desk today, if you like."

Rob stood and marched out of the office, swearing he wouldn't give his father the satisfaction of seeing the tears burning in his eyes. Rationally, he consoled himself with the knowledge he'd done his level best to succeed and just hadn't measured up to Henry's sky-high standards. He knew H.D. would have his replacement hired and trained in the wink of an eye, because business was business. He also knew Henry would be thinking of Benjamin being ready for mentoring in a few years, and maybe the third time would be the charm for a Demeter boy. Bottom line? Rob wasn't Tom. He didn't blame H.D., nor was he particularly going to miss working at the company.

It was just that his father's disapproval was always devastating.

Rather than dwell on his failure, Rob drove straight from the firm to the local recruitment office, surprising himself as much as the bored buck sergeant on duty. "I want to sign up," announced Rob. The sergeant lay aside his WordSearch booklet and pulled the application packet from his files. It was 1976. For all intents and purposes, Vietnam was over. Rob was signing on to a peacetime Army. His plan was to survive basic training, enhance his financial education, obtain valuable job experience in a regimented work atmosphere, ride out the next three years and hope all hell wouldn't break loose in the Mideast during his tour of service. He visualized the G.I. Bill helping pay for a master's degree and a house of his own in Greenstone. It was a means by which he could show Henry Demeter he didn't need his help, that he was capable of making his own mark in the world. Rob figured to be discharged before President Carter left office.

Except it didn't work out that way. Much to his surprise, Rob found his niche in military life. He signed on to become a Financial Management Technician, and after basic in Ft. Ord was dispatched to MOS training at Ft. Hood. The curriculum there was a refresher of most of what he'd learned at the University of Colorado and later at Foothills Investment Services of Greenstone. Accounting principles and procedures, statistical analyses, record-keeping, auditing techniques. In the meantime, he found fulfillment and contentment within the Army routine, the barracks inspections, physical training, guard duty, standard reports and examinations. Rob cruised through his classes and graduated with honors. He was given an assignment to Colorado Springs, at Ft. Carson. He inquired if he had any right of refusal, and was advised he did. When asked where else he preferred to be stationed, he said tartly, "Anywhere out of Colorado."

They shipped him to Korea.

During his first tour, Rachel sent him care packages and news from home. He was in Korea for about a year when he heard Tom and Vi split up after seven years together. "Nobody seems to know why," his mother wrote. "It's a shame, is all." Rob thought he had an inkling of what caused the break-up. Tom was not the most faithful of boyfriends, he knew. Rob also didn't agree it was a shame. Another year passed, and he received word when Tom left Greenstone and moved to some coastal village in Florida, sight unseen. "Good for him, I say," Rachel wrote. "Although I miss both of you tremendously, I'm elated you've each found your respective pathway to independence. I still see Violet from time to time. We remain good friends. She seems a bit lost without Thomas, but I am confident that she, too, will find her own way." Ben was at the university. Henry remained at the investment firm.

For the first and only time during his enlistment, Robert toyed with the idea of taking his honorable discharge and coming home to Greenstone to take a shot at wooing Violet. It was an enticing daydream, and he even embellished it with a fantasy of returning to Foothills Investment Services, this time fitting in perfectly with his newfound maturity and worldliness. Then, as Tom would have put it, he 'woke up'. What the hell was he thinking? Even while Vi was with Tom, she'd barely acknowledged Rob. He might have chased her to the ends of the Earth in true Hollywood leading man style, but that was not Robert Demeter, that was not in him at all. Instead, he decided to re-up another three years for a small bonus and an extra stripe. He viewed this decision as an insurance policy against making a huge fool of himself, against going off half-cocked for a girl who had no idea he existed. It's a thin line, he told himself, between being in love and being an embarrassing numbskull.

In 1980, Rob was transferred to Germany. Later that same year, Rachel wrote to report Violet was gone, presumably from Greenstone, possibly from Colorado. She'd left no forwarding address, had said nothing to her friends before disappearing. Rachel hoped she was 'following her bliss', and said while she would miss Vi from her life, she was confident "that young woman will always land on her feet." She added news about Benjamin working at the firm since graduation. Henry guessed Ben's easy-going nature would help him acclimate to the demands of the workplace, but Rachel wasn't so sure that was the case. The relationship between Henry and Ben, she wrote, was 'growing increasingly strained'.

I'll bet, Rob thought from across the Atlantic Ocean.

Another letter from his mother the very next year reported that Ben, too, had vanished. Unlike Vi, he'd left a short note which, while couched in vague and mysterious language, was clear about him leaving town for good. "I love you, Mom, and I love Dad, too," Ben said in his farewell letter. "This has nothing to do with you guys. I need to do this for myself." Whatever 'this' was, however, was not explained and remained an enigma.

"Now you are all gone and somewhere off on your own," Rachel wrote to Rob, "your father and I are left with one another and our memories of raising you. Were we a happy family, Rob? My sense is that all you boys grew up to become fine men, but perhaps also damaged in some subtle manner. However, don't mind me. I'm just alone in this big house, being sentimental and missing my sons. Forgive me and write soon. Love, Mother."

How many of those letters had he received from Rachel over the years as he'd hopscotched from one country to the next, to all the bases in all the many cities? Meanwhile, not a postcard from Henry, not a measly word except for what his mother chose to convey secondhand. Rob continued to travel and to re-enlist, staying with the Army through Carter, Reagan, and Bush. In all that time he'd refused to take leave to visit Greenstone, and so the summers and holidays passed for many years without him seeing his parents. Rachel continued to write, but her letters arrived less often the longer he stayed away.

Rob sweated out flare-ups in Iran, Israel, Palestine, and the major scare with Iraq, but felt fortunate that, in sixteen years, not once had he been asked to soldier in a war zone.

When the Democrat's dark horse from Arkansas received the presidential nomination and went on to win the election, the lifers who were among Rob's best friends were so appalled they threw a party in the theme of a funeral. After twelve years of Republican rule, the unthinkable happened. The American electorate lost its ever-loving mind. Rob and his buddies boozed long into the night. When it came time to fall out for morning formation, many of them reported to sick bay rather than their workstations.

A few months later, Rachel wrote, notifying him that Henry was dead. "Come home," she implored. He did, wondering if his brothers would come, too.

~ * ~

"I'm going home, Mrs. Zimmer," Rob now told his assistant.

She tilted her chin at him from her own desk. *He looks exhausted,* she thought. *He looks like he's carrying the weight of the world on his back. Something in his eyes makes him look a hundred years old.* "There's nothing left for me to do here."

"No, sir," she said. "Good afternoon, sir."

Chapter Fifteen

Vi was in bed when Rob phoned twice, leaving his loving message on the second call. She didn't hear the phone ring or her husband's message, but not because she was asleep. To the contrary, she was wide awake, musing about Rachel being gone and how much she was going to miss the old woman. She was also thinking about God, how His actions were sometimes so closely mirrored by the Devil's that it was nearly impossible to tell them apart. Also how just two or three moments of stupidity could come to define an otherwise devout and exemplary life. She knew it was cold outside, but the sheets and blankets were wonderfully warm. She felt like she'd been bee-stung and pleasantly paralyzed, unable to rise.

Another reason she didn't hear the phone ring was because she was not in her own house, or in her own bed.

She hadn't wanted to come here, not today. She knew it was wrong and probably sacrilegious, screwing out of wedlock on the day of her mother-in-law's service. Then Rob rushed out of the house to 'check in' at the office, and Tom and Ben took off for breakfast to spend a little time together. *Good for them*, she thought, *they can use time alone together to talk.* Vi told herself she only needed to burn off some nervous energy. She convinced herself she was just going out jogging for a little while.

What she really craved, though, was human company, someone to talk to who wouldn't look straight through her or push her away. Worse yet, someone who wouldn't treat her like a fragile female. Someone who would listen to her, who might touch her and make her feel beautiful for a couple hours. She drove herself to this secluded rolling part of town, parked her car, and ran the hills of the neighborhood until she could feel her flesh burning pink beneath her jogging outfit. She didn't run up to the church this morning. She didn't think she could bear her own thoughts up there.

When she completed her run, she trotted breathlessly back to her car, then hesitated. All she had to do was unlock her door and drive home. The choice was that easy and that hard. She thought she could leave right up to the moment when she turned and headed up the walkway to his house. As she rang the doorbell, she didn't allow herself to think about what she was doing. His face when he opened the door was surprised, but pleased. He was wearing his rust-colored terrycloth robe and he motioned her inside, apologizing for not having shaved. "Late night," he muttered, and then pulled her to him, kissing her roughly. Violet tasted his mouthwash, felt his stubble scratch her neck, felt his arousal through the robe. In a matter of seconds, he'd led her down the hallway to the bedroom and whisked off her sweatpants and panties. She protested she needed a quick shower first, but before she knew it, she was flat on her back on his bed and his mouth was on her. She didn't care about the shower anymore because he didn't seem overly concerned with her hygiene.

Now she lay on her lover's big bed, him fast asleep beside her and purring like a puma, she cursing herself for being a fool and a hypocrite. In her postcoital daze she felt guilt for betraying Rob again and for feeling so much pleasure when so much was wrong, wrong, wrong. Her mouth was dry and her breasts sore. She wanted cold water. She swung her legs off the bed and stood, wrapped a tan towel around her waist, and moved into the kitchen.

About a week's worth of mail was spread haphazardly across the dining room table. Her housekeeping instincts kicked in and she began to make neat piles. There were *Sports Illustrated, U.S. News and World Report,* credit card offers from three different banks, a Disabled Vets postcard addressed to RESIDENT PARKER, a Lands End catalogue, a mailer from the local congressman announcing a town hall meeting, a gas bill, a trash bill, weekly ads from King Soopers and Albertsons, and other assorted junk mail. Vi surveyed the kitchen, mentally noting cleaning and organizing tasks for the future. The cabinets could use a new coat of varnish, the stove was due for a major scrubbing, the floor was in dire need of mopping and waxing. In her mind, the evidence cried out for a woman's touch.

Not that she was volunteering for the role. She already had a sloppy husband, she thought ruefully as she searched for a water glass. As Rob was calling home, trying to reach her, leaving her a message, she'd been busy being ravished from behind, she on all fours on the bed, her lover gasping, plunging in and out of her, his strong hands on her bare haunches, pulling her to him. She'd been too wet to care about God or Robert or anything except the powerful motion and delicious friction which overrode all senses, obliterating any moral misgivings she might have had just minutes before. He drove himself deep inside her, his thrusts becoming more and more rapid, less calculated, more frenetic. All tenderness was gone as they both gave in to the furious energy of the animal grinding. Vi wanted it to last for hours, his urgency, his hands grabbing at her hips, running up her naked back to clutch at her shoulders, his fingers caught in her hair, his hands cupping her breasts and belly, returning to her rocking hips.

"Call me if you need anything," Rob was saying into the voicemail at home at the very moment his cuckolder exploded inside his wife with a cry. Violet could manage only a helpless "Oh!" at her own climax. Her whole body shuddered and went limp. She saw pink and green filaments of light shooting across the back of her closed eyelids.

She found a glass and filled it with tap water, room temperature. She swallowed half of it in one gulp and refilled the glass. The bay window in the kitchen looked out over the sloping backyard where the lawn was white with a crust of snow and the mulberries were stripped of their leaves. Vi preferred Greenstone in the cool of early spring, the time of resurrection, with cowbirds and lazuli buntings warbling after a late afternoon thunderstorm. She could spend hours out in her gardens. Outside, two chipmunks squabbled at each other in one tree, while a woodpecker watched them from another.

"Fellows, didn't you get the news?" Vi called to them through the window. "Winter's here. Time to head south. Time for hibernating."

"You're talking to chipmunks now?"

She jumped a little at his voice. Water spilled over the lip of the glass and onto her chest. Self-consciously, she dabbed at her breasts with the towel, and he laughed. "Want me to get that for you?"

He was standing in the hallway, wearing only a towel that identically matched hers. On him, it seemed like a washcloth. He was a huge man and looked even bigger with no clothing on. Vi couldn't believe she hadn't heard him padding down the hall. "Thought you were sleeping," she said.

"I must've dozed off. Either that, or I was in a coma. You trying to kill me?" He grinned. "Although, what a way to go, huh? By the way, do you know you're bleeding? You must've started."

Violet followed his gaze down to her towel and saw it was splotched with bright burgundy stains. "Oh my God," she cried. "I am so sorry."

"You should see the sheets. It looks like a war zone in there, girl." He approached and wrapped his arms around her. "Can I have some of that?" he said, meaning the water. She handed him the glass and he drained it. "I hope it looks worse than it feels. Are you okay?"

"I've had bad cramps the past few days, but not anymore. Must've needed a friendly probe."

He bowed ceremoniously. "Happy to be of service. Here, let me get some more water for you." He moved to the sink, asked, "What time's the memorial, again?"

"Two o'clock."

"Should be crowded. Rachel was one popular lady in this city."

"Yes, she really was. For good reason. You'll be there?"

"You know I wouldn't miss it. Friend of the family and all."

How does it come to this? Vi asked herself. He'd said it so nonchalantly, and she'd accepted it so readily. "Friend of the family." "Wife." What did those words mean when friends cheated, and wives lied? How casually we sometimes double cross our better selves. How recklessly we put our loved ones at risk for a moment's coarse pleasure. Worst of all, we know what we're doing, the wrongness of it, and we do it anyway. That's the blemish on the human soul. That's the hell of it.

"I don't have much time," she said quickly, not wanting to pursue that train of thought, not now. "You mind if I hop in the shower first?"

"No, go on. I'll make some coffee. I've got some work to do anyway."

It was a man's bathroom, blue and green color scheme, spare and functional. Vi started the shower. The hot water felt purifying on her skin. She shut her eyes and emptied her mind, or tried to. She knew a hundred meditative tricks, but none of them seemed to make a dent in her malaise. *Forgive me, Lord*, she prayed. *I know I'm a sinner. I acknowledge and renounce my sins. I am heartily sorry and I am thoroughly ashamed. Just please let me get through today, God.*

She soaped her arms and tried a breathing exercise designed to help 'center' her. She pictured herself as a tree, with her legs as mighty roots reaching deep into the earth so nothing could shake her. The smell of soap and shampoo was soothing. The act of self-cleansing felt righteous. Still, nothing mitigated her dull sense that a reckoning was at hand, and that it was coming soon. This charade could not go on forever. There were too many dangling threads, unresolved conflicts, secrets and misunderstandings.

Too many mistakes, she thought. *Too many damned sins.*

Rachel had been a mother-figure for her almost from the moment Vi had stepped into the Demeter house as Tom's girlfriend. It was the rarest of life experiences. One meets a person for the very first time, and an instantaneous bond is formed. There's recognition there, not as in a vague dream, but more as a low-grade electrical tickle, faint but real voltage between two old souls. In 1971, Rachel was approaching forty and Vi was just fifteen. Their age difference meant nothing. Rachel welcomed her into their clan as warmly as if Vi was a long-lost daughter. All night, she asked Vi friendly and knowing questions, showing interest in her answers. Rachel's direct gaze left the impression she could envision the strong woman Violet might one day become, and was vested in watching the journey unfold.

Otherwise, Vi remembered the night as unbearably awkward. Rachel made a simple dinner of pasta, salad, and good bread, and the evening got off to a fine start. However, as warm as Rachel's reception had been, it was neutralized by Henry's extreme cold front. His pale blue critical eyes seemed to stare x-rays through Vi and expose…what? Her cheap character, her low pedigree, her already-checkered history? She'd never met anyone so openly contemptuous and hostile. Henry actually crinkled his nose at her, this bad smell which suddenly entered the house with his son.

"Oil and water, little miss," he confided to her later, after she and Tom had been dating for several years. "That's what you and I are. We don't mix. We don't like each other, and we never will."

So much for social amenities, thought Vi.

Henry Demeter was an unremittingly cynical man who expected nothing from most people, and consequently brought out the worst in them. It was hard to understand Rachel putting up with his bullshit for two minutes, let alone twenty years. Harder still to fathom was the biological connection between H.D. and his three outwardly normal sons.

Tom was nothing like his dour father. He was fun to be with, witty, athletic, and attractive. His unorthodox sense of humor made him popular at school, especially with the girls. His brothers seemed ordinary enough, too. Ben was shy and cute, where Rob was so transparently smitten with her. he could hardly look her way without blushing. There was something slightly off-putting about Rob, though. *He seems tightly wrapped*, she thought at the time. She made a mental note to have little to do with him in the future.

During dinner, Henry jawed about his day at work, complaining bitterly about the morons who worked for him, the simpleton customers who had no conception of a dollar's value, and Greenstone's venal leaders with whom he consorted because "after all is said and done, business is business."

"Hard workers, every last one of them," he said about this last group. "Nothing wrong with working hard. But do you know what the hardest work of all is? Can you guess?" He fixed a stern gaze on Vi and recited, "'Thinking is the hardest work there is, which is probably the reason why so few engage in it.' Hah! Truer words were never spoken, little girl. Particularly for this backwater town."

"Henry Ford, right, Dad?" Tom interjected.

He turned to Vi with a dangerous grin. "Henry Ford is in Dad's pantheon of Great American Capitalistic Pigs. Oh sorry, did I say 'pigs'? I meant 'heroes'. Who else is in that Mt. Rushmore of yours, Dad?"

"Tread lightly, son," his father grumbled. "Rachel, this bread's a bit garlicky, don't you think?"

"No, I don't."

Good for you, Mrs. Demeter, thought Vi.

"And can you two save this bickering for another time? We have a guest tonight and I'm fairly certain we can find a more benign line of dinner conversation, can't we? I fear we're not making much of a first impression on Violet."

"I'd say the Vanderbilts, right, Dad?" Tom went on as if his mother hadn't said a word. "J.P. Morgan, the Mellons, all the Rockefellers. Smart guys, every last one of them."

Tom was insulting his father by mocking Henry's own words, Vi realized with a shock. Even Rachel seemed stunned at her son's audacity.

"Henry Ford, though, he was the philosopher king of the moneymakers, wasn't he? First off, all you Henrys have to stick together. Second, he's the assembly line pioneer. We've got him to thank for oodles of mass-produced junk we don't need, for lousy customer service, for the death of the American artisan. Thirty years from now, this country is going to be one coast-to-coast strip mall…"

"You're so far wrong you don't even know it. Try interchangeable parts," Henry pointed out impatiently. "Decent working conditions. Living wages and fair benefits for employees."

"An ignorant consumer base," countered Tom. "Corporate welfare and tax breaks for the rich. A lockstep, Levittown mentality across the land."

Vi giggled as Tom mimicked a Southern preacher's delivery.

"Tom, any citizen is free to start his own company. Great men don't play outside the rules so much as they create their own. Let's see how high-and-mighty you'll be when it's you needing to earn a living," Henry said in measured tones. "When you're sitting behind a desk or working with your bare hands out in the hot sun. When you're trying to squeeze the most out of every dollar you make, just to stretch it from week-to-week." He wagged a fork at his son, a strip of lettuce stuck to its tines. "Just remember that it's 'capitalistic pigs' who provide the jobs in this country. The same 'pigs' manufacture the clothing you wear and the car you drive. They distribute your God-awful music and your precious liberal books. They build your house and fix your plumbing and deliver groceries to your local market."

"Those are some busy porkers," Tom observed lightly. "Oink, oink."

Vi was delighted by this give-and-take at the Demeter table. She'd never heard anything like it, especially within supposedly harmonious families. In time, the other boys joined in the fracas. Ben took his lead from Tom and joyfully argued against any position Henry took. He was loud and preposterous, as would be expected from any fourteen-year-old boy. Rob mainly sided with his father, and Vi could see right away that he did so to win favor, not out of conviction. At one point just before dessert, the dialogue deteriorated into a shouting match. Vi's face must have shown alarm because Rachel leaned over to whisper, "You should be grateful. They're on their best behavior tonight because it's your first time."

My first time, Vi thought, hearing the phrase's unintended double meaning, doing the math in her head. She'd been fifteen at the dinner, and had not been a virgin for almost two years. Having discovered the powers of sex and prayer early in life, she'd grown into an abnormally attuned adolescent. Maybe that was what Henry detected and distrusted from the moment he'd laid eyes on her.

"Hello? Are you drowning in there? Leave a little hot water, please. I've got to shower, too."

"Almost done," she called, remembering it was his bathroom, but still annoyed at having him interrupt her thoughts.

Thomas, Robert, Benjamin. In the beginning, how could she have known their fates would be intertwined with hers for the rest of their lives? She thought she'd put the brothers behind her when she'd fled Greenstone in the early eighties. Rob joined the Army. Tom and she broke up, then he vamoosed to his beloved Florida shortly after the split. Ben had not been pleased with her, and in fact had been instrumental in driving her

146

out of town.

Rachel had been the only Demeter left to say goodbye and wish her well. They'd had lunch at a small Mexican cafe downtown, spinach enchiladas and margaritas. Vi was fine during the meal, then broke down after Rachel went home.

Vi rambled for a long while afterward, California, Oregon, Nevada, Utah, Arizona, New Mexico. A dozen years passed before she knew it, during which she had a slew of good times, acquired plenty of friends, and dated a smorgasbord of attractive men. Vi was seeking meaning, trying to get right with God, but it wasn't unfolding the way she'd planned. Her restless heart refused to settle. Instead of finding peace of mind, she felt more out-of-place and unraveled than ever.

One day she received the news of Henry dying. She was living close to Tucson at the time. Somehow Rachel tracked her down. In dry tones, she reported her husband suffered a massive stroke which killed him at his office. "I thought you should know," she told Vi. "You and Henry never got on very well, I know. I always considered you family, though, and thought you deserved to know. Rob and Tom will be coming home for the funeral."

"What about Ben?" Violet asked cautiously.

"We don't know where Ben is," Rachel said mildly. "How have you been, dear?"

She'd been a basket case, but she wasn't about to confide to Rachel during this mourning period. Vi would've described herself as being at a crossroads, but she'd been at so many crossroads over the past twelve years the phrase had lost all definition for her.

What the hell is wrong with me? she thought for the billionth time. *Why am I so anxious? Why can't I ever feel at peace?* None of which she said out loud. "I've been good, Rachel," she lied. "I'm so sorry for your loss. I'll be there as soon as I can."

"Oh, you don't need to worry about that, Vi. I know you have your own busy life now. I wouldn't expect…"

"I'll be there," she said again. Her 'own busy life' at the time consisted of 'not much'. She found herself looking forward to seeing Rachel again, even during this difficult time.

Vi bought a one-way plane ticket, Phoenix to Denver, and thought of her trip as a sort of homecoming. *How sad is that?* she thought as the plane soared over the red mesas and Rocky Mountains. *After all my travels, Greenstone is the only place I think of as home.*

Henry's funeral was a huge affair, a celebration of his ramrod life, a tribute to all he'd foreseen and accomplished. He was eulogized as what he'd hoped to become, a great man. There were more than enough speakers at the ceremony, and Vi was spared having to express a few of her own less-than-precious memories of the munificent H.D. "I'll always remember him as a hateful, negative, domineering control freak," she might've begun, and that wouldn't have been proper for the occasion.

In deference to Rachel, she kept her lip buttoned. She'd only been to a couple of open casket funerals and was relieved when she learned Henry had been cremated. Rob and Tom returned to pay their respects and tend to their mother. There hadn't been much time for Vi to interact with either of them, they were both so occupied with logistics, Tom with socializing, Rob with everything else. She was amused to watch them behaving as grown-ups and wondered if they thought the same of her.

Tom was still Tom, and it was easy for Vi to recall how much she'd been in love with the jerk at one time. They took pains to say hello, promised to get together later on, then studiously avoided each other the remainder of the day.

Rob, too, was very much the same as she remembered. He stared intensely at her when he didn't think she was looking and averted his eyes when she glanced up at him. He was still a very closed-off guy, perhaps too much his father's son after all. However, Vi found herself admiring his take-charge manner, the way he arranged the proceedings, anticipated needs, and addressed budding problems before they became disasters. She had dated enough screwballs and dim bulbs, parasites and fuck-ups to appreciate the maturity it required to do what Rob so easily seemed to accomplish. It also didn't escape her notice that Rob looked fitter now than he had in his younger days. His shoulders were wide, his waist trim. Apparently, the military had been a good option for him, in more ways than one.

"It's good to see you again, Vi," he said after the service, between tasks. He couldn't quite meet her eyes, and he turned beet-red when she hugged him. "Are you in town long?"

"I'm thinking of moving back to Greenstone," she said, searching his eyes. "Permanently."

What? she asked herself. *Where the hell did that come from?*

He nodded. He didn't seem surprised at all. A thin line of perspiration outlined his upper lip. "Mother would like that. She's always been fond of you."

"I'm sorry about your dad," she said, hoping her insincerity wasn't too obvious.

"Thanks. He was…well, he would have appreciated all this…you know how he was…"

Vi nodded. It was the first time all day she'd heard Rob stammer or display any uncertainty.

"Anyway, I probably should get back to the guests. Lot of work to do. Thanks for coming, Vi. I'll see you before I go."

He turned and melted back into the crowd, leaving Vi with a small grin and an unexpected warm feeling. *I'll be damned,* she thought. *After all these years, he still has a crush.* To her surprise, she found herself flattered.

After the funeral, after the winding drive up to the shelter where Henry had asked his ashes to be scattered, after Rob returned to his unit at Ft. Hood and Tom went home to Florida, Rachel helped Vi find an apartment in town and the two women cultivated their renewed friendship. They didn't always see eye-to-eye, but each woman had a healthy respect for the other, and they simply enjoyed one another's company.

"Hanging out," Vi called it when they met for a meal, played tennis, ventured into Denver to catch a concert or take in a museum's new exhibit. Rachel didn't know why Vi was so unhappy so much of the time, but she enjoyed broadening the younger woman's horizons, acting the roles of sounding board and guiding angel in Vi's life.

For her part, Vi surely appreciated Rachel's counsel, generosity, and abiding fellowship, but couldn't understand why she didn't believe in God. Rachel refused to talk religion with Vi, it was her only off-limits topic of discussion. Vi feared Rachel might fall into a period of deep grieving for Henry, perhaps become reclusive. Those concerns, however, soon proved to be baseless.

Rachel grieved, but if anything, she threw herself more vigorously into her volunteer work, her clubs, her network of friends and community associates. She'd never admit it, but in a way, losing Henry took a great load off her shoulders. *Had set her free,* Vi thought. H.D. always seemed more married to his job and his cronies than he was to his wife. With him gone, Rachel now looked younger at sixty-two than she had at forty-five.

When the Foothills Investment Services of Greenstone had trouble locating a suitable candidate to replace its founder and president, the late lamented Henry Demeter, word quickly reached Rob in Texas, who lost no time in applying for the position. With his education, work experience, military background, and lineage, his hiring was close to being a sure thing. After sixteen years in the U.S. Army, Rob put in for an early and partial retirement to accept his new civilian job. His request was summarily granted. He packed his few belongings, cleared the last few hurdles to discharge, and headed home to Greenstone.

It took him about three months to get up enough nerve to call Vi. She accepted a dinner-and-movie date, as much out of courtesy as curiosity. Now, twisting the shower faucet off and toweling herself dry, she tried to recall the turning point when she realized Rob had shifted from casual dating to slow courtship. His advances were so cautious as to be nearly unrecognizable. She thought she understood he was trying hard not to make any mistakes, not to blow what little chance he thought he had at winning her. It was sweet but maddening. Rob approached every date like she was a live hand grenade, or a wild-eyed porcupine. Vi found herself taking the initiative from hand-holding to first kiss to sleeping together. Once she'd gotten him into bed, he'd been a surprisingly capable lover, not too imaginative but with lots of stamina, energy, and, when it counted, gentleness.

Rob proposed on New Year's Eve, 1994, less than a year after Henry's death, scarcely six months after he and Vi began dating. "I know it seems rushed, kind of out of character," he said, still bashful around her when he was trying to be serious. He fumbled open the little box with the diamond ring inside. "I've never been more sure of anything in my life, Vi. What do you say?" For once, his gaze was direct, his pale gray eyes boring into hers.

What she *wanted* to say was, "Dear God and holy shit. Can life get any weirder than this?" At one time, she'd been convinced she would wind up as Mrs. Thomas Demeter. Afterward came a period when it appeared she and Ben might transcend their friendship and...Well, that was a long time ago, when she still believed in fairy tale marriages and happy endings. Now she had Rob's sudden proposition to consider. Vi had to confess, it was an intriguing offer. Rob grew up to become a self-assured man in a respectable, well-paying position in town. He wasn't bad-looking and if she was looking for stability, well, she couldn't ask for a more grounded, even-keeled husband. Also, he *was* a Demeter. Rob was so in love with her she thought they could get married, live together and she could learn to love him in a deeper way. It would be a late first marriage for them both. Perhaps they would avoid the problems younger people suffered through. Vi was thirty-eight and she wanted to start leading a real life. She wanted to be *normal*. She told herself she *deserved* to be normal.

Vi said yes, and she and Rob announced their engagement to family and friends on January 1, 1994.

Rachel's reaction to the news was oddly muted. Vi was taken off guard by the older woman's narrowed eyes and slightly pursed lips. Rachel didn't disapprove, but neither was she turning cartwheels at the prospect of wedding bells. "I'm happy for you both," she congratulated them, but Vi detected a hint of coolness. Her son was marrying her good friend, but Rachel treated the engagement as if it were a distant cousin getting hitched to a total stranger. Was she dismayed by Rob's choice? Did she think of Vi as a wonderful companion, but a less-than-desirable daughter-in-law? Or did she just judge it a poor match between two very different personalities?

Then at the end of February, after being gone for over a decade, Benjamin Demeter returned to Greenstone from God-knows-where.

Vi swung open the bathroom door and steam billowed out into the hallway. Turbaned and wrapped in towels, she strode barefoot out to the kitchen where her lover sat at the dining room table, hunched over a blue folder, engrossed in thought, his tiny glasses comically out of place on his serious tiger face. He didn't register her presence right away, so she took the luxury of watching him for a long moment, admiring his conked hair, the athlete's muscles on his shoulders and back, sadly thinking it would soon be over between them. It couldn't last because it was impossible and because nothing like this ever lasted. This affair was as vulnerable to rust and ruin as everything else.

"Huh?" He jumped a bit when he realized she was eyeing him.

"Just admiring a work of art. How can you concentrate like that?"

"It's a big important account, that's why. I *have* to concentrate. How are you feeling?"

"Doing all right, except I need to get some female supplies on the way home."

"Okay, information overload. Not necessary."

She leaned over and kissed him on the forehead, nose, lips. "Part of me is pretty sore," she said.

"Mm-hm. I can relate." He smiled, stood up, took her in his massive arms. "Listen, I don't mean to kill the romance of the moment, but I have to get ready, too. I'll say goodbye now, since you probably won't be here by the time I get out of the shower. See you at the service?"

"Speaking of service…"

"Right, very funny. We don't have time. I'm warning you, don't do that."

"You mean this?"

He let out a small groan. "Yeah, that's what I mean. Come on, now, behave. Better get out of here before I attack you again."

Vi stopped, reluctantly. "All right, all right. I've been warned. I'm getting dressed now. Guess I'll see you later on. Try not to think of what we could be doing with a little more time."

She kissed him once more and turned back down the hall. Halfway to the bedroom, she turned her head for one last look. Clifton was standing by the window, towel tucked carelessly around his big waist, his ridiculous glasses riding the tip of his nose, staring out at the yard like a cat might stare at a butterfly. He was squinting, leaning forward.

"What's out there?" she called.

He turned his head to the sound of her voice and flashed her an enormous grin.

"What're you looking at?"

"Nothing special," he told her, and when she shot him a puzzled look he added, "I was trying to see what you were seeing."

She nodded. "If you find it, let me know, will you?"

Chapter Sixteen

That morning, Tom picked up Ben at his apartment. The plan was to stop somewhere for breakfast, then kill some time before Rachel's service. Tom thought they'd visit Sweet Lou's Records & Tapes, and rummage through the endless bins of used LPs. Vi had lent him her and Rob's emergency car, a sturdy little Accord with two hundred thousand miles on it. The vehicle was as reliable as the turning of the seasons.

"We just keep the oil changed, and it keeps on running," she told him, handing over the key.

Tom planned to delegate the decision of where to have breakfast to Ben. His head ached prodigiously, epically, and he didn't want to have to engage in active thought, did not wish to make any unnecessary decisions on this fine sunny morning. His cure for hangovers was black coffee and silence, liberal portions of both.

Tom was introduced to Mr. Whiskers, who yowled at him the minute he set foot in the apartment. "Nice to meet you, too, you mongrel," he said pleasantly. "Is she pregnant?"

"No, just fat," Ben told him while scooping out a can of salmon pate.

"Salmon. For a cat. What're you living on, peanut butter and jelly sandwiches?"

"No," Ben protested. "I don't like peanut butter."

"That's good to hear."

"I eat a lot of chicken pot pies, though," Ben informed him. "Macaroni and cheese. Sometimes I bring something home from work. I can make Hamburger Helper, too."

"Huh."

Tom didn't care for cats, but for Ben's sake he was willing to feign affection. Vi and Rob informed him the irritating pet was very important to his brother. Naturally, Mr. Whiskers saw straight through Tom's phony front. The cat made sure she sat in Tom's lap, purring loudly, shedding profusely. When Tom, in an attempt to be friendly, scratched her rump, she hissed, whirled, and nailed his hand with her claws.

"Ow!" he shouted, more surprised than hurt. The damn creature had drawn blood.

"Mr. Whiskers!" yelled Ben. "That wasn't very nice." The cat stared blandly at Ben, signifying her supreme indifference to what humans defined as 'nice'.

"Ben, I'm fine." Tom was at the kitchen sink, dousing his hand with cold water. "Get me a little band-aid and let's go. You pick the spot. Mr. Whiskers, pleasure meeting you."

The cat didn't acknowledge him. She flipped her tail and waddled off to the sofa, ready for a nap after all her hard work. She would eat her salmon when Ben and the interloper left, in the privacy to which she was accustomed.

Ben chose Crazy Gunther's, a farmhouse out on the eastern edge of Greenstone which had been converted into a charming old-fashioned waffle house. Tom knew the place from his college days, when he'd fuel up on their colossal bacon, cheddar, and avocado omelets before a full day of classes. The thought of all that butter and grease now made his stomach flipflop, but Gunther's served coffee which satisfied half his requirements for recovery.

Tom drove the weaving road out to the restaurant, into the countryside. The snow had mostly melted, and the open fields on both sides of the two-lane were brown with tangled brush. This was a pretty ride in spring, he recalled, these same fields nourished by sun and rain, overrun with daisies, sweet alyssum, prairie clover and purple horsemint, white phlox and silver lupine. The foothills rose in the west, the eastern plains sprawled as far as the eye could see. Ben sat quietly in the passenger seat, mindful of his brother's headache, taking in the scenery.

"Ben, you ever miss driving a car?" Tom asked.

He was interested in Ben's answer, but he was also talking

because his tongue felt furry and dense from the previous night. He felt the need to exercise it.

"I don't think so, Tom," Ben replied in his quizzical, earnest voice. "I can't really remember driving. I remember getting my license, and I remember being behind the wheel a couple of times. I think I drove into Denver once. I have my trike now. That gets me anywhere I want to go."

"Sure it does. Lots more fun than the internal combustion engine, I bet. Less expensive, too."

"Huh?"

"Pedaling. Keeps you physically fit, I imagine."

"Oh yes, Tom," Ben said seriously. "I am in excellent condition, physically."

They arrived at the restaurant and Tom swung into its dirt parking lot, which after the snow was more of a muddy pit. Gunther's investment in the farmlands had not gone so far as to include an asphalt lot for his customers. Story was he'd been a sheriff who'd put in his twenty years, retiring while he was still in his forties and before he got himself killed in the line of duty. Evidently, he'd had a few close calls over the course of his career, one of which had turned him prematurely gray. He was done with all that stress, and with dealing with 'society's garbage', 'young punks', 'gangbangers', drug dealers, petty thieves, 'violent psychos', and his least favorite, 'stupid fucks'. At first, he'd wanted to use his life savings to open a topless joint several miles outside of town. His wife got wind of that pipedream and quickly vetoed it.

"You think cops are tough? Try arguing with a cop's wife," he hooted. "With a frying pan, she talked me out of it."

His alternate plan was to start the restaurant, which had been going strong now for over twenty years, six days a week, closing only Mondays, open for breakfast and lunch.

"Watch your step, Ben. Looks pretty slippery," he said.

Wouldn't that be great? he thought. *Take Ben out for breakfast and have him slip and fall in this sea of mud. Maybe hit his head on a rock again. That would enhance my reputation as Mr. Irresponsibility, wouldn't it?*

"Careful," he winced when Ben's shoes skidded a bit getting out of the car.

Ben grinned at him, steadied himself, shot him a thumb's-up, and gingerly made it to the safety of the entrance.

Crazy Gunther's was not crowded, being between breakfast and lunch rushes. They sat at a booth and the waitress brought water and menus right away. Ben ordered orange juice and hot chocolate. Tom asked for coffee. Out of habit, he took an extra second to appraise the server's legs, hips, and chest. He guessed she was in her mid-thirties, plain-looking and small-breasted, but with smooth arms and calves. There was a flirtatious tilt to her mouth. She noticed him noticing her and held his eyes for an extra second.

"Cream and sugar?" she said with a drowsy half-smile.

"No, no thanks. Just black."

"You got it, sweetie. Be back in a sec for your order."

When she was out of earshot, Ben leaned over the table and said, "She likes you, Tom."

"Mm. You think so?"

"Oh yeah. Everybody likes you. Especially women."

"Is that a fact?" Tom said with a forced smile. Ben's syntax sounded memorized, as if he was parroting something he'd heard. "Well, what can I say, Ben? Rob got the brains and the know-how, you got all the charm, and I was left with the good looks."

"Vi says you're a womanizer." Ben stared benignly out from his pale eyes. "She calls you a pussy hound and, and a scoundrel."

"Violet's a bitter, middle-aged woman, Ben," Tom laughed. "She say anything else?"

Ben opened his mouth to continue, but at that moment the waitress returned. She hovered. "You boys decide yet?"

The question was for them both, but her eyes were locked onto Tom's. Tom heaved an inward sigh, wished he weren't so fluent in the encryptions and semaphores of sex, nudged himself to check in with Donna when he got back to the house.

Oblivious, Ben ordered a meat-lovers' skillet breakfast with home fries slathered in onions and green peppers, plus a side of blueberry pancakes drowned in maple syrup, topped with whipped cream. Tom didn't know whether to lecture him on the dangers of heart disease, or to tell Ben he was his new hero.

"How 'bout you, hon? See anything you like?"

A younger version of Tom would have leaped at the suggestive bone she'd thrown him. No doubt he would have made a glib response, "Yeah, but it's not on the menu" or, more directly, "I'm hungry, but I can wait to eat till you're off shift." Together he and she would traipse back to his apartment or her trailer where they'd bump uglies all afternoon long.

"The good old days," Clifton called them, when fucking your brains out with a friendly girl was the ultimate goal. It was the measure of a fine way to pass the hours, numb the senses and avoid thinking seriously about your future.

"Hon? I'd love to stand here all day with you, but my boss is mad-dogging me, y'know?"

She cocked her head toward a glowering twerp standing behind the cash register. Her boss looked all of fourteen years old. In his too-large white shirt, clip-on tie, and ill-fitting trousers, his attempt to look menacing was hilarious. Tom gave a short laugh, and the waitress graced him with an impatient, give-me-a-break-mister, look.

"Sorry," Tom said, holding his hands up. "More black coffee, please, and, um, maybe some rye toast? No butter, though, just leave it dry."

She regarded him up, down, and sideways, nodding slowly. "Okay," she drawled with a knowing grin. "Somebody had a rough night, huh?"

"Something like that."

Her grin became sympathetic, downright sisterly. When she reached down to collect their menus, Tom spotted her wedding band. She noticed him noticing and gave him a sheepish grin Tom recognized as telegraphing, "Yes, I'm married, but I'm not obsessed about it."

"I didn't know you were feeling so bad," Ben commented after she'd gone.

"Nothing major. I was out late last night with Cliff. Had a little too much to drink."

Ben nodded. "Clifton's a good guy."

"Yes he is. Now let's talk about you."

The café was noisy with the din of background chatter and bad Christmas Muzak. Just then, a grating, smooth jazz version of "Little Drummer Boy" piped in and Tom winced. "How's work? Rob tells me you really like it at Maggiores."

"It's okay. I do the place settings and clean up and help wherever they need me. I like it. I like the people I work with. Well, most of them." His face darkened. "There's this one guy. A cook. I don't like him."

"What do you mean? Does he bother you?"

"He bothers everyone. He's an unhappy person, I guess. That's what Cynthia says. He's unhappy, so everyone around him has to be unhappy, too."

"And Cynthia is…"

"She's a waitress. She's really nice. So's everybody else, except for Phillip."

"Phillip's the asshole?"

"Yes." Ben paused as the waitress returned with their drinks. To Tom's relief, this time she didn't linger over them. "I don't know what to do about this guy. Rob says it's all part of learning to live in the community again. He says we all have to learn to deal with jerks. He says if you have to work with a jackass, you have to find a way to make it click."

"That's good advice. So what do you want to do about this Phillip character?"

"I want to punch his face in," Ben said with no change in inflection. "I want to hit him until he stops making fun of me. I want to hurt him bad. But Rob says I can't do that. He says that'll only get me in trouble."

"Rob's right, Ben."

"He says if I do anything stupid like that, I'll lose my job and my apartment. I'll have to go to a board-and-care and be monitored around the clock. I might have to take more medication and be all drugged up all the time. Rob says I might even go to jail if I hit anyone else."

Evidently, Rob learned one of Henry's lessons well. *In order to ensure compliance, paint a doomsday scenario and scare your man into behaving.* "What are you going to do?"

"I'm going to eat my breakfast," Ben said, perfectly deadpan.

Tom saw the server returning with the toast and Ben's meal. She also plunked down bottles of ketchup and Tabasco sauce.

"Anything else for you boys right now?"

"Thanks," Tom said without making eye contact. "We're good."

She loitered by their table for a split second, then scampered off as a party of eight entered.

"Place is filling up," Tom noted. "So, Ben. What are you doing, besides working?"

"I'm on a bowling team. I swim down at the college. Mm, taking care of Mr. Whiskers, of course."

Unconsciously, Tom massaged his injured hand.

"I listen to my music, all the good oldies. And I'm looking for a nice church. So far, I haven't found one I like." He raised a forkful of eggs to his lips, hesitated, and went on. "Some of them are just too big. I feel lost in them. There was a couple where I didn't understand what was going on. In one, the preacher talked about President Clinton and sin, instead of God. Another one, they kept bugging me to go on a retreat, volunteer for a car wash, or join their softball team. I didn't want all that. I just want to go on Sunday and be close to God."

"You always had that need, Ben. You were the only one in our family who seemed to have that in you. You must've been fourteen, fifteen when you started hauling around a Bible. We had no idea where that came from, but you were serious about it. You had a million questions, even as a kid. Do you remember?"

"I remember thinking it was the only thing that helped me make sense of the world. I remember wondering why Mom and Dad never introduced us to religion. And I wanted to be a minister." He met Tom's eyes. "At one time, I wanted to have my own church and spread the Word. I remember when you started dating Vi…"

"Whoa, you can remember that?" Tom asked. "Rob said the accident wiped out most of your memory."

"Vi was the only one who understood me. She would talk about God's plan, the universe, good and evil. Man's sinful nature. Free will. Staying humble. She was the only one who took any time with me. She treated me seriously." He stopped to drink some juice and to collect his thoughts. "She was your girlfriend, Tom. What happened? How come she married Rob?"

Tom fingered his toast, which was charred and inedible. It was hard to believe the kitchen hadn't burnt it on purpose, maybe upon the urging of a certain mean-spirited waitress. He downed the coffee, which was marginally safer.

"Ben, I remember being glad you and Vi liked each other right away. That was important to her, to be accepted by you and Mom right from the beginning. You're asking some good questions and I'm afraid I don't have all the answers. Vi and I broke up because I was selfish and self-centered. I wish I didn't have to face that, but it's true. Also, we were young. We were really two different people, and it took us six or seven years to find that out. How much can you remember?"

"Not much," Ben replied. "There's high school, and maybe a little past then. And the last few years."

"In between?"

Ben shrugged and developed a keen interest in his plate.

Tom said, "Dad wanted to take me under his wing and teach me the business. Just like he wanted to teach Rob and you. Except I couldn't imagine a worse fate than staying in Greenstone and being chained to an office every day, nine-to-five. Might as well shackle me to a dungeon wall and leave me there to rot. I wanted to get the hell out as soon as I was through with college. Vi didn't agree. She wasn't siding with Dad, but she saw the firm as being an excellent career opportunity. Security and comfort for the future, all that happy sappy crappy. She wanted to get married, have a big church wedding. I just couldn't see it. It was a pretty awful time. Are you sure you don't remember any of it?"

Ben shook his head. He had already demolished half his skillet breakfast and was digging in on the pancakes. Tom shook his head in admiration and continued.

"It probably wouldn't have worked out with us, anyhow. I was too restless for her. I wanted to tell jokes, entertain people and make them think at the same time, travel the country. And get paid for it," he laughed. "I had an idea for a documentary, *This Hard Life.* Y'know, my claim to fame? Ha. I was so sick of Greenstone. It just felt so small town, so narrow-minded and limited. Also the winters sucked out loud. I'd start freezing in September and couldn't warm up until May." He took another slug of the battery acid coffee and was careful with his next words. "Vi said religion didn't matter, that it wouldn't come between us, but I could tell it was going to be a sore point for years to come. Her faith is so important to her, and I respect that, even envy that. But it wasn't in me. I started seeing other girls, just for shits and grins. Naturally it didn't take long for Vi to catch on. Eventually she got sick of playing second fiddle to my sex drive. Can't say I blamed her." More black coffee. "Toward the end, I think she may have been seeing someone of her own."

Silence lay between them for long seconds. Finally, Ben said, "I started to say something before. About my memory."

"Yeah?"

"I think it's coming back. I mean, some of it, anyway."

Tom made a half-hearted attempt to nibble some toast, but it was like chewing charred drywall. He searched his brother's face "What do you mean?"

Ben frowned and finished off his potatoes before answering. "I'm starting to remember pieces of things, Tom. Nothing definite. Nothing that makes any sense, either. I can't put any of it together. Not yet, anyway. But I'm remembering…stuff."

"Like what, Ben?"

Twilight, and blue slate all around. Green ice cracking. A wind that was not a wind. Awareness, not-awareness, then awareness. Wood beams, stone benches. The metallic wash of clouds above. Tornadoes of ash, the sickening undulation of the hills, a terrible vertigo.

The vortex of voices. No, no, no, no, no.

Aloud, Ben said, "Stuff about the shelter, I think. It's all mixed up in my head, though. It comes at me pretty fast and jumbled. It's hard to fit any of it together…"

"The shelter?" Tom prodded.

Green ice cracking. Black snow and liquid music.

"Ben?"

Ben ran a hand across his mouth, rubbed his jaw. "Yeah. Like from when we scattered Dad's ashes up there. I can see everybody's face and tell how everyone was feeling. Mom was so sad, but it was like she knew everything was going to be okay. Rob looked terrible when the ashes fell into a pile instead of flying away. It wasn't his fault. The wind just quit blowing. I could see he felt bad, though. Tom, you were there, too. You looked like you couldn't wait until everything was over, then you could leave again…"

"Ben?" Tom was frowning.

"Yeah?"

"You can't remember all that. You weren't there." Ben's expression remained flat. Tom said, "You didn't come home for Dad's funeral, bro. Maybe you've heard the story so many times, you can visualize everything. Or somehow it's become part of your dreams."

An animal howling. A wind that was not a wind. Crickets and cicadas and long spaces between sounds. Ben shook his head vigorously. "No. I was there."

"But…" Tom stopped himself.

No sense in forcing an argument, he thought. Ben strongly believed he'd been at the shelter when their father's ashes had been strewn. Therefore, in his own mind, maybe that became his reality. Nothing Tom said would shake his conviction. So, was this part of the head injury? Internalizing family stories, projecting and inserting himself into them, crafting a fixed delusion? Curious how Ben could live independently with such a skewed sense of the true facts.

"Tom, will you tell me something?"

"If I can, sure."

"Why don't you believe in God?"

This caught Tom off-guard. His response was clipped. "I don't have any reason to believe in God. I think it's superstitious bullshit. Maybe a better question is, why do *you* believe? Especially you, who was every reason to doubt?"

Ben's gaze remained steady. "You shouldn't answer a question with another question," he said quietly.

Tom noted with interest that a new firmness had crept into his brother's voice, a steely tone which hadn't been there before.

"I wish I did believe in God," he said, measuring his words. "I envy you your faith, Ben, I really do. I just don't have it in me. You know, I believe everyone has to find his own personal god. I hike, I read poetry, I try to connect with people on a human level whenever I can. That's my religion, Ben. Life is an amazing gift, and I revere it in my own way. I'll even concede there may be some guiding universal force or intelligence behind the workings of the world, some super-principle of physics we can only guess at. I won't call it God, though. And I can't worship a so-called superior being. If that makes me rebellious or childish, then so be it. I think you have to be a little desperate to buy into the story of an invisible all-powerful king in the clouds. Desperate, or crazy."

He grinned, hoping to take some of the sting out of his rant.

Ben stared philosophically into his hot chocolate. He wore a little smile of his own suggesting he had a wonderful secret to tell, but that his words were about to land on deaf ears. "It sounds prideful to me," he offered. "It sounds like your rational mind is so blind it refuses to yield even the possibility of divinity. Your mind is so stuffed with reason that it's lost its capacity to feel humbleness. Tom, we're all of us His children. There is no shame in kneeling before Our Father, in acknowledging His greatness. Is that so hard for you to accept?"

His eyes were suddenly bright, his smile wide, and Tom at once recognized the expression. This was Ben in his twenties, before the head injury.

"To all things, there is a purpose, Tom," Ben continued. "Fortune and treasure, as well as war and hunger. Children dying. Charmed lives. All of it, part of the great tapestry."

"Your accident," Tom said harshly. "It's called an accident for a reason. It's random, Ben. There is no larger meaning to it. You were in the wrong place at the wrong time and you stepped into some shit. What's the purpose there? What's the celestial message? Why were you hurt? Why you? The answer is, there is no 'why.' It was just a stupid accident."

Now Ben had the beatific look of a gentle man of wisdom,

maddeningly serene and patient. "I've thought often about my fate, Tom. Naturally I've wondered as to my role in God's ultimate plan." His smile faded a bit, became slightly crooked. "I have to confess, I don't know why me. I don't know how it came that I slipped on that patch of ice and lost my balance. I don't know why my head hit a particular rock, or why that blow affected the specific areas of my brain that it did. I can't begin to fathom why Our Lord has orchestrated events in this fashion, or what purpose it serves to have me disabled, to lose my memories. I'm not sure it's even intended for me to understand. The predator has no idea why it hunts. It just does. The rocks don't know why they exist. They just do." He shook his head and pushed away his plate. "No, I only wonder because I'm human and can ask myself the 'why' and 'how' of things. In the end, those questions don't matter. Those questions come from pride and ego. They need to be placed aside to get to the truth. What's important is it's all part of the master plan, and we all have our part to play. My body and mind serve His higher purpose. That's all I need to know. It's the only explanation that makes sense to me."

"Ben," Tom said quietly, studying his brother's face. "Do you hear yourself?"

"Yes, of course."

"You're talking like you did when you were younger. Before your accident."

Tom leaned back in his chair, trying to collect his thoughts. Around him, Gunther's was filling up, the early lunch crowd barreling in, noisy and hungry. He grew conscious that a loop of Christmas standards had replaced the muzak and was now quietly playing in the background.

"Your vocabulary, the way you're building an argument... We used to debate like this all the time. Over beers, mostly. Rob's never mentioned this before, that you can..." *Can what?* he thought. *Can talk intelligently, and not in the stilted and childlike sentences of the mentally impaired?* Tom struggled to gather his focus while Burl Ives was exhorting him to have a holly jolly Christmas. "How often does this happen, Ben? Are you even aware of the difference?"

Ben stared blankly at him. "You're making it sound like I'm two people. I don't understand what you're asking me. Are you just trying to change the subject?"

"No, no, not at all."

It struck Tom then. Ben's eyes and expression were those of a mature forty-year-old man. The confused boy sitting across the table from him just a few minutes ago was gone. "Ben, let's rewind a bit. Tell me again what you can remember about the shelter."

"Why? You told me I wasn't there for Dad's services, so I guess it must've been my crazy imagination, right? You think because I've got a head injury that..."

"Forget all that for now," Tom snapped. "Just tell me again. I'm listening this time."

Ben took a deliberate moment to finish his chocolate and carve out a hunk of pancake. He eyed his brother as he chewed, and Tom saw wariness there but also the dawning gleam of something else. It was as if Ben was seeing himself new through his brother's eyes, and the image was not what he'd expected.

"You said I wasn't there," he pouted, and for a moment Tom thought he'd clam up, or revert to his simple state. Soon, though, Ben put down his fork and shut his eyes. "I can see all of you, standing around by the shelter wall. Rob's holding a box covered in silver foil. Dad's ashes are inside. Rob looks really nervous, like he gets when he wants to make sure things go exactly right. Vi's next to him, and she keeps touching his arm lightly. Trying to reassure him, I think, trying to keep him calm. You're off to one side, over by the shelter itself, standing apart from them. You have one foot up on a stone bench and you're looking up at the wood crossbeams, kind of lost in your own thoughts. Mom's near Rob and Vi, and she's whispering something to Vi. There's some kind of music being played, but I can't tell what it is or where it's from." Ben's face tightened as he tried to retrieve the memory, then relaxed when he let it loose. "Rob calls you over, but you don't hear him. Or else you're ignoring him. Then Vi says, 'It's time,' and you respond to her and make your way over to them. Then all of you join hands and form a little half-circle. Rob leads the family in saying a prayer."

Tom leaned forward on the table and tented his fingers. "Where are you, Ben?"

"I'm not there," Ben said, his eyes still closed. "I mean, I'm not there at the shelter with you all. I'm off in the distance somewhere, being quiet. Observing."

"You mean you're there in spirit?"

To Tom's surprise, Ben's eyes flew open and he broke out laughing. "No, not in spirit," he chuckled. "I mean physically. I'm watching all of you. I'm about a hundred yards off, uphill. Kneeling behind a stand of trees." He sobered, then corrected himself. "I'm *hiding* behind a stand of trees."

"Excuse me?"

Ben's body gave a little shiver. "I'm uphill from you, and I'm hiding behind some trees. I don't want you to know I'm there."

Tom knitted his forehead. "What else do you remember about that day?"

"I remember Rob trying to toss the ashes in the air to catch the wind. The sky was wild and most of the time there was a brisk wind. I tensed up against the trunk of an old pine, expecting to see a cloud of ashes carried down the slope, just as Rob intended. Then, without warning, the air turned absolutely still. The ashes spilled out of the box and fell straight to the ground. Rob was so embarrassed. The rest of you looked shocked at first. You began buzzing about what to do. You were trying to help, but it just made things worse for Rob. I felt awful for him."

Tom wanted to ask a million questions, but he was afraid of breaking the spell. He held his tongue, hoping Ben was like most people who couldn't stand silence, and would keep talking.

He did. "I remember thinking Dad's ashes looked like black snow falling. They lay on the ground, on the blue slate all around. You looked disgusted, Tom. And it was heartbreaking watching Mom. I hadn't seen her for years, so she'd aged anyway, but the scene with the ashes was like a kick in the stomach for her. I wanted to run down the hill and throw my arms around her. Why didn't you do that, Tom? Mom needed your support, and you stood there like a statue, like you were waiting for a bus that was running late."

Without guilt, Tom remembered all too well his irritation with Rob for his ineptitude, with Vi for her prima donna act, with Henry for dying, with the gray mound of ashes laying there on the ground, with himself for being back in fucking Colorado, with all of it. Unfairly, he'd even resented his poor mother, who'd just lost her husband of forty-three years. Come on, though, theirs hadn't been a romance for the ages anyhow. You couldn't even say they'd been the best of friends. Truthfully, it had become a pure business arrangement. Henry gained the appearance of respectability through his marriage, Rachel benefited with lifetime financial security. Had Scrooge shed a single tear when Marley passed on? No doubt Rachel had needed someone to hold her and prop her up. At the time, Tom's thought was to let Rob handle it. After all, he'd been running the goddamned show, hadn't he?

Now his irritability was amplified by Mel Torme singing about some turkey and some mistletoe. Ben was shooting him accusatory looks across the table, which didn't sit well with Tom. His voice was cold when he said, "So you saw everything, Ben? You saw everything and did nothing?" Much to his surprise, Tom realized he'd stopped questioning and had bought into Ben's story. *My God*, he thought. *It wasn't a dream or a delusion. He really had been there.* "What were you doing, anyway? Nobody knew you were back in town. Why were you hiding from us?"

Ben blinked as if he'd been slapped. A cloudiness filmed his eyes. He looked like a man emerging from a trance. He tried to refocus his gaze on Tom and said dully, "I don't know. I can't remember that part."

"Oh, you don't know. That part you can't seem to recollect," Tom said acidly. "So let me try to recap this for you. We, your family, hadn't heard from you in years. Our father had just died. We couldn't contact you, had no clue where you were living or what you were doing. Mom was devastated thinking you wouldn't know H.D. had croaked."

Tom tried to remind himself this wasn't Rob or Vi he was addressing. This was his baby brother with his diminished faculties. He knew he should ease off some, should spare Ben the full force of his sarcasm. He couldn't mitigate his anger, though. He wasn't in the mood to exercise his better judgment. Instead of pulling back he gave his emotions free rein.

"Apparently, you didn't give a flying fuck about what any of us thought, did you? You snuck back into Greenstone and you skulked around us on the day of our father's funeral. You hid from us, Ben. What was that all about? Why wouldn't you want us to know you were back?"

"I don't know," Ben repeated helplessly. "I told you, I can't remember that part. Everybody tells me that I disappeared for years, but that's all blank for me. The only thing I know for sure is it has something to do with Vi."

"Vi?"

"Yeah. I have a strong feeling about her being involved. What could that mean, Tom? You know her as well as any of us. What does she have to do with anything? What does she have to do with me?"

Tom considered that life was never as mundane or uncomplicated as it seemed on its surface. You never could predict when your world would be turned upside-down, or when what you thought you knew for certain would explode and reconstitute in the most unlikely form. Here, for instance, in Crazy Gunther's, over pancakes and bad coffee, with your kid brother dialing in, then tuning out on his own disrupted memories, telling you a version of an event you thought you knew inside-out. The image of Ben concealed from the family behind a screen of pine trees was mysterious, strange, unexplainable.

Yet, what right did Tom have to pry? He had no room to talk. He himself had cut loose from Greenstone years before and rarely looked back. Since moving to Florida, he'd made marginal efforts at communication with the family, but otherwise his and Ben's situations were similar.

Except Tom articulated his every grievance and motivation, while Ben had disappeared in secrecy, in silence.

Besides, the Demeters knew Tom was living in the Sunshine State, but had no clue as to Ben's whereabouts. They didn't even know if he was dead or alive.

Also, by the way, what did Ben think Vi had to do with anything?

"There was a wind, then the wind stopped," Ben murmured. "Vi said, you're not aware, but then there was awareness, and then not-awareness."

"Ben. Hey, Ben."

"Gee," Ben chanted lowly, singing along with Perry Como, "the traffic is terrific."

It was a peculiar sight watching the transformation, witnessing the dimmer switch turned down and the light slowly fade from Ben's eyes. Tom felt his anger ebb as his brother's features slackened, losing the animation which had been there only minutes before. His face again became that of a simple man with few worries and fewer memories. Was he truly a split personality, or was this labile display a sign of healing, of Ben gradually returning to himself? At the moment, Tom decided on two matters. First, he wasn't going to tell the rest of the family about Ben's Jekyll-and-Hyde act. Second, he was chagrined to admit he liked this damaged version of his brother better than his healthier, but more pious, former self.

"Are you almost finished?" Tom asked. "Would you like dessert before we go? Something light, maybe, like a giant slab of lemon meringue pie and a glob of vanilla ice cream on the side?"

Ben laughed. "No. I'm full."

"You still want to hit Sweet Lou's before heading back to the house?"

"You bet. Let's go."

It was as if nothing out of the ordinary had occurred. Tom paid up front, just as Der Bingle was warming up to croon a faux hepcat rendition of "Rudolph." As they exited, their waitress called from behind the counter, "So long, boys. Come back any time. Hey, how was your toast?"

"About as good as your tip," Tom shot back, and had the satisfaction of seeing her grin vanish. He'd taken a page out of Henry's book by leaving her a single nickel for poor service. *Petty,* he admitted to himself. *Satisfying, though.*

Sweet Lou's Records & Tapes had been an institution in Greenstone since forever and a day. It was a two-story brick building painted in greens and yellows, situated in the city's artsy foothills district. Like many of the older structures in town, it boasted a whole history as some other function. In Lou's case, it was constructed back in the early 1920's as a tack and feed store. The building held an ancient musty smell, which Tom attributed to the lingering body odor of sweaty, old-time Colorado cowpokes.

However, since he'd been a kid, Sweet Lou's was the best place outside of Denver to search for and purchase LPs. The store was crammed full of crates and bins and bookshelves loaded with old records, including a broad selection of 78's and 45's. Lou's also stocked used and new hard-to-find CDs, cassette tapes, music books, t-shirts, posters, and numerous other memorabilia. There was a beat-up Mr. Coffee and home-baked oatmeal raisin cookies for the customers. A dog on its last legs named Humphrey had the run of the place. For the tactile consumer who enjoyed browsing at a leisurely pace, it was vinyl nirvana. Tom knew its days were numbered. Real estate was getting too valuable and it was only a matter of time before the big box stores would infiltrate even this funky neighborhood. He was glad he wouldn't be around to see its demise, probably sometime within the next decade.

There was no actual Lou presiding over business. If he'd ever existed, he'd boogaloo'd off to the Great Jam Session in the Sky long ago. The sole clerk was a bookish and sleepy-eyed little hobbit whose nametag identified him as JERRY. Jerry was the kind of useful music nerd who couldn't tie his shoes without supervision but could readily name the original lead guitarist for Captain Beefheart, or explain in detail the offbeat time signatures employed by Dave Brubeck's quartet.

Tom didn't require access to Jerry's vast and arcane body of knowledge. He only needed to ask for directions to the used punk section, which turned out to be upstairs. Ben remained on the ground floor, hunting down vintage recordings of Eddie Cochran, Carl Perkins, Link Wray, Little Richard, Duane Eddy. It was music born right around the time he himself came into the world.

Chapter Seventeen

Rob reflected that the Honorable Bradley Spinwell, six-times elected mayor of Greenstone, was one of the best people persons he'd ever known. The mayor stood gripping the podium at Helm's Mortuary. With his cowboy boots, conservative dark blue suit, bolo tie, and silver hair, he looked every inch the prototype for the rugged Midwestern politician.

Spinwell had been a land developer before entering the public service arena and he was foursquare for Greenstone's progress, particularly the types of progress aimed at expanding the tax base and perhaps lining his own double-dipping pockets. Some claimed he had designs on the local congressional seat and lusted to represent Greenstone in Washington, D.C. Rob's own opinion was it was all idle talk and didn't regard the mayor as a serious rival. Hizzoner had it pretty good here. Why move to the House and start over again as low man on the totem pole?

Mayor Spinwell had a deep voice and, in a room this size, didn't require the microphone provided. He'd been invited to sing the praises of the late lamented Rachel Demeter, Greenstone icon, widow of Henry Demeter, mother of the Foothill Investment Service's president, social and political gadfly, and do-gooding volunteer extraordinaire. While he was first and foremost an astute businessman, Spinwell also possessed the excellent instincts of the populist huckster. Promise the people what they wanted, within reason and without cutting into any potential profit to be made. The mayor's abiding creed was 'give them a hell of a show'. When the electorate asked for new parks and upper echelon retail stores, free summer concerts as well as a new youth library, well that's what they got. No quibbling and no questions asked. If the people went apeshit at a city council meeting over the number of homeless people lollygagging downtown and sleeping in bus shelters, a strict ordinance outlawing loitering would be swiftly passed and vigorously enforced. If a group of leading citizens cajoled him into scheduling a cameo at Helm's Mortuary to say nice things about the recently deceased and much-admired Mrs. Demeter, why then, that seemed a simple enough request to accommodate. It was well worth the time invested for the goodwill his appearance would generate.

The rest of the eulogizing panel included the president of the community college, the nondenominational pastor of Greenstone's largest food bank and resource center, the director of the regional art museum, an officer from the Friends of the Library, the owner of several local car dealerships who also happened to be one of the area's biggest philanthropists, a realtor who'd been buddy-buddy with Henry Demeter, a board member from the country club, and other notables. Interspersed among the VIPs would be Rachel's friends and neighbors.

The room was medium-sized and bare except for the podium. About a hundred thinly-padded metal folding chairs were set out and there was a forest of flowers on display. People were asked to make donations to the American Cancer Society in lieu of the flowers, but many of Rachel's well-heeled friends and colleagues sprung for both.

Violet sat front and center, Tom on one side of her, Ben on the other. Rob sat facing them, near the podium and next to the speakers. Automatically, he scanned the crowd for familiar faces. Curiously, he didn't see their friend Clifton seated anywhere. *Odd,* he thought, *but maybe he's just running a little late.*

The service was standing room only. The plain but elegant blue urn containing Rachel's remains was placed on a small table in front of the podium, along with a photo of Rachel from her late thirties or early forties. In it, she struck a regal pose, Queen Rachel.

Tom made the family's opening remarks. As usual, he struck the proper tone for the occasion. He was solemn, but also gently humorous as well as appreciative to everyone who turned out to celebrate his mother's life. When Tom finished, Rob took his place at the podium and introduced Mayor Spinwell.

The Mayor cleared his throat and began. "Citizens, we gather today to honor the memory of one of Greenstone's finest and most ubiquitous citizens, the great Rachel Demeter."

"Ubiquitous, yet," Tom whispered to Vi.

She raised her eyebrows at him, aiming for playful. "We're in for a long haul," she whispered back.

Was it Tom's imagination, or did she seem a bit frayed at the edges? He knew Violet was a master at disguising her emotions. Now though, some inner disturbance appeared to seep through her social mask. Tom knew if he asked her what was wrong, she'd laugh and brush him off with, "Nothing, silly" or "Duh. It's a funeral, right?" or some other flip response. However, her aura didn't lie. She wasn't vibrating in her chair, nothing so obvious, but Tom felt her uneasiness all the same.

It would indeed be a lengthy ceremony. By its conclusion, there'd be thousands of kind words of remembrance, people would be squirming uncomfortably in the metal chairs, and not a single soul would mention that Rachel Demeter perished due to a deliberate overdose of prescription drugs. That would be indelicate, not at all in good taste. In accordance, neither Rachel's obituary nor her death certificate would reveal her final act of independence. Afterward, few would pause to reflect on the rumors of her taking her own life.

~ * ~

Except for Ben. The idea of his mother committing suicide troubled him profoundly. He was hard-pressed to explain why. He fingered his rosary, mouthed a "Hail Mary" to himself, asked God for guidance, understanding and mercy.

He found himself studying Vi's profile as if she were the Rosetta Stone to all his hundred thousand questions and quandaries. Her face always struck him as a mixture of appetite and innocence. He knew, in his heart of hearts, that somehow she was the key to all his missing years. *How could that be?* he wondered, and time after time came up empty for answers. His brother's wife. His other brother's former girlfriend. The favored daughter Rachel never had. A poison thorn in Henry's side.

Why did everything revolve around Violet?

The earlier conversation with Tom was still fresh in Ben's mind, and it acted like a twig stirring up sediment in a shallow creek. Cloudy memories swirled. He retreated into himself until the mayor's words sounded far-off and muffled.

With a pang, Ben summoned up an old picture of Vi with Tom, the older brother he most idolized. They were young, just starting out in life and discovering each other. Ben was pleased at their happiness but seeing them together also scooped out a hollow place in his chest. He watched how Vi touched Tom when they danced together, the way Tom looked straight into her eyes when she laughed at one of his jokes. Ben was all of fourteen years old, and he was sure he would never meet a girl as full of life as Vi. There'd be times when he'd have a few precious moments alone with her, like when Tom was on the phone with a school friend or playing basketball while Ben and Vi watched from the bleachers. Those were times when Ben absolutely came alive, feeling almost immortal in her company.

They'd talk freely about the Demeters, Rachel's kindness and Henry's iron-fisted tyranny. Vi wondered how they could stand one another, how they'd met, why they'd married. "They were probably in love," Ben said. "Oh, love," Vi laughed. Wide-eyed, she added, "Can you picture them having sex? I mean, really." Ben had been shocked because (a) they were his parents, and (b) it was unpleasant to imagine H.D., an old man at forty-five, naked and convulsing on top of the forever young Rachel. Ben changed topics then, talked about world affairs or the banality of politics. Most of the time, though, they'd talk and connect most intimately over God.

Vi came from God-fearing stock. While her faith had been sorely tested by her parents' odd beliefs and odder behaviors, it was burned into her. Her teenaged self stayed busy synthesizing a new religion out of the old, one which fit well with her modern views and experiences.

Ben, however, came to God from out of a spiritual vacuum. The Demeters attended church, but even as a boy Ben realized it was a social rite for Henry, not an act of piety. Rachel seemed indifferent to going, bored by any talk of dry doctrine or even the Bible. His brothers approached the church by two different paths, neither of which was favorable. Rob was tolerant, neither for nor against any creed, dumbly accepting religion as a simple fact of existence, like a mountain, or an accepted way of "doing things as they've always been done," like voting Republican. Tom, on the other hand, openly mocked the church, although in a strange way he seemed to take it much more seriously than Rob.

"You're a seeker, Ben," Vi told him once, which struck him as a true statement. Since the age of eleven, it seemed he'd been on his own quest to decode and comprehend the world on his own terms. To Ben, the only unifying principle appeared to be God. God was the sole explanation which made his life and the lives of others coherent and meaningful. God tied together the physical and moral universes. Rob always treated Ben with a distant, brotherly respect, but avoided engaging him in theological debates. Rob also had a mind confining his interests to worldly concerns, and his brain just couldn't grasp the notion of a higher power. Tom gently chided Ben's earnestness and was glad to play Devil's advocate in their discussions.

Only Vi spent time nurturing and reinforcing his beliefs. She talked with him about the Bible, the Ten Commandments, Jesus Christ, the dangers of moral relativism, the holy purpose of serving Him before self, the rewards of accepting deferred glory over the pleasure principle. On those occasions when they talked long into the night, out on the Demeter's back porch or in their living room, Rob would politely excuse himself to engage in work he'd brought home. If Tom were present, he'd hang in for a while to play the role of agnostic sparring partner, but eventually extricated himself from the conversation to go watch sports.

~ * ~

Tom now leaned back in his creaky chair, Vi's thigh pressed against his, and thought about his brothers. Another of H.D.'s favorite sayings came to him. "A camel is a horse designed by a committee." He mused on how much the sentiment applied to his family. Rachel and Henry had been complete temperamental opposites, and all three boys turned out unique, as if each had been adopted from a different

176

dysfunctional family.

If there was a God, He might have amused himself by assembling the Demeters willy-nilly, without regard for compatibility, cherry-picking them from random gene pools. It made Tom examine, for perhaps the ten thousandth time in his adult life, the curious concept of family. He'd never bought into the lie that 'blood was thicker'. Since leaving Colorado, he'd carefully recruited and cultivated an extended family of his own choosing. It struck him that he'd never thought of Rob and Ben as his true kin. They'd gotten along all right as youngsters. "Made it out alive," as Tom liked to say. However, they may as well have been a trio of strangers growing up in the same house with their well-intentioned but basically aloof adult guardians. Tom would add, with a wry grin, "Or what the rest of the world calls 'parents'."

Vi shifted in her seat. Tom reflected on how the three Demeter sons orbited her in one way or another this past quarter-century. Her attitudes and opinions about how crucial it was to subscribe to Christian tenets in these confused modern times should have painted her as a thoroughly unlikable hypocrite.

In his experience, she'd been pious and promiscuous, devout and devious, sacred and scurrilous. She was also unapologetic about her contrary behaviors without coming across as arrogant. She fully expected to be taken for who she was, dualities and inconsistencies included, always authentically Violet. It could truly be said she walked comfortably in her own skin, and her unquestioning self-assurance was finally what had prompted Tom to back away from their relationship. Her talk of a fallen world seemed to excuse or explain away all bad behavior and evil ways, so long as you bet the house on Jesus Christ, the only begotten son of God. Vi saw herself as a poor sinner, too impulsive for her own good, prone to temptation. Tom could see her as a candidate for divine forgiveness. He wondered, though, about the cold-blooded murderer who kills as a young man, then 'finds God' when he's old and imprisoned?

"There are no atheists in foxholes or jails, are there?" Tom would argue. "Does that mean there are no guilty men, as long as they have Jesus in their hearts?"

"If a man repents and accepts Jesus, and it's not a sham, then yes, he can be saved," Vi explained serenely.

"Uh-huh. And what about his victims? What's their salvation? Where's their justice?"

Vi did her Mona Lisa impression. "They may or may not have been saved, depending on what they believed at the times of their deaths."

"Yeah, but they were innocent."

"Nobody's innocent, Tom. There can be no presumption of justice for anyone in this sinful world."

"Well, that's fucked up," he told her, effectively ending another of their theological discussions.

He broke up with her despite the gymnastic sex, their more-or-less common ideals, the laughs, the crackling chemistry between them. In the end, he couldn't see himself hitched to a Jesus freak for all eternity. He knew she'd always have her hidden agenda of trying to convert him. To 'perfect' him. She denied it, but how would she feel in ten or fifteen years, stuck till 'death do us part' with an unrepentant heathen? Also, Tom was young. He couldn't know yet that compatibility such as theirs was a rare bird. His expectation was to play the field for a while, eventually finding another girl who was as smart, funny, and in tune with him as Vi. By the time he realized what they'd had was exceptional, the damage was already done and there'd be no going back for them.

"I'll always love you," he told her on their last night together.

He had no idea how true his words would turn out. Her dark eyes filled with tears, her bottom lip trembled slightly. That was all the emotion and all the satisfaction she'd give him. She turned away and walked out of his life, just like in a B-movie.

Shortly afterward, Tom moved to Florida and started over again.

And Vi? He knew she'd found another guy soon after their break-up. A mystery man. Not even Rachel, who knew everything in Greenstone, knew who he was. Later, and without a word to anyone, Vi vanished for a number of years. Just as mysteriously, she then resurfaced at H.D.'s funeral. After which, inexplicably, she'd married Robert.

~ * ~

Now Vi listened to the tributes and accolades for Rachel. She delivered up a silent communiqué of her own. *Oh, Rachel. I wish I'd been a better friend. I'll always be grateful for your generous spirit and your beautiful friendship. Thank you for your sons. Thank you for standing with me against your horrid husband. Thank you for recognizing my sins and for not judging. Thank you for saving my sanity more than once.*

Her mind sleepwalked through the clumsy elegies and fumbling anecdotes, all sounding the same, like the drone of a power saw. Suddenly the image of the church on the hill leaped into her mind. It should have comforted her, this place of peace and devotion. Why then did it materialize in her head like Frankenstein's castle, terrifying under a limitless Western sky, illuminated in bursts of dry lightning? Faith, she knew, *was* frightening. You gripped onto God for dear life, and He squeezed you back so hard He left you breathless and with bruised ribs. One man's ladder was another's stumbling block. Vi acknowledged her sins and accepted she was a sinner. She also knew that, when the Son of God died on His cross, all her sins were absolved. She knew, when her time on Earth was through, her path would lead her Heaven-bound. Yet, she remained dogged by feelings of unworthiness.

Now Grace walked slowly to the podium. The housekeeper's hands trembled and her voice shook as she read from notes on a sheet of loose-leaf paper. She praised Rachel as a kind and generous employer. She revealed that Rachel had once loaned her money for a new car, no questions asked. Grace's eyes shone with tears when she talked about the birthday when Rachel took her to a local dinner theater to take in a production of *Camelot*. The young actors did double-duty as waiters. Sir Lancelot served their table, brought them their chicken Kiev and iced teas, flirted with them and, at Rachel's request, sang a snippet of "If Ever I Should Leave You" *just for them*. After the show, Rachel called over assorted cast members, Lancelot included, to sign Grace's program.

"I'll never forget that," Grace told the mourners. "Those kids, they were so talented. They were thrilled to have Miss Rachel ask for their autographs. And I was thrilled to have them sign. I still have that program. Someday I'll get around to having it framed."

The housekeeper smiled and gazed out at the front row of seats.

"Your mother was so proud of her boys," she declared, turning her head to include Rob. "She was always bragging about you. 'My three big, good-looking sons,' she'd say. 'My joys.'" Fat tears slid down Grace's cheeks. She sniffed and wiped them away with a pink handkerchief. Rob looked on with a mixture of sympathy and impatience. He knew Grace's own adult children had had their troubles. The boy was in jail, the daughter in and out of rehab. "Your mother loved all of you so much. Thank you for letting me speak."

Then, as a final awkward tribute, she hummed a few bars of "If Ever I Should Leave You," her eyes misting, her lips quivering.

At last Grace stepped down, helped to her seat by Violet. Vi patted the housekeeper's big shoulders and gave her a brief hug before sitting. It was Connie Worthington's turn to speak. Connie described herself as one of Rachel's "oldest and dearest friends." They'd known each other since grade school, had grown up together in Greenstone, and remained friends through "thick and thin." Together, they shared stories about boyfriends, marriages, children, illnesses and surgeries, successes and setbacks. Mrs. Worthington positioned herself behind the dais and gave a self-conscious little laugh.

"We all knew Rachel as a super-volunteer, a pillar of the community, a do-gooder extraordinaire. Saint Rachel, right?" A titter swept through the room. "There'll be enough along those lines today. Most of you know I prefer to swim against the flow sometimes. So I decided to talk a little out of school today. Now, for those of you who didn't know her all that well, I'm here to tell you Rachel had an impish side to her. Oh, she kept it hidden from the public eye. But she was a high-spirited old gal. In fact, in her younger days, she had a mean reputation as a scamp and a practical joker."

At this, a look of consternation crossed Robert's face. He frowned up at Connie Worthington. He hated surprises, and he had a sickening premonition this woman was about to throw a wicked curveball into the so-far dignified services. In contrast, Tom leaned forward in his front row seat, his lips stretching into a wide anticipatory grin.

Mrs. Worthington launched into a tale from college days, when apparently, she and Rachel took full advantage of Greenstone's numerous happy hours. On one such afternoon, classes over for the day, the springtime sun warm with no breeze blowing down the canyons, the girls decided to sip margaritas at the outdoor patio of the popular Creekside Inn. The clear, shallow waters of Greenstone Creek ran alongside the restaurant, six or eight feet below patio level. Connie and Rachel were camped out at a small table near the railing so they could watch the lazy current flow. Now and then, inner tube enthusiasts floated by, waving and hooting at the Creekside's patrons. The boys were shirtless, the young women clad in cut-offs and bikini bras. All of them were loud and laughing.

Midway through their second margy, the girls felt as placid and drowsy as a pair of sun-dazed lizards. They were partially sheltered from the sun by a broad and colorful Cinzano umbrella. Connie had been droning on about a handsome basketball player they both knew. Slightly bored, Rachel took to tossing tortilla chips over the railing and into the creek. She liked watching them drift downstream like little boats. When she grew tired of that, she chewed her straw and let her eyes wander over the patio. She regarded the red-and-blue umbrellas. A sudden light came into her eyes.

"Wouldn't it be grand," she asked Connie, "to take one of these umbrellas down to the creek? We could flip it upside down in the water and ride to the very end."

Connie agreed it sounded like great fun indeed. She saw only two drawbacks to Rachel's little fantasy. One, she was uncertain as to how reliable a flotation device the umbrella might be, especially if it was expected to bear both their weights. Two, neither of them owned a Cinzano umbrella.

Rachel shrugged. "We could just take one of these," she suggested reasonably.

"You're not serious. That would be stealing," Connie said, a little shocked by her friend's attitude.

Rachel turned her face to the creek, a small smile playing on her lips. "Oh, we'd give it back," she told Connie. "We'd only be borrowing it for a while."

They both burst out laughing and attributed their giddiness to the alcohol. They ordered another round of margaritas.

Another two weeks passed before they summoned enough courage to execute the heist. Rachel headed straight to the patio while Connie waited below on the narrow banks of the creek. Smiling, Rachel asked the waiter to bring some tapas and a carafe of sangria. He smiled back at the charming girl and left for the kitchen. Once he was gone, the patio was nearly empty. *Good,* she thought, *few witnesses.* It took some doing, but Rachel managed to unscrew the hand-tightened wingnuts at the base of the umbrella stand. Carefully, she wrested the shaft up through the hole in the center of the table, then tilted the umbrella over the railing. From there, it was child's play to let gravity do most of the work and settle the Cinzano into Connie's waiting hands.

Amazing, but the inverted umbrella proved sturdy enough to carry them both down Greenstone Creek. They had to bail water from time to time, and their vessel spun in the slow eddies because they'd forgotten to take along slender tree limbs to use as poles and oars. Otherwise, their trip was without hazard. The girls bobbed along in the amiable silence only good friends can know. Their blue-and-red craft followed the creek's gentle meanders as the afternoon light dappled down through the cottonwood canopy. The banks were lush with cattails, willows, maidenhair fern, columbines. At one bend, the water was a pale gold and sparkly with bubbles from an underground spring. Rachel said it was like floating through champagne. They drifted past a spot where a little lagoon had formed in a swirl of purples, maroons, and deep blues. There were no rapids, just a lazy, even flow to the creek which Rachel called 'slow-pids', which Connie called 'stu-pid'.

In less than an hour, the girls ended their run in a shallow green pond which Rachel noted was "More like a puddle with delusions of grandeur." The Cinzano bumped ashore on a strand of dirt and stones worn smooth, white as milk. The girls whooped. They were wild-haired and slightly sunburnt. Their trousers were soaked to their bottoms. They felt happy and totally free. Slipping on their sandals, they started walking the two or three miles back to Connie's car, parked on a side road around the corner from the Creekside Inn.

"Rachel always said everybody needed to seek out a river every now and then. It was good for the soul, whether or not a person understood why."

"Didn't you return the umbrella?" Vi called out with a laugh.

"Why, hell no," Connie replied. "After that stunt, we didn't dare show our faces at that restaurant ever again."

Connie Worthington stepped down, having significantly lightened the mood in the room. Her homage was followed by another monotone eulogizer, this one the director of a non-profit employing developmentally disabled adults and promoting the teaching of independent living skills to these clients. The man's homage was carefully scripted and of cookie-cutter quality. He reported Rachel had been an energetic and effective organizer of their annual auction, a passionate philanthropist, a down-to-earth community activist, a humble thoroughbred of a human being. Listening to the speaker drone on, Tom thought, *And blah, blah, blah.* He leaned over to whisper to Violet.

"I know this sounds awful, but I'm bored to tears," he confided. "Think I'm going to slip outside for a cigarette."

"Didn't you try quitting years ago?"

"Yeah, I did," he admitted. "Didn't take. I just need a break from all this flattery and ass-kissing. Come on with me, I'll let you gulp down some secondhand smoke."

Vi said thanks, but no thanks. As Tom headed for the door, he felt Rob staring at him. Tom ignored him and walked outside.

The afternoon air was freezing. Tom jammed his hands deep in his jacket pockets and blew out plumes of breath-steam. The mean snap in the air likely meant a storm was on its way. Tom was ready for all this to be over so he could jet his way home to Florida. He didn't want to linger in Greenstone one minute longer than good manners demanded, and he sure as hell didn't want to see the airport snowed in. He missed his own house, his own routine, the warmer climate. Also, he realized with a start, he really missed Donna.

Although he did have to admit that, objectively speaking, it was beautiful here. Had he been more the nostalgic type, he might've recalled a near-idyllic childhood amid Greenstone's rolling streets, the pine wilderness and wonderful hiking trails winding through the foothills, the white serenity of the city after a snowfall. In fact, he did sometimes describe his old hometown as "all Currier and Ives." Because he wasn't a sentimentalist, though, the words came out mocking rather than fondly. Tom would be quick to note that he thought of Greenstone winters as little as possible, and when he did, he mostly recalled the icy roads, slashing winds, dismal gray skies, the dreary months of despair and restlessness.

He took his last few puffs and was about ready to make his way back indoors when the yellow Karmann Ghia pulled into one of the few remaining open spots at the far end of the parking lot. Tom had to laugh as he watched Clifton slowly unpack himself from the toy-like vehicle, noting the big man's wince as he limped his way to the funeral home. Clifton fiddled with his glasses and topcoat, trying to stay warm and seemingly lost in his own thoughts. He didn't notice Tom until he was almost upon him.

Tom grinned broadly. "Well, well, looky here. See what the cat dragged in."

Clifton held up one fat warning finger that signaled, *Don't even think about it, pal.*

Tom nodded. "Better late than never, amigo. If it's any consolation, I'm not feeling real lively myself. Guess neither of us can drink for shit anymore."

"Guess not." Cliff's eyes slid away, and Tom thought he saw a shadow there, something Cliff wasn't saying. Something he might be *hiding,* although that didn't make much sense to Tom.

Clifton growled, "Mind if we skip the small talk and hustle inside? I'm freezing my ass off out here."

"Sure, sure," Tom said, his grin fading.

Weird vibe, he thought. He stubbed out the cigarette and tossed the butt into the coffee can used as an ashtray. "I'm right behind you. Fair warning, these services aren't exactly electrifying."

Clifton grunted, swung open the door, and moved inside. He didn't bother holding the door open for Tom, who caught it before it swung shut and opened it again. *What the hell...?*

~ * ~

Rob spotted Clifton entering and selecting a seat in the last row. The big man squirmed, appearing cramped and ill at ease. That made some sense, the folding chairs were hardly the epitome of luxury. Still, Rob strongly suspected Clifton's discomfiture was based on something more. The big man fidgeted and seemed to go to great lengths to avoid eye contact with Rob. Also, he'd practically *slunk* into the service. He hadn't made any effort to say hello to Vi or Ben, not to mention ignoring Tom who walked in right behind. *Yes, odd,* thought Rob. *Maybe he's just being respectful, doesn't want to call attention to himself. Yet....*

Now that he thought about it, Vi also seemed a little high-strung. She was socially adept enough to feign sober conduct for this occasion, but Rob knew his wife well enough to feel her edgy aura. There was a touch of falseness in her laugh, and when she thought no one was looking, her eyes darkened, turning inward. Across the room, Rob tried to read her thoughts, but failed to zero in on the source of her uneasiness.

He couldn't help but form a nascent suspicion. His wife's out-of-character behavior, Cliff's awkwardness. *Could it be...?*

~ * ~

Meantime, Tom returned to his seat next to Vi. His own thoughts matched his brother's observations. Experience told Tom that Vi was feeling hinky. She may not have wanted to confide what was eating at her, but her body language broadcast her anxiety loud and clear. *Hell, it's like she's sitting on a bed of thorns,* Tom noted.

Now some old biddy he didn't recognize was holding forth at the dais. He stifled a yawn and whispered to Vi, "I miss anything earth-shaking?"

Vi managed a wide social grin. "Listen and learn," she told him coyly.

The speaker looked to be Rachel's age, give or take a few years. She had a pixie face enveloped by a blue-white corona of carefully coiffed hair. Her skin was remarkably free of age-lines and her cheeks heavily rouged. She wore a hesitant smile.

"Some of you know me. My name is Rita Tomlin," she began. "I told Rachel I would never tell this story. In fact, last night I actually prepared a few other remarks. More formal and, well, respectful, I guess you'd say. Then I got to thinking her children deserved to hear something fun and playful and true about their mother. So this story presents a different side of my good and brave friend.

"Most of you know Rachel was fiercely opposed to the ongoing operations at the Flatirons nuclear plant."

Heads nodded all around the room. The plant had been built thirty-five miles east of Greenstone a decade before. Rachel was known to be vehemently anti-nukes, especially when it came to her own backyard. To Henry's chagrin, she was outspoken about her views, bitterly debating anyone who would argue that the plant brought good-paying jobs and clean energy to the Rocky Mountain region.

"It was just a few years ago that she and I signed on to take part in a demonstration out there. You see, we were both veterans of those kinds of protests. We were active in water conservation efforts, preserving the no-kill animal shelter, those sorts of things. We figured this would be old hat for us and go pretty much as advertised. We'd do some marching, hold up some signs, chant our objections, make our points, maybe get interviewed by the local news folks. Then we'd ride home, pour ourselves a glass of wine, and rest our aching feet.

"Well, evidently that wasn't enough for some of the organizers. There was a lull in the event, nothing much happening except we were all standing around and chatting among ourselves outside the perimeter of the facility. Tell you all the truth, things were getting a little dull. Also, we didn't feel like our message was getting through.

"Then one of our leaders gets this bright idea. 'Hey,' he yelled to the thirty or forty of us gathered together. 'Let's take our clothes off and march a couple times around the plant. That'll get their attention.'"

At this, a horrified expression blazed across Rob's face. For a moment, Tom thought his brother was going to leap up, shoo Rita Tomlin away from the podium, and hurriedly thank everybody for coming. As Rob leaned forward and started to stand, he caught sight of Vi. She was shaking her head at him. She beamed him a gentle smile and mouthed,

"It's all right." He cast her a despairing look, but swallowed his panic and remained in his chair.

Mrs. Tomlin continued. "Naturally, I was mortified. All around us, the protesters, mostly young people, started shucking off their shirts and blouses and pulling down their pants at record speed. Noble cause or not, they seemed very eager to show off their beautiful bodies. It was one big excuse for everybody to get naked! Rachel and I exchanged a look and, to my surprise, she burst out laughing. Then she walked over to the leader who'd started the whole mess. Gene, I think his name was. Gene was in the middle of removing his own socks…they were green with a diamond pattern, isn't it funny what sticks in your memory? Anyway, he was startled by Rachel's approach.

"She asked, 'Can I ask you a question, young man?' Gene stopped undressing and gaped at her. 'Sure,' he said. He didn't seem to know where to place his hands.

"Rachel smiled sweetly and looked him dead in the eye and said, 'Do you think it would be appropriate for us to keep our shoes on? The ground's pretty rough around here. I wouldn't want to cut my feet up on these rocks.'

"Well, I couldn't believe my ears, but I wasn't half as shocked as our fearless leader. At first he seemed struck dumb. But after a few seconds, he nodded and said, 'That's a good idea, Rachel. Just the shoes, though.'

"That's all your mother needed to hear."

Mrs. Tomlin addressed Tom, who wore a broad grin and leaned way forward in his chair. He hadn't heard this story before.

Rob, on the other hand, was not grinning. Rob looked like he might have a stroke any minute.

"I don't believe I've ever seen any man or woman get undressed as fast as Rachel. She had her clothes off and folded into a neat pile, bra and panties on top, in less than thirty seconds, I'll bet. Then she slipped her feet back into her sandals and started egging me on to take it all off. I just couldn't. I'm afraid I was way too self-conscious to follow her lead. Today, I regret not being a more courageous friend. Rachel just laughed at me, called me an uptight old lady, and ran off bare-assed to join the others. Goodness, they were a sight!"

By now, most of the mourners were chuckling appreciatively. Those who weren't sat rigidly with their hands folded and their mouths pursed. Rob shook his head slowly from side to side, wondering when the services had spun out of control, calculating a way to ease them back on track. He could see Vi would be no help at all; she was among those laughing the loudest.

Now Tom asked with obvious delight, "My God, what did my father say about all this?"

Rita Tomlin's hand flew to her mouth. "Oh, he was scandalized all right. If your mother could've gotten away without telling him, she sure would have. But she had too high a profile in town. There was no way to keep the news from Henry, someone was bound to tell him eventually. He was outraged, humiliated, and irritated, all at the same time. To tell you the truth, Rachel thought he was more upset with her participating in a 'liberal' protest than he was by her public nudity."

~ * ~

I know how he felt, Rob thought. His face had gone a flaming crimson. *How much longer can this thing go on?*

Dennis Mooney was next. Mooney was the editor-in-chief of the *Greenstone Sentinel.* He was a short, pudgy griffin of a man with a penguin body, bat-like facial features, and tiny pigeon feet which carried him to the podium in tiny mincing steps. He faced the mourners and nodded somberly at Rob before beginning. When he spoke, his voice was oddly fluty and high-pitched. Otherwise, he seemed comfortable with public speaking.

"Rachel," he intoned, letting the gravity of her name settle heavily in the minds of her friends and family. "Rachel Demeter. What a pure pleasure and privilege to have known this remarkable woman. She had what I would characterize as a quiet courage and a questing nature that invited admiration from nearly everyone who crossed her path. Was she a first-rate intellect? Maybe not, maybe not. But she possessed a moral compass and assertive nature second to none, by God. Believe me, I've known some VIPs and big shots in my time. Rachel Demeter took a backseat to nobody.

"I remember the time she wrote a letter to the editor expressing her support for a national healthcare system." Here, Mooney paused and uttered a snort of laughter. "Understand, this took considerable guts. She was Henry Demeter's wife, and Henry ran Foothills Investment Services, one of the most respected businesses in town. Henry firmly believed government ought to keep its blundering mitts out of the medical markets. If pressed, he might admit the present system had some minor flaws and could stand a little tune-up, but that its fundamentals were sound. He believed only private enterprise should be permitted to tinker around with proposed improvements.

"As always with Rachel, she wasn't going out of her way to be controversial or ornery or defiant. She simply insisted on expressing her honest differences of opinion, regardless of how that was perceived by the community. Or by her loving spouse." Mooney chuckled. "Listen, her letter was well-crafted, logical, and reasonable. She wasn't one to foam at the mouth over her causes. Henry, however," and here the mourners joined the editor in knowing laughter, "well, he wasn't too happy with his wife's position. It was hard to tell which made him unhappier, her publicly supporting Hillary Clinton's agenda, or them not presenting a united front to their Greenstone peers and business associates.

"Now, Rachel knew she was semi-protected from criticism due to her social standing. But you could see how certain people who disagreed with her struggled to be cordial. Some would tease her about becoming a socialist. 'Healthcare's not free, you know,' they'd bait her. 'Just who do you think will have to pay the costs for a national healthcare program?' She'd smile pretty then, widen her eyes innocently, and reply, 'Why, I'm sure I'm not smart enough to be able to answer that. I don't have the faintest idea of how to make the arithmetic turn out. But other countries manage quite successfully, don't they? So there are some blueprints out there. We don't have to start from nothing. And if the United States is made up of *exceptional* people, as all us good Republicans believe, then some of our financial people ought to easily figure out how to afford to provide such a basic human service to all our citizens.'

"Oh, woe to the man or woman who attempted to dive deeper into policy and philosophy with her. When it came to her passions, you did not want to get into the weeds with Rachel Demeter. She was too well-versed about the causes she cared about. By the way, that caution not to mess with her extended to Henry. I've been to parties and fundraisers where he would chide her for her 'simplistic' worldview, saying things like, 'Why should the successful have to subsidize the poor?' and 'You don't want to live in a nanny state, do you, dear?' Invariably, Rachel would refuse to back down. She'd gently poke holes in his righteousness, carefully outline how her solutions were nearly always the humane choice in addition to being, far and away, the most cost-effective, then finish up with that mischievous, persuasive smile of hers.

"God, I'm going to miss her." The congregation nodded in sympathy when tears pooled in Mooney's eyes. Unashamed, the editor let the tears track down his cheeks, and a quaver crept into his voice. "On top of being a fighter and an advocate for justice, Rachel Demeter was foremost a decent, absolutely charming woman who can never be replaced. You boys," he said, sweeping his hand over Rob, Tom, and Ben. "You were blessed to have her as your mother. So long, Rachel. I'm certain that, even now as we speak, she's standing at the pearly gates giving St. Peter an earful about her ideas for improving Heaven's infrastructure…"

Mooney was the last scheduled speaker. When he concluded, the crowd burst into enthusiastic applause. Rob stood up then and stepped to the dais. In dry tones, he thanked everyone for coming, gave extra thanks for those who had spoken, and half-heartedly encouraged people to stay, mingle, help themselves to refreshments. A little self-consciously, he added, "Goodnight, Mother. We love you."

He was immediately mobbed by mourners wanting to express condolences, offering to help clean up, hoping to share other anecdotes and memories of Rachel to her eldest son.

"That was beautiful," Ben piped up. His eyes were damp and shining with emotion.

Tom still couldn't get their breakfast together out of his mind, the way Ben slipped in and out of memories and self-awareness.

"Mom would've liked it. People loved her so much."

Clifton walked over, joining their little circle. He focused on Ben and took it upon himself to respond. "That's right, Ben. Rachel was a very special lady. She deserved this special send-off. Right, guys?"

Uneasily, he glanced at Vi and Tom for reinforcement. Vi said nothing and made a show of looking away. Tom noted the fleeting shadow of injury cross Clifton's face, and again thought, *What the hell...?*

"Christ," he said, partly to cover his confusion. "I need a cigarette."

Vi placed a hand on his elbow. "And I need a drink. Let's see how fast we can get the fuck out of here." With a self-conscious grin, she added, "Respectfully, of course."

Chapter Eighteen

In his sleep he suffered night sweats. In his dreams he was freezing. He was hiding, then he was in plain sight but wishing he was hiding. He feared frostbite but found the extreme cold also forced a clarity of thought.

All around him, he could hear green ice cracking.

In his dreams it was twilight, and there was a tall man and a woman standing in the fading light, silhouetted by a red setting sun. There came the far-off howling of a timber wolf, and voices rising. Blue slate everywhere. A wind that was not a wind busking out of a wild sky. Blue snowfall.

The unchangeable gospels of rock and stone. Hymns to the holy undulations of the hills. A choir like a vortex of voices, *no, no, no, no, no, no.*

Wood beams, stone benches. Clouds scudding and congealing, the tarnished skies a chiaroscuro of shadows and movement.

I loved you.

His slumbering body was racked with night sweats, his skin cold and damp all over. His toes were icy and tingling, his fingertips numb. The cold was perfect for awareness. Then came a wind that was not a wind, followed by not-awareness.

Tornadoes of ash spinning off a mountaintop. The metallic wash of towering, terrifying clouds. Rock and stone and green ice cracking.

Long spaces between sounds. One voice saying no snowflake ever blames itself for the avalanche. Another voice singing a cracked old tune. More voices whirling together, gathering strength, and forming a vortex. Screaming *no, no, no, no, no.*

~ * ~

"Hello?"

"Hey there, girl. It's your lover boy, checking in from the Centennial State."

"Lover boy, huh? Which one might you be?"

"Ouch. You sure know how to bruise a guy's ego. Very funny."

"Thanks. How'd the services go?"

"Surprisingly, not too awful. I'd describe it as above average. I heard a few stories about dear Mama that I never could've guessed."

"Oh yeah? Like what?"

Thomas sighed. "Like I'll tell you in detail once I get home. Right now, I'm bushed. Besides, you need to hear these tales over a bottle of wine."

"It's a date, stud. I'm counting the days. Your family holding up okay?"

"Not too bad for a manic-depressive clan. Really, everybody's fine. Although I picked up on some weird vibes today, especially with Ben. I sat with Violet and even she seemed a little off."

"What do you mean?"

Tom heard the sudden tightness in her voice. It happened every time he mentioned Vi's name. He supposed he couldn't blame Donna.

"Skip it. It's probably nothing. Everybody's nerves are frazzled. It's probably normal shit for a funeral. Let's save it for when I'm home."

"Over a second bottle of wine?"

"Now you're talking. How's work?"

"Oh, you know, just another day in the life of an angel of mercy," Donna said with a yawn. "Saw a mean case of MRSA. Kid with a broken arm, might be a children's services referral. Treated a baby with croup and a sky-high fever. Couple of morons came in with drug OD's. Let me see, what else? Oh, yeah. There was a guy with a small screwdriver stuck inside him. The doctor had to perform an impromptu extraction. High point of the day."

"A what?" Tom laughed. "What'd he do, swallow it?"

"It was up his ass," Donna told him matter-of-factly. "Use that fertile imagination of yours."

"C'mon, you're not going to leave me hanging? You've got to tell me this story."

"Maybe when you get home, cowboy. Good excuse for a third bottle of wine, dontcha think?"

"You nurses have all the fun."

"Tell me about it."

"Hey, I really miss you, baby," Tom heard himself blurt. He rubbed his tired eyes. "Seriously, I can't wait to walk in the door and feel you in my arms again." When a couple of beats passed and Donna didn't respond, he asked, "Baby?"

Her voice came back low. "I'm sorry, I thought I was talking with my boyfriend, Tom Demeter. Who are you?"

"Now what's that supposed to mean? I can't say something sweet without you getting all sarcastic?"

"You're not exactly the sentimental, smooth-talking type, darlin'. What's next? Flowers and chocolates?"

"Maybe," Tom pouted, then repeated, "I just miss you, that's all. I'm ready to wrap things up tomorrow and wing my way home Friday afternoon. What's wrong with that?"

"Not a thing," she said softly. "I miss you too, you know. Sure you're not just horny?"

"Oh well, there's that." Donna could feel his grin long-distance. "You're still picking me up at the airport, right? Maybe you'd better have a mattress strapped to your back."

It was the old joke between them. On cue, she replied, "Yeah, and maybe you'd better be the first one off the plane." They both laughed as if they were hearing the punchline for the very first time.

They said their goodbyes. Tom put down the phone and gazed off into space for thirty seconds or so. Sometimes, despite his cultivated cynicism, he could still surprise himself. No, he hadn't expected to miss Donna so much. Even more peculiar, he hadn't planned on saying so to her.

Was Cliff right? Was he becoming just another domesticated

softie? Was that necessarily a bad thing?

Tom was convinced he wouldn't be able to turn off his whirling brain tonight. He yawned, wondering how tomorrow's scattering of Rachel's ashes would play out. Twenty minutes later, he was asleep. He slept soundly. Dreamless.

~ * ~

Rob sat by himself, lights off, out on the porch. The door to the house was partially open. It was late and Violet had asked, *Aren't you cold?* Those were the first words she'd spoken to him since the memorial ended. In a flat voice Rob told her, *Yes, I'm cold.*

She'd mingled with the mourners afterwards, leaving him to manage the final logistics. Now she asked, *Do you want to come inside?*

During the ride home, she hadn't said a word, instead flipping on the radio and humming along to a classic oldies station. "Unchained Melody." "Smoke Gets in your Eyes." "The Great Pretender."

No, he told her, *I think I'll stay out here a while. Don't worry. Go to bed. I'll be in soon.*

At home, Vi busied herself in the kitchen, still humming a few tunes like "Who Wrote the Book of Love?" and "I Heard it Through the Grapevine". She fixed herself a whiskey sour.

Want a blanket? He turned to look her in the face, but her back was to him. *No thanks,* he said to the blanket offer. *I just want to be alone for a few minutes. Collect my thoughts. Clear my head.* Turning to him, Vi nodded, but it didn't escape his notice that her forehead was knit into three puzzled creases. She said good night and retreated to their bedroom at the far end of the house.

Left alone with his thoughts, and unaccustomed to introspection, Rob moved back into the living room once Vi was out of sight. He struggled to piece together the events and emotions of the day.

Part of him was still indignant at the inappropriate testaments to his mother as a young umbrella thief and a nude anti-nukes activist. He'd been deeply embarrassed by the revelations and by the laughter in the room. It was supposed to have been a solemn occasion, for God's sake.

"That's my mother you're gossiping about!" he wanted to shout. "This is a memorial, not a comedy club."

Mainly, though, his thoughts centered on his unease at the tension in the room. Tom was Tom, on-the-surface charming and even somewhat helpful in restoring order with his closing remarks. "It's easy, just like herding cats," he'd told Rob. "More like nailing down Jell-O," Rob grumbled, eyeing the unruly guests irritably.

Tom laughed and offered, "With this crowd, it's more like nailing down jellied cats."

So yes, Tom was Tom, and Rob had to admit grudgingly that, for a change, he was glad to have his brother in the room.

However, there was something decidedly out of plumb with the rest of the family. Also with Clifton, their old beloved family friend. A friction in the air, but nothing Rob could put his finger on. Not knowing what was off, however, did nothing to appease Rob's nagging doubts, shapeless suspicions, and growing sense of dread.

Somehow it all centers around Violet, he thought uneasily. *My wife. What am I supposed to make of that?* He looked around at the walls of his living room, but they held no answers to his question.

~ * ~

Clifton thought, *Maybe I'm just being paranoid, but I swear Rob knows. He was glaring my way all afternoon.* He sipped at his Jameson's and replayed the day's scenes in his aching head. Hell, it felt like *all* the Demeter brothers were giving him the stink-eye. The big man squirmed in his chair. He asked himself, *Am I that transparent?* From time to time, he'd risked glancing Violet's way for…what? Reassurance? A small smile of support? A conspiratorial wink? Vi was Mt. Rushmore. She kept her gaze fixed dead ahead, not once granting Cliff even a sideways peek. Studying her stony profile, he realized, despite their long friendship and recent physical intimacy, he didn't know her at all. He didn't have a clue what she might be thinking.

How the hell did I dig myself this deep a hole? He was accustomed to being the smartest guy in the room, biochemical engineer, savvy businessman, music aficionado, sports trivia expert, talented student of human behavior and motivations. He prided himself on faithfully applying his critical thinking skills to his decision-making process. He viewed himself as analytical, extremely cautious about keeping his life ordered and objective. That said, how had he managed to get himself embroiled in such a classically moronic situation? It wasn't like he hadn't examined all the angles, seen all the obvious pitfalls, agonized over the probability of people getting hurt somewhere down the line.

Yet, still he'd lumbered headlong into this star-crossed, delicious, and thoroughly addictive predicament.

Exactly when had he allowed his reptile brain to take over? Clifton could remember few other times in his life when he'd felt so out-of-control. True, his appetites were enormous. Always had been. He'd spent small fortunes on food and drink, he craved adventure, he could carouse with the best of them. However, he'd made sure to stay within certain *parameters.* This love triangle shit was something new and totally unexpected. The cold-blooded voice in his head that rasped *I want, I want, I want,* proved too strong for him to resist.

Still, with all the single, attractive, and available fish swimming in the great female sea, somehow he'd seen fit to screw around with a married woman. Not just any married woman, oh no. Let it be said when Clifton Parker fucked up, he fucked up royally. The married woman had to be a longtime friend and, to boot, her husband also happened to be a buddy.

Clifton shut his eyes, willing himself to fall asleep and trying not to think how all of this was bound to come crashing down on him and the Demeters sooner or later. Sooner, he feared.

~ * ~

Violet sat up in bed alone with her cascading thoughts, while her husband brooded in the living room, stubborn and shivering. She pictured Rob with his arms folded tightly across his chest, his jaw set, his angry eyes staring into the darkness.

She thought, *This isn't like him. It's not in his character to dwell on things. It's almost like he knows something.*

She thought, *Rachel, I miss you so much already, old friend. Who else can I open my heart to?*

She thought, *Dear God, I have sinned, and I am heartily sorry. Have mercy on my poor soul. For the life of me, I can't see my way clear of this. You know I've made some terrible, selfish decisions. Now I feel like my transgressions are all coming home to roost, and I'm afraid.*

Vi shifted uncomfortably against her pillows. Her body felt red and raw all over. She blamed the central heating, it dried out her skin something awful in the wintertime. She'd already scratched one leg bloody. Now there was a chafing halfway up her back, driving her mad. She couldn't angle her arm high enough behind to reach it.

She thought, *An itch that needs scratching, just out of reach. Story of my life.*

She thought, *Dear God, I don't want to lose my husband.*

What did Rob suspect? Vi was fairly confident he didn't know about Clifton. He *couldn't* know. She'd been so very careful covering her tracks. She'd had plenty of practice. Since they'd been married, she'd had other affairs, sometimes physical, more often emotional. It wasn't that she didn't love Rob. She loved him in her own way, she told herself, and in all the ways that mattered. It was just, all her life, she'd find herself imagining the bodies of other men. She speculated about being touched by their hands. *Fantasies,* she thought. *Temptations.* She flashed back to her old pastor's booming voice. "Violet, there's a lot of *longing* in *belonging.*" *Yea, verily,* she thought now. *That old blue flame of desire has been licking at my flesh since I was a pre-teen. Lord have mercy.*

The itch, yearning to be scratched, just beyond her reach.

She thought, *Forgive me, Father, for I have sinned.*

She thought, *Dear God, can it be that Ben is starting to remember?*

At the service, the climate in his blue eyes kept shifting, like fast-moving clouds sailing through a placid sky. When Ben looked her way, Vi could read dawning in his face, along with confusion, hunger, and flickers of anger. She pictured his damaged brain as an electrical storm, crackling with random memory shards, sparking with haywire emotions.

Fuck, what if he remembers everything?

As soon as the thought surfaced and tried to draw breath, Vi pushed it back down. She shoved it hard and tried to hold it in the underwater murk of her subconscious. Tried to drown it. It couldn't be suppressed, of course. Some thoughts breathed on forever. Some *sins*. If you cut off their air, they could no longer shout, but they could hiss and whisper till the end of time.

Violet thought, *That's the ultimate punishment, never forgetting.*

She thought, *Dear God, does he remember New Mexico? What about the day of the accident?*

Desperate, she made the oldest, most common plea in the world. *Dear God, if You will walk by my side through this terrible time, if You can see me through, I promise I'll do better. I'll be good. I swear, I'll change.*

Chapter Nineteen

Mid-morning, the four of them drove to the shelter together, Rob coaxing the big Lincoln up the snow-dusted hills. His eyes diligently followed the road, both his capable hands clasped on the steering wheel. Clifton followed in his Karmann Ghia.

Tom's mind turned back to springtime rides up into these ancient mountains. On family outings, when he and his brothers were in grade school, before Henry took to working seventy-hour weeks at the office, they'd passed cherry orchards and grape vineyards, quarter horses in fenced yellow yards. As the ground began angling upward, fault lines, rock formations, and vermillion crossbedding patterns appeared. From the creek, red boulders lifted above the current. The waters boiled around the knees of boys and girls in short pants, holding poles, carrying their wickerwork creels. Sprawled along the banks were families with colorful blankets pooled beneath their supine bodies. They ate their lunches of brown bagged egg salad sandwiches, peanut butter cookies, deviled eggs, sour pickles, macaroni salads, potato chips. Their radios squawked with poor reception, bad pop music and local sports shows.

The Lincoln continued to climb, slowly, doggedly. *If this were late spring,* thought Tom, *the hillsides would be bright with yellow roses.* They might see chipmunks and badgers outside the car windows. They might hear chickadees and nuthatches. There were several isolated homes custom-built along the slopes, the beautiful, simply-designed homes of Greenstone's well-to-do. Wild rhubarb and lilac bushes grew around their tiny yards when the weather turned warmer. By May, there'd be dozens of rock climbers out and about. College kids and tourists might be panning for gold. A few mountain bicyclists would share the twists and turns of the road with the regular traffic.

Here in winter, though, it was all barren and bleak. When they arrived at the shelter, they discovered a mess. Beer cans and broken bottles littered the flagstone patio and surrounding landscape, along with empty chip bags, cigarette butts, one left-handed red-and white mitten, a Ralphie the Buffalo windbreaker, vomit drying on the blackberry thickets. All the lovely detritus of whatever celebration occurred the night before.

"No used condoms, anyhow," Tom noted.

Vi snorted. "Silver lining."

"This is terrible," Rob complained, scowling, taking in the wreckage. "Mother deserves a cleaner send-off. Something more dignified."

"Like what, Rob?" asked Vi. "This is exactly where she wanted to be laid to rest. Near and dear to her precious H.D."

"Yeah, Mom was never big on ceremony. Anyway, she carried her own dignity wherever she went," Tom chimed in. "This time, just make sure you actually scatter the ashes, Rob. Not like with Dad."

"Uh-huh." Something in Rob's tone put Tom suddenly on guard. His older brother was stoic and stiff-necked. Now he gave his wife and Tom a hard stare. "For once, can you two put a lid on it? And fuck you, Tom. You think you can do a better job with Mom's ashes? Be my guest." He held out the urn.

"Children, children," pleaded Clifton. "Stop bickering, please."

Tom backed off, both hands held high in surrender. Rob was gratified to see his brother's smirk disappear. He turned on Vi, said pointedly, "Any other unhelpful comments? If not, the adult will now take charge. Let the mourning begin."

The day was cold but thankfully dry, and the wind whistled through the treetops, high-pitched and somehow accusatory. Cliff pursed his lips, playfully mimicking the sound. Vi shot him a black look and he stopped. Tom considered wetting his finger in his mouth and holding it aloft. Mindful of Rob's foul mood, he refrained from the joke.

"All right," said Rob. He stood beside the stone wall and held the urn out at a forty-five-degree angle. The wind blew steadily. There was little chance of him repeating the fiasco with H.D.'s ashes. "Let's get this done, shall we?"

"Hold on a minute, Rob," Ben spoke up.

All eyes turned to him then, making Tom think of synchronized swimmers, or cornstalks bending in unison in a spring breeze. The youngest brother's eyes were clear and fixed on Rob and Violet.

"What is it, Ben?" Vi asked. "Is there something you'd like to say? Maybe a few words for Mother?"

"No. I mean, yes!" he snapped. "I do have something to say, but not about Mother. Not yet, anyway. That can wait." Ben's mouth hung slightly open, but his eyes burned and now fastened onto Vi's. He said, "I remember."

"Remember what, Ben?" she said.

Tom came alert to the small catch in her voice. Rob moved slowly away from the wall, shifted the urn to the crook of one arm, placed one hand on Vi's shoulder.

"What do you think you remember, little brother?" Rob asked carefully.

"Everything." Ben placed two fingers on his forehead and gingerly rubbed a quarter-sized spot between his eyes. "Mostly everything, I think."

A wind that was not a wind. An animal crying out.

Rob cleared his throat. "Can we maybe talk through this later? Ben, would you mind waiting? We came up here to lay our mother to rest, not to do the usual family dysfunction thing. C'mon people, this is Rachel's day. She deserves something…"

"…more dignified," Tom finished for him. "Yeah, we get that, Rob. But we have some time. Let's give Ben a minute to express himself."

"Yes, right now," Ben said excitedly. "Before it all fades again."

"What the hell, Ben?" Clifton prompted. "What is it?"

The transformation, Tom thought, was astonishing. His younger brother stood tall before them, most signs of his infirmity melting away like a snowflake on hot pavement. There was no trace of bewilderment on Ben's features, no slouch to his posture, no fog in his eyes. Years fell away. Tom could've sworn he was looking at his brother from fifteen years earlier, when Ben had been strong, smart and full of promise.

"Like before the accident." Tom hadn't meant to say it out loud, but knew he had by the way everyone's head whipped his way.

Ben threw back his head and laughed. "Accident!" he roared. "Yes, let's talk about my accident. Rob, Vi. What happened that day?"

Falling and blackness. Awareness, then not-awareness.

"Ben…" Vi began to protest.

"Don't." Ben jabbed a finger at her. "Don't you dare."

"I'm not…"

Rob interrupted her. He spoke quietly, directly to Ben and into the charged atmosphere. "We were up here, the three of us, paying Dad a little visit. You, me, and Violet. It was a day like this, sunny, breezy. You'd been back in town for a while, Ben, after being gone so long. You never bothered to explain where you'd been. You just showed up. Full of attitude, too, I might add. You had some ill-informed ideas about the company, some notion of your rights and how you'd been cheated out of your fair share of things." Rob's face darkened. "You had some misconceptions about Violet, too, I recall."

Ben grinned at that, and Rob wondered if he was the only one who noticed the nastiness in the new grin. "I told you, Rob," Ben said in a low, even voice, "I remember almost everything. I don't know how long it's going to stick with me, but believe me, it's crystal-clear right at the moment."

"Well then," Rob spluttered. "Why don't *you* tell us what happened that day?"

A look flashed between him and Vi. Tom thought she seemed nervous. Rob's expression was flat, unreadable.

Ben stuck both hands in his pockets. He rocked back and forth on his heels. "You made a good start, Rob. You're right, the three of us drove up here to pay our respects to dear old Dad. We stood right over there." He waved to indicate the spot. "Because that's where you'd dumped Henry, in one big gray sticky mound, right? Only by then he'd been blown away, or washed away, so your screw-up didn't matter much anymore.

"So we moved apart from each other, each of us finding our own quiet space to meditate, to think deep thoughts about our dearly departed father." Ben gave a harsh laugh. "The old bastard was one mean, manipulative, poor-excuse-for-a-parent SOB, wasn't he? You turned out a lot like him, Rob."

"Ben, don't do this," said Vi.

"Sticks and stones," Rob said. "I grew up, that's all. Don't blame me for not staying stuck in childhood like you and Tom."

"Hey, hey," Tom protested. "Why are you dragging me into this?"

"You grew up," Ben went on with his new small evil smile aimed at Rob. "You grew up to become Mr. Go Along To Get Along. You were always the good son, weren't you? Followed all the rules, nodded your bobble-head at every word H.D. spouted, served your country as an obedient little soldier-boy. Saved our father's company from the clutches of your immature little brothers."

"For God's sake, Ben," Rob spat. "You were gone, nobody had any idea where you were. Tom didn't want anything to do with the company. If I hadn't stepped in, Father's life work would've fallen apart. How could I let that happen?"

"Here he comes to save the day! It's Super Rob! He can fix anything!" cried Ben. "Yeah, we're all lucky to have you around, Mr. Wouldn't Say Shit If He Had A Mouthful."

"Ben, that's enough." Vi again, shaking her head. "Can we please, please not do this?"

Ben shot her a searing look, a strange mix of loathing and affection. To Rob, he said, "Oh, and let's not forget, you stole my girl."

"Your girl?" Tom frowned.

"Maybe I'm being unfair. Vi's always been her own girl, am I right? Do you all know the old blues song about the three-handed woman? 'She's right-handed, she's left-handed, and she's underhanded.'" He laughed, then addressed her directly. "You've never felt loyalty to anyone, have you, sweetie? Not even in your high school puppy-love years with Tom. Not with me, afterward and in New Mexico. Surely not with Mr. Stick In The Mud Husband now. And damn sure not with whoever you're currently screwing on the side."

Tom thought, *New Mexico? What the hell?*

An angry clamor arose, Vi, Rob, and Tom all yelling together in indignation, outrage, denials, perplexity. Clifton watched, goggle-eyed, disbelieving. He'd known the Demeter clan for decades. He'd been closest with Tom, of course, playing ball, day-drinking, chasing girls, debating politics, arguing over music. However, as time went on, he'd grown close to the others as well. Ben was the smart, optimistic, perpetual-motion kid brother. You could wind him up and he'd talk your ears off for hours, pepper you with questions, display a voracious curiosity about the ways of the world, tell you all about what he planned to accomplish when he grew up. Even Rob, *cuckolded Rob*, he thought with a pang of shame, even Rob functioned as a distantly tolerant older brother, occasionally dispensing advice, loaning money, and providing guidance.

Cliff remembered feeling terrible when the accident robbed Ben of his personality and potential. Then again, he also recalled Vi describing Ben in a different light before the fall as intense, sarcastic, quick-tempered, selfish. Clifton could honestly say he'd never seen those qualities in Ben.

Now Ben's ugly new smile was broader than ever. "Truth hurts," he observed to no one in particular. "You know, part of me doesn't blame you, Rob. Dad croaked and opportunity knocked. The business needed a steady hand. I wasn't around and by then Tom was in Florida, wanting nothing to do with running the family store. Your so-called military career was stuck in neutral, and you happened to be in the right place at the right time. I know Mom appreciated you stepping in, too. No hard feelings there."

"No hard feelings?" Rob blurted. "Are you kidding? You totally resented me. You were gone for years, no word from you at all, then you popped up out of nowhere, nursing your little grudges, demanding your share of the inheritance."

"Wait," Tom said, shaking his head slowly. "All that time you were gone and nobody knew where you were? You chased Vi down to New Mexico?"

"Tom, Rob." Vi swung her gaze from brother to brother, former love to current husband. "This all happened a long time ago. Can we please not rehash the past any more than we need to? What about Rachel's ashes?"

"They'll keep." Tom stared hard at her, questions and suspicions flaring in his eyes.

Rob only said, "We'll talk about this later, okay?"

Ben seemed amused. "You're a piece of work, big brother. All I wanted was a partnership. I wanted us to work together and share the fruits of our labor. That's all I asked."

"Demanded, you mean." Rob corrected him.

"Whatever. I wanted what was rightfully mine. Now I admit, I probably came on a little strong. But that's because I felt cut out by you. Disrespected. I thought you'd be glad to see me back in town again, happy to take me on and work alongside me to make the firm a success." Ben's face darkened. "But the look on your face... Then to find out you'd somehow found the balls to talk Vi into marrying you..."

"Careful. Step lightly, Ben." An edge formed in Rob's tone, and Clifton found himself thinking, *This is so surreal. And will wonders never cease? Is Rob actually growing a spine?*

Ben laughed. "I was jealous, sure. It struck me as so absurd and unfair. Made me see red. Probably didn't help my attitude. Then, when you were so resistive to taking me on at the company..."

"That wasn't Rob," Vi broke in, and her voice was hard and saw-toothed. Everybody turned to listen. "You're not remembering that correctly. Yes, your brother had reservations about working with you, but he also felt he owed you a chance." She straightened her shoulders. "I was the one who talked him out of it."

For a moment, Ben appeared confused and shaken. "You?" he said, temporarily off-balance. He managed to gather himself and resumed his light, taunting tone. "You? The love of my life? Say it ain't so, Vi." Vi stared back at him, eyes smoking. "Mind telling me why?"

"You know why. I didn't want you around us to poison the well. That was my main reason, but I might've felt different if I thought you had an ounce of business sense that could be an asset to us. But we all know you had more ambition than talent, right, Ben?"

He turned his face away, petulant. "If you say so, baby."

Vi smiled, all frost and ice. "I'm not your baby. Get that through your thick skull. We broke it off in New Mexico and that was end of story,

Ben. I never expected you to follow me back to Greenstone. What the hell were you thinking?"

"*You* broke it off, dear. It wasn't a mutual decision. *You* broke *my* heart. Besides, this is my hometown, too. You might *think* you and Rob run things around here, but you don't run me."

"So, what? You came looking for some little boy's idea of getting even?"

"People," Rob interjected. "Mother's ashes? Can we follow through with what we came up here for? There's time for all this nonsense later…"

"Hold on a second," Tom spoke up. "I want to hear this play out."

"Why?" Rob asked coldly. "It's none of your business."

"It's family. That makes it my business."

"Oh, you're big on family now, are you?"

"Stop it!" yelled Vi. "All of you. Rob's right, let's get on with what we came up here to do. Ben, you've said enough hurtful things. New Mexico was a lifetime ago. It was over and done with long before you decided to drag your sorry ass back to Greenstone. Fact is, you came skulking around for a few weeks, hiding from us, spying on us, before we had a clue you were in town. Fact is, you tried to bully and beg your way into a partnership position with Foothills Investment Services. Fact is, after we turned you down, you continued to make a nuisance of yourself, pouting for months, pestering us with your passive-aggressive bullshit. Which, by the way, I still don't understand. You managed to latch onto a decent job here, had just signed a lease on a place of your own, and were starting to get on your feet. But you couldn't let things go, could you? You had to keep picking away and picking away…"

"It was humiliating, that's why," Ben interrupted, his face red. "The family business, my name on the shingle, and I couldn't have any part of it. I was completely shut out. You think I didn't hear people laughing behind my back? You know how this town is, all whispers and gossip. Rob, it wasn't fair."

Rob looked up, startled.

"No matter about our family history, we're brothers, man. You should've found a way to make room for me in your life."

"Oooh, it wasn't fair," Vi laughed. She stamped her foot. "Rob and Violet are so mean. What are you, five years old? Fact is, life's not fair, you big cry baby. Fact is, you would have been a disaster working at the firm. The only thing you're capable of running is your mouth. There's no doubt in my mind you would've found a way to drive your father's life work into the ground."

"Fact is," Ben shot back. "You betrayed me. Both of you. Vi stabbing me in the back was bad enough. But Rob, we're blood. How do you sleep at night, knowing how you fucked me over?"

Before Rob could respond, Tom cut in. "Time out," he said. "I'm getting dizzy trying to keep up with this soap opera. Let me ask you all something. While this drama was unfolding, did nobody think about calling me and filling me in? I mean, I understand I'm in Florida, and I've made no bones about wanting nothing to do with family. I get that. But seriously, Ben suddenly appearing and back in Greenstone, that didn't warrant a phone call? A postcard? Something?"

"No," Vi told him. "No, actually we didn't give you a second thought."

"Why would we?" Ben asked. "About the only thing we all seem to agree on is that you were out of the picture, Tom. By your own choice, I might add."

Tom stared at Rob. His older brother wouldn't meet his eyes, but his slight nod was all the confirmation Tom needed.

"All right," he said in a small voice. "Guess I know where I stand. Thanks for the honesty, y'all."

"Any time," Vi said, then faced Ben. Before she could say whatever it was she had to say, Tom spoke up again.

"Ben," he said matter-of-factly. "I wonder if you'd tell me something? As long as we're all being, y'know, so honest and everything."

Ben beamed a sneer at his brother. "Can't hurt to ask."

"It's about your accident," Tom went on casually.

He was gratified to observe a fleeting look of alarm cross Vi's face. Rob remained stoic, but he clutched the urn of ashes tighter to his chest.

"I've always been curious, especially now knowing some of the dynamics of your homecoming. So let me make sure I'm understanding correctly. Rob, or Vi, or both rejected your demand to become part of Henry's precious company? That made things pretty tense between the three of you for a while?"

"That's fair to say," Ben said, smirking. "A real understatement, in fact."

"But some time passed by and one day you all decided to let bygones be bygones and go visit H.D.'s ghost together up here at the shelter?"

Rob cleared his throat. All eyes turned to him. "That was different," he advised Tom. "Our conflict had been strictly business. The trip to the shelter was to honor and remember our father. Vi and I thought it might be a healing gesture to invite Ben along."

"Sure, sure," Tom said, nodding. "Although, truth be told, the 'conflict', as you say, was both business and highly emotional. I'm considering how Ben still felt for Vi. But, hey, never mind that," he went on as his brother and Vi began to argue. "So, you all drove up together, kinda like we did today, with the intention of remembering H.D.?"

"That's right," Rob agreed, narrowing his eyes. "What are you getting at, Tom?"

"And sometime while you were up here, Ben slipped and took a bad fall? I want to make sure I've got that right. Ben fell and cracked his head on a rock?"

"Yes."

"And as a result of his injury, this traumatic head injury, his intellectual functioning became severely impaired, impacting his memory, his impulse control, his whole ability to function normally in daily life?"

"Intellectual functioning," Ben repeated, a dark gleam in his eye. "My, my. Listen to you, big brother. You know how to say it, don't you?"

Tom smiled. He addressed Ben directly. "This is my understanding, mind you, so please feel free to tell me if any of this is inaccurate. So after your hospitalization, and after a period of physical and emotional rehab, you were able to improve your, ah, functionality enough to manage to live semi-independently, as well as work part-time at the restaurant? With Rob and Vi vouching for you, right?"

Ben stared at Tom, wary. "Pretty much right on target," he said with a slow snarl. "This trip down Memory Lane is getting mighty boring, though. Do you have an actual question, Tom?"

"I do. I have two actual questions. First one is a two-parter. Ready?"

Ben's grin remained fixed in place, but Tom noted with satisfaction that his arrogance seemed to slip a notch.

Rob looked on poker-faced, tight-lipped.

Vi's eyes were jumpy.

"Ben, tell me, does your functioning level always vary? Or is this a more recent development?"

"I don't know what you mean," Ben said, aiming at nonchalance. He crossed his arms across his chest, almost hugging himself. Tom thought he spotted a dangerous light appear in his little brother's eyes.

"Oh, I think you do. For instance, right now you seem pretty clear-headed to me. You're able to recall episodes from the past. You've been articulate about your anger. You had that same clarity yesterday at breakfast. Briefly, but it was there. It comes and goes, though, doesn't it? Most of the time your brain is still stuck in a lower gear, isn't it? I wonder what it's like, being in a kind of sticky fog, where your motor skills don't work properly, and your thoughts get all muddy." Tom shook his head. "Must be so hard to live like that, especially knowing how you were before…"

"Don't do that! Don't you dare feel sorry for me!" Ben exploded. "You have no right, Tom. You don't know anything about me."

"Okay, that's enough." Rob stepped forward. "Can't you see you're upsetting him? Enough, Tom."

"Yes, enough," came Vi's weak echo.

Tom ignored them. "I'm glad to see your anger, Ben," he said mildly. "Maybe that rage will help you focus when you hear my second question."

"You better listen to them, Tom," Ben growled. He dropped his arms and let them fall to his sides. Both hands had balled themselves into fists. "Don't push me. I'm warning you."

"You're warning me?" Tom repeated with what he knew was an infuriating game show host smile. "Do you want to hit me, Ben?" Playfully, he jutted his chin at his brother.

"I don't do that anymore," Ben told him. A dull curtain began clouding his eyes. He bit his lower lip hard, a trick he'd learned to help keep him 'in the moment'.

"Because that would be inappropriate, right?" Tom needled. "That would be bad behavior, and bad behavior might lead to you losing your freedoms, Ben. If you lashed out at me, that would be considered a serious relapse, wouldn't it? Think about it. No more apartment, no more job, no more Mr. Whiskers."

"Stop it, Tom," Vi cried. "Stop goading him. What's wrong with you?"

"Yes, Tom, what the hell are you trying to do?" Rob joined in.

Looking on, Clifton was captivated by the play of emotions flickering across Ben's face. He saw defiance, fear, anger, confusion, a childlike gape of hurt and helplessness, an adult's calculated hostility. He looked ready to erupt. His eyes darted everywhere, leapfrogging from Tom to Vi to Rob before lighting again on Tom, his new tormentor.

"What do you want to know?" he snapped. "What's your fucking point?"

Tom met his eyes, then exhaled a long breath. "What happened that day, Ben? The day of your accident, I mean. You said you remembered almost everything. What do you remember?"

"We've told you," Violet broke in, her voice raised. "He was walking down the trail with us. His foot slipped on some loose pebbles or a patch of moss or something slick. He fell and he cracked his head open. That's what happened. You weren't there, Tom. You were never there when it counted. You didn't see your brother laying there, twitching, moaning, all that blood…"

"Vi…" Rob placed his free hand on her shoulder. As if he'd flipped a switch, she quit talking.

Tom didn't look at her while she spoke. His eyes still held Ben's unsteady gaze. "Yeah, I've heard that story. Sounds like you were lucky

Rob and Vi were with you that day, huh? Otherwise, you might have bled to death, right here at the shelter. And gosh, afterwards when they helped you get your own apartment, and Rob went to bat for you at the restaurant…"

"Lucky, yeah," Ben murmured, shutting his eyes.

"Ben?"

"That's what happened, Tom," Ben told him, eyes still closed. "That's what they said happened, so it must have gone down that way. I don't…I thought I remembered something, but it's fading again. I hate when my mind does this. I hate it, I hate it, I fucking hate it…"

It's not an act, Tom decided, studying his brother's face. *He really does seem to pass in and out of his mental fog. I'm watching him regress, and in a moment he'll be gone again.* Aloud and gently, he said, "Ben? Benjamin? The accident. What can you tell us about the accident?"

"Shut up, Tom!" Vi yelled. "Can't you see you're upsetting him? Can't you just shut up and leave us alone?"

"Oh." Ben's eyes flew open. He turned Vi's way. "That's what you said that day, Vi."

Everyone stopped breathing. Ben regarded them curiously, through his haze of memories.

"You said, 'Shut up, Ben. Just shut up.'" He frowned, concentrating. "I was coming down the trail, like you said. Walking behind you and Rob. We were arguing, as usual. I was complaining about being left out of the business again. Rob, that's when you said, 'For Christ's sake, for once can't you just let it go? We're here to visit Father.' And Vi was yelling, 'Shut up, please shut up…'"

"That's when my foot slipped. I could feel myself tipping off-balance, down the slope…"

"That's when you fell," Rob prompted.

"Um, yeah. No, wait a minute, that's not right." Ben's eyes brightened. "I stumbled, and I almost lost it. Somehow, though, I was able to stay on my feet. I remember thinking, whew, that was a close call. Then…"

The sound of green ice cracking. An animal crying out.

"Then I heard sounds and looked around. There was screaming, and a figure coming out of the forest at me with one arm raised high. It was like a demon from a dream, everything shadowy and in slow-motion. There was an arm raised high in the air, the sun right behind it, blocking my vision. There was…"

A wind that was not a wind.

Ben swallowed hard. "At the end of the arm was a hand, and its fingers were wrapped tight around something, I couldn't tell what. Something hard and sharp and jagged. It was…" He shook his head violently and moaned. "No. No, no, no, no."

"Say it," Tom coaxed. "What was it?"

"A rock." Ben stopped short, blinking his eyes rapidly. The last wisps of murkiness dissipated. He faced Rob and Violet in disbelief. "It was a rock. I was stumbling forward, about to fall, and you had a rock in your hand."

Falling and blackness. Awareness, then not-awareness.

"You, you ran at me, and you raised your arm, and when you got close enough, you brought your arm down fast."

"You son-of-a-bitch!" cried Tom, launching himself at Rob.

He grabbed the front of his brother's shirt and pulled hard. "You cowardly, selfish prick. Who the fuck are you, Rob? What kind of man blindsides his own brother? Then lies about it afterward, for years? Was H.D.'s firm so goddamn important to you, you had to have everything? Even if that meant bashing in your baby brother's brains?"

"Stop, Tom," pleaded Rob. "Be careful. Mother's ashes…"

"Yes, stop," Ben said in a suddenly calm voice. "It wasn't him."

"It wasn't…what? What'd you say?"

"It wasn't Rob," said Ben, shifting his gaze to the right of the grappling brothers.

Violet stood with her back to the shelter's slumpstone wall. Her expression showed equal parts resignation, resentment, and righteous fury. She held her spine straight as a broom handle. She placed her hands on her hips and stared at Tom. Rob tried flagging her attention, but she ignored him.

"It was me," she declared, and was shocked at how small her voice sounded.

She cleared her throat and tried to look defiant. At this long-dreaded moment of truth, she promised herself she wouldn't show weakness. She wouldn't give any of them the satisfaction. She looked directly into Ben's eyes. The realization was there even before Vi spoke. "I had the rock. I'm the one who struck you. You remember, don't you, Ben?"

"Yeah," he said, scowling, rubbing his chin. "Yeah. Now I remember."

Clifton took a half-step toward her. "This is crazy. Vi, you don't need to..."

"This is none of your business, Cliff. Stay out of it."

The frost in her tone stopped him in his tracks.

Facing Ben, she went on. "You just wouldn't quit, would you? You couldn't take no for an answer. You wouldn't listen to me when I told you things were over. You didn't listen to Rob when he tried to explain about the company. You wouldn't shut up and you wouldn't go away. The situation was getting more and more toxic. There was no good way to resolve it."

"You hit me with that rock," Ben said, bemused, touching the spot on his head. "I didn't fall. You hit me."

"Hang on a New York minute. Rewind, please."

Tom studied Ben for a moment, then addressed Vi. "What do you mean he wouldn't listen to you about things being over?"

Vi glared but said nothing. Into the silence, Rob said to Tom, "You can piece it together, I'm sure. It started with New Mexico. Apparently, Ben always had a crush on Vi. When you two broke up they dated in secret for a few months. When Vi left for New Mexico to start over, Ben followed."

"Not at first," Vi continued. "He showed up a few months after I'd moved. Tom, I was still hurt from splitting with you. Still feeling a little shaky, trying to learn a new city and build a new life. When Ben appeared, I was so glad to see a familiar face from home. He was sweet and sympathetic and said all the right things those first few months. At first, when he told me he'd always had feelings for me, my guard went up. After a while, though, it seemed only natural for us to get closer to each other."

"You hit me," Ben interjected, wearing a wounded look. "It wasn't an accident at all." *Green ice cracking and rippling hills.*

Violet sighed. "No Ben, it wasn't an accident. Just so you know, I didn't plan to hit you. It's just the way things turned out. You weren't listening, damn it. You didn't want to hear we were done. You kept saying you wanted to get back together. You weren't respecting Rob and me as a married couple."

Rob coughed theatrically and shifted Rachel's urn from one arm to the other.

He said, "You were becoming overly aggressive, Ben. You started screaming. You were raving about the business, about being cheated out of your heritage. I offered you a more-than-fair settlement to keep the peace, but you wouldn't be reasonable."

"So Vi hit me with a rock?" Ben asked wonderingly. *Blue slate all around. A rock and a howling wind and a wild mountain sky.* "Then told everybody I had an accident? That I fell?"

"I'm sorry, Ben," said Vi. Then she shook her head. "No, hell, I'm not sorry. You were upset and I thought you snapped and were coming at me. I didn't have time to decide anything, I just reacted."

She heard her voice rise toward shrillness and told herself to stay centered, stay in control. Still, she could feel the blood thundering in her ears. Tom studied her closely, as if she were a strange animal on exhibit. She said, "What are you looking at?"

"All these years," Tom mused. "Excuse me a second. I've got a pretty good imagination, but I'm having a hard time wrapping my head around this. All these years, you've been feeding me this bullshit story about Ben's tragic accident and how you two rode in on a white horse and made sacrifices to look after him and…" He stopped. Shut his eyes. Opened them again to blaze out at Violet. "What the fuck? Who *are* you, Vi? How do you call yourself a Christian after what you did to Ben? Plus the lies, not to mention the weirdness of you screwing all three Demeter brothers…"

"Enough, Tom," Rob warned. "You're way out of line, even for you."

"*I'm* out of line? Jesus, are you listening to yourself? I'm out of line, that's a good one."

"Can everybody be quiet, please?" Ben whimpered. "I'm starting to get one of my really bad headaches." *No, no, no, no, no...*

"I think that's a very good suggestion, Ben," Vi said calmly. "What's past is past, everybody. What we all need to do is take a deep breath and finish honoring Rachel's memory. Later, we'll start planning for tomorrow and the next day and the day after that. Agreed? I'm not denying there are a lot of hurt feelings here to deal with, my own included..."

"Your own." Tom gave a bitter laugh.

Her mouth grew taut. "I don't usually like to be blunt, but let's have some honesty here."

"Because honesty's your strong point."

"H.D. still holds power over you. Over all three of you. He's been gone a while now, but his ghost haunts your souls. He's crippled you, each in your own way, and I'm afraid it's a permanent laming. Which is a terrible shame, because you're remarkable men with so much unrealized potential. You're all just so hard to live with."

"You mean sleep with?" Tom, again.

"I told you," Rob growled. "Enough."

"Yes. You need to stop being childish, Tom."

"What are you going to do, Vi? Hit me with a rock?"

There seemed to be nothing left to say. The five of them fell silent almost as one, as if obeying an invisible signal. A breeze riffled the leaves of the pines and the red alders. A chorus of birdsong rang out sharp and loud. Clifton, Violet, and the three brothers retreated into themselves, thinking their secret thoughts, trying hard to rein in private feelings.

It was Rob who broke the spell. He cleared his throat and said, "Well, people, we didn't come up here to squabble..."

"Squabble?" Tom blurted. "You call this a squabble?"

"We came here to honor Mother," Rob went on determinedly. He raised the urn for everyone to see. "Shall we?"

"Sure, let's do it," Tom said gruffly. "Let's get it over with."

"Not exactly a reverent attitude," Vi observed tartly. "Don't you think Rachel deserves better?"

"Why don't you keep the lecturing to yourself?" Tom shot back. "She wasn't your mother."

"No, but she was my friend."

"Please, everybody." Ben pleaded. He seemed close to tears. "Can we just do this?"

"We can." Rob lifted the urn higher, just above his head. He waited while the breeze gusted and died, gusted and died. He waited patiently, timing the gusts, vowing he wouldn't be responsible for replaying the H.D. debacle. The breeze came up again and he made his decision. He tilted the urn. Rachel's ashes swirled out on the air currents and were borne off into the woodlands beyond the shelter. They flew, they scattered throughout the woods, they settled softly onto the forest floor and into the mossy bark of the trees.

Rob's face broke into a huge smile. Tom nodded, patted his brother's back, and said stiffly, "Okay. Nicely done this time, Rob. Thank you."

A few reflective moments passed. At last, Vi said, "Well, that's that. Rest easy, Rachel. We all love you and know you're safe now, nestled in God's light. Is everybody ready to go? Ben? How are you holding up?"

Ben mustered a wan smile. "I'm all right, Vi. Thank you, Rob. That was beautiful."

Rob blinked, taken aback. In just minutes, Ben had regressed. He showed no trace of the anger and awareness which had shattered the mood of the afternoon. *Does he even remember?* Rob thought. All he said, though, was, "Thanks, Ben. I appreciate you saying that."

"Time to go, then," said Vi.

"Yeah, let's ride," Tom chimed in.

"So long, Rachel," Clifton was surprised to hear himself say. "Your spirit lives on with your boys. You'll be much missed."

"Yes, she will," agreed Tom. "Now let's vamoose, before we all start blubbering."

With that, they clambered into their respective vehicles and started their descent back to Greenstone. Back to their new lives, whatever those might look like.

Chapter Twenty

That evening, Rob stood in the doorway of the guest bedroom, arms folded, watching his brother pack. He said, "You know, you really don't have to do this."

Tom didn't respond He didn't trust himself to speak. He didn't dare make eye contact with Rob. In a frozen silence, he flung his clothes and grooming supplies into the suitcase, hoping his brother would take the hint and leave him alone.

"Plus," Rob went on, clearing his throat. "Plus, I'm worried about your flight tomorrow. They're saying a major storm's moving in tonight. Fifty-fifty chance they'll shut down the airport, Tom. If they do fly, it's bound to be a hairy trip for you with all that snow and wind coming off the Rockies."

No reply.

"So what I'm saying is, maybe you ought to check into postponing your flight a few days, just to be on the safe side. Just until the weather clears out. You're welcome to stay here through Monday or so. The motel's pretty pricey, especially its weekend rates. Besides, that would give us all a chance for the emotions to settle down. We've got a lot to discuss, don't you think?"

Tom zipped and buckled the straps on his suitcase. He fixed his brother with a polar stare. "Are you serious?" he said evenly. "If you are, you're dead wrong, Rob. You and me, we don't have a goddamn thing to talk about."

Rob returned Tom's glare with his own mild gaze. He nodded thoughtfully, and Tom could see the wheels turning in his head, looking to change the subject. "Give me a little time," Rob said calmly, watching

Tom retrieve his coat from the closet. "I need to talk with a few people, gather the paperwork together, go over some figures. It shouldn't take long. A week, maybe two. When I have the numbers finalized, I'll contact you about the estate, okay?"

Tom buttoned his coat, hoisted the suitcase, and walked to the door. "You're incredible, you know that?" he said. Rob made no effort to move. "C'mon, step aside. I've got a cab coming."

"No, you don't." Violet appeared behind Rob. A shadow from the hallway fell across her cheekbones and her lips. "I called and canceled for you. We need to talk, Tom."

"Aw, hell," Tom croaked. "Just let it go, will you, Vi? Just let *me* go."

She shook her head, slowly but with finality. "Not until we talk. If you still want to leave when we're finished, Rob will drive you to the motel." She put a hand on her husband's shoulder and spoke in his ear. "Honey? Tom and I will be out on the porch. Would you be a sweetie and fix us a half-pot of decaf?"

For a fleeting second, Tom thought he recognized refusal in his brother's eyes. Refusal, and maybe a weak protest that he not be excluded from any intimate conversations taking place beneath his roof. The idea of objection flared up, then just as quickly vanished. Rob tightened his jaw, nodded curtly, and walked off to the kitchen to follow his wife's bidding.

Tom left his suitcase on the floor and went with Vi out on the porch. He watched her slide shut the glass door. It was cold, maybe the coldest night of his Greenstone stay. Vi turned, but instead of facing him she cast her gaze out into the black universe, up into the wilderness of stars. He didn't say a word. He was determined not to make this easy for her. For centuries, there was silence between them.

Finally, she spoke. "Your brother is just devastated by all this," she said softly. "You can't begin to imagine the hell he's been in since this afternoon. He's…"

"Which brother?" Tom interrupted, acid in his voice. "Are you referring to Ben? Because, yeah, I'll bet he's pretty torn up, all right. What would that be like, do you think? Your memories come flooding back at you, all at once, and you realize your sister-in-law isn't what she makes herself out to be. In fact, turns out she's a bit of a witch. On top of that, your big brother looks like he's been a selfish coward all along. All that on the day when Ben's saying goodbye to his mother. You're right, that would be hellish."

Vi didn't budge and kept her eyes trained on the Great Beyond. The full moon winked in and out of a bank of dark-gray snow clouds, curling shadows over her stoic profile. She drew in a long breath. "Actually, I was talking about Rob."

"Oh, Rob." Tom spat out the name. "Guess I misunderstood."

"He has feelings, you know," Vi said. "For the most part, he keeps them to himself. I keep telling him he's going to grow himself an ulcer if he doesn't let the emotions out once in a while. All the stress at the office, and Rachel passing so suddenly, and now this…" She sighed. "He's a grown man, though. He does what works for him, like we all do, I suppose. I'll tell you one thing, he's got the lowest blood pressure of anyone I know."

Tom studied the side of her face, wondering at her nonchalant manner. He said, "Before you interrupted us, Rob was baring his soul to me. He talked about the weather, my travel plans, the cost of the motel and reviewing Mom's will. Profound, spiritual stuff like that."

She nodded, and Tom recognized the gesture as a fair duplication of Rob's nod. "It's not his way to be emotional," Vi told him, a weary tenderness in her voice. "You know that as well as anyone. To Rob, things are what they are. He just takes life as it comes to him, the highs as well as the lows." She raised two fingers to her lips and nodded again. "Maybe especially the lows. I've never known a man who could sail through sorrow and hard times like your brother. He accepts it all at face value. He puts his head down and works his way through the thorns. It's an amazing quality."

"He's amazing, all right," Tom retorted.

She ignored his sarcasm. "No really, it's his gift. A lot of people look at him and think he's just a shallow guy. I admit, I thought the same when I was younger. Just the opposite is true. Rob runs deeper than you'll ever know, Tom. He's strong in ways that I never believed a man could be. That's not the way you see him, though, is it?"

"Nope. To be honest, I see him as being a pussy-whipped drone, at the beck and call of his manipulative wife."

Clouds shifted. A great shade eclipsed Vi's face and reaction. When she replied, her voice was steady. "You look at him that way because you're a small and fearful person, Tom. You can only feel strong when you're putting someone down. You know I love you, but really, you're a frightened little man. I mean, you're clever and witty, sometimes a lot of fun to be around. But you have no idea how to live in the real world, do you? You're always fantasizing a better tomorrow, and meanwhile you dream inside your own head and disconnect yourself from ordinary life. I'm just starting to realize what a selfish and unhealthy way to live that is."

Tom felt the blood rush to his face and was grateful it was too dark for Vi to see his anger. Through clenched teeth, he managed to say, "Is this what you wanted to talk about?"

"I have this idea," she went on. She craned her neck and aimed her eyes at the heavens. "I'm considering the idea that human beings, every one of us, may be some sort of lower-level angels. We're far from perfect, and sure, we're stuffed full of sin and temptation and cruelty. Still, each of us also carries within us a holy spark. I believe that may be the reason why we can be redeemed, Tom, in spite of our bad thoughts and terrible behaviors."

For the first time, she swung around to face him. In the play of dancing shadows and wan moonlight, he could clearly make out her luminous eyes. "Can you tell me you believe in forgiveness?"

"Vi, are you crying?"

"Allergies," she snapped. With her sleeve, she brushed at her eyes. "Answer my question. Do you believe in forgiving someone when she falters? Can you absolve someone for her stupidity, for a careless moment's transgression?"

"Someone?" he repeated. "Like we're talking hypothetically? Come on, Vi. We've known each other too long for this bullshit. Especially after this afternoon, don't you think?"

Violet didn't flinch. Instead, she squared her shoulders and took a half-step forward, bringing her features into the house lights. Tom thought she looked ten years older than she had at the shelter today. He saw by the straight line of her lips she was growing impatient with him. "Simple question, Tom; do you believe in forgiveness?"

"Oh, sure I do," he told her lightly, weighing out his words before speaking them aloud. "As you know, though, I'm not a Christian like you. So I don't believe in *unconditional* forgiveness, Vi. You know, confess all your sins, go say eight Hail Marys and four Our Fathers, and we'll call everything even-Steven. In that context, I think forgiveness is a highly over-rated virtue. Maybe even a weakness. What do you think? I'd go so far as to say there are times when damnation and condemnation are absolutely appropriate responses to shitty actions. 'Like when?' you may ask. How about when 'somebody' bashes in her brother-in-law's head out of fear, envy, avarice, and rage? Should that certain 'someone' be forgiven?"

"Tom, you can't know how awful I feel about Ben."

"Oh, you mean Ben's 'accident'? Isn't that what you and Rob call it?"

"I think about Ben every day of my life. I do penance every single morning, noon, and night. I know it's not enough; it's never going to be enough, but what more can I do? I swear I'd give anything to have that afternoon back, to have the chance to handle the situation differently."

"Yeah, but you can't, can you?" he said, stone-faced. "You want to criticize me for not living in your 'real world', for putting too much stock in the idea of a better tomorrow? At least I don't pretend to feel bad about my past and mistakes that can't be changed."

"Damn you, I'm not pretending."

"The hell you're not. The only reason we're talking like this is because you're scared for your own salvation. Or probably more like saving your own skin. Face it, Vi, you got busted and now it looks good for you to express remorse. Oh, don't worry, I'm not running to the police or the adult protection people or Ben's social worker. Part of your punishment is having to live with your own sorry self. You want redemption from picking up a rock and ruining Ben's life forever? Well, fuck you, and fuck your redemption, Violet."

The moon climbed its slow arc in the sky and burrowed deep into the thickening clouds. Again, sword-like shadows crept across Vi's face, transforming her body into a full silhouette. She muttered something beneath her breath.

"What?" Tom demanded. "What did you say?"

"I said, Rachel would've forgiven me."

He wanted to spring at her. He wanted to knock her to the porch's wooden floor and kick her, kick her in her head and in her soft parts, kick her until she cried out sharply in pain, kick her until she screamed for mercy, kick her until she stopped making any sound at all. The raw violence of his reaction frightened him. With an effort, he forced himself to remain still and silent. He was afraid that, if he wiggled a single finger or uttered one tiny peep, all his self-restraint would vaporize. He might uncoil and explode on her like a runaway thresher. A sour taste rose to his mouth. Tom hadn't felt this red surge of animal rage since his adolescent years. He'd *never* experienced it toward a woman.

Vi didn't seem to notice. In a low voice, she continued. "Your mother was the most spiritual person I ever met, Tom. She had class and kindness. She was a true lady in the best sense of the word. She confirmed my idea that we're all wounded angels. Only she was a rank or two above most of us." Vi's face remained hidden, but Tom could hear the small self-satisfied smile in her words. "Remember when we first started dating, way back when? Rachel was the only one out of all you Demeters to make me feel like I belonged. Like I deserved a place at your table. She could sense what it was like to be the outsider, to feel lost in this fallen world of ours." Briefly, she shut her eyes, picturing Rachel's warm grin and welcoming presence. "She was the first woman I'd ever met who knew exactly who she was. She knew me, too, without any judgment or phony sympathy or nosiness. She simply accepted me into your clan for who I was and who I wanted to be." Vi paused a beat, then added, "She would've forgiven me, Tom. Why can't you?"

While Vi had been rhapsodizing over his mother, Tom managed to calm down a bit. Now his anger returned full force. "Seriously? She would've forgiven you for destroying her youngest son's life? For settling into a lifelong financial arrangement and a loveless marriage with her oldest son? And she would've been happy that you fuck other men behind Rob's back on a regular basis? Is that what you're telling me, you crazy, batshit, self-deluded…?"

"Better stop before you say something you'll truly regret, Tom."

She held her hand up to him like a crossing guard. *A gesture to halt children,* Tom thought, amused despite his anger.

"I'm not saying Rachel would've liked any of this. I'm not saying she would've approved of my choices. What I am saying is that she would have shown me some mercy."

A bar of moonlight lit upon Vi's nose and jaw. Tom could see she was wearing a faint, serene smile. "See, Rachel knew I was a good person, Tom. She would've acknowledged that I've sinned, but she was wise enough about human nature to separate the person from the behavior. Don't you know that about your own mother?"

Tom said nothing. He tried to ignore the red curtain rippling before his eyes and focused on remaining still.

"I always admired Rachel," Vi went on. "I wanted to emulate her. Still do. She set a high bar, but maybe someday…" Her voice trailed off.

The moonbeam shifted higher, to her hairline, and Tom saw her eyes were steady on his. "Please don't judge me, Tom. You've known me a long time. You probably know me as well as anyone, Rob included. You know who I really am. You know my *soul.* Can't you forgive some of the things I've done?"

"I don't think so," Tom told her, shaking his head. "Listen to yourself, for Christ's sake. You call yourself a good person, in spite of committing some awful, rotten actions. It sounds like you expect me to look at those acts as isolated instances, or freak occurrences. Crimes of passion, maybe. But at some point, Vi, what you do makes you who you are. You've done a lot of talking, but what bothers me is what you aren't saying. What I don't hear from you is acknowledgment of you doing anything wrong. I don't see any sign of regret, I don't even hear a promise to behave better in the future." He felt his heart start to race and took a moment to breathe. "You're right about my mother. She *was* a remarkable person. Part of that was because there wasn't a pretentious bone in her body. Also, she didn't hide behind any religion. Oh, and she didn't hurt people and try to persuade them that she was really, at heart, a swell human being. Or a...what did you call it? A lower-level angel?"

There was a rapping on the sliding door. They turned to see Rob peering out at them with a questioning look. Through the glass, he mouthed, "Coffee?" Tom shook his head and, after a small hesitation, Vi followed suit. Rob nodded, expressionless, and retreated into the semi-darkness of the house.

"Rachel was one-of-a-kind," Violet said dreamily once Rob disappeared. "A very unique woman. Another part of what I wanted to tell you is I'm so sorry she's passed. Also, you know, that I'm worried for her immortal soul."

Tom stared at her. "Excuse me?"

"Because she killed herself," Vi said, turning away. "That's a mortal sin, Tom. It's sad, but it means her soul is forever banned from entering Heaven. I'm not smart enough to know whether her spirit goes to Hell, or if it wanders in limbo for all eternity. What I do know is she'll never find her permanent rest. There's no salvation for her. And I'm very, very sorry about that."

Tom remained quiet for a long twenty seconds. He looked past Vi out into the night sky, thought about death and the void and what limbo might feel like. He could easily have hurled Violet over the railing and broken her neck. Crueler yet, he could have smashed her skull in with a huge rock.

When he trusted himself to speak without screaming, he said in a hoarse voice, "Well, good thing Mom didn't believe in any of that superstitious mumbo-jumbo. Neither do I, by the way. When you're gone from this world, you're just gone. Just for the sake of argument, though, are you suggesting somebody can lead an exemplary life here on Earth, full of love and sweetness and selfless acts, and still be denied access to paradise because they choose to end their mortal suffering?"

"It's not my doctrine," Vi said. "But yes. Suicide is forbidden. Only God can determine when your time is up."

"On the other hand," Tom continued, hearing the ragged edge creep into his voice, "someone could, say, commit numerous adulteries and permanently cripple her brother-in-law, but as long as she claims to repent, she gets the golden passport to the Promised Land?"

"It's not that simple, Tom. It has to be genuine repentance, not just lip service. The short answer is yes, though. That's the way it works. That's the ultimate forgiveness."

"You're going to have to pardon me for saying this, lady, but that is one seriously fucked-up theology."

Violet only nodded at his words. She backed several steps away from Tom, into the cloaking shadows. She said, "There's something else I need to say."

"Because with you the fun never stops. Go ahead, I'm all ears."

She made a deliberate show of turning her back to him. "I've thought about this long and hard, Tom. I want you to know this isn't easy for me," she said slowly. "I've come to the conclusion it's not healthy for Rob and me to have you in our lives. This has been a challenging week for all of us, but you being here has been a major complication, especially for Rob. I know he's your brother, but…"

"Don't sugarcoat it, okay? Rob and I have never been the best of buddies, right?"

Her shoulders sagged. "I know I've said this before, but I've often thought it must be so tiresome to be you, Tom. You hold onto your grudges and grievances forever. They just seem to eat you alive. You carry all that bile around just under your skin… Well, that's your business, I suppose. It seems to me a lonely way to live, but that's who you are. I can tell you, though, being around you is toxic for Rob and me. We can't tolerate it any more. I'm guessing, once you leave tomorrow, you won't be returning to Greenstone?"

"You're guessing right," Tom said to the back of her head. "I've got zero reason to come back to this town."

Vi nodded slightly. "And we have no desire to visit you in Florida. So, problem solved, it sounds like."

"Problem solved," he repeated tonelessly. "Are we done now?"

It was her turn not to respond. Above, the cloudbanks came undone and drifted south, slowly, eventually unveiling the moon. Lunar light, amber and orange, spilled over the porch. At the same time, Vi turned and took several steps toward him. Tom saw her clearly for the first time that evening. Her forehead was smooth, her brown eyes untroubled, her cheeks shining with color. She looked as though she didn't have a care in the world. Her lips moved, but he couldn't make out what she was saying. His ears felt plugged with water, and the only sound he could hear was the agitated rush of his own rivers of blood pumping through his body.

He said, "I didn't catch that. What were you saying?"

To his surprise, Vi graced him with a quick and dreamlike smile. She said, "I was just praying."

"Praying," he repeated dully.

"Yes," she said. "Praying to thank God for how He shines his lamp on the righteous path for us, just when things seem blackest. Just when we feel we might be lost forever. Blessed is He who forgives our transgressions and creates in us our clean hearts."

Tom cleared his throat but said nothing. He watched the moon slide behind another cloud. He couldn't look at her.

"I'm praying for Rob tonight," she continued. "Praying for his pain to be soothed, and for our bond as husband and wife to be restored. I'm praying Cliff finds the answers for his own confused and lonely heart. I'm praying for Ben, that he finds peace within himself, and that his healing stays on track. Most of all, though, I'm praying for you."

"Yeah?" Tom snapped. "Don't do me any favors, Vi."

Her composed mask slipped a notch. Her eyes blazed out a charged look. "It's not a favor, damn you. Honestly, do you deliberately misinterpret everything I say? I'm approaching you with love, Tom. The power of prayer *is* love. While I can't have you in my life, you'll always be in my prayers. I'll never wish you harm or misfortune."

"Spare me," he said coldly. "Let me rephrase what I just said. Don't bother to pray for me. Don't waste your breath. Got it? No wait, maybe that's still not clear enough. Let's try this." The showman in him instinctively hesitated two beats, calculating the impact of his next words on her, his audience. "Go fuck yourself sideways, and don't you *dare* pray for me."

She didn't quite flinch and, if she blanched at all, it was impossible to tell in the moonlight. Her lips trembled some, and for a moment her eyes seemed lost. She aimed for a poised recovery, reassembling her smile and asking softly, "Tom, do you remember telling me you'd always love me?"

"I do," he said with no hesitation.

Six or eight hours earlier, he wouldn't have believed he could ever fall completely out of love with his old girlfriend, with his younger brother's one-time lover, with his older brother's wife. She'd had that strong a hold on him all these years. Now here she was, standing before him, and he was stunned to discover he felt nothing. Maybe less than nothing. Just a yawning, aching emptiness where his feelings for her used to be. He thought Vi could slip out of her clothes right there on the porch and stand stark naked under the stars, calling out his name in lust and desperation, and still he'd remain unmoved. He went on in a flat voice, "I was wrong. I couldn't imagine any circumstances that could ever make me not want you on some level. But guess what? We're done. You're dead to me, Vi."

Her mask vanished. She stared at him incredulously. "You don't mean that. I understand, the shock of this afternoon, of course you're furious and upset. But we had something…"

"Once upon a time, yeah. But now what's this mindfuck game you're playing? Didn't you just get finished telling me you couldn't have me in your life anymore? What, did you think I was going to pine for you? Shit." He surprised himself by laughing out loud. He gestured toward the sliding door. "Your husband's lurking around somewhere inside. Get him out here. I'm ready to go."

He had to give her credit. She gave him one last steady look, then held her head high as a queen as she walked by him to slide open the door. Tom let out a long breath. He stared up at the hide-and-seek moon until his brother appeared on the porch. Rob had put on his jacket and was jangling his key ring.

"Sure you won't stay the night?"

"Yeah. I'm positive."

"All right, then," Rob said lightly. "Ready to ride?"

Tom nodded. "Let's hit it."

The two of them moved inside. Tom grabbed his bags, waving his brother off when he offered to help carry something. He asked, "How far would you say the motel is from here?" He felt Violet's eyes crawling over his face.

"Oh, less than five miles. This time of night, maybe ten minutes, tops."

"Good. Hey, Rob?"

"Yes?"

"Just to be clear, for that ten minutes, I don't want to hear a goddamn word out of you."

Rob stared back at him.

"I just want you to play chauffeur and drive. Are you following me?"

"Yes, I'm hearing you." Rob's eyes swam with questions, but he otherwise remained expressionless.

"Just drive and keep your fucking mouth shut," Tom said wearily. He walked slowly to the front door without giving Vi so much as a sidelong glance. "Now let's go."

Chapter Twenty-one

The plane ride home was long and uneventful. Tom sat in an aisle seat and spent most of the trip hooked up to headphones, zoning out to the comforting music of his teens and twenties. He thanked the gods he didn't believe in that he wasn't sitting next to a chatterbox. From takeoff to landing, the woman in the middle seat was engrossed in a Danielle Steel book.

The pilot touched down without incident and the mad rush for the exit was on. Tom let the crowd surge past. When at last he walked out onto the tarmac, he was struck by the difference between the cold dry air of Greenstone and Florida's sticky and springlike weather. Seventy degrees, to quote the weatherman. It felt like home.

In the terminal, Donna stood in the waiting area, arms crossed and one foot tapping impatiently. When she spotted him, her face broke into an endearing grin.

"Not exactly the first one off," she noted, just before the kiss.

"No mattress," he countered.

They walked arm-in-arm down to the baggage carousel and waited twenty minutes for it to start spinning. In the meantime, Tom sketched in the highs and lows of his trip. He kept his voice low and matter-of-fact. Donna wasn't fooled. Her eyes went wide. All she could say, repeatedly, was, "I don't believe it. I can't believe any of this."

In the car, she sat in silence while he settled in beside her. Her hands gripped the steering wheel tightly. Tom could see the machinery of her mind whirring, trying to digest his story.

"You planning on white-knuckling it home?" he said mildly.

"You have to admit, it's all pretty fantastic," she said.

"It is, isn't it? If I hadn't gone through it myself, I wouldn't believe a word."

"I mean, I'm even factoring in your family's normal weirdness. This goes way, way beyond anything you've ever told me."

"Yeah. It raises the ante on freaky, even for the Demeters."

Donna drummed her fingers on the wheel. After a moment, she asked in a small voice, "What about Violet?"

"Are you planning to start the car up any time soon? Because I tell you, I'm pretty played out. I just want to get home, honey. I feel like I could sleep for a week straight."

"Sure." Donna turned the key and the engine caught. "But don't dodge the question, mister," she added as she backed out of the parking space.

Tom stared straight ahead. "What about Violet?"

"Yeah, that's what I asked."

"It's odd," he said, bringing two fingers up to brush his lips as he considered his response. "The entire flight back, I was thinking more like, 'What about Ben?' And 'What about Rob?' Both have to live with the consequences of what Vi did." When Donna didn't say anything, he went on. "I can't begin to predict what's been going on in Ben's head the past forty-eight hours. And Rob? How the hell does he live with her? Or with himself?"

Donna steered out of the parking structure and merged smoothly with traffic. "Are you pleading the Fifth, Mr. Demeter?"

"What? Oh, Violet, right." He shut his eyes, inhaled deeply. "Who knows what's going to happen with her? Our last conversation was like a dialogue from an insane asylum. I didn't know her at all, and I don't know what she's become. It's like she's got alligators and snakes swimming around in her swampy brain. She's got religion, but no soul. That vacant, blissed-out smile of hers really gave me the creeps."

"I guess I meant more like, how do you feel about her now?"

"Oh, baby. I don't feel anything for her. Not a goddamn thing. It's like someone or something came along with an emotional Shop-Vac and suctioned out her life force. She's a dry and hollow woman, and I'm done with her."

232

"Just like that, huh?"

"Say again?"

"Hang on a second." A lunatic in a silver Lexus inexplicably swerved in front of them, no turn signal, then slowed to a crawl. They watched the driver juggle a roadmap and a hamburger while his car battled to stay within the lines of its new lane. "Honest to God," Donna muttered, accelerating and blowing past the Lexus on the right. Tom grinned when the driver, a mild-looking middle-aged man in a shirt and loosened tie, flipped them the bird. "Does Motor Vehicles give a driver's license to just anybody these days?"

"Temper, temper, honey. If it's all right with you, I'd like to get home in one piece."

"Oh, like that was my fault? Listen, Tom, let's be honest with each other," she said evenly, resuming her line of questioning as if there hadn't been the slightest interruption. "We're talking about a woman you've been infatuated with for most of your life. First, you were childhood sweethearts, right? Then she married your brother, which you've never really gotten over. Now you find out she had a secret involvement with your other brother. At this point, I understand you've got to be a little shellshocked. But you're telling me, all of a sudden, you don't have feelings for her anymore? Just like that?"

"Yeah," said Tom wearily. "Just like that. Just like flipping an off switch. Donna, I know that's hard for you to swallow…"

"Well, yeah," she said, her eyes on the highway ahead, alert for other stunt drivers. "You've carried that torch for years, Tom. It's been tough sometimes, trying to live up to the great mythical Violet Inverce. If you're done with her, I'm glad. But it is a little unreal."

"This whole fucking week's been unreal." Tom pinched his eyes.

He turned to study Donna's profile. She was focused on the road, frowning slightly, alert for the next kamikaze motorist to cross her path. He fought the urge to lean over and kiss her cheek. He was surprised by how much he'd missed her this past week. Just being with her again brought him a sense of peace. He felt a small joy rising in his breast.

Her radar went off and she sensed him gazing at her. "What're you grinning about? Don't make me nervous, I'm trying to drive."

"It's good to be back, Donna," he told her. "With you, I mean." The words fell into the comfort zone between them, made a rattling sound like pebbles tossed into a deep canyon.

She stifled her first impulse, which was to offer up a quick, snarky rejoinder. She was hearing something new in Tom's voice. From the corner of her eye, she saw he was regarding her with study in his eyes. And tenderness. Donna said, "I missed you, too, babe. I'm so sorry about your mom."

"I'm sorry you two never met. You would've liked her," Tom said. "And trust me, she would've adored you. Hey, hey, watch the road. You see that idiot in the red Accord? I swear, Honda drivers are the worst."

He shut his eyes and leaned back on the headrest. He yawned. "Worse comes to worst, it's all grist for the mill. I've got a lot of new material to play with, that's for sure. Give me six months, I'll have a whole fresh act to take on the road. Hell, I'm even thinking of doing a follow-up to *This Hard Life*. Maybe call it *This Crazy Life*." His eyes remained closed. The car rocked in a lulling rhythm. Tom felt a fog moving in. "Did I tell you, I'm thinking about quitting cigarettes again? I think I can do it this time, for real." He yawned. "Lots to talk about, honey. You and me and where this is all going. Can't do it now, though. So tired."

He heard Donna say, "We can talk when we get home, or tomorrow morning. There's no rush. Why don't you…?" Sleep crept over him then, and the mists lifted him up and carried him off to a dreamless land where the only sound was the low hum of tires covering ground.

~ * ~

Business was booming at the investment company. The office was on fire with activity. In Greenstone, and in fact all across the country, it felt like the economy was starting to turn a corner and gain some momentum. Consumer confidence was on the rise. Ordinary people were starting to think about buying new cars, refinancing their homes, upping their savings for colleges and retirement.

Sitting in the oxblood leather chair which belonged to his father, sitting in Henry's old office, Rob stared blankly at his computer screen and tried to think of one good reason why he shouldn't take the rest of the day off. For the life of him, he couldn't concentrate. It was only late morning, but he felt oddly disconnected from himself and his surroundings. For weeks now, ever since Rachel's memorial service, he'd been listless and inattentive at work.

Ever since the catastrophe at the shelter.

He swiveled his chair and faced out the window. Even on his best days, he didn't fully appreciate the magnificent view of the foothills. Today was worse, though. Today he saw nothing except his own morbid thoughts.

He brooded over the way things ended with Tom. Rob had difficulty reconciling himself to the idea they were brothers and they'd never again speak to one another. *It's just not right*, he thought. At the very least, the terms of their estrangement had been poorly negotiated. Uncharacteristically, he indulged a fantasy, wishing he had a time machine to dial back a month or two and, as he often told himself, "fix things." If this was golf, he thought stupidly, he'd simply request a mulligan.

Also, there was Ben. He'd had another incident at work, a physical harassment complaint filed against him by a fellow employee. Now there was a written warning in place, and another outburst was liable to cause him to lose his job. Then what?

Rob sighed and tried to ignore the pressure starting to build behind his eyes. He'd feel better if his baby brother would even pretend to care about his own well-being. Lately, Ben seemed to be clinging to his anger, even reveling in it. His self-described "moments of clarity" seemed to be cycling faster and faster. Rob wasn't at all sure where they were leading. *Nowhere good,* he thought dismally.

One thing for certain, Ben couldn't keep expressing his frustrations by exploding on people. That was unacceptable. Rob acknowledged the dynamics were changing swiftly, and Ben was remembering more, but also having more challenges in controlling his mood swings. Rob and Vi talked briefly about the costs and responsibilities of assuming legal guardianship. However, neither had the stomach for limiting Ben's freedoms and risking an escalation of his resentment. Besides, they weren't communicating too well themselves about their own issues. The one thing they could agree upon was they needed a new strategy with Ben.

Rob didn't stir when Patty Zimmer entered his office. His back was turned to his admin assistant, his head cradled in his right palm.

~ * ~

If she hadn't known him better, Patty would've said her boss was daydreaming or taking a lazy moment to enjoy the view of the foothills out his window.

"Mr. Demeter? Rob?" She was carrying a stack of documents, fastidiously rubber-banded together.

"Mmm?" He swung around to face her.

"I just wanted to remind you, the McBride retirement account paperwork is done. You just need to review it." Rob gave her a groggy smile and a slight nod. She waited for him to say something. When he didn't, she went on. "That's the one you asked us to expedite. Remember? It's all here for you. Mr. McBride's asked to come in later today to finish up with signatures."

"Thank you, Patty. I appreciate all your good work in pulling this together." He smiled at her again, and this time it was closer to his genuine smile. Patty felt a pang of relief. "I'll look it over in a bit. You can put it on the desk."

She did as she was asked. "Can I call Mr. McBride and ask him to come in before we close up?"

"If he can be here around half-past four, that would be perfect. Would you please shut my door on your way out? I'd like a few minutes to work some things through by myself."

"Certainly, Mr. Dem...I mean, Rob. Let me know if you need anything else."

"I will, Patty. Thank you."

She wanted to ask if he was all right. She wanted to ask what in the world had him so off-balance, so lost-looking. She decided it wasn't her place. He was the all-business boss and she the employee, that was all. She backed out of the office, closing the door quietly behind.

~ * ~

Rob spun his chair around again and returned his gaze out the window. Had Patty asked her questions out loud, he undoubtedly would've answered he was fine, he was pretty much always fine, and why was she asking? As to what was tugging at his attention, he might've chuckled. *Am I all right? No? What's wrong? Oh, just everything.*

His mind raced through the events of the past few weeks, the revelations, the ruptures throughout the family, the alarming feeling of being out of control. He saw himself *fading*, for lack of a better description. He prided himself on his self-appointed role as the solid, sensible one, the guy who held everything together, the man everyone could depend upon. Now? He felt he was on his way to becoming an invisible man, a ghost husband, a spectral brother, a phantom employer, an apparition in the community he'd always considered his home.

What a joke, he thought bitterly. Where the hell had his good intentions gotten him? Who were these people whom he loved and trusted his entire adult life? One brother who hated his guts and never wanted to see him again. Another whose secrets had fractured the stable world Rob thought he knew, whose disability hung like a stone around Rob's neck, whose recovering memories might turn into a coming storm in the weeks and months ahead. An old family friend who slept with his wife. A beloved mother laid to rest. A job he was frankly bored with and ready to shed like a snakeskin for a different path. A father who'd demanded much from his clan, who in life had been perpetually disappointed in his sons and, in the afterlife, was probably laughing his ass off at the mess they'd made of everything.

Also, his wife, Violet, the center of this cyclone, both a unifying and destructive force for the Demeter family. What to do about Violet?

All right, enough. Get a hold of yourself, he told himself sternly. This ruminating about things, it wasn't like him. After all, wasn't he a problem-solver? His self-image was of a man who had the ability to deduce and analyze. He prided himself on being solution-focused when confronted with unpleasant and entangled circumstances. It was what he did. Tom used to poke fun at his older brother's seriousness. He'd say, "Hang on a second, everybody. Let's give Rob a minute to overthink this." Once upon a time there'd been grudging respect, maybe even some envy behind the joking.

So again: what to do about his wife? She was like a Rubik's Cube in female form, his Violet. Always had been. Somehow, for all his analytical skills, he'd never totally solved her, those colored blocks never quite aligning. Initially, he'd been intrigued by and attracted to her mysterious ways, challenged by her quiet refusal to be 'figured out'. Gradually, though, he found himself less enamored of those qualities, then vaguely irked, and now, in light of recent developments, seriously doubtful about their future together.

Vi's affect in the days following the afternoon up at the shelter baffled him. A strange, out-of-place serenity seemed to settle over her like an obscuring mist. Her voice softened. She chose her words carefully. Her demeanor was gentle and reasonable. She'd taken to wearing a cautious and fixed half-smile whenever Rob happened to catch her eye unexpectedly. It was, he thought, like watching an android version of his wife, one which could duplicate the speech and mannerisms of Violet while displaying an aura of something not-quite-right, something artificial mimicking human interactions. She floated dreamily about the house as if their lives had not just gone through a monumental shift, as if by sheer force of will she could preserve the illusion all was well. Their conversations were now overly cordial. He felt he was constantly stepping on eggshells around her. Perhaps more honestly, he was hyper-alert to the landmines buried beneath their words.

It was, he considered, probably a blessing there was so much to do. For the time being, they could lose themselves in everyday details and errands.

One good thing, she'd ended the affair with Clifton. That helped some. In Rob's mind, Cliff was the worst kind of Judas. Had Rob suspected him at any time? *Perhaps*, he admitted to himself. *Perhaps I did.* In fairness, he also conceded that, in matters of infidelity, it always took two to tango. He couldn't help noticing how nonchalant Vi was about the betrayal. Incredibly, she hadn't apologized, and she seemed without any sense of the damage her impetuous actions inflicted upon their marriage. Like a wildfire or a terrible flood, she wreaked chaos without seeming burdened by any hint of a conscience.

She's a child is what she is, Rob thought. A little girl in a woman's body. Thoughtless and selfish, yes, though somehow charming as well. With reluctance, he had to acknowledge the puzzling, maddening pull she still held on his heart. If for a moment he could shunt aside his jealousy, he might easily understand how hard Clifton had fallen for her. Which didn't excuse their duplicity. However, objectivity was Rob's strong point and, objectively, he had to admit he understood. Maybe that was why he'd ignored his suspicions about their affair. *Maybe in this case,* he thought, *it took three to tango.*

"Does it bother you," he'd started to ask one night, shortly after the shelter debacle.

He'd been alone out on the deck, lost in a whirlpool of emotions. The night was cold, clear and quiet. He'd come inside after a quarter-hour of sifting through his racing thoughts.

He poured himself a half-glass of merlot and took it with him back to the bedroom. Vi was still up, reading a magazine. He felt ready to talk with her, but when he tried to speak, he was embarrassed to hear his voice shaking. She watched him, her eyes neutral, guarded. Waiting. He tried again. "Does it bother you we don't make love much anymore?"

She regarded him with dry eyes. "You mean, have sex?"

Her bluntness took him aback, but he nodded.

"Oh Rob, how do I answer that?" She sighed. "If we're going to commit to staying together, of course we can talk about having sex more often. If that's what you want."

"If that's…?" Rob shook his head, struggled to find the language he needed to clarify. "Look, if we're going to move forward together, be a team, I mean, both as a married couple and career-wise, all those plans we've made…" Babbling. Again, he paused. He perspired inside his shirt. His face reddened. He fumbled for more words. "Don't you know, Vi, it's the touching that matters. You don't touch me anymore."

For a second, he thought he'd struck a nerve. When she spoke, her response surprised him. "Dear God," she began in a whisper. "When do I stop paying penance for my transgressions? Tell me, how is it fair for me to be so condemned? What's the appropriate punishment for the sinner who makes two or three stupid choices in her life? Rob, I know I'm a good person. You can't make me feel like I won't be redeemed at the end of my days. I will not be denied entry through the gates of paradise because of a few silly, mortal missteps..." Rob watched her eyes soften. A few tears welled up and trickled down her face. "What do you want me to promise, Rob? That I'll resist base temptations from now on? That I'll rebuke my own weak nature? That we'll be man and wife, forever and ever?" She smiled. Her tears stopped flowing. "Of course I promise, darling. I repent and I promise. Blessed art thou, and blessed art us."

He didn't know what to say. She mistook his silence for acceptance and gave a hesitant smile. "We're going to be fine, Rob," she'd said, reaching out to take one of his hands in hers. "Wait and see. Together, we're going to fix everything. You're going to run for office like you've talked about, and I'll be right by your side. We'll figure out how to handle Ben. Don't worry about anything. We just need to be patient and stay steady with each other. It's all in God's hands now."

Still wordless, Rob nodded. Half of him was grateful for Vi's optimism and confidence. The other half? Dubious. Distrustful. He thought, *The rock that changed Ben's life...that was in your hands, Vi. Can you not own that? Don't you feel anything except 'God's plan' about your role in this story?*

Now, watching the afternoon sun dip toward the Flatirons, Rob recalled how that evening had been the pivot point. The scales had fallen from his eyes and he couldn't kid himself any longer about his life, his marriage, his future. Once he'd turned that mental corner, he was free to do what he did best. He recalculated his situation, calmly, unsentimentally. It proved easier than he imagined. On paper, the pros of staying together far outweighed the cons. *Devil's in the details,* he thought, then added, amused, *That's what H.D. would say, isn't it?*

Rob lost track of time. How long had he been staring out his window, as if the mountains contained the answers to all his questions and worries? He remained lost in his fog until Patty buzzed him to announce Mr. McBride was in the lobby, having arrived several minutes early for his four thirty appointment. "Should I tell him it'll be a few minutes?" she asked.

"No," Rob said, rubbing his eyes. He shut the blinds and clicked off the office lights. He gathered up the McBride papers. "I'll be right there. We'll be using the conference room, Patty."

Business and busyness are the balms, he heard H.D. say in his head. *No time for melancholy when there's work to be done. Go on now, be a serious man.* Rob nodded and forced himself to focus. He went out to his greet his customer.

~ * ~

Clifton Parker? He missed Violet, and lamented losing his long friendships with the Demeter brothers. He had a favorite pub a mile or two outside the Greenstone city limits. It was the kind of unremarkable place frequented by blue collar men searching for anonymity and solitude. A universe away from downtown's upscale drinking establishments. Most days after work, he'd make the drive, find a single, out-of-the-way table, order a beer and an appetizer, then lose himself for an hour in his own moribund thoughts. He pondered how swiftly life could go to shit, wondering if and when he'd ever recover his sense of equilibrium again.

~ * ~

Several days after the New Year, a cold snap descended upon downtown Greenstone. Its streets and sidewalks glazed over, the air felt brittle as glass. In contrast, Maggiore's kitchen was sweltering. The dinner rush was on. The place was packed with customers using their Christmas gift certificates, looking for a post-holiday evening of comfort food and inexpensive red wine.

The waitresses ran helter-skelter. The shift manager sweated into his white shirt and barked directions to his staff. Ben kept happily busy busing tables, restocking clean plates, glasses, and silverware steaming hot from the dishwasher, monitoring the salad bar. There were three cooks on duty tonight, and two of them hustled to keep pace with the orders.

Phillip, the third cook, alternated between loudly cursing the work volume and trying to corner Cynthia every time she appeared to check on an order.

"C'mon now, little Cindy, quit breaking my balls here," he pleaded. "Why won't you go out with me? Give a poor working guy a break, would you?"

Cynthia recently moved out of her father's home and into her own apartment with a friend. Her new independence and escape from a probable abusive situation had given her a new level of self-assurance, which her co-workers noticed in her eyes and in the way she walked. Now she leveled a frosty stare Phillip's way. "For the thousandth time, don't call me Cindy," she told him. "And really? You won't even quit bugging me on one of our busiest nights ever? You know my answer, anyway. Now where's my order for Table Four?"

"Cynthia, Cynthia," Phillip crooned. "It's a new year, little darlin'. New opportunities, new resolutions. Say yes, baby, and…"

"Hey, Phil!" bellowed one of his fellow cooks. "How 'bout doing some work instead of flapping your gums? We're dying here."

Phillip didn't deign to glance his way. He kept his eyes on Cynthia's and took a meaningful step toward her. She didn't back away and he grinned. "Feisty," he said, and took another step. "That's my tough girl."

Cynthia didn't move, though something in her face tightened. By the time she realized Phillip wasn't just teasing, he'd crossed the space between them and seized her. Quickly, he used his size and leverage to push her backward pinning her to the wall. She went to scream and he clamped his left hand over her mouth while the fingers on his right hand fumbled at the top buttons of her blouse.

"Ah, not so tough now. Listen, all I want's a peek," he whispered, his breath hot in her ear. "You don't mind so much, do you? Hell, you're barely putting up a fight, sweetie."

"What do you think you're doing?"

The voice was sharp, outraged, and it startled Phillip. For a moment, he relaxed his grip. Cynthia stamped hard on his foot and executed a spin move, reversing their positions, throwing Phillip momentarily off-balance. Another second and she broke free, racing out the door leading outside to the break area. Phillip swore, then glared at the figure who challenged him.

"You," he muttered. "I might've known. Don't you ever listen, shit-for-brains? How many times have I warned you to stay out of my business? Now get the hell away from me before I punch your fucking lights out. I got work to do."

Ben didn't budge. He stood his ground and regarded Phillip with a flat baleful stare.

What's different about this retard today? Phillip thought.

The way Ben held himself seemed more poised, made him appear taller somehow. His eyes, too…they seemed clearer, didn't they? Less cloudy with confusion. Even intelligent.

Angry.

Before Phillip could ponder this line of thought any further, Ben was on him. He whipped the cook about-face, wrenching one arm behind his back and placing him in a quick chokehold.

Christ, he moved so fast, Phillip thought, panting to catch his breath. Ben frog-marched him not-so-gently into the main kitchen area.

They all stared, the busboys and the waitresses, the prep guys and the two other cooks.

Phillip felt his face burning. He yelled, "What the fuck you all looking at?" Ben tightened his grip and nudged him forward. "Let me go, goddamnit. Can't you see how busy we are?"

"I don't think you're going to have to worry much about work anymore," Ben said in a raw whisper. "After Cynthia tells the boss about you and files harassment charges, I predict your days here are done. Good riddance, too. My guess is, you won't be missed much."

"You freak," Phillip squawked, his voice rising. "Can't you fight fair? Turn me loose and I'll kick your disabled ass from here to Denver, I swear to God. If you weren't such a gutless piece of shit, I would…Wait. Where are we going?"

Ben said nothing, but in a moment it became obvious he was leading Phillip to the big industrial stove.

The cook dug in his heels and struggled against Ben's efforts. Ben simply tightened his chokehold. Phillip gasped. He quit resisting and allowed himself to be nudged forward until the two of them stood in front of the stove.

"Little help here," Ben called.

One of the busboys, a cheerful kid named Timmy came to his side. This was Timmy's first job, and he was eager to show he was a good team player.

"Do me a favor, Timmy. Light number three there," Ben instructed, indicating one of the front burners.

Timmy gave him a searching look. After a moment, he shrugged and did as he was told. A circle of blue flames sprang up.

"Turn that up to high, would you, Timmy?" Ben asked in the most reasonable of tones. Phillip gurgled for air as Timmy twisted the dial obediently.

"Yeah, that's perfect. Thanks, Timmy. You can go back to work now."

Work was the last thing on Timmy's mind. He retreated to the dishwasher and the big sinks where his co-workers crowded together, wide-eyed, waiting to see what would happen next.

"I don't believe I've ever noticed, Phil," Ben said nonchalantly. "You right or left-handed?" Another gurgle. Ben loosened the pressure on his windpipe. Phillip croaked a reply.

"Right, okay." Ben removed his chokehold and let his hand travel lightly down the length of Phillip's right arm. He gripped the cook's wrist and urged it slowly forward. By the time dim-witted Phillip realized what Ben was planning, it was too late. Ben was too strong for him to put up any resistance besides a weak mewling sound.

"Ben, c'mon man," the cook pleaded. His hand was inches from the ring of flames. "Jesus Christ, Ben, don't do this. Please don't burn me." His face was shiny with sweat.

Ben said nothing but seemed to hesitate a half-second. A dull scrim briefly filmed his eyes. Although he didn't release his grip, he looked lost for a moment. The exit door creaked open and in walked Cynthia. Her face was puffy and her mascara smeared. She took in the scene at the stove and frowned. A hard light appeared in her eyes.

"Ben, what are you doing? Let him go." Her lips were tightly compressed. "This isn't you, dear. Let him go."

Without releasing his hold on Phillip, Ben turned to look at her. "But he's always bothering you. He's an asshole, isn't he?"

Cynthia gave a little laugh. "Yes, he is. But I can take care of myself, Ben. Even he doesn't deserve this. Watch now, you've almost got his fingers in the fire."

"Ow, ow!" Phillip yelled. "Listen to her, man. You don't want to do this, right? You're a good guy. Please stop."

"Besides," Cynthia added. "If you hurt him, you're the one who'll be in trouble. He's not worth it, honey."

"You want me to let him go?"

"I'd like you to let him go, yes."

As soon as Ben relaxed his grip, Phillip broke free and spun away from the stove. He nearly barreled into his co-workers, who hurriedly backed away from him. The cook cradled his tender right hand. He looked ready to cry. When his eyes found Ben, his whimpering turned into a roar.

"You stupid, crazy son-of-a-bitch! You're the fucking asshole, not me! You think you're gonna get away with this? You can kiss your shitty job here goodbye, for starters. Then I'm gonna sue your dumb ass for assault. When your brother hears about this, look out. My guess is he'll take away your crappy apartment and lock you up somewhere for good. Where you can't fucking *burn people!*"

"That's enough, Phillip," Cynthia broke in. "It's time for you to go home now. You're the one looking at unemployment."

"Yeah? Well fuck you, bitch, and everybody who looks like you. This wouldn't have happened if you weren't such a fucking cockteaser." The cook sobbed and rubbed his hand gingerly. "This hurts," he whined.

He faced Ben again. "Yeah, you're about to lose everything, retardo. Your job, your home, and hey! What are you gonna do without your precious little pussycat, huh?"

Up to this point, Ben had been listening docilely to Phillip's tirade.

His expression had been bemused, like a child being scolded for something he hadn't realized was wrong. At the mention of losing Mr. Whiskers, though, his face colored and a fire sparked in his eyes. He uttered a low growl and moved toward the cook. Phillip blanched and stumbled backward. His elbow grazed a cast iron frying pan and sent it clanging to the floor.

"Ben, no," Cynthia said, and Ben became a confused child again, stopping in his tracks. She turned to Phillip. "Go home," she told him again. "We're done here."

"You all saw what happened," Phillip said to the thinning group of his co-workers. "You're my witnesses, right?" When he received no words of reassurance, he hung his head. "All right, all right. Thanks for the fucking support, everybody. I'm going now."

When he was gone, Cynthia sighed and addressed the remaining crew. "Show's over, kids," she announced. "Back to work. We've got a lot of hungry and impatient customers out there."

"Cynthia?"

"Yeah, Ben?"

"Are you okay?"

"I'm okay, Ben. Thank you for trying to make things right." She walked over and hugged him hard. "Are *you* okay?"

He seemed to study the question. "I don't know," he said after a pause. "I'm not sure what just happened. I think Rob and Vi are going to be mad at me when they find out. I'm not really going to lose Mr. Whiskers, am I?"

"No," she said softly. "You're going to be fine, Ben. Come on, now. Let's get back to work. It'll help us both to keep busy and not think about this anymore."

Ben nodded. He liked the idea of not thinking about Phillip and the stove and having Mr. Whiskers taken away from him. For now, anyway. He left the kitchen carrying an empty plastic tub and began busing tables.

~ * ~

Violet stood outside the church, panting from her run. It wasn't especially cold, but nonetheless she felt herself trembling. Her head spun and her eyes watered. Her breathing was shallow. Her lower back ached, a souvenir from her recent bout with cramps. It was late afternoon and the air held a greenish, pre-storm tint to it.

She thought she'd feel better after running, but she still felt out of sorts. Actually, she wasn't sure what she felt. She stood in the enormous shadow of the church and felt like a stranger shivering inside her own skin.

She and Clifton were through, that much was certain. They hadn't spoken about breaking things off but reached a mutual silent agreement to end the affair. Vi was a little surprised at how relieved she was it was over. She loved jogging through his neighborhood, though, so she parked her Accord several blocks away from Clifton's familiar yellow house and continued her routine.

She understood now was the time for her to be moving on. Of that, she was certain. If only she could define what 'moving on' looked like. Her entire sense of who she was and where she stood had been flipped topsy-turvy these past few weeks. Rob's new coldness toward her. Thomas' harsh rejection. Ben's here-again-gone-again fits of memory. All the secrets that were peeled back and exposed. "Like dry rot," was Tom's caustic observation. Naturally, the disastrous revelations at the shelter had been a tremendous shock to them all.

Violet couldn't grasp the strange pull this church had on her imagination. If it was peace of mind she was seeking, there was little to be had here. The building was a chilly piece of architecture, more like a citadel than a place of worship and forgiveness. She felt as if she couldn't and shouldn't enter through its tall double doors. Was her faith wavering again? She didn't think so. Maybe it was evolving, though, which struck her as a natural and sensible process. This wasn't the profound doubt she'd experienced as a young adult. Rather, it manifested as a devotion which allowed room for questioning, and for a shift away from the black-and-white Biblical lessons of her childhood. It occurred to her there were too many soft spaces between Heaven and Hell, sin and salvation, the sacred and the profane. It was no wonder how beliefs broke apart and believers fell hard through the resultant cracks.

From now on, she resolved to pay closer attention, to slow down her judgments, and try to better analyze her own thoughts, feelings, motives. She congratulated herself on this new determination and felt encouraged about the future. "And you know," sayeth the old pastor's voice in her head, there's a lot of *courage* in *encouragement.*"

Vi told herself she believed absolutely in the promise of redemption and the power of everlasting faith in Jesus Christ Almighty. She also believed in self-preservation and forgiveness. The way onward, she knew, was to trust in God's plan for her. She knew He loved her and that was really all that mattered.

Suddenly Tom's voice was in her head, mocking as always. "How convenient," he jeered. "Rationalizations. Self-delusions. Situational ethics. It's all in God's hands, isn't it? That way, there's no free will, no accountability for your shitty behaviors."

The winter sun was doing its best to chisel through the gloom of the day, through the threat of rain. High on the hill, Vi turned full circle to take in her surroundings. The church made her feel as if she herself were a well-armed fortress, strong and ready to defend her life from the world's storms. She jogged in place to stay warm, vigorously pumping her arms. She reckoned she was mostly at ease with herself and her actions. She made a conscious effort to shut out unwise thought patterns. Why put herself through pointless suffering when there was nothing to do about the past? Why torture others? What was done was done. Amen.

Yet, she asked herself, how could she not reflect on paths taken, choices made, happenstance, world events, personal experiences, and the people you encountered during your life? How could she, Violet Inverce, traveling her own unique path through the universe, have ever expected her own existence would be so closely bound to the Demeter clan? Who could have guessed she'd be loved by the three brothers, shaped by Rachel's kindness, and forged by Henry's hostility?

There wasn't a crystal ball big enough to forecast all the outcomes and consequences of those interactions, was her rueful thought.

So now what? She hated how things had fallen apart with Tom. He said he never wanted to see her again. Probably for the best, but also hard to accept. Vi understood his anger, but not his condemnation. She knew he'd loved her fiercely.

Tom and Rob shared little in common, but Vi believed neither could help loving her all these long years. For Tom to claim he'd turned off his feelings like he would a faucet was unfathomable to her. Yet, there was no mistaking not only his words but his last actions. He'd been clear. He was done with her, walking away, shutting her out, cutting off all contact. Was her ego bruised? Did that partially explain her discomfort with the rift? No. Vi convinced herself she could live with his rejection, especially since the son-of-a-bitch would be two thousand miles away in Florida and would never darken her door again.

Stop dwelling on Mr. Thomas Demeter. He's gone, it's over, and he no longer matters.

Ben presented a more difficult challenge. These days, his memory waxed and waned in rapid cycles. Now that the awful central truth of his condition had been exposed, it was his unstable emotions which most worried Vi. There was increasing evidence of Ben's self-control slipping more often in the weeks following the scene at the shelter. His new awareness of what he'd lost and the role Vi played in changing his life forever played hell with his ability to 'regulate his anger', in the words of his therapist. Reports of irrational outbursts and aggressive behaviors grew more frequent. What if he lost his job, or was evicted from his apartment? Already, his landlady had called Rob twice about Ben shouting at neighbors.

Worse, what if he ever decided to go public? His story would be met with skepticism, of course, and nothing he reported would be grounds for opening a criminal investigation at this late date. That wasn't the point, though. The accusation itself would be enough to ignite a firestorm of gossip and probably derail Rob's political aspirations. Therefore, the whiff of scandal had to be prevented at all costs. Vi knew she needed to develop a canny and delicate strategy in her future dealings with Ben. She also knew she held a trump card over the youngest Demeter. Ben needed Rob and Vi to continue watching over him. His independence was a fragile thing and he remained highly dependent upon the sister-in-law who was responsible for his vulnerability.

Vi calculated that Ben possessed more control over his behaviors than he let on. She sensed his rages were not altogether spontaneous. His temper tantrums danced right up to some invisible line he knew not to cross without jeopardizing his freedom. Ben naturally blamed Vi for the injury which changed the course of his life. He clung to his bitterness toward Rob for choosing to protect Vi and to betray his baby brother.

Fair enough, thought Vi. Ben was not stupid, though. Even in his foggiest mental state, he comprehended his situation. He knew he couldn't broadcast the truth of what had happened at the shelter without losing his own safety net. He didn't want to be placed in a group home or, worse, institutionalized.

Besides, thought Violet, *hadn't he brought his own misfortune upon himself? By his greed, and his unwillingness to leave us alone? If only he had never come back to Colorado...* Wishful thinking, though, and she refused to go down that path.

Rob? What about her husband? Where did she stand with him? She sighed inwardly, resigned to their marriage becoming a long-term project. Understandably, Rob was hurt, confused, and angered by her actions. Discovering the affair with Clifton badly rattled his normal composure. He might channel H.D. with quotes like, "Sunlight is the best disinfectant," and "You're only as sick as your secrets," but still, this was Clifton.

"Obviously, he was never much of a friend. I feel stupid trusting you," Rob kept saying to Vi, shaking his head. "After what happened with Ben, I thought we were in this together."

He'd always viewed himself as her protector. In return, he expected her loyalty and gratitude. She acknowledged it would take him some time to get over this episode. She'd need to be patient.

Immediately and without thinking twice, Rob cut ties with Clifton. Now Vi could see the wheels turning in his head, processing the data, weighing the pros and cons of staying with her. Methodical, as ever. She wasn't worried. The facts and circumstances were on her side. When all was said and done, and emotions were subtracted from the equation, there was very little downside to repairing the marriage, to restoring their partnership. After all, their finances were complicated and intermingled.

They held a common interest in Ben's well-being and in curating what he might express in the future about the accident. The community already saw them as an attractive young power couple. Violet had been discreet with Clifton, and with her other flings, about which Rob remained ignorant. There was, she thought, no benefit to confessing *everything* to her husband. There would be no public disclosure and humiliation. If Rob were to run for state office as discussed, Vi knew she would be an asset with fundraising, giving supportive speeches on his behalf, helping to capture the female vote, working the phones, wooing the power brokers as needed.

Rob's strengths? He was a competent, if not superstar, executive. He was sincere in his desire to enter public service. He believed in his policy stances and felt qualified to fairly represent the good constituents of Greenstone. Initially, Vi worried he might be too laid back and willing to compromise for the rough-and-tumble political climate in Denver. Lately, though, he'd displayed a toughness she'd underestimated in all their years together. Add to the mix that Rob found himself getting a little bored with the family business, so running for office became an even more attractive and exciting option. The pay for an assemblyman wasn't much, but the prestige was priceless. Also, how many times was the House a steppingstone to higher office? If Violet let herself fantasize a bit, she had no trouble envisioning herself in the governor's mansion, maybe six, eight, ten years down the road.

First Lady of Colorado. It had a pleasant ring to it.

So yes. She and Rob would work hard to get through this painful time, iron out their differences, improve their communication, rebuild trust, and make adjustments to create a stronger marriage, an ambitious future. Given time, Tom would slowly become a distant memory. Eventually, care for Ben could be farmed out.

Dusk prepared to settle over Greenstone. The sun sank. In its descent it painted the western skies and evening cloud cover in royal purples, roses, citrons. *Beautiful,* she thought. Although there was no denying the entire scene at the shelter had been ugly and painful, she accepted the reality of struggle. Nothing came to anyone easily. Nothing worthwhile, anyway.

She appreciated the idea of contentedness being a mirage, that it might be a virtue to feel a little dissatisfied about your place on the planet and with your strivings. Oysters formed pearls due to irritation from grains of sand, correct? Afterward, did the oyster feel *content?* Did oysters have souls to feel pride, happiness, a sense of accomplishment? Here, Vi felt torn between doctrines. As a Christian, she believed only human beings possessed souls. However, as a living organism, she had trouble embracing the concept of soulless animals.

In the gloaming, the church seemed to loom over her on powerful haunches, more reprimand than redemption. It was a Sphinxlike reminder she was simply a creature of sin, no more, no less. What wasn't fair, she thought, was being disproportionately defined by those sins. Horrific though they may have been, they were also infrequent, common impulses, lapses of judgment and weakness by which she felt harshly judged. *How is that just?* she wanted to scream at the church and at God. All at once she was a little girl again, nine years old, praying, pleading with her parents, *I'll be good, I promise, I'll be good from now on.* Standing in the church's parking lot, Violet realized she was shaking, ashamed of and embarrassed for her craven nine-year-old self. *Jesus, how pathetic was I?* As an adult, she'd mastered the trick of partitioning off troubling thoughts and traumatic memories, of barricading inconvenient feelings so she could forge ahead. How else could a person *fucking function* as needed to get what she wanted? It was her grand plan in life, to shunt aside her past and remain purposeful in her actions. She saw little reason to deviate now.

Light follows darkness, she thought with satisfaction. *Same as it's always been. We'll get through this, Rob and me.*

Violet turned her back to the church and surveyed the rolling hills and houses of the neighborhood below. Clifton and Tom were in her past. She needed to stay present with Ben, for the time being, at least. Most importantly she wanted to lean to the future alongside Rob. She pulled the hood of her sweatshirt over her head. Her legs felt strong and rested. She trotted to the edge of the parking lot and hit her full stride just before reaching the streets spiraling downhill. Her head was clear as she jogged back to her own world, her mind fresh as a new morning filled with blue light and bright promises.

About the Author

Rod Williams has published poetry, short stories, and music reviews over the past twenty-five years. His first novel was *An Americana Singer for the Twenty-first Century* (2014), followed by the anthology *Celestial Springs and Other Stories* (2015). Both are available by contacting Rod at joyousshambles@gmail.com. *Americana Singer* is also available at Amazon.

Rod has been a member of numerous writing groups and organizations. He founded and hosted a spoken word series, has co-edited various anthologies featuring regional authors, and taught creative writing classes for a variety of organizations. His story "Butter, Salt, and Onions" won first place in the Fiction category of The Professional Writers of Prescott (Arizona) in 2014. Two of his stories were performed live as part of The New Short Fiction Series in North Hollywood, California in 2018.

Rod and his wife currently live near Eugene, Oregon.